ALWAYS FRASER

A. K. STEEL

Always Fraser
Copyright ©2021 by A. K. Steel

All rights reserved. No part of this book may be reproduced or transmitted in either electronic, paper hard copy, photocopying, recorded, or any other form of reproduction without the written permission of the author. No part of this book either in part or whole may be reproduced into or stored in a retrieval system or distributed without the written permission of the author.

This book is a work of fiction. Characters, names, places and incidents are products of the author's imagination. Any resemblances to actual events, locations, or persons living or dead is purely coincidental.

The author acknowledges the trademark status and owners of products referred to in this fiction which have been used without permission. The publication and use of these trademarks is not authorised, associated with, or sponsored by the trademark owners.

Published by A.K. Steel

Edited by Contagious Edits

Blurb by Contagious Edits

Cover Design by Opium House Creatives

ABOUT THE BOOK

Finding Mr Right is one thing... but making a relationship work is another matter entirely.

Fraser Davis has everything going for him. He's successful, driven, and attractive. And doesn't have any trouble finding women willing to warm his bed. Long-term relationships? Not for him. No woman will ever be able to compare to Elena, the one who walked away.

Elena Walker has spent years trying to get over her teen crush, her brother's best friend, Fraser. But when life throws him back in her path, she'll have to come to grips with knowing that her feelings run deeper than she'd like to admit. Family drama, childhood pacts, and past mistakes, not to mention an endless supply of trust issues. Nothing about this is going to be easy.

Moving on is not an option. For Elena, it has always been Fraser.

Always Fraser is a steamy, angst-filled romance that will leave you breathless.

PROLOGUE
ELENA

I run through the door to the Dragon's den. Coffee in hand, notepad tucked under my arm. The escaped tresses of my hair dripping down my face. I try to flick them behind my ears with my free hand, but it's no use. I'm a total drowned mess. I'm normally annoyingly punctual to the point that I'm early. It's a pet hate of mine when people are late, but the universe is not on my side today. I'm ten minutes late which earns me a filthy look from the Dragon herself. It's really not my fault because Sydney is experiencing a summer storm with torrential rain. The forecaster said we're expecting more rain today than the whole of December, and of course, it's the day the battery in my Getz decides to cark it! I didn't have time to call the repair guy and get it fixed, so it was the bus for me, and because of the weather, of course the bus was late.

I take my seat next to Janie and she offers a sympathetic smile. These meetings are never fun and I'm already off to a bad start. The Dragon is still on her phone, but I can only imagine what's to come. First thing Monday morning is our weekly meeting with our boss,

Bridget. I think it's supposed to be some sort of a pep talk, to get us motivated, but it's more like a roasting. Her office is sterile and cold, just like her. It's hard to believe she's an interior designer, or *was* before she landed the gig on TV and started ordering the rest of us to do everything for her.

The Dragon hangs up her mobile, throwing it down on her desk. She takes a deep breath and stares us down. "That was the network. Our ratings are terrible! If we keep this up, the network won't give us another season and we will all be out of a job! Elena, you and Janie need to pick up your game. Our next project has to shine, it needs to be off-the-charts chic. Something people haven't seen before. Do I make myself clear?"

"We did everything you asked of us for the last job. Maybe if you let me go with some of my own ideas, we could change things up a little," I stress with a quivering voice. Shit, why do I let her get to me?

"I don't want your excuses! Go above and beyond this time or you'll be the first to go, Elena."

"What do you want us to do differently that will make it more modern and fresh? After all, this is your project, and you don't like the ideas I bring to you."

"Please bore someone else with your silly questions, I have a hair appointment."

She waves us off out of her office.

I slump back to my desk, my familiar space in this office full of grey cubicles. It's only 9:45am on a Monday and I already feel totally defeated. I don't even know where to start.

The woman's a total narcissistic bitch. She wants control over everything but won't lift a finger to do any of the actual work, leaving us unable to come up with any innovative ideas ourselves, but still having to do all the work to make it happen.

I have been working for the home renovation reality TV show "Project Reno" since I finished my interior styling course nearly five years ago. I used to love this job. It was an amazing opportunity for someone fresh out of study. Most of the other girls I graduated with still haven't found work in our industry and I'm travelling around Australia, redesigning and fixing up people's homes. It's a great job for a stylist.

Our last host was fantastic to work with. We coordinated every project together and our trips away were always a blast. I couldn't believe my luck. I had hit the career jackpot!

Then last year our host announced she was pregnant and taking two years off. That was when Bridget started (aka the Dragon by the rest of our team). It's been downhill ever since. She's demanding, unorganised, and won't lift a pretty manicured finger to help with anything. I can't even count the number of times I've had to work through the night to play catch-up because of her. She's all about having the perfect face for TV. While the rest of us do all the work, she claims to have done it as the face of the show.

For the last few months, I've been fantasising about starting up my own interior styling business. I've been squirreling away any extra pay I have left at the end of the week, hoping that maybe in 12 months I'll have enough to go out on my own. If I have to do all the work, I might as well be getting the credit for it.

I get to work examining our design brief and sketching up the drafts for our next project. It's a four-bedroom, one-bathroom house in the country. The house looks quite quaint from the outside, but it's majorly run down. Our team will have to work our magic on the interior and exterior to get it ready for sale. It's going to need a paint job throughout and a new kitchen and bathroom, then furnishings to style. Not a massive job for us, but still big enough that I need to be organised. Luckily, I have three weeks to plan and prepare for it.

Janie, my design assistant pops her head around my cubical, and she looks worried. "Elly."

"Yes, Janie? What are you hiding?"

She dumps a massive pile of tile samples on my desk. "The Dragon wants you to ring around and find the best price for one of these samples for the Roberts' reno. We're on a tight budget and it needs to be ordered by 3pm today. They have moved our next show forward to next week. I'm so sorry, Elly, I will help however I can."

I glance at my watch. It's 1pm now. Shit, there is no way we're going to get this all done. I'm sure she could have had me ring around this morning when I asked what was on for today. As if she just found out now that they moved the job. But of course, this morning she was more interested in starting the day ripping into us for our bad ratings.

"Thanks, Janie," I grumble, feeling defeated already.

She offers me a sympathetic smile before returning to her desk in the cubicle next to mine. Her long strawberry blonde ponytail bouncing as she walks. Janie's still young, she came to us fresh out of design school at the beginning of the year. But she has an amazing work ethic. I don't know what I would do without her. Her bubbly, enthusiastic personality gets me through the never-ending demands we have thrown our way.

My phone buzzes and Jessie's name lights up the screen.

"Hey, babe," I answer excitedly. I needed to hear his voice; he will change this shitty mood I'm in.

"Hey, Elly, just checking what time you're going to be home for dinner. I can get it started if you like?"

"Think you're going to have to eat without me. We have a job that's been moved forward to next week now. I'm really behind. I have no idea what time I'll be home."

"Don't worry about it, baby. It's your job, it's important. What days will you be away?"

"It's the whole week, Sunday till Sunday. Shit, I just remembered we have our anniversary next week and you said you had something special planned. I'm so sorry."

"Don't worry about it, we can do something for that the following week, I can move things around. I'll have something for you to heat up when you get home. Oh, and the car repair guy has dropped in to check out what was wrong with your car. You just needed a new battery, so it's back up and running now."

"Thanks, I don't know what I'd do without you!" The smile returns to my face, knowing no matter how shitty my day is, I have him to go home to tonight.

"See you later. Love you."

"Love you too. I'll message when I'm leaving."

I don't know what I would do without him. He's such a thoughtful man. Always calling to check on me. I met Jessie the first week that I moved to Sydney to study. It started as a one-night stand. I was trying to get over someone else. I guess you could say, he was my rebound. But I'm not really the kind of girl who does the whole one-night-stand thing, not well, anyway... so within weeks we were dating. We have been inseparable ever since. Next week is our sixth anniversary.

A year ago, he proposed and we're getting married in

three months. I'm so excited for the wedding. It's going to be on the beach in my hometown, Byron Bay, and I'm actually taking a month off work. I don't know what I'm more excited about, the wedding or the time away from this dungeon! *Stop daydreaming about the wedding, Elly, we have a list of suppliers to start ringing.*

I hang up the phone from the last tile supplier and take a deep breath. "I need coffee if I'm going to get through this afternoon—you want one?" I call out to Janie.

"Sure, thanks, Elly," she answers, not stopping to look up from her computer.

I retreat to the break room and make two cups of coffee, inhaling the aroma as I take my first sip. God it smells good. Life is better again. *Okay, Elena, you've got this. Smash out the rest of today's jobs as quickly as possible and get home to your man.*

I hustle over to Janie's desk with her coffee and renewed determination to smash this job out. She's not at her desk so I leave her coffee and turn to see her walking back from the Dragon's den, struggling with a pile of magazines and fabric samples.

"What next?" I groan.

"She needs to see you in her office now."

What now? I walk into her office, not knowing what to expect, because you can never tell with her. She looks up at me from the magazine she's looking through.

"I've decided the tile sample you picked is all wrong for the look we're going for. Start again and find me something better," she scoffs with a wave of her hand. She hasn't even bothered to look up from her magazine.

"But it was from *your* shortlist?" I protest, now getting really agitated with her.

"Yes, and I have now decided it's wrong." She looks up

at me, her icy gaze chilling me to the core. "Go find me something better, Elena." She dismisses me again with that flick of the hand.

I have to bite my tongue. So many thoughts come to mind. All the things I want to say to her right now. I want to rip into her. Tell her to shove her job where the sun don't shine. But that's just a fun scene I play over in my head. I haven't got the guts. So, I turn and walk out of her office, head down, shoulders slumped, defeated.

I start again with the list of suppliers from earlier, trying to come up with something different.

An hour's past and I'm happy with my progress. These new samples that have just arrived in my inbox are going to be perfect. One of them is fresh from the designer, not even been released in the shops yet. So our show will be first to use it in the country. Can't get any fresher than that!

Janie stands in front of my desk, just back from the Dragon's den, looking like she's about to burst into tears.

"What's wrong, Janie? Has she started breathing fire?"

"It's going to be a late night, Elly. She wants the whole job planned today because she's going to be out of the office tomorrow with beauty appointments in preparation for the show," Janie whimpers, dumping all the magazines and samples on my desk.

"What do you mean? We have all week!"

"She wants it done today so she doesn't have to stress this week. She said her viewers can tell from her face when she's stressed, and she wants to look perfect for the show."

For the first time in five years, I see red. I've had enough. I can't deal with this bitch anymore. I push out from my desk like a raging bull. Ready to fight to the death. The matador has been waving a red flag all day, tormenting me... and I've hit my limit.

"I'm done with this!" I get up and storm into her office. Janie grabs my arm as I stomp past her.

"Don't do anything you're going to regret, Elly. We'll get it all done, we always do." Her eyes plead with me to calm down, but it's too late. I can't hear reason anymore.

"I can't work with her for another day. She's not going to do a thing for this project, then next week, once the show airs, she'll be on social media telling everyone how wonderful she is," I almost yell as I pull out of Janie's grip.

"It's your funeral," she calls as I storm off.

I push open the heavy door to the Dragon's den and storm in. She's at her desk, filing her nails. Are you fucking kidding me!

"What is it, Elena? I'm very busy."

"Yeah, it looks like it!"

"What's that supposed to mean?" she hisses at me.

"You're in here doing your nails, while Janie and I do all the work. I'm not staying back tonight to get this job done. So you can have your beauty appointments tomorrow. Do them after work like the rest of us have to."

"Do you think you have a choice, my dear? I'm your boss and I can do what I like. You can either fall into place and do as you are told... or leave. There are plenty of other girls lining up to take your place. You're nothing special, you know." Her expression unfazed by my anger. Surely she can see the steam coming from my ears. My body is tense and I can feel how hot my face is. Did she really just say I'm replaceable? She would be screwed without me.

My mouth is moving before I have time to filter the words from my brain. "Good luck finding someone with my experience at such short notice. I'm done," I yell. I turn and storm off. I've got to get out of this place before my tears start flowing.

"You walk out that door and you're done in this industry. I'll drag your name through the mud."

I keep walking. I'm not giving her the satisfaction of seeing how upset I am. I'm walking out of here with my head held high and some dignity.

I pack up my desk quickly, shoving the few personal items I have in my bag. Janie's by my side.

"What did you do, Elly?"

"I quit. I'm sorry if it leaves you with all the work, but I can't work with her anymore." A tear escapes down my cheek as regret kicks in. I swipe it away; I'm not crying here.

Janie wraps her arms around me. "It's going to be okay, Elly. I'm sure you've got a plan, haven't you?"

I shake my head. "Nope, no plan. I wasn't expecting to do that!" I hug her back. "See you, Janie, good luck with the Dragon." I grab my bag, the potted plant, and the photo of my family from last Christmas, the only personal items I had here. I hold my head up high and power walk straight for the elevator. I can't believe I just did that. Jessie's going to kill me. With the wedding in just three months, we need all the money we can get. Fuck, Elena, why did you do that!

My heart is racing as I stand looking at the front door to our apartment. I'm soaking wet. I waited for the bus for half an hour in the pouring rain, after calling Jessie non-stop to come save me. His phone must be on silent or something. He didn't answer. How am I going to tell him how stupid I've just been? I check my watch. It's 4pm so he should be home at this time in the afternoon. He works from home, designing websites. There's no avoiding it, I have to tell him now.

I put the key in the lock, slowly opening the door. It's quiet, unusually quiet for Jessie. Normally he would have music playing while he works, how odd. Maybe he's out meeting a client? That's good, I need to get out of these wet clothes, and a shower would be amazing before I have to tell him the bad news. I dump my overfilled handbag on the lounge and drag my wet tired body up the stairs to our bedroom. While I shower, I'll work out a plan. If I can work out a plan before Jessie gets home, I can show him this will all be okay.

I'm about to push open my bedroom door but the sound I hear stops me. What was that? It sounded like someone moaning. What the fuck? I push open the door and my body breaks into a hot sweat at the sight. Jessie's nearly naked body bent over... head buried in some girl's pussy! What the actual fuck is going on!

The air is thick with the smell of sex and deception. I taste bile in my mouth and feel like I'm going to be sick. He's really going to town on her, his head buried deep between her legs, his fingers moving back and forth as he finger-fucks her at the same time as he laps her up. The brunette underneath Jessie writhes, her eyes rolling back in her head. Her fingers threaded through his hair.

They haven't even noticed I opened the door. I clear my throat loudly and her eyes rise to see me. He turns his head from his task. His dark eyes widen in fear when he sees me standing in the doorway. He jumps back from her like he's been bitten on the arse by a red-back spider.

"Elly, w-w-what are you doing home?"

My head is spinning. What is going on? My Jessie with his head in some chick's pussy. This isn't happening. I want to scream but I can't. I'm numb. Everything is playing out in slow motion. I can just hear the sound of my heartbeat, thumping in my head.

What's he saying to me? Pull yourself together, Elena. He's waiting for me to say something, but what do I say? This is fucked. You fucking arsehole. How could you do this to me? I take a deep breath and say the first thing that comes to mind.

"Wow, I guess me walking in on you must have ruined the surprise. I can only assume this must be some sort of wedding present for me, you getting lessons on how to give head properly before we got married." I smile at him sarcastically, my eyes boring into him.

The brunette is already up, trying madly to pull on her clothes. She's shooting me a filthy look I can only assume is for interrupting them before he got her off. Sorry I'm such a fucking inconvenience, slut.

"I'm out of here, babe. Call me when you have sorted this shit out," she scoffs. Tossing her long dark hair over her shoulder as she grabs her bag and struts out the door, as if this is a normal situation and she hasn't just been caught with my fucking fiancé.

Jessie hurries over to me, reaching for my hand. "Elly, I'm so sorry, you weren't supposed to be home till late." His eyes plead with me to understand.

I push him away. "Don't touch me, don't ever touch me again. How does the fact that I'm not supposed to be home, make it okay for you to be doing that! How could you do this to me? Who is she?"

He takes a step back and shakes his head. "She's no one, she's just a client I've been building a website for. It just kind of happened. It doesn't mean anything."

"How long has this been going on?" I scream at him.

He looks down at the floor. "Not that long. I was going to stop when we got married."

"What does that even mean? Like things will be different once we're married."

"I love you, Elly, I'm sorry, you were never meant to find out. I just needed to have one last fling before settling down. The thought of being with only one person for the rest of my life was kind of scaring the shit out of me."

"Is that right. Well, you don't have to worry about that anymore. You can have as much pussy as you like." I pick up his pile of clothes from the floor and throw them at him.

"Get the fuck out... get out!" I scream at him as I push him out the door.

He stumbles backwards. "Okay, Elly, I'll go. I'll come back in a couple of hours when you have settled down. I promise this was nothing. It's you I want to marry and spend the rest of my life with." He stands there looking sad and pathetic. I have no idea who this man is anymore.

"Just get out!" I slam the bedroom door shut and pick up a photo of us from my bedside table. It's been turned upside down, I assume so his quick fuck didn't have to see it while they fooled around. I throw it across the room, smashing it into thousands of tiny pieces. I can hear the front door open and close. He's gone. My life as I know it is over. I slide down onto the floor and the uncontrollable sobbing starts.

Eventually, I open my eyes and pick myself up off the floor. It's getting dark outside. I don't know how long I've been sitting here for, but I can't stay here any longer. Not if he's coming back tonight. I weave through the broken glass, heading straight for the shower. The hot water streams down my back.

As the steam fills the air, my walls go up. Who the fuck

does he think I am? Some pushover? Has he met me? Maybe that's who I've become with him. Someone who lets her fiancé cheat on her and turns a blind eye. No fucking way! I'm going to pack my stuff tonight and I'm out of here. What have I got to stay for anyway? I've got no life here now. He was my world. Over the last six years, my friendships have dwindled down, and I didn't care, because I had him. He was my best friend. How wrong was I. Now I have nothing, no friends, no job, no Jessie.

CHAPTER ONE

ELENA

Sweat beads on my forehead. I wipe it away with the back of my hand as I roll on the last stroke of paint. I'm done! I drop the roller in the tray underneath me and jump off the ladder, stretching my arms over my head. My back is killing me. I need to book in a massage this week, if I can make it out of my safety zone of my parents' house. I take a step back so I can inspect my handiwork. Much better!

The dark blue my childhood room was painted in, from my moody teenage days, was just depressing. When I was a teenager this room was my sanctuary from the bitches I was dealing with at school. A place to look up at the little glowing stars I had all over the ceiling and dream about how awesome my future was going to be as an interior stylist when I got out of this town.

It was also a place to think of *him*, the boy that filled my dreams, the one I wanted so badly but could never really have. He was perfect. Not just because he was six-foot-two with abs of steel, the cheekiest smile you have ever seen, and grey eyes like silvery moons that twinkled with mischief, but because he was my hero. From the day we started high school, he was there looking out for me. No matter how bad things got, he was always there to stick up for me. Without him and my brother Drew, I wouldn't have made it through high school.

It's weird being back in this room. It brings back all the feelings from the past. The ones I had buried long ago. I was so busy with my life in Sydney, I had almost forgotten how obsessed I was with him... Almost.

The last three months have taken a toll on me emotionally, and I have spent way too much time in this room locked away from reality, just thinking. I thought I would be able to pick myself back up and get on with my life, no problem, but even leaving the house has become a challenge. The more time I spend in here, the harder it is to leave.

Today is a new day, and I've woken up with renewed purpose. I'm not feeling sorry for myself anymore. Today is the first day of my new, more exciting life, so why not start with a room makeover. I think my parents were glad to see a glimpse of the old me coming back to life. An hour after I announced to them that I was making over my room, my dad was there with a tin of paint, paintbrush, and roller.

It's now an off-white which is perfect with the rustic beach-coloured timber floor. I spent the morning online shopping, and I've ordered a new bedroom suite and white linen bedding. I splashed out and got the most gorgeous handmade jute rug that will finish off the room perfectly, and some pop art for the walls to add a splash of colour. I've probably overspent, but I figure I deserve it under the circumstances.

When the money came through from Jessie buying me out of our apartment, I had enough to do whatever I wanted. The rest I will save for starting my business. It's the most excited I've been since I dragged my sorry arse back home to my parents' place in Byron Bay three months ago.

Not quite where I thought I would be at 25, back at home starting all over again. I was supposed to be getting married this weekend, but I'm not letting that get me down anymore. The way I see it, this was just a sign that my life with Jessie was going to be shit and I'm better off without him. That's what I keep telling myself anyway. That is until I jump on Facebook and see all my friends' perfect lives. If I see one more happy post from someone I went to high school with, saying how terrific their job is or that they just got engaged or their awesome new house is ready to move into, I'll be sick. I haven't even bothered to call any of them. I know I should maybe attempt to get out of this house, but it's too embarrassing.

Maybe my life being turned upside down just when I thought it was all coming together is punishment for being such a terrible teenager. I have to watch everyone else live their best lives while mine has completely turned to shit. Man, I was an awful teenager. When I look back at the way I acted towards my parents, it would not have been a fun time for them. Just another reason I'm not having kids of my own anytime soon. If they turned out anything like me, I'd be screwed.

I'm one of three kids. The only girl, with a twin brother Drew and an older brother Theo. I always kind of felt like the odd one out. The boys were smart, sporty, and popular. They had it all. Then there was me... the arty one, who never fit the ideal student type and didn't get good grades. I completed my schooling hiding out in our art studio, sketching or creating with my best friend Indie. That's if we were at school. We were pretty good at missing our most hated subjects and no one seemed to care too much, so we never got caught. Not the perfect little student that my principal mother expected me to be. Luckily, she was at the primary school, so she didn't know the half of what Indie and I got up to.

I love my mum dearly and we're quite close now, but she has never really understood me. She was too busy fussing over my perfect brothers, especially the golden child, Drew. Lucky for me, I've always been Daddy's little girl, so he is always on my side and there to get me out of trouble when I go too far.

"Elly, are you finished up there?" Dad calls out from the kitchen.

"Yeah, I'll be down in a second, Dad." I grab the roller and the paint tray and head down the hall.

"What's up, Dad?" He sits at the breakfast bar drinking his coffee and looking over the plans for our beach villas, his latest project.

"I've got an appointment this afternoon at the station, but I have just heard from the architect who's working on our beach villas, and he wants to come by and do a site check with his builder this afternoon. Can you show them through? It might be a good opportunity to show them what you have been working on for the interiors as well."

"Yeah, no worries. It's not like I was doing anything else anyway. Did something happen at work?" I have always worried about him working in the police force, and I know Mum has had many sleepless nights worried about him as well, you just never know what they're dealing with. And now Theo has joined, I have to worry about him as well.

"No, nothing out of the ordinary."

I drop the paint tray on the countertop and wrap my arms around him. "Okay, but you know you can talk to me if something's worrying you, Dad."

"Everything's fine, baby girl, nothing to worry about," he says, turning to hug me back and tuck some stray hair behind my ear. "I still can't believe you dyed it bright blue."

I shrug, "Needed a change, not like I'm leaving the house at the moment for anyone to see what I look like anyway."

"Whatever makes you happy, honey."

"Thanks, Dad. Good work changing the subject too. But we're still talking about you. What made you want to retire out of nowhere and build these beach villas in our backyard? I mean, it's not a bad idea. Byron is buzzing with tourists now so I'm sure it will work for you. It's just, you love your job."

"It's just time. I can't work in the police force forever. I want to have an easier life for a bit. This is something your mother and I have been discussing for years, and now's the time." He slides his chair out and hops up and empties his coffee in the sink.

"The boys from The Green Door will be here in an hour so you better get yourself cleaned up. You have paint in your hair. Did you use your hair as a paintbrush? White strips over the blue is a good look," he laughs as he wraps his arms around me, giving me a squeeze. "It'll be a great opportunity for you to show off your talents and build a portfolio of your own. You might even get some work out of it?" Dad's always on my side, trying to help me through whatever project I'm working on.

"Thanks," I smile up at him. He's a big man, and for his age he's still super fit. All the men in my family are tall, over six feet, and obsessed with keeping in shape. At his age, he's still up every morning at six for his run, then off to the gym. If you didn't know him, he would be intimidating, but to me he's just a big teddy bear. I hope he's okay.

"The plans are on the kitchen bench if you want to go over them again before they get here." He grabs his keys and walks out the door giving me a wave.

"Thanks, Dad, see you later."

An hour later, I'm towel-drying my hair. Was that the doorbell? I quickly pull up my ripped jeans and chuck a singlet over my bra. The architect is early, how annoying. My hair is a wet mess. I drag my fingers through it as I sprint down the hallway in a rush and open the front door.

"Hi, sorry, I wasn't expecting you till later." I'm almost breathless from the run down the hall. The view I'm treated with is a surprise, he must be the builder. There's no way this guy's the architect. You can tell he works outdoors, with tanned skin, a broad chest, and arms that look made for heavy lifting. Don't even look, Elena. Remember you're sworn off men, they're all lying, cheating arseholes.

"That's okay, I'm a bit early. I came straight from another job. I'm the builder, Blake. Our architect has been held up with another project, so he won't be able to make it." His dark eyes burn right through me. Have I pissed him off somehow? I don't think I was who he was expecting, he doesn't look happy about it.

"Did I interrupt something? Your hair is dripping everywhere."

My wet hair has run all down the front of my singlet top leaving it soaking wet. "Oh, yeah, it is, just jumped out of the shower." I flip my hair up into a bun, out of the way as the beads of water run down my back.

"Lucky it's hot today," I say with a shrug. "I'll show you through to the building site." I gesture for him to follow me into the house.

"Is Jim going to be here, or should I come back later?" he mutters awkwardly, still standing in the doorway.

"Sorry, he's had to go out, so he's left you in the capable hands of his daughter. Hope that's okay? I know the plans as well as he does. We've been working on the ideas for the design together."

"Oh, okay. Yes, of course, sorry. I didn't catch your name?" He is so serious and looks annoyed to be dealing with me instead of my dad. Well tough luck, buddy, I know this stuff as well as any man so you're just going to have to deal with me.

"I'm Elena." I reach out and shake his hand with a firm handshake. "Come on and I'll show you through to the site." I walk him through the house and out onto the back deck to the backyard.

"Impressive yard," he calls back to me, taking a look around.

"Yeah, it was the best place to grow up. My brothers and I spent most of our time out here."

"Yeah, I can imagine. So, Jim wants the villas built starting from this line?"

"That's the one. He's got some grand plans for an outdoor patio and pool area once you're done, so it can cross over the line. Is that all going to work?"

"No worries. I'm just going to take some measurements and have a look around. You can go inside, I don't need you for this. I'll let you know when I'm done."

"Oh, okay, I'll just be inside then." I probably should ask him if he wants something to drink, but his attitude towards me has kind of pissed me off so I'll just make one for myself instead.

I sit at the kitchen counter inside, waiting impatiently for Blake the builder to finish up. This guy is insanely hot, but he seems like kind of a dick. Oh well. Luckily I'm not looking anyway. I inhale my coffee, it smells so good.

I look over at the yard. It really is huge. We were so lucky as kids to have this as our playground. I can't imagine what it's going to look like with these three beach villas all lined up. The pool will be nice when it's finished. I'm looking forward to that part. As kids we had it all. A massive trampoline and a swing hanging from the mango tree, and when it rained, we would get a little creek flowing down the back. We spent most of our time out there playing. My older brother Theo was the leader of all the mischief we got up to, and my twin Drew and I just followed along. The number of times I got the blame for something he orchestrated. Somehow Mum always believed him.

The tree swing was my favourite. I wouldn't admit this to my brothers, but I would sit in that swing and imagine we were in a fairyland. I was the fairy princess, of course, and all of my fairy friends lived up in the mango tree above. Their tiny houses were the mangos. It makes me sad to think it's all going to be torn down in the next few weeks. It feels like everything in my life is changing so fast at the moment. Things that used to feel so comfortable and safe are gone and now this yard will be too.

I'm an emotional mess. Why am I crying over this? I swipe away the stray tear that escaped with my hand. I've got to pull myself together. I'm so emotional at the moment. What's wrong with me? I never cry.

"Elena, I'm all done." I flinch, spilling my coffee all over the countertop.

"Sorry, you scared me." I was in my own little world and didn't even see that Blake had come back inside and was standing right in front of me. I hop up and start to wipe up the mess.

"Sorry, are you okay?" he asks, trying to help clean up the mess.

"Yeah, I'm fine, you just startled me."

"It looked like you were upset about something."

"I'm fine... It's just all the changes to our house. You know, all the memories. I can't imagine coming down here every morning to see villas instead of the yard we grew up in." I don't know why I'm feeling this way. I'm a total mess, how embarrassing.

"You still live with your parents?" he utters in surprise, throwing me a raised brow in question.

"Don't be so judgemental! I am recently back living with them, yes," I protest, standing my ground. Who does this guy think he is?

"I didn't mean anything by it. I was just surprised. You seem like the independent type who's got it all together, that's all."

"I am! But things haven't gone my way lately." I sigh sadly.

"Shit happens. It couldn't be all that bad, though, could it?" He offers me a kind smile. "Sorry I was kinda in a bad mood when I arrived here today, family stuff, I shouldn't have been so rude to you, though. I feel bad now."

"It's okay, don't worry about it."

"So, what brings you back home living with your parents, then? If you don't mind me asking." He smiles; his face has softened, and his eyes are now warm and friendly. Maybe I was too quick to judge this guy.

I sigh. "My life kinda fell apart in the space of a day. I was living in Sydney working my dream job as an interior stylist until I threw it all away because I couldn't work for my dragon boss anymore. Then, would you believe in a cruel twist of fate, I arrived home early to walk in on my fiancé with his face buried in another girl's pussy! Pardon my language. This was three months before we were supposed to get married." His face says it all, shock, pity, sympathy. "So, yeah, I'm back at home living with my parents. It's not ideal, but sometimes, as you say, shit happens!"

"Wow, that's quite the day from hell! I'm sorry, Elena. Me and my big mouth, I shouldn't have said anything. I don't have much of a filter. Sometimes I open my mouth without thinking."

"It's okay. Don't worry about it. You weren't to know. I guess my life does look pretty sad right now. I was supposed to be up here getting married this weekend, and now I'm hanging out with my parents, watching Netflix." I finish cleaning up the spill. "Did you need to go over the plans? I was hoping to show your architect some of the samples I've got for the bathrooms."

"That's okay, we don't need to finalise any of that yet. You can talk to him about it later. So, you're an interior stylist?"

"Yeah, I've mostly worked as a stylist and assistant to the head designer on that TV show Project Reno. That's why Dad asked for my help with this project. I've helped them with the renovation for most of the house already. But this was an exciting new project he sprang on us, and it's nice to have something to work on until I get myself sorted out and get my own business up and running."

"Oh, really, you worked on a TV show? That would've been all right."

"You'd think so, hey, but in the end, it was long hours, a lot of travel, and no recognition for a pretty shitty wage. It was time to move on. I should've just waited until I had some sort of a back-up plan."

"If you have a portfolio of some of your work, I could show it to our architect. Sometimes we need help with the styling for the sale of some of the larger projects. I know he's been looking for the right person to take over that part."

"Really? That would be amazing. I can show you my work right now if you want," I blurt, probably a little too excitedly. I really do need my luck to change, though.

Seeing my excitement, he offers me a bigger smile this time. His smile is gorgeous. He really should do it more often. "I've got no idea about all of that, you're better off talking to him. Come into the office on Monday morning, I'll let him know you're coming." He hands me his business card.

"Thanks, that's really nice of you." I take the card from him and put it in my pocket. He's looking at me like he wants to say something else. "Did you get everything you needed? Are there any questions you need me to pass on to Dad?"

"Oh no, it was all pretty straightforward. Just tell Jim I'll email through the final designs, and if he can approve them this week sometime, I'll get them into council so we can get started as soon as possible."

"No worries, I'll show you to the door." I walk over to the door, holding it open for him. As he walks out, he turns to me again. What's the go with this guy? First, he's all serious, then he's lost for words.

"Elena... if you're looking for something to do this weekend..." he mutters, looking down, suddenly shy, "I've only been in Byron for six months myself, so I haven't really settled in, other than hanging out with my business partner. Maybe we could hang out, if you like? I know you have just come out of a pretty serious relationship, so not a date or anything, maybe just as friends. If you want to hang out with someone your age rather than watch Netflix with your parents, that's all." That's a surprise, not what I expected him to say at all.

"Sure, why not? It's been a long time since I've been out in Byron. You can show me the hot places to go."

"Okay, perfect, I'll pick you up from here at seven then?"

"Sounds good. Thanks, Blake, see you then."

Well, that was interesting. A night out as 'friends'. I thought he would have run for it when I told him my shitty life story. Maybe my luck is changing. I knew today was going to be the start of something better, and it looks like I was right.

CHAPTER TWO

ELENA

I peek through my bedroom blinds to see a white ute pull up in front of my house. How predictable, a builder driving a white ute. I quickly lace up my black Doc Martin boots. I don't want to keep him waiting too long, or he'll get chatting with my parents and this will all go to shit before it's begun. I check out my reflection in the mirror.

Man, I love these boots, I look hot! Jessie always wanted me to wear heels and look like a girl when we went out, so I did. I hadn't even realised how much of a doormat I had become. Everything he suggested, I did without a second thought. The more I think about it, we were never a good match. I just fitted into his life and became what he wanted me to be. Never again. I have learned from my mistakes, and from now on I'm living life my way. Strong, independent Elena is back, and the world better watch out!

I walk down the hallway with a little skip in my step. I'm so excited and nervous. It's been a long time since I've been out with someone new. Mum and Dad have opened the door and are chatting to Blake. He radiates this fantastic self-confidence as he shakes their hands. Man, he looks good in black jeans and a button-up. Dad lays the plans out on the dining table and is talking his head off about his latest ideas.

"Hey, Dad, put them away, he's not here for work." Both men look up and give me a stern look.

"What, he's not," I smile over to them with a super sweet smile. That tells them I'm cute but I'm going to get pissed really soon if we stand around too long looking at plans. I'm ready for a drink and I'm starving.

"Hi, Elena, it's okay. Just a couple of things to go over, we won't be long," offers Mr Serious with a little smile. Tonight's going to be interesting.

"You look nice, honey," Dad adds. "I'm so glad you two hit it off and decided to have a night out." He turns his attention back to Blake. "Look after her tonight, though, Blake. No funny business." He's always looking out for his baby girl even when I don't need it. Seems he still thinks I'm 16. No funny business, is he serious?

I'm in skinny black jeans and a hot-pink silk cami. I'm wearing my favourite hot-pink lipstick and my hair is swept up into a high ponytail that runs all the way down my back. It's the best I've looked in months. Getting dressed up with a full face of makeup was kind of my thing. I was one of those kids who got in trouble constantly for breaking into Mum's bathroom cabinets and playing with her makeup, leaving bits of it smudged into the carpet. I was a shocker as a kid! Tonight, all done up, I'm finally feeling like myself again.

"Thanks, Dad. You know I can look after myself, though, right? Poor Blake doesn't need the whole speech about you being a cop in this town." Blake doesn't look worried. Actually, he doesn't strike me as the kind of guy that is scared of much at all.

"Of course we do, Elly, you have always been our Miss Independent," Mum laughs as she hugs me goodbye.

"See you guys later, don't wait up," I call out, heading outside and giving them a little wave, making it clear we're not hanging around to chit-chat about the building plans tonight. Blake takes the hint and follows me out like a good boy.

"Miss Independent, hey? Is that the family's nickname for you or something?" he teases.

"What? Mum just calls me that because my brothers are such mummy's boys. I don't need anyone looking after me. I can, and always have, looked after myself."

"Is that right? You're not one of those girls who think all men are jerks and women are better off by themselves, are you?"

"I don't know. If past experiences are anything to go off, that might be right," I say with a shrug. "I guess I'm just not looking for a saviour to swoop in and take care of me. If I look after myself, then I'm all I need."

"Funnily enough, I feel the same about women," he adds.

"Well, I guess it's lucky we're just planning on being friends then. That way we can just be ourselves and have some fun. What have you got planned for tonight?"

"Well, I thought I'd show you a typical Saturday night with the boys. Do you like pizza?"

"What kind of a question is that? Of course I love pizza! Then what?" I lean up against his ute as he goes around his side to jump in.

"Then maybe go to a bar, play some pool and have a few drinks. What do you think?"

"Perfect. Just what I need." I smile.

We jump in his ute and it's just a quick drive to the local

pizza place, Angelo's. This place hasn't changed since we used to come here for family birthday dinners when I was a kid. Still the same cosy atmosphere with red booth seats and checked tablecloths. I hope their menu's the same too. The waiter shows us to a booth and places the menus in front of us.

"The food smells delicious." I probably should have eaten more today so I don't look like a complete pig.

"What do you feel like?" he asks, looking over the menu.

"One of everything, I'm starving." I grin.

"You couldn't handle one of everything, you're tiny!"

"Ha, you'd be surprised what I can handle. I had to keep up with my brothers. Everything was always a competition, including how much we ate," I laugh. Being in this restaurant brings back so many happy memories of us as kids. I have no idea why I used to compete with the boys so much, but I can't back down from a challenge. And more than once that ended badly for me.

"Well, let's just start with a couple of different pizzas and a garlic bread, then we can always get more if you want later."

"Sounds good. You can pick. I'm not fussy." The waiter comes over to take our order, then Blake heads to the bar to order some drinks. I take that opportunity to check my phone for the millionth time today. I don't know why I keep torturing myself, but something about today being the day I was supposed to be getting married has me stupidly wishing Jessie would message me, begging for forgiveness.

The night it all ended, he messaged to see when I was coming back, then that was it, nothing else. He didn't fight for us, and I found out a month later the prick let the chick he was cheating on me with, move into our apartment. The one we had bought together. That's when I asked him to buy me out of the mortgage. I wanted nothing between us. But for some reason, I just hoped he would message today. It's pathetic. That's it, I'm turning it off now for the rest of the night. Tonight, I'm moving on and having fun with Blake the builder.

"You okay?" Blake hands me a massive glass of wine.

"I am now, thank you." I take the glass and have a big gulp. It's so good and just what I need. I finish the glass and place it on the table.

"Lucky I got the bottle," he laughs at me, taking my glass and topping it up. "You okay? Did something happen while I was gone?"

"No, all good, I'll drink this one more slowly," I sigh, a little embarrassed.

The garlic pizza arrives and I'm straight in there. "Yum, this smells so good and looks just how I remember it."

"You've been here before?"

"Yeah, it was my family's favourite. We came here for any big family occasions, like birthdays."

"Must have been where all the local families went. My business partner introduced me to it because this is where his family came too."

"Oh really? It was probably pretty popular when we were kids. It must be so nice having your own business. How long ago did you set it up?"

"I met my business partner back in Newcastle. We often worked on the same projects and we were both looking for a roommate at the same time, so we moved in together and were roommates first. We had both had a shit week at work and were over working for someone else. My mate took a trip home for the weekend and returned with a business proposition for me. He had a good mate from school that was a developer here in Byron and had the money to start us off. The offer was too good to refuse and neither of us had any reason to stay in Newcastle, so the three of us went into business together." He's so proud and confident when he talks about his business.

"That's so inspiring. You're lucky you have each other. I would love to start my own interior styling business. I just keep losing the nerve to do it."

"Sometimes you just have to start, you can figure out the rest as you go. I'm so glad we did, it's changed all of our lives. The business took off straight away when we landed a large government contract because they loved our eco-friendly edge. So we now have 20 employees and more contracts than we can keep up with."

"That sounds amazing, I don't even know where to start!" I laugh.

"As I said the other day, bring your portfolio in on Monday and we can work out if you'll fit in with our aesthetic, and, if not, I'm sure I can point you in the right direction to get started."

"Blake, why are you being so nice to me?"

"You look like you could use a friend, we've all been there."

"Thanks, you're a nice guy. Very serious, but nice," I say with a lopsided smile. He raises his dark eyes from the pizza he's just bitten into.

"Hey, what do you mean serious?" he grumbles.

"I don't know, just an observation. You just seem kind of serious and structured, like everything needs to be perfectly organised and in place for your world to be okay."

"So, I like things organised. Drink up. I'll show you I'm not Mr Serious all the time. I can be fun too," he says with a mischievous smile. And when he says it like that, I totally believe him. Maybe I have judged him too early and he has a completely different side to him.

We finish up our food in record time. I don't know if Blake was aware, but it was definitely a competition, and I won by two pieces.

"You want to just head over to the bar? I can walk you home later. I feel like I need a drink tonight too."

"Long week, hey? Lucky I wore my walking boots," I laugh as we walk out of the restaurant. I'm a little tipsy from the wine already. "So what's your deal anyway, Blakie?"

He shoots me a puzzled glare at my cutie nickname for him. "No deal. What do you mean?"

"Well, you're an attractive guy, with a decent job. I would think girls would be throwing themselves at you. How are you single?"

"I don't have girls throwing themselves at me," he grumbles, with a stern look like I have somehow insulted him. "I'm kind of in the same situation as you. I had a long-term girlfriend back in Newcastle, but it was a long story. Things got kind of complicated and she had feelings for my business partner as well as me. He didn't feel the same, but it tore me apart. So I broke it off not long before we decided to move here and I haven't really wanted to date again."

It's the first time I've seen him drop his tough, serious persona. She must have done a number on him to still be so hung up on her. I can see how wounded he is.

"That's shit, Blake, I'm sorry. Chicks can be such skanky bitches!" I offer a sympathetic smile.

"Yeah, it's been a while now. I thought I was getting over it, but she's been calling me again lately, wanting to try again. There's no way I'd go there, after how it ended, but it's hard to move on when she's still calling. I was glad we had plans tonight. I need a distraction."

"I can definitely organise that! I can be very distracting." I smirk.

"I'm sure you can," he smiles sexily.

"We need another drink." I grab his hand and power walk through the door at the bar and straight to the bartender. "Four tequila shots, please," I say to the bartender with a broad smile.

"What are you doing?" Blake whispers to me.

"Erasing our memories, for tonight anyway," I say with a wink, as the bartender places the shots down in front of us. I hand Blake two and then grab two for myself, clinking his glass. "To forgetting the past and living in the now." He gives me a slow smile and throws back the shots one at a time.

"I think you're going to be trouble, missy."

"Trouble's my middle name. Now come on, let's play pool. I'm going to kick your arse and loser gets next round, and that's going to be you!" I say, nudging his arm.

"Ha, bring it on baby, I never lose." He takes the cue, stepping up to break.

"Neither do I, baby," I tease him.

Three rounds of pool later and Blake's up two. Tonight's going to cost me, he's a lot better than my brothers and I'm out of practice. I used to kick their arses, but it's been a while, or maybe I'm just a little too tipsy to play. I'm having so much fun with him. It feels like before I moved to Sydney when I used to hang out with Drew and his best mate. Other than Indie, I always got on with boys over girls. There's no bitching or trying to outdo each other. Girlfriends are just hard work. I can just relax and have a good time when I hang with the guys.

He sinks the black to win the third game.

"Ha, not fair, you must be cheating," I say, stomping my feet like a toddler having a tantrum.

"Sore loser, are we?"

"No, just not used to it, that's all." I'm pouting now, normally pool is my game but he's just too good. Think we might need to change things up a bit. "I'll get this round, but no more pool. Let's play something else."

"What? Are you going to make up a game so you can win?"

I shrug my shoulders, "Maybe?"

"I'll get this round, I don't want to take all your money tonight. You go find us somewhere to sit."

"Don't get too cocky, you just got lucky. No more tequila, though, get something else." I make my way over to a leather lounge in the back corner. I'm surprised I can get a seat, but it's quiet here for a Saturday night. At least compared to what I remember it being like when I was 18, anyway. Blake returns with two bright blue cocktails.

"What are these?"

"I have no idea. I got them because they match your hair." His whole face lights up when he laughs. It's the most natural I have seen him. He's finally starting to relax around me. I think he's getting kind of drunk too. I can't help but laugh back. I don't even know why.

"I guess my hair is kind of ridiculous at the moment. I needed a change after... well, you know the story."

"What made you go with bright blue?"

"I don't know. I just wanted to be as far from what he wanted me to be as possible. When I was younger, I used to love experimenting with my hair. It was all different colours. Pale pink was my favourite. That's how it was when I met Jessie, but he soon talked me into stock standard blonde. I guess I didn't even realise how much I changed myself to be who he wanted me to be."

"I like the blue, it suits you. You're kind of different from any of the other girls I know. You could never be just another boring blonde."

Now I can feel my face heating up. He's too cute to be saying nice things to me. "Thanks."

"So, what's this game you've got planned?"

I sit up in my seat, crossing my legs, and clap all excited remembering the game. "It's kind of a getting-to-know-you game, called Two Truths and a Lie. You tell me three things about yourself. Two are true, one's a lie, and I have to guess which one is the lie. If I get it right, you drink, and if I'm wrong, I drink."

"Okay. Sounds interesting. Why don't you go first so I can see how it works."

"Okay, let me think... Okay, I've got it. One, I'm a twin. Two, when I quit my last job, I told my boss she was so conceited she should go fuck herself. Three, I wasn't ready to get married and I'm secretly glad I walked in on Jessie and that girl."

"Okay, well I know you have two brothers, though I'm not sure if they're the same age as you. You sound like the kind of girl who would speak your mind so I'm sure you ripped into your boss. I reckon it's the first one, I can't see you as a twin."

I'm laughing hysterically now, slapping my hands on my legs. "Wow, you must think I'm a mega-bitch if you think I told my boss to go fuck herself! I'm sweet and innocent. I would never say that," I add, batting my eyelashes at him. "Not to her face, anyway! I have a twin, so you better drink up."

"You have a twin! That must have been cool. Growing

up, I always imagined what it would have been like to have a twin. I've only got an older sister; she's six years older and I don't really know her. My family aren't all that close." He skulls his drink. "Oh, this was a bad choice, it's awful, so sweet. So, you're glad you're not getting married?"

"I don't know, I wanted to. I mean, I thought he was the one, but the closer it got, there was this niggling feeling like something wasn't right. Maybe I wasn't ready, or he wasn't the one. I couldn't put my finger on it. Something was just off. You know? Man, that sounds so bad. I think it's the alcohol talking."

"It doesn't sound bad. Sounds like your intuition was trying to tell you he wasn't right for you."

"Yeah, maybe? Anyway, it's all done now. Right, it's your turn. What exciting truths have you got for me?" I ask with my biggest smile. This game is fun. I almost want to pat myself on the back for coming up with the idea.

"Okay, I don't know how exciting they will be. I'm not all that interesting, but here goes: One, I've never been outside of Australia. Two, I cheated on my final exams for high school. Three, I've had a threesome."

"Oh, I don't know, there's no way you cheated on your final exams, you're too organised and smart for that. Hmm..."

He's raising his eyebrow at me now, trying to throw me off. "How do you know? I could have."

"Hmm, I reckon you have never had a threesome."

He throws his head back, laughing at me.

"What?" I say.

"Tricked you, now drink up."

"What? Okay." I skull the blue liquid. "Yuck, that *is* sweet. Wow, I can't believe you've had a threesome. Sorry," I laugh, "but Mr Serious seems kind of vanilla."

"You shouldn't be so quick to judge. I'm more fun than you think," he says with a wink.

I'm now sitting up giving him my full attention, he just got a lot more interesting. "I want details!"

He's squirming under my gaze. "It's a long story."

"I've got all night, baby. Tell me, I need a good dirty story. This is the longest I've been without sex since I was a teenager and I'm not coping." I can't believe I just said that out loud! What's this blue stuff, truth serum?

He raises his eyebrows at me. "Fuck, you're so forward, aren't you!"

"What!" I nudge him with my arm. "I'm not really, I think I'm just a little tipsy. Come on, tell me, I promise I won't tell anyone." I draw a cross over my heart so he knows I'm serious.

He laughs at me again, "You're like an excited little kid."

"Now you're starting to work me out, but that doesn't get you off the hook. Tell me, I can beg all night."

"Well, it's kind of a complicated story but I'll keep it short. That girlfriend I was telling you about..."

"Yeah, the one that had a thing for your business partner. It was with your girlfriend? Wow!"

"Yeah, that one. Lexi's her name. We had been together for a while and I was her first, so she hadn't really... you know, explored sexually, at all. She kept telling me of these fantasies she was having of threesomes. I was imagining, you know, two girls, so I was up for it. But kind of thought it would never happen. They were just, you know, fantasies. Then one night we were hanging out with my roommate..."

I think I know where this is going. I bring my hand up to cover my mouth in shock. "You mean your girlfriend, your friend, and you?"

He clears his throat, getting annoyed with me, "Let me tell the story!"

"Sorry, go on, I won't interrupt anymore."

"Anyway, we were hanging out drinking one Friday after work and it kind of just happened. She started it and we went along with it."

"Did you and your friend?"

"Fuck no. We both did her."

"Oh, okay, like at the same time? How does that even work?" He runs his hands through his hair getting frustrated with me.

"And you called me vanilla?"

"Ha ha, so funny. I just want the details."

"I fucked her pussy, while he fucked her in the arse. Is that detailed enough for you?"

"I didn't even know that was a thing. I'm obviously watching the wrong porn," I mutter, covering my mouth again, half mortified, half turned on. "And then what, how are you still friends? How on earth did you look at each other the next day?"

He runs his hands through his hair again. "I don't know, we just kind of pretended it didn't happen, didn't talk about it again, until a few months later when she told me she was in love with him as well. She said she was in love with both of us and didn't know what to do. I was in shock. I probably should have seen it coming. When I look back now, I can see the signs were all there, but at the time I had no idea. So I ended it with her and we moved here.

"Did your mate know how she felt?"

"Yeah, he's my best mate, we tell each other everything."

"Wow, that's crazy, Blake. I'm sorry I made you tell me, I feel bad now. I thought it was just some random sexy story."

"Don't worry about it. It kind of feels good to talk to someone about it, you know?"

"Yeah, I do." I check my watch and it's after 1am.

"They're going to be closing up here soon. You want to keep playing while you walk me home?"

"You want to keep playing after that?" He laughs at me.

"Yeah, I'm making a new friend. I like hearing your stories. Makes me feel like I'm not the only one who's got a shitty life."

He laughs at me again. "You're a strange one, Elena. Come on, let's go."

"Blakie, if we're going to be friends you need to call me Elly." He nods his head, and we link arms as we walk out the front doors onto the beach.

"You're going to have to hold me up. I'm a little drunk," I giggle. He's gone quiet now, deep in thought. Maybe I shouldn't have pushed him to tell his story.

"We can walk up the beach. I know a shortcut home." We stumble over to the beach and both take off our shoes. Then I grab his arm again.

"Okay, I think I need to even up this game," I tell him. "One, I'm allergic to peanuts. Two, in high school, I was secretly in love with my twin brother's best friend. Three, I've had a threesome."

He gives me a sideways glance. "Well, I know you haven't had a threesome after our last conversation, 'Miss Vanilla', so that was a bit easy."

I just laugh at him and nod.

"In love with your twin brother's best friend, that sounds complicated. How did you keep that secret? I bet that would've been hard."

"It was so hard. He didn't have the best home life, so he was around our place a lot, like every weekend, and sometimes through the week too. When we were younger, the three of us hung out, riding our bikes or playing in our yard making up games. We were even on the same soccer team until I got too good for them," I laugh. "I'm not good at sports at all! Then once we got to year nine, Drew and his friend were popular with the girls so they would hang out with their girlfriends. It was awkward and didn't help that I was in love with him, so I made some new friends." We stop walking when we get to the front of my house.

He brushes the hair out of my eyes. "You never told him how you felt?"

"He knew. After our graduation, we talked about it, and swear you will never tell anyone?"

"I will never tell anyone whatever it is you're about to tell me."

"We kind of slept together. No one back here knows, not even my friend Indie. My brother would have killed us if he knew. It was so hard. He said he felt the same way, but it could never be anything other than friends because of my brother. And that was the end of it," I shrug. "What ya going to do? It was just a high school crush and I haven't seen him since. Thanks for holding me up all the way home."

"No worries, I promised your parents I would look after you, and had to get you home safe. Your dad's kind of scary."

I laugh, "Only to men who do the wrong thing by me. I'm sure you'll be fine. How are you getting home now?"

"I live the next street over, so I'll just walk, all good. Go get to bed, sleep it off, and if you're a good girl, I'll come to take you for breakfast in the morning."

"Thanks, Dad," I laugh at him and stumble backwards, falling into the garden, laughing hysterically at myself.

"Whoops, Dad's going to kill me, this garden is his pride and joy."

Blake reaches down and pulls me up. "Thanks for a fun night. You made me forget." He's still holding my hands in his, and I look up into his eyes as he stares back at me. My head is spinning and I'm not sure if I'm reading this correctly or not. Should I just kiss him? Then he quickly lets go of my hands and takes a step back.

"You're a mess, get to bed." My ego is a little bruised, but he's probably right. I salute him then stumble to my front door, fumbling around for my keys. Thank heavens I'm not in heels or I'd be on my arse again. I make it in the front door, turn and wave goodbye. What a night!

CHAPTER THREE

ELENA

Oh, my head hurts. I try to open my eyes but the light burns. Why didn't I close the blinds last night? I need something for the pain and fast. I slowly open my eyes and let the light sink in, then sit up and pull back the sheets. Why am I naked? Oh my God, I didn't bring him back to my parents' place, did I? How mortifying.

I check my phone. Ahh, it's 11:30am. I've missed half the day already. I haven't slept in that long in forever. This room is doing things to me. Could be the paint fumes mixed with alcohol, though, I guess. What on earth did we get up to last night? I remember dinner, playing some pool, losing, drinking a lot of shots, then it's all a bit hazy. I pull on my PJs and dressing gown and tiptoe down the hall. The timber floor is cold under my feet, but I can't find my slippers, so I'll have to just suck it up. Painkillers are more important right now.

Luckily there's no one in sight. My parents must be out. Thank heavens! I don't want Mum and Dad to see me like this. I grab the painkillers and a glass of water and head straight to the bathroom. I need a shower.

I throw back the painkillers and jump out of my robe. Turning on the shower, the hot water hits my back, and my body slowly returns to the land of the living. After an extra-long shower, I head back into my room. My head's still pounding but it's bearable now. I need clothes. As I stand in my wardrobe trying to decide what to wear, my tummy rumbles loudly. I need food, I'm starving!

A message pings on my phone and I check to see that it's Blake:

Blake: How's my drinking buddy holding up this morning?

Elena: Better after a shower and some painkillers. What about you?

Blake: Never been better. I feel kind of bad you got so smashed on my watch. I'm coming to take you for coffee to make it up to you.

Elena: You don't have to do that. I'm a big girl and I can take care of myself. Plus, pretty sure this was all my fault anyway!

Blake: Ha ha, definitely was, but I'm out the front already so I'm taking you out.

I look through the blinds. Shit, he's here!

Elena: Okay, give me a minute, I'm still in a towel.

Blake: No worries, I'll wait for you out the front.

I need clothes quick. I pull on a pair of denim shorts, a bra, and T-shirt, grab my thongs and bag and run to the bathroom. I quickly chuck on some foundation and lipstick then pull my hair up in a messy top bun. I'm out the door within five minutes. That's pretty good for me.

Blake's standing by the mailbox looking way too good after a night out drinking. He's going to think I'm a total mess.

"Hey," I say, feeling a little shy after last night and having blurry memories of what we actually got up to.

"Hey, yourself. You look good for someone who got home at 2am and drank the better part of a bottle of tequila."

"Thanks, I think. Was it really that late? Maybe you can remind me how I got home? My memory is a little blurry after we started playing pool."

"That bad, hey? Well, it was your idea to wipe your memory. Don't worry, you didn't do anything to embarrass yourself. I'm sure your Dad's plants will be just fine." He points to the mess in the front garden. "You took a tumble."

I slap my face. "Oh no, how embarrassing." I pause for a minute trying to think of how I ask this next question. "Did we...?" I gesture between us.

"I was a perfect gentleman. I'm not into taking advantage of girls when they're fall-down drunk."

"Oh, okay, that's good. I mean, I would want to remember, that's all." My tummy rumbles again, so loudly I'm sure Blake heard. "Where are you taking me for breakfast?"

"I haven't noticed it before but there's a café on the corner up the road. Do you want to give it a go?"

I chuck my thongs on the ground and wiggle into them. "Anywhere. I need coffee and food ASAP." We start walking up the hill to the café. "So, anything I should know about last night? Did we just play pool? How did we get home so late?"

Now he's giving me a mischievous smirk and I know I must have done something. "We played pool and some game you made up, Two Truths and a Lie or something?"

"Oh my God, what did I tell you?"

"Well, I know all your long-lost secrets now. You're very

chatty when you're drunk. Something about a peanut allergy and that you're a twin."

"I'm very chatty all the time. Well, that's not so bad."

"So, is your twin still living at home as well?"

"Ha ha, you're so funny. I get it. I'm a loser living at home. And no, he's off living the dream life. On the world surfing tour, he's currently ranked number eight. Definitely the more successful twin."

"Nice, that's pretty impressive. Bet you miss him?"

"Every day. We were super close before I moved to Sydney. We still message most days when he's not too busy with his exciting life."

"Must be nice having a family that's so close. My family is kind of fucked up, we're not close. My dad calls on occasion but it's normally for a favour I'd rather not do. Or to try get me to move back to Sydney and help with the family business, and there's no chance of that happening."

"Really? That sounds sweet your dad wants you to be involved in his business. Is he a builder like you?"

"Ah no. It's not the kind of family business you would want to be involved in, and definitely not sweet. You're lucky to have the family you do," he says, with sad eyes.

"Yeah, I know, even if they drive me nuts sometimes." We stop when we get to the café on the corner of the street and take a seat out the front. "I never even noticed this place before and it's right up the street." The smell of fresh coffee and bacon waft through the air. "It smells so good. I'm starving."

"It smells amazing! Now I know it's here I'll be here all the time. We're living just around the corner. Until we get ourselves better set up here, so it's close. I'll go order the coffee. Do you want anything to eat as well?"

I quickly glance over the menu. "I'll just have the

sourdough with avo, thanks." Hopefully, that will make me feel better. He heads inside to order our food. He's so nice buying me breakfast. I wish I could remember more from last night. I wonder what else I told him in that game.

Blake returns with our coffees. "They'll bring our food out in a bit. They're super busy."

"Thank you." I scoop the mug up and inhale the smell. "How good is the smell of coffee. I hope this makes me feel better. What on earth did we drink last night other than wine and shots of tequila. I can't even remember when I felt this badly."

He laughs at me.

"It's not funny. How are you okay?"

"I'm twice your size, and you were determined to drink everything in sight."

The waitress arrives with our food, and I'm surprised to see it's a familiar face, one I haven't seen for a long time.

"Hey, Elly, I didn't know you were home. This must be your fiancé." Ah, I knew this was going to happen sooner or later. It's why I've been avoiding leaving the house.

"Hey, Indie." I jump up and hug her. "It's so nice to see you. This is Blake, a friend of mine, not my fiancé. He's the builder working on Mum and Dad's renos."

"Oh, that's lucky. Nice to meet you, Blake," she says, blushing.

"Ahh, yeah, hi. Indie, is it? Nice to meet you too," he replies.

"What are you doing home, Elly? Having a holiday from your perfect life in Sydney?"

"Ah, not quite, I've moved back in with Mum and Dad for a bit. Things didn't work out with Jessie and I needed a break from Sydney. Just looking for some work so I can stay here a bit until I figure out what's next. How are things with you?"

"Yeah, same old stuff, commissioning some art, but I need this gig just to tide me over. If you need work, we've got a waitress job going if you're interested? It could be like the good old days."

"Really? Yeah, that would be great, thanks."

"Drop by tomorrow afternoon. I can show you the ropes and we can catch up properly when it's not so busy."

"Thanks, Indie. It's so good to see you."

"See you later, Blake," she says shyly.

"I'm sure I will, Indie." He looks up from his food and offers a little wave and smile.

I sit back down, legs folded, and grab my coffee. "Friend from high school."

"Oh, okay. Looks like you scored yourself some work."

"Yeah. Might get me through till I get my business started anyway. Indie's a talented artist. I'll have to show you her work sometime." I bring the toast up to my mouth and bite into it, smashing the first piece as soon as I can. "This is yum." Blake has an egg-and-bacon roll that he is devouring just as quickly. "Yours looks good too."

"It's so good, maybe I should've got two," he mutters into his roll.

The food is making me feel so much better. Something comes back to me from last night. "So... I'm curious, since I can't remember much from last night, what secrets did you tell me?" I say, raising an eyebrow at him.

He leans back in his chair, hands behind his head looking way too relaxed. He thinks he's off the hook. "Luckily for me, you can't remember, and I think it's best we keep it that way."

"I'm remembering something about you in a threesome. Is that correct?" I smirk.

He crosses his arms across his chest. "Nope, your memory must be tricking you." A message pings on Blake's phone. He grabs it out of his pocket and checks the message. "That's just my business partner. I've got to get going, we have a project we have to get finished this arvo."

"Saved by the bell, hey?" I stand up and hug him. "Thanks for breakfast and a fun night, I think?"

"It was fun. We can do it again if you want. See you tomorrow when you drop off your portfolio."

"Sounds good, see you then." He walks off around the corner and I make my way home.

This is so frustrating. I've been sitting on my laptop trying to work out a business plan for hours, but seriously, this is not my thing. As much as I hate to admit it, I think I'm going to have to ask for help.

I'm dreading dinner tonight. I still don't feel that crash hot after last night. I have managed to avoid my parents all day by locking myself in my room. But it's 4pm now, and soon my brother Theo and his fiancée Fiona will be here for Sunday family dinner, so I'm going to have to crawl out of my bedroom cave eventually.

I love my big brother but he's such a mummy's boy. Ever since he moved out, he's been coming every Sunday for dinner. I won't admit it to the rest of them, but it is kind of nice to have family around. I didn't realise how much I missed them all.

There's a knock at my bedroom door and Mum pops her head around the door. "Hey, Elly, you okay? You've been in here all day." She comes in and sits on the bed next to me.

"Yeah, all good, just been trying to work out my business plan." I sit up and show her my laptop screen. "I'm not getting anywhere."

"Thought you might've been too hungover and trying to avoid us since you didn't get in till two?"

"Did you wait up?"

"You weren't exactly quiet when you came in. You were singing and crashing into the walls." She laughs at me.

I smack my head. "Sorry, Mum, that's so embarrassing."

"Sounds like you had a good time. I'd say that's a good thing, honey. You know, if you want to bring boys home it's okay with us. We like Blake, he's a nice boy. You don't have to worry about all that. Your father and I don't mind, we know you're a grown-up now."

Oh my, I'm way too tired and old to be having this conversation. I need to find a place to live as soon as I can. I need to change the subject. "Did I tell you I got a job today? You remember Indie from school? I ran into her when I went for a coffee and she offered me a job. So I might be out of your hair sooner rather than later."

"That's great, honey, but don't feel like you need to rush. You can stay as long as you need to. It's been nice having you home." She puts her arm around me and pulls me into her.

"Thanks, Mum, but you know me, I need my 'independence'," we both say together.

"Yes, I know, but the offer stands as long as you need it. Now come downstairs and help me get sorted for dinner. Your brother will be here soon and apparently they have news." She pats her belly and raises her brow.

"You think? But they're not married yet."

"That's my guess."

Interesting. They're not mucking around, they only just

got engaged. "I'll just have a quick shower then I'll be down to help."

I walk into the kitchen to see Theo and Fiona are already here.

"You're finally gracing us with your presence, sis."

"Hey, guys, what's going on with you?"

"Well, we were waiting for you to get here so we could tell you all some exciting news," Theo announces, standing behind Fiona with his arms wrapped around her. They look so in love.

"We're having a baby!" Fiona yells excitedly. "Sorry, Theo, you were taking too long."

We all hug and congratulate them. Mum takes Fiona under her arm and they go off excitedly into the study to look at the ultrasound images. Mum's been dying for a grandchild, and that gets me off the hook for a little while longer.

I grab two beers from the fridge and hook arms with Theo. "Let's sneak outside before Mum makes me help."

He takes the second beer, giving me his signature cheeky wink.

"Wow, Theo, that's exciting news, you're going to be a dad."

"Yeah, it was a bit of a surprise. We were going to wait till after the wedding, but that can wait now. We're both so excited."

We sneak out to the back deck and sit in the swinging egg chairs. "Can you believe our yard's about to be turned into holiday accommodation?" I whine, with a pout.

"Yeah, I know, there's so many good memories out here, but I think it'll be good for Dad. He needs a change, he's not himself lately."

"Yeah, I noticed that too! Do you think he's all right?"

"I think he's just ready for a change, something more positive. Working on the force can be mentally draining, I would know, and he's been there for nearly forty years. It's a long time to be on the force."

I can't stop picking at the label on my beer. It's annoying me. "Yeah, that's probably it."

"Everything all right with you, sis? Mum tells me you went out with some guy last night. I think she's marrying you off to him already."

I roll my eyes at him. "Of course she is! He's not some guy, he's just our builder, Blake, and it wasn't a date, we just hung out."

"Likely story. But do you mean the builder from The Green Door?"

"Yeah, I think that's what the business is called. Why?"

"Do you think that's such a good idea? You know his business partner, the architect, is Fraser, right?"

"Fraser who?" I sit up as my heart starts to beat a little faster at the mention of that name. The name that is etched in my heart and always has been, even though I know nothing can ever happen with him.

"Fraser Davis, Drew's best mate from high school. That's why Dad chose them for the job."

"I didn't even realise he was back home." I can feel my face heat at the mention of his name. We're both back in the same town again. How do I navigate this?

"Yeah, he's been back a little while. I caught up with him last week. He was always so protective of you in high school. I'm pretty sure he's not going to be happy about you dating his business partner."

"Theo, that was years ago. He doesn't even know I'm home. I'm sure he's not going to care. Besides, Blake and I are just friends, not dating or anything," I say, trying to brush it off as nothing, but it's not nothing. It has never been nothing when it comes to Fraser.

Oh my God, realisation dawns on me at what Blake told me last night. Fraser Davis is Blake's roommate and business partner. That means Fraser was the one Blake's girlfriend fell in love with. This could be a whole lot of fucked-up awkward. Luckily, we didn't do anything last night. I think.

I can't believe he's back home as well. I was so obsessed with Fraser in high school, he was the star of my diary. And entered my thoughts quite a few times over the years. Hearing his name takes me back to that night after graduation. But that was just one night. Long ago. So much has changed since then and I'm sure when I see him, whatever it was we had back then, will all feel like some silly high school crush. Intensified by the fact he was Drew's best friend and totally out of bounds. One thing's for sure, it's going to be weird seeing him again, and there's going to be no avoiding it with him working on this job for Dad.

Theo is smugly smiling at me. "What?" I say, agitated.

"Nothing. You went awfully quiet, that's all. He's single, if you were wondering."

"I wasn't even thinking about him."

"Yeah, right. You know Drew and I read your diary in high school, right? You were in love with him," he teases.

"You read my diary? You dick!" I throw the cushion from my chair at him.

He laughs his head off, "Yeah, we did. It was all, Fraser Davis is so hot, I can't wait for him to realise we're soul mates and we will get married and be together forever and always."

"I didn't say that." I jump up and storm off.

"It was something like that," he calls after me.

"I can't hear you," I call back, covering my ears.

I head inside to grab my phone. I can't believe they read my diary. They never said anything to me about it back then. I'm surprised at Drew, we told each other everything, or so I thought. I'm going to text him now. I have no idea what time zone he is in today, and I don't care if I wake him.

Elena: Thanks for not having my back when we were kids! You're not my favourite brother anymore!

A message pings back straight away.

Drew: Hey, what did I do now?

Elena: You and Theo reading my diary.

Drew: Did he tell you that? I never read your diary! But Theo would have for sure, thinking it was his right as the oldest to know all the facts of our lives.

Elena: Lucky for you. All right, you're back to being my favourite brother. How are you anyway? I miss you.

Drew: Well, I've got good news then, I'm coming home this week for our birthday!!

Elena: Really? That will be amazing. We haven't had a birthday together for years.

Drew: I've got a bit of a break in events, so I'll be home for a month. It'll be good to catch up with you. Did you hear Fraser is home too?

Elena: Yeah. Just found out.

Drew: It'll be like old times. Anyway, got to go, sis, see you on Wednesday.

Elena: See you then, bro.

Mum and Fiona are back in the kitchen preparing dinner.

"So nice of you to come and help us, Elly."

"Sorry, Mum, I'll help now." I grab a chopping board

and sit next to Fiona at the breakfast bar. "Your fiancé is a dick!"

"What did he do now?"

"He's just informed me he used to read my diary when I was a kid and he's using it against me!"

"Totally a dick move! But not that surprising for Theo. He can't help himself when it comes to sticking his nose in other people's business." She rolls her eyes. I don't know how she puts up with him.

"Mum, did Drew tell you he's coming home for a month?"

She stops washing the lettuce and looks up at me. "No, when's he coming?"

"On Wednesday this week, I just talked to him."

"Nice of him to let me know. Typical of Drew." She goes back to preparing the salad, mumbling to herself. "You know what, Elly? We should have a party for your birthdays. When was the last time we were all here at the same time? We could have it in the backyard before they dig it up for the holiday villas."

"I can help you organise it if you want," Fiona offers, looking up from her cutting duties.

"Yeah, sounds good, Mum. I'll see who's around and let you know."

Two hours later and we're just finishing up with our dessert, Mum's famous chocolate cheesecake. It's seriously the best thing you can put in your mouth. I'm hoping Theo doesn't eat it all so there's some left over for tomorrow.

The rest of the dinner was pretty uneventful, and I'm exhausted after last night. I wonder if it's too early to escape back to my cave. "Thanks for dinner, Mum. I'm going to head up to my room and keep on working on my portfolio for tomorrow. See you guys later in the week." Don't know why I'm even bothering to do my portfolio now I know the architect is the one and only Fraser Davis. I'm pretty sure working with him is going to be a bad idea. A really bad idea.

"She's probably just rushing off to write in her diary," Theo teases, laughing at his own joke.

"Real mature, Theo," I snap, slapping him on the back of the head as I walk past. That will stop his laughing. I say my goodbyes then make my way up the hall to my room. So tomorrow I'll see Fraser again. As I lie on my bed, the last conversation we had plays over in my head:

"I can't believe that just happened. I thought the chemistry we had was all in my head. Now I know it wasn't, you feel it too."

"It's been there all along, gorgeous, I just knew we couldn't go there. So I've been trying to fight it."

"Why tonight then?"

"You walked into the party looking stunning on his arm and something took over me. I couldn't ignore the way I feel about you anymore."

"So you were just jealous because I was with someone else?"

"No, that's not it. I just realised how I felt, I knew I had to have you."

"And now what? We can tell Drew and actually be together?"

"Elly, you know you mean the world to me, but we can't tell Drew. Your brother's my best friend and he will kill us, and if he doesn't, he will probably never talk to me again." I can still feel his strong arms around me, hugging me as he whispers the torturous words, breaking my heart forever.

"Then why did you just let this happen... it was you who started it, you kissed me, why would you let it go this far if it

wasn't going anywhere?" Tears fall from my eyes. I can't stop them. This hurts too much.

"You know I want something more too, gorgeous, but we can't. Just stay with me tonight, let us have this." *His lips are on mine again, desperate, wanting. I pull back from him and I can see the hurt in his eyes.*

"Are you serious? You knew what tonight meant to me, I'm not just one of the sluts you normally bring home! I was waiting for the right person, you knew that!" *I sit up, now madly pulling on my clothes. I can't believe this is happening after I trusted him.*

"I know you're not. This was really special to me too. I don't want to lose you because of this, you mean too much to me."

"Too late, Fraser! What, I'm supposed to watch you with other girls now and pretend I'm okay? When I know what we have here is real, but you're just too scared to tell my brother? Sorry, I can't do it!"

"You think it's not hard for me too?" *He pulls me back down on the bed, trying to kiss me again, but I push him away.*

"You've made your choice, Fraser. Don't tell me we can't but continue to kiss me, it's so unfair. I can't do whatever this is between us anymore. I leave for Sydney next week and that's it. I need to move on from you. It hurts too much to be so close to you and not be with you."

"You're moving to Sydney and didn't tell me?"

"I hadn't made my mind up until tonight, but I am now. There's nothing keeping me here."

"If that's what you want, Elly, then that's how it'll be."

I grab my bag and walk out of his bedroom. I'm never going to recover from this. My heart shatters into a million tiny pieces.

And that was that. I lost more than just my virginity that night, I lost one of my best friends. I haven't seen him since. Of course Drew still talks about him, but once he was on the surf tour, they didn't see each other as much and we all just got on with our own lives. I wonder what he looks like now. I have to admit I have stalked him a couple of times on Facebook, but not for a few years.

Tomorrow will be interesting.

CHAPTER FOUR

FRASER

"Sophie, wake up," I call, slapping her on the arse. "You need to go, I'm late for work."

Sophie's sprawled out over my bed, naked as the day she was born, and she's not moving at all. Sunday night drinks with her was a bad idea. She begged to see me again, and after the wild night we had on Friday, how could I resist—or should I say, how could my dick resist? I've been seeing her for a few weeks. There's not much conversation between us. Not to stereotype, but she's kind of a dumb blonde, but the sex is fucking hot so I keep going back for more. "I'm jumping in the shower," I call back to her. She's starting to wake now finally.

I hop in the shower and the warm water breathes new life into me. My body's waking up for the day. I think back to poor Sophie. I know she's getting attached, I can feel it, so it's inevitable that this arrangement we have needs to end soon. I've been like this since high school. It's just easier. You get too attached to anyone and you're just in for heartache. I learned that the hard way, watching my dad pine after my bitch of a mother when she took off with another man.

I thought I had something with someone once, but she turned out the same as my mum and left. So that shit's not going to happen to me again. I'll have my fun then move on when I'm bored or they start getting too attached, then I'll find someone new to play with. The girls know that's the way it's going to be from the start, so if they get hurt that's on them. I know I sound like a selfish arsehole and I probably am, but this works for me.

I turn off the shower and dry off, trying to pull myself together, ready for a massive day that I'm already late for.

I glance at my car clock as I pull into our parking lot of our building. It's 11am already. I'm running so late; Blake is going to be pissed. He likes everything running to our schedule and now our whole day will be off. I have a shitload of work that has to be done today as well. I'm going to be here till late now. That's what you get when you rock up late to work and it's your own business—the work still has to be done. We share this office with our third business partner, Ash, he's the developer. But he is very rarely in, preferring to work from home unless he has a meeting, and he could care less what time I'm in.

I push through the double mahogany doors to our office and round the corner, stopping dead in my tracks. Blake's office blinds are open, and he's in there with a girl. Not just any girl. *My* girl. It's her.

I can hardly believe my eyes. It might have been years since I've seen her in the flesh, but I know that body. I memorised every inch of it in high school. She's standing at Blake's desk, leaning over slightly, looking through a folder on his desk. Her black jeans are so tight they look painted on. She's not the young girl I knew back then, all shy and innocent. I can tell that by just looking at her and watching the way she interacts with Blake.

She has confidence about her as she flicks her hair over her shoulder and chats to him. She's animated like she's telling a story, and she's sexy as fuck. I watch them for a while, trying to process what's going on here. They're deep in conversation, and now she's laughing at something he said. I know Blake, he's not that funny. What's going on between them? What's she doing here in our office?

I shake my head as if to erase what I've been watching. Who knows how long I was standing here spying, but I better stop watching them like some weirdo before I get caught. I walk into my office, which is adjacent to Blake's, and dump my coffee cup, and the work I took home with me over the weekend, on my desk. I check myself out in the glass door and walk straight to Blake's office. I knock once on his door then walk in, not waiting for a reply.

I want to know what she's doing in his office and now. I'm not a patient man. Lucky Blake's used to me by now, after living with me for years, and now sharing an office too, he knows I'm not waiting for anything.

"Hey, mate. Sorry I'm late. What's going on here? Did I miss the memo?" They both turn to look at me. Fuck, she's stunning. She's even better than I remember. With long hair, a strange colour for her. Blue? But it suits her, frames her oval-shaped face. She has such pretty features she could get away with anything.

She was always a little different to the other girls at school. They used to make fun of her because she was different, but for me, it's a massive turn-on. Her pouty red lips turn into her trademark massive smile as soon as she sees me. You don't forget a smile like that. It was the first thing that attracted me to her all those years ago. She would flash that smile and you would have to smile back. It's contagious. But it's those eyes, they draw me in every time, they're somewhere between green and blue, and when she flutters those long lashes I'm gone. She hasn't even said a word and already I know it—I'm screwed when it comes to her.

Blake clears his throat. "Fraser, good morning." He's checking his watch as we have a silent conversation with our eyes.

Yes, I know, I'm late, get on with it. Though why is she here? I turn to look back at her, and her gaze roams over me, those eyes drawing me in already. I've got to stop looking at her, but I can't.

"This is Elena. I forgot to tell you yesterday that she would be dropping in. She's an interior stylist and brought in her portfolio to show you, for some of the styling jobs."

Before I know it, she jumps up and wraps her arms around me, pulling me into her body. I can't help but inhale her scent. She smells amazing. She smells like summer, vanilla and coconut maybe. It must be her hair, it's intoxicating.

"If it isn't *the* Fraser Davis. So nice to see you again after all this time."

"Elena Walker, nice to see you too."

Blake is now standing up looking completely confused. "You two know each other?" He gestures between us.

Elena giggles. "We did a long time ago."

"Her twin was my best mate in high school. You know, Drew the surfer, he's stayed with us before."

"Yeah, of course, why didn't I connect this all up sooner?" Blake's eyes have gone wide and he's looking at Elena like she's in trouble for not saying anything.

"I didn't work it out either until last night, when Theo said Fraser had moved home and you work together."

She leaves my arms and I feel the loss straight away as she moves over to sit on Blake's desk. I don't like this. They look all cosy.

"How do you two know each other? And how did I not know about it?" I motion between them.

"We met last week when I went to measure up for the Walker job. Jim was out and Elly was helping in his place."

"And then Blake showed me a good time on Saturday night, followed by breakfast Sunday morning," she taunts with a cheeky smile, bumping Blake's arm. If I didn't know better, I'd think she was trying to bait me, and it's working. What the fuck is going on? Are they together? I shift my stance and cross my arms. I'm starting to get pissed.

Blake can see my change in mood. "That's not exactly how it went now, did it, Elly?"

"What... oh fine, we've just been hanging out. I've been bored out of my brains at home with Mum and Dad, and Blake kindly offered to take me out for the night."

"I see. Well, did you want to show me that portfolio? You can bring it into my office and I'll have a look through now, if you like?" I say, gesturing towards the door.

"Sure, thanks." She turns to look back to Blake. "I'll come to grab you for lunch when we're done," she says, with that massive smile I thought she saved only for me.

"Thanks, that would be good." He goes back to working on his computer.

I wait patiently for her as she slowly makes her way to my office, then I close the door. I don't want Blake to hear this conversation. She places her portfolio on my desk and takes a seat, looking very carefree and relaxed. Just as she always used to. That was something I used to like about her.

She had a calming presence over me, one of the only ones that could calm my crazy.

Except when she was making me jealous, like now.

"What's going on here, Elly? I thought you were living in Sydney with that arsehole, what's his name, about to make the biggest mistake of your life by marrying him. Then I arrive at work this morning to find you all over my business partner." I sit across from her, giving her my 'I'm not happy' glare. If I was going to see her again this was not how I wanted it to happen.

"Wow," she says, straightening up in her chair and crossing her arms, "you haven't changed a bit, Fraser. Still think you have some kind of say in how my life should be? Stop looking at me like that. If you must know, I left Jessie three months ago because he cheated on me! Oh, and I wasn't all over Blake, I was showing him my work."

"I see, well, you're better off without him anyway. From what I hear from Drew, he was a total dick. What's going on with Blake? Are you sleeping with him?"

"Um, totally inappropriate for the office, Fraser! Do you really expect me to answer that?"

"Yes, it's my office, I can ask what I want." I'm getting angry now. Why won't she just tell me what's going on? I want to know what I'm up against. Blake and I have had trouble in the past with girls, and I don't want this to become a problem.

She rolls her eyes at me, obviously annoyed at my questions. "Not that it's any of your business, but no! We're just friends, he's been nice to me, that's it. What's your problem anyway? I'm 25, pretty sure I can sleep with whoever I want. Thought you would have grown up and moved on from all your jealous mood swings by now."

"Not when it comes to you, obviously," I huff.

She rolls her eyes at me again. "Well, you might have to sort that problem out. I thought I was here to show you my portfolio so I could try and get some work, but if you're going to be a dick, I don't want to work with you anyway." She grabs her portfolio and stands to leave, heading for the door. But I get there first and put my arm over the door so she can't open it. She looks pissed. Really pissed. Shit, I've gone too far.

"Sorry, Elly, I was just surprised to see you after all this time, that's all. I didn't mean to have a go at you."

"Yeah, well, you did. My life is already shit enough, I don't need you making me feel even worse. Why do you care if I'm seeing Blake, anyway?"

"I don't, I was just surprised, that's all. I'm sorry things have been shit for you lately. Come sit back down. I'll have a look at your portfolio and see if we can work something out."

"You have no idea how shit, Fraser. I feel like my whole world has fallen apart." She slowly walks back to my desk, taking a seat.

I flick through her work. "So, you worked as the assistant stylist on Project Reno for the last four years, but weren't you just helping out the designer? Have you ever managed a project of your own?"

"I was managing *all* of the projects on my own. That's why I left. My boss was a total narcissistic bitch. She was great on camera, but she didn't do anything behind the scenes. So, yes, I can handle any project by myself. That's why I'm here. I'm starting my own interior styling business and I was hoping you guys might need a freelance stylist. Blake said sometimes you work on larger projects and need someone to style for sale."

I look back over her portfolio, flicking through the pages

of work. "Everything I can see here looks really good. Your style would suit our aesthetic perfectly. But I need to ask you something, and I need you to answer honestly. Do you think we can work together with our history?"

She looks down at her hands for a minute as if contemplating how to answer, then her eyes lift and look straight into mine. "Without a doubt. When it comes to my work, I'm a total professional. Besides, there's nothing here but two old high school friends who now work in the same industry."

Good answer, but I can see in her eyes that there is more here. The chemistry that we had back then, it's still here. I can feel it. I haven't felt like this since I gave up on us all those years ago, and I know, when it comes to Elly, I'm in big trouble. But just like when we were kids, when it comes to her, I can't help myself. I want to see how this is going to play out. "Okay, well, if you're sure?" I ask.

She nods her head.

"We have a smaller project for some townhouses in Broken Point that need styling for sale. They go to auction next month so you would need to get started straight away if you're interested."

"That sounds perfect. Yes, I'm interested, thank you."

"I'll email you the project brief and budget. You will need to include your wage when working out how you spend your budget."

"Okay, perfect. I don't have a business card yet. Can I just write my number and email down somewhere for you?" She scribbles it down on a scrap of paper from her bag.

"I'll put it in my phone now so I don't lose it."

"Thank you so much for this opportunity, Fraser. I can't tell you how much I appreciate you taking a chance on me." She smiles. Fuck, she's gorgeous when she smiles.

"No worries. I'm sure you'll do an amazing job."

She gets up to leave then turns just before the door, catching me watching her. "Drew's home this week and Mum's organising a birthday party on Saturday night for us, if you want to come? I'm sure Drew would love to see you."

"I spoke to him last week, and he didn't say he was coming home. He didn't tell me you were home either, though."

"He's hopeless! Don't worry, he forgot to tell Mum as well, she only found out because of me. Thanks again." She smiles.

I watch through the open door as she walks back into Blake's office. There's definitely something more than just friends going on there, and I don't like it. I need to set him straight quickly. If I can't have her, he can't either.

Elena

I walk back into Blake's office, and he looks up and smiles the instant he sees me. "You ready for lunch?" I ask.

He motions for me to sit on the brown leather lounge in his office. "I've just got to finish sending one email then we can go."

I sit scrolling through my phone while I wait. Fraser looks the same but also so different. He's bigger than I remember. I mean, he was always kind of built, even in high school, but now his arms are massive, and you can almost see the outline of his six-pack through his shirt. I would love to run my hand over his chest. His dark hair is different too, not the short and spiky haircut he had going on. It's now longer in the front. He looks good, too good.

I'm not sure why I'm bothering to scroll through my

phone, I'm not taking anything in. All I can think about is him and how this morning went differently than how I planned in my head. I'm not sure what I was expecting. Fraser has always been jealous when it comes to me dating, one of the reasons I moved so far away after high school. He wanted to keep me close but not be with me. I had to move away so I could start over without him around. I'm not letting him do that to me again. I'm here for the long haul now. I love it here in Byron and I'm so glad I came back home. Once I get a bit of money together and start this business properly, I'm moving out of Mum and Dad's and putting my life back together here. He's just going to have to grow up and deal with seeing me with other men, because I'm sure he's dating half of Byron.

My phone lights up with a number I recognise, but I'm not sure if I should answer or not?

Blake looks over his computer at me. "You going to get that?"

"It's my old work," I say, pulling a scared face.

"Find out what they want."

I answer, my voice unsure and a little shaky. "Hello."

"It's Bridget, the network has asked that I call you and see if you would consider your old job back," she barks. Still the same old Bridget, no warmth or emotion in her voice, just straight to the point. It must be killing her to make this call. She will never admit that she is wrong, but just by the fact that she is calling now, I know it's all turning to shit over there.

"I'm confused. I thought you said you could replace me in a heartbeat," I say, a little smugger than I intended but it totally serves her right.

"Well, it seems I may have underestimated the job you were doing. We have had all three of your replacements quit within weeks of starting. And the suppliers are being difficult to work with."

"Have you ever thought that's because you're difficult to work with? Sorry, Bridget, I wouldn't come back even if you doubled my salary. Maybe this is karma saying you need to change the way you work with people. Good luck with it all."

I hang up; I don't need to hear her reply. It feels good to know she had to come crawling back, but I'm well and truly done with that life.

"Everything all right?" asks Blake.

"Yeah, get this. That was my old work wanting me back!"

"Bet it felt good to turn her down."

"Yeah, it did." I smile. Funny how things worked out today. I have been offered work and hope for my new future, and the past is testing me, seeing if I'll take the easy road and go back to what I know.

I wonder how poor Janie is, so I send her a quick text.

Elly: What's going on? The Dragon just rang and offered my job back.

Janie: She's trying to save the sinking ship, but I think it's too late.

Elly: What, the show is going to be axed?

Janie: I'd say so. We have two jobs left, then nothing else booked. It's not looking good.

Elly: I'm sorry, Janie.

Janie: It's okay, I was ready to quit anyway. This way I'll get a payout until I work out what to do next.

Elly: Good luck with it all. If you ever feel like leaving the city, let me know. I'm sure I could find something here for you.

Janie: Thanks, I'll definitely think about it.

"Okay, I'm all done, let's go," Blake says, jumping up from behind his desk.

I follow behind him and catch a glance at Fraser in his office; he's trying to pretend he's working but it's obvious he's watching us. We head out of the office and start walking down the street. "Where do you want to go?" I ask.

"I'm taking you to Daisy's Diner, they have the best burgers in town."

"Nice, I do love a good burger."

We make it to the end of the street and the cutest little burger place with a flashing neon sign. This place is definitely a new addition to the Byron eateries. It's all decked out like a 1950's diner, with vinyl booth seats in pale pink and blue, and a pink-and-white checkerboard floor. It's so retro cool. I can see myself eating here a lot. We find one table left at the back. It's really busy. This place must have good food too. It looks like it's the place to have lunch for anyone who works around here.

I look through the menu, and everything looks so good. "I'm going to have the Southern fried chicken, what about you? It's my shout to say thank you for helping me get some work."

"You don't have to do that," he says.

"Yeah, but I want to. You've been so nice to me and you didn't even know me, I really appreciate it."

"Okay, thanks. I'll have the double beef and bacon with chips and a Coke."

"Not that hungry then," I tease. "I'll be back in a sec." I go to the counter and order our food and return with two Cokes.

"So, Blake, looks like you'll be seeing me a lot more."

"Fraser has offered you some work then?" He smiles.

"Yeah, he's sending me the details, some townhouses that need styling."

"That's great. He seemed kind of pissed that we knew each other. Was everything okay?"

"Yeah, he just needs to get over himself," I say, rolling my eyes.

"Elly, you probably don't remember this from the other night, but when we were playing that game, you told me you were in love with your brother's best friend in high school. That was Fraser, wasn't it?"

God, I'm so embarrassed, I bury my head in my hands. "I told you that? What did you give me, truth serum or something? I don't think I've ever told anyone that."

He laughs at me, "Maybe it was that blue cocktail thing?"

"It must have been. I'm never having one of them again," I laugh back. "You know I'm not still in love with him, though, right? That was years ago."

"Are you sure? It's pretty clear there's something between both of you. I've known Fraser for a while now, and he's never reacted like that with a girl."

Our food arrives and we start eating, quietly lost in our own thoughts.

"These are the best burgers," I mumble into my food. Probably with the sauce running down my chin.

"They are, hey?"

"So, if he's your business partner, he's the one that you split with your girlfriend over, isn't he?"

"Yeah." He nods.

"Wow." He's not making eye contact anymore, just eating his burger quietly. Maybe I shouldn't have brought that up.

"Blake, are you okay? You've gone all quiet on me."

"Yeah, it's just I like hanging out with you. Your smile's infectious, and you're pretty cool for a chick."

"Me too, Blake. I'm feeling better than I have in months."

"Yeah, but now I know that you and Fraser have a history, we can't keep hanging out. Things are going to get messy. I could see how jealous he was, and I can't afford to go down that road with him again."

"We don't have a history, we were just friends, you don't have to worry about Fraser."

"Yeah, just friends." He raises a suspicious brow at me. "I don't think that's how he sees it. I saw the way he was looking at you."

Is it that obvious or did I tell him more than I can remember the other night? "He's just a control freak. It's what he used to do to me in high school too. He'd scare every guy off who looked my way but didn't want me for himself. He just wanted to make sure no one else could either. You don't have to stop being friends with me because of him."

"It's not that easy and you know it," he grumbles, looking defeated.

"Yes, it is, he doesn't get to control who I'm friends with. Besides, I'm pretty sure you're into my friend Indie."

He looks up from his food, surprised with my question. "Who?"

"Don't play dumb with me, mister, I have eyes. I know you two were eye-fucking the shit out of each other the other morning at breakfast." His expression has changed to a small smirk and I know there's a story there.

"You know nothing, Elly." He smiles.

"Oh, I know plenty, Blake, and I will get it out of you." I laugh.

"Not today, baby. I gotta get back to work, thanks for lunch." He stands to leave.

"Next time, Blakie." I smile. "See you later. Actually, you should come to my party Saturday night, it's my birthday. Indie will be there," I tease. Well, I don't technically know if she will, but I love playing matchmaker and it's now my mission to get them both there.

"Yeah, maybe. See you later, Elly." I think I almost see him blush. I'm so right about this, I know it.

"Okay, I'll text you the details, hopefully you can come," I call as he walks out.

A COUPLE OF HOURS LATER, I WALK UP THE STREET TO the Hilltop Café and Indie's face lights up as soon as she sees me. "Hey, Indie, thanks so much for this."

"No worries at all, chickee, it's going to be like old times," she giggles. "It's so good you're home. After I show you through, stay for a bit. We need to catch up properly before the after-school rush starts."

"We so do, I've missed you."

She shows me through the café and talks me through all the processes and the menus. It's all pretty basic. Indie and I worked at a café together every Saturday morning when we were at high school, so it's nothing new.

"Come on, you make us a coffee to practise and we can sit and have a catch-up. I'll get us some cake too."

"Ooh, yes please. Hopefully it all comes back to me, it's been a while."

"It's not rocket science, I'm sure you'll be fine," she laughs at me.

Two attempts at making coffee later and we're sitting

down with our coffee and cake. It was a little harder than I remember.

"Sorry, I didn't call much. Life just got crazy, you know?" I say with a small smile, grabbing her hand across the table and giving it a squeeze. We were so close, and I know she has been through a lot over the last few years.

"It's okay, I didn't either, but it's nice to have you home now." She smiles back.

"I'm going to stay this time. I'm starting up an interior styling business."

"Really? That's so exciting."

"Hey, I checked out your Facebook page after I ran into you the other day. I want to use some of your art for my first freelance job. Would that be okay? Your art would be perfect with the look we're going for."

"Really? That would be amazing. What do you need?"

"I'm not 100% sure yet. I'll have a look over the brief and let you know."

"Who are you working for?"

"Remember Fraser Davis from high school? He has an architecture business here in Byron now, with the builder I was here with the other day. You remember Blake."

Her eyes raise to mine, and bingo! I knew there was something there, and she has just confirmed it. "Fraser and Blake, hey? That should be interesting," she says, raising her eyebrow at me.

"What? Why does everyone keep saying things to me like that?"

"No reason."

"Anyway, what happened with Hayden? I always thought you two would get married and have babies.

"How did you know we split?"

"Facebook. What happened? If you don't mind me asking?"

"He broke it off, wanted to experience different things. He was scared that, being with me since high school, he was missing out on something."

"Wow, that's harsh. I'm sorry, Indie." Her green eyes are glassy, and I can see she's still hurting. I wrap my arm around her and give her a comforting squeeze.

"Well, Indie, babe, we're in this together now. Who would have thought that at 25 we would still be no closer to knowing what to do with our lives than when we were 18."

She has a little giggle. "Yeah, I know. It's okay, Elly, it was a while ago, and the more I think about it, he was right. We were just going along with it all because it was easy and comfortable. We weren't in love anymore. I'm glad he had the guts, I didn't, before we got married and had kids. It could have been such a mess."

"Yeah, true." I sit and sip my coffee while I think about how I can change our luck with men. "This cake is so good. I'm going to get fat working here." We both laugh.

"You, my dear, will never get fat. If I remember right, you used to eat as much as Drew and still not put on a thing! It is good, though, hey? My boss Rachel makes all the food here and her cakes are to die for. She's out at the moment but I'll introduce you tomorrow."

I roll my eyes at her. It used to be a bit of a joke at school that I could eat whatever junk I wanted and not get fat. "I'm sure it'll catch up with me one day." I clap my hands all excited, "I've just had a thought. We're both single girls, we need to go out and celebrate. Drew will be home on Wednesday. We should go for drinks Thursday or Friday night, what do you say?"

"Yes, we so should. I haven't been out in forever. I can do Friday night, don't have to work Saturday."

"Perfect. Oh, and you have to come to my party on Saturday night too. Mum's organising it because Drew's home and we haven't been able to celebrate together for a while. And Blake will be there."

She rolls her eyes at me. "Who?"

"You're as bad as each other, I'm going to get to the bottom of whatever is going on between the two of you."

"There's nothing to get to the bottom of. Can you believe your dork brother is some big surf star travelling the world and followed by thousands on Instagram?"

"I know, right? What do you mean followed by thousands on Instagram?"

"He's like one of those influencers or something, Elly. Haven't you seen his page?"

"No, but there's no way he's an influencer. He's totally against all that shit. What, you follow him?"

"Everyone we went to high school with follows him. He got out of here and made it big. Plus, your brother's kinda hot!"

"Uh, yuck. You know he's my brother, he's not hot, he's a dork." She's cracking up at my face now, and it feels like we're taken back to the good old days, hiding out in the art studio creating, so we could avoid the school bitches.

The café is starting to fill up with people and the girl behind the counter looks flustered.

"I'll be there," calls Indie, sounding excited. "Do you want me to ask Rachel about the cake? She does birthday cakes too."

"Yeah, that would be perfect, thanks."

"I better get back to work, we're getting busy again. You

okay to start tomorrow at ten? You can do a quiet shift to start with."

"Thanks, Indie." I hug her goodbye and head off down the street. After today, I can take getting a job off my to-do list.

CHAPTER FIVE

FRASER

I jump up from my desk excitedly. I haven't seen this idiot's face in forever. "Look who the cat dragged in. Drew Walker, it's really you, in the flesh, not some superstar on my screen, with his girly haircut and all."

"Girly haircut, speak for yourself! I've missed you too, mate," he laughs, checking out the place. "Sweet office."

"Yeah, it's not bad, hey. It had to be something nice; you can hardly trust someone to design and build your house if their office is ugly as fuck."

"True, I guess." He shrugs, taking a seat.

"What's been going on with you, man? I've been following you on the tour this year. Number eight, hey, you've got to be happy with that!"

"Not till I'm number one, man. I'll be happy when I'm number one."

"I'm sorry, Mr Perfection, I forgot you are the most competitive person I know, second only to your sister."

"Yeah, right, you know I'm more competitive than her. Don't suppose you want to come for a surf with me while I'm home? I got to keep it up."

"No way. You'd kick my arse. I haven't been out for ages."

"It'll be wicked, you should come."

"I'll think about it."

"Elly tells me you've given her some work. She's excited about it. Thanks for that, man, she needed her luck to change."

"She's earned it. Her work is really good, and it sounds like she had a shitty time with her last boss. She deserves a go. No special treatment."

"Yeah, sure, everyone knows you've got a soft spot for her."

"Of course, I will always look out for her, she's your sister. She's nearly finished the project I gave her a month to work on, in less than a week. So far, her work speaks for itself. So, you seeing anyone?"

"Everyone," he laughs. "I'm in a different country every few weeks. It's a single man's dream."

"I bet. You'll have to take me with you," I laugh, but the truth is, all I can think about since she was in my office on Monday is Elly—his twin sister and the only girl I really can't have.

"You're not seeing anyone? Fraser Davis without some chick hanging off him, there's no way."

"You're so funny. Of course I'm seeing someone, but she's no one special."

"Nothing much has changed then."

"When are we hitting the town?"

"Elly wants to go out Friday night, you free?" he asks.

Does she now! This should be interesting. A night out with the Walker twins, just like old times. "Yeah, sounds good, man."

"Okay. I guess I'd better let you get some work done, but I'll see you Friday," he says, getting up to leave.

"Yeah, man, see you then."

Elena

It's finally Friday night. I've spent this week learning how to use the extremely sensitive coffee machine at the café. You wouldn't think it would be that hard, but that machine hates me! The boss, Rachel, is lovely and very patient. I'm sure she should have already fired me. I've had a shift there every day, just for a few hours, which is perfect because it gives me time to work on the styling project for The Green Door guys.

Drew's been home for two days and it's been amazing. Just like old times; man, I have missed him. We're not the type of twins that know each other's thoughts or anything, but we have always been close and it's so nice to have him home for a while. He's back to his usual self, though, eating all the food in the house, making everything a competition, and talking nonstop about how awesome he is at surfing.

Tonight, we're going out with Theo, Fiona, Blake, and Fraser, so Drew can catch up with the boys and I can party with Indie. That girl needs a night out more than me and that's saying something.

"I'm so excited we're going out tonight, chick. It's going to be like old times, it's so weird," she calls excitedly from in my wardrobe, where she's fixing her makeup in the mirror.

"I know, it's just what we need, a night out to check out the local talent. We're hooking up with some hotties tonight, Indie, and getting you over what's-his-name," I say, giving her a cheeky wink.

We're both dressed to impress tonight. Indie has been here for an hour getting ready. Her short dark hair is curled slightly, and her green eyes really pop with the smoky eye shadow. In high school, we used to spend hours in my room playing with makeup and creating different versions of ourselves. She's the kind of girl who can pull off any style and look like a completely different person every time. She has an amazing bone structure and a body to die for. Tonight, she's rocking an edgy short black dress that shows off the intricate flower tattoos that trail down her right arm.

"Did this hurt?" I ask, as I run my hand over her tattoos. "I've always wanted to get one, but I've been too scared. You know how I am with needles."

She laughs at me, "Honestly, anyone else I'd say do it, it doesn't hurt that much, but not you, Elly. Witnessing you freak out getting your year-nine immunisations as you passed out in front of the hottest guy in school. Hilarious, but not something I want to see again."

"Ha ha, so funny, some friend you are. As I remember, you were pretty happy with me that day because it got us out of the last class of maths."

"You're right, I was, it was still funny, though. If you really want one, I'll take you. I know a guy and I can hold your hand. It's nothing like an injection, just stings a little and kind of feels warm but doesn't hurt. You would be fine."

"Maybe I will."

"You finished in there? I want to get going," Drew calls through my door.

"Yeah, be out in a sec."

We stand back and admire ourselves in my full-length mirror. "We look good, Indie girl, let's go party."

We walk up the three blocks from our house to the bar where we are meeting the others. Drew and Indie are chatting the whole time about Drew's favourite subject, him surfing and how awesome he is at it. I tuned out a while ago. I'm so nervous about how tonight's going to go. I haven't talked to Blake since Monday, and Fraser and I have emailed back and forth, but it's just been purely professional about the townhouse project. I'm just hoping we can all have a fun night with no drama and maybe I can play matchmaker.

We walk into the bar and see the others already have a table. Drew nudges me in the arm. "Thanks, sis, for taking so long to get ready, the boys are already into it. I'm going to have to catch up."

"I'm sure you'll catch up in no time." He takes off to join them, and I offer a little wave. I'm not ready to go over there yet. I need something to relax me. Everyone's here—Theo, Fiona, Blake, and Fraser. Fraser has some blonde sitting on his lap. Nice, after the talk I got when I dropped into his office the other day, about hanging out with Blake. Looks like it's going to be just like old times. Fraser with his double standards, sleeping with everything that moves, and me a slut for going out for lunch with someone.

"Drink first," I grab Indie's arm and I head straight to the bar.

"Two beers, please." I'm going to try not to get drunk tonight. I don't want to make a complete fool of myself again in front of Blake.

"What's going on, Elly?" Indie asks, looking confused.

"Nothing, it's just all got a little complicated already."

"Ah, okay. Are we right to head over now?"

"Yeah, okay. You've got to meet Blake properly. He's such a nice guy. I reckon you guys will hit it off."

"Oh, he's the builder you were with on Sunday at the café, right?"

"Yeah, don't play dumb with me, you know who he is."
"Is something going on between you two?" she asks.
I shrug. "Nope, we're just friends."

We walk our way through the crowded room, over to the others and say hi. Pulling up seats down the end of the table where Theo and Fiona are sitting.

"This is my sister-in-law, Fiona, and you remember Theo." I gesture to them both.

"Hey, girls, drink up so we can dance. I want to go for a dance while I still can!" Fiona says, patting her belly.

I hate dancing, but sitting at this table feels so awkward, too many boys. I'll gladly get up and dance to avoid the weirdness. The boys appear to be deep in conversation, laughing and listening to some story Drew is telling. Blake won't make eye contact with me at all, and Fraser has been giving me a filthy look since I walked in. I don't know what his problem is, he's the one with some chick on his lap.

"How do you girls know each other?" asks Fiona.

"We went to school together," Indie replies with a little smile. I forgot how shy she is around new people.

"And Indie has just got me a job at the café she's working at."

"It's not my full-time job, I'm an artist. It's just hard to get enough work to pay all the bills, so for now, I have to work at the café too." We finish up our drinks. "What do you do, Fiona?"

"I'm Theo's partner, we met at work."

"Wow, working as a police officer must be crazy," adds Indie.

"Yeah, most of the time it's pretty uneventful, just filing reports, it's not a big deal."

"Aren't you scared now because of the baby, though?" I ask.

"You sound like your brother. He wants me to go on leave now. He thinks it's too dangerous for me to be working."

"Don't you think he's right?" I ask, as she rolls her eyes at me.

"Not you too! He's just being overprotective, you know how he is. I've been doing this job for long enough to know I'll be fine."

"Fair enough. You shouldn't have to give up your job just so you can have a baby. I get it."

"Come on, girls, you finished your drinks, let's dance." Indie looks scared. She's not much of a dancer either. Fiona grabs our hands and drags us to the dance floor, so it looks like we have no choice.

"Come on, Indie. We have to get out there if we're going to fuck our exes out of our systems." She just gives me a little shrug.

"How are you so perky, Fiona? I thought pregnant people were supposed to be all tired and boring," I laugh as she drags us through the crowd. As we get closer, the music gets louder. Maybe a dance is just what I need.

Fraser

I see her as soon as she walks through the door. She's fucking gorgeous as always in a leopard-print skirt and a black singlet, with her tits on full display. Why does she have to wear such sexy clothes? She's killing me already. It pisses me off, she must know it's going to attract the wrong type of attention.

Blake is sitting next to me and looks over to them as well. We had a little chat this week. Apparently, what she said is true and they are just friends, nothing else. He has his eye on someone else and I have to believe him. She and her friend head straight for the bar. She hasn't changed a bit. She'll need me to walk her home by the end of the night. She'll be blind drunk.

Sophie's pissing me off tonight too. I don't even know why I brought her. Why she insists on sitting on my lap like a little kid, I have no idea.

"Hey, man. So good to see you." I reach over Sophie and shake Drew's hand. "You remember Blake, my flatmate from Newcastle, and this is Sophie."

"Yeah, mate, how are you? I hear you're the builder working on my parents' place. It should be a good project for you guys, hey?"

"Yeah, your dad's a great guy. It'll be nice to bring his grand plans to life."

"I'll get the next round. What you drinking, Drew?" Theo announces.

"Whatever you are, bro." Theo heads for the bar then returns shortly with a tray of beers. I don't know how he's getting served so quickly, no one else is. Must be one of the perks of being a cop in this town.

The girls walk back from the bar and sit down at the other end of the table, giggling and chatting. "Drew, who's Elly's friend?" I ask.

"It's Indie, you know, from high school. She looks different, hey, fucking hot! I had to do a double-take when she turned up on the doorstep tonight."

"Yeah, I had no idea that's who it was! Wow."

"Too bad I can't go there, since she's Elly's friend. You know, the pact," he says.

"Yeah, that's right, the pact! I'm sure you'll have found someone else to go home with by the end of the night."

"I'm counting on it."

The girls head for the dance floor and it's hard to see Elly from where I'm sitting. I don't know why I care, but I want to know what she's up to. Having her in the same town again is messing with my head.

"Hey, Soph, why don't you go dance with the other girls?"

"No, thanks, they look like total bitches!"

"You don't even know them." Man, she's pissing me off. I need to get her off my lap.

"I'm going to take a piss." That should work, that way I can see what the girls are doing on my way.

"Oh, all right, hurry back," she whines with a pout. Then pulls out her phone to scroll through. She'll be fine for a while, she's attached to that thing.

I walk through the crowded room. It's really busy here tonight. I have to push through people to get closer to the toilets. When I get through the crowd, I can see the girls on the dance floor. Elly's dancing around with her eyes closed. She's totally unco. I think back and I'm not sure I've seen her dance before, now I know why. I laugh to myself. She still looks sexy as fuck, though; I'm in big trouble.

I walk out of the toilet and look for her immediately, where is she now? She's dancing with some guy. Who is that? What the fuck, I was only gone for a minute. I can feel my heart starting to beat faster and I crack my knuckles to try and ease the tension I'm suddenly feeling. Two guys have started dancing with her and Indie. One is all over Indie, and the other's looking at Elly like he wants to eat her. He better just keep his hands to himself. If he lays a finger on her, he's not walking out of here without a black eye. I slowly make my way back to the table.

"You all right, mate? You look pissed," Blake asks.

"Yeah, I'm fine," I nearly bite his head off. Cracking my knuckles in my hand again, I pull up a seat where I can keep an eye on her. Sophie's back trying to sit on me. I just shake my head and pull up a seat for her next to me.

"Drew, can you see this shit?"

"What?" He turns to look in the direction I'm looking.

"Your sister!" I point to Elly on the dance floor.

"She's a big girl, Fraser, I'm sure she can look after herself," he grumbles, irritated with me.

"What's your problem tonight? You're being a dick!" Sophie yells at me.

"You don't have to stay," I tell her.

"Whoa, are you serious? I came out tonight with you and your friends because I thought that's what you wanted. You have been short and distant all night, what's..." as she's talking my head off, I see the bastard wrap his arms around Elly and start grinding up against her from behind. That's it, I've had enough of this shit. She may have no respect for herself, but I'm not sitting here and watching this. Why aren't her brothers stopping her? I push my chair back and stalk towards the dance floor.

Drew calls out to me over the crowd. "Where are you going, man? She's not going to like you getting involved."

But it's too late. I make it to where they're dancing, and she looks up to me with fear in her eyes. "What the fuck do you think you're doing?" I yell.

"Dancing, Fraser, you should try it, it's quite fun." She laughs nervously.

"I think you're done, you're making a fool of yourself." I grab her arm to pull her off the dance floor.

"Go back to your little girlfriend, Fraser, you're not needed here." Now I'm pissed off. *Not needed here!*

"Hey, buddy, the lady says to leave her alone, you need to back off," says the smug dick dancing with her.

"You're the one that needs to back the fuck off, buddy. She's coming with me," I snap.

Blake's by my side. He's always got my back, and he looks pissed too. "Come on, girls, why don't you come and have another drink with us," he adds, trying to defuse the situation before it escalates.

"Nah, we're having fun, Blake," says Indie.

Blake's got his serious dad face on and stands in between me and the girls. "Come on, Fraser, let's just leave them to it, they're clearly happy dancing."

"I don't care, this fucker thinks he can touch her like that," I mutter to him angrily. Pushing past him.

"Who are you calling a fucker? You really should listen to your friend and sit down before I knock you down."

I can feel Blake's hand on my arm trying to pull me back and Elly is pushing me away. Then the fucker puts his arm around Elly, licking his lips. Taunting me. That's it, he's gone. I pull out of Blake's grip and push Elly out of the way before my fist connects with his face. His mate jumps in and thumps me in the jaw, then Blake grabs him, holding him back. The fucker gets up.

"Come on, man, these chicks aren't worth it." They take off before the bouncers step in.

"You four, out," we hear someone yell, as a middle-aged, overweight man wearing a security uniform comes into view. Is he for real?

"What? We didn't do anything, sir. It was all him," Elly shouts, glaring at me. She's pissed.

"I saw what happened. You were a part of it, miss, you're all out," he barks, pointing to the door.

She throws me a filthy look and Indie takes her hand,

pulling her outside. We follow the girls out with the bouncer close behind us. Drew sees us and catches up before we make it to the door.

"Our bags, Drew," Elly calls to him.

"I'll go grab them. Be back in a second," he yells back, running back inside.

Once we're outside, Elly turns on me, pushing me up against the wall, hitting my chest. "You fucking arsehole. Why did you do that! We were having a good time! What's your fucking problem?" She's fuming mad. Her eyes bore through me with anger.

"You! You're my problem. You always have been." I grab her wrist to get her to stop her lashing out at me.

"What? I didn't do anything." She's struggling to get out of my grip but that's not going to happen. If we're both going to live in the same town again, she needs to listen to me. Cause I can't do it again, watch every fucker around going for her. I can't just stand back and watch this time.

"You're out here dressed like this, you're looking for trouble."

"No, Fraser, this is just what all girls wear when they go out. Take a look around. Even your girlfriend is in something much skimpier than me, and I bet you thought that was hot. You don't get to do this to me again!" she yells in my face, she's so mad.

"Do what?" The way she's looking at me in such close proximity, I just want my lips on hers. No other guy should be able to put his hands on her. I should be able to protect her. The world should know she's mine and always has been.

Drew arrives outside with the girls' bags, Theo and Fiona following close behind him. I drop Elly's arms as she takes a step back.

"You need to grow up, Fraser, and realise I'm not yours to protect," she whispers angrily, as she walks to her brothers. "Thanks, Drew. I'm so sorry to ruin your night out."

"It's all good, sis. It's not ruined, just added a bit of excitement. Let's go somewhere else and continue. Sophie's gone, though, mate. She took off while you were fighting," Drew calls.

But I don't care. Sophie doesn't mean anything to me, and she knows that, that's why she took off. It's Elly that has my stomach in knots every time I see her. She fucking drives me crazy and I don't even know why. We can't get through a conversion without ripping each other's heads off. "I'm done for tonight. Sorry, Drew. I'll catch you tomorrow." I can't be around her anymore tonight.

CHAPTER SIX

ELENA

Mum is running around like a mad chook trying to get ready for the party and has sent Fiona and me out for flowers. She said the house isn't ready for a party until there are fresh flowers throughout the house, and we're glad to get out of there.

We walk through the door of our local florist and I'm immediately hit with the beautiful fragrance of fresh flowers wafting through the air. I don't think I've ever actually been in a flower shop before. This place is like a tropical rainforest with plants hanging in pots from the ceiling, stunning orchids cascading from vases, and roses as big as my hand. "I could stay in here all day, couldn't you?" I say to Fi.

"It smells amazing, hey. What are we supposed to get?" she asks.

I shrug. "I have no idea about flowers. I thought you were listening to Mum's requests."

"She said something about fresh eucalyptus. That's all I remember, Elly."

"Ooh, I love these. They're so fluffy. We have to get some of these." They look so cool I want to feel them, and as

I reach out to touch it a voice calls from behind me, "Chrysanthemums," making me jump and turn to see a lady behind the counter. I didn't even see her there. The florist would be in her late 40's with long dark hair running down her back and a T-shirt that reads 'I'm a florist. I'm used to dealing with pricks.' She's staring at us from her place behind the counter where she's stripping roses. She doesn't look impressed that we have interrupted her work.

"Can you help us, please? We have no idea what we're doing here," I ask.

"That's kind of obvious. Of course I can help. What do you need?" She fakes a smile.

"We have been sent by Mum for flowers to make the house fresh for a party. Maybe a couple of big bunches."

"Including some eucalyptus, please," Fiona adds, luckily. I nearly forgot that bit.

"Do you have vases to put them in?" the florist asks.

We look at each other and shrug. "I'm sure she would. She often has flowers in the house."

"Okay then. I'll make them up now. Come back in about ten minutes and they will be ready to take home," she says with a flick of her hand, dismissing us.

"Okay, thanks." She was kind of rude or maybe she was just annoyed we had no idea.

We wander up the street and Fi stops when she sees a baby shop. "Can we go in? I haven't bought anything for the baby yet. I've been too scared to."

"Of course, let's have a look. Theo is so excited, hey. He's such a big kid himself. I feel sorry for you. You'll have two children to look after."

"He is excited! He's started acting really overprotective of me, though. I was glad to have a little space from him today."

"You have to get this. It's so cute." I hold up a little cream onesie with rainbows all over it.

"We don't know what we're having yet. It's too hard to buy clothes until we do."

"Yeah, true. When do you find out?"

"At week 20, so, like, six more weeks."

"I'm pretty sure it's a girl." I smile, I can see it already. I'm going to spoil my little niece.

"What makes you say that?"

"I don't know. Just a feeling. You've got to get something."

She picks up a cute bunny rattle. "Maybe this little rattle. It's so tiny and cute," she says in a cutesy baby voice.

"Yes, I'll get it for you as your first present." I grab it from her and walk up to the cash register. "We'll have this one, please."

I hand it to her after I've paid. "Your first official baby present," I say, with a massive smile. "I'm so happy for you and Theo, and now I'm finally getting the sister I have always wanted."

She wraps her arms around me, "I feel the same, little sis. We'd better get back to the florist. She'll be wondering where we went."

We arrive back at the florist and see two massive bunches of flowers waiting on the counter for us. "They're absolutely stunning," I say to the lady behind the counter. "Thank you." I tap my credit card to pay and we make our way out to the car, trying to wrangle the massive bunches into the back of the car without completely destroying them.

On the drive back to the house, I keep thinking about all the craziness of last night. It all happened so fast. Fraser punched that guy, and we were kicked out before I even knew what was going on.

I've got to text Blake. I feel so bad we didn't get to talk last night. After the crazy fight on the dance floor, he took off after Fraser, leaving Drew, Indie, and me to make a quick pit stop for ice cream on the way home. It would have been a good night except for jealous Fraser rearing his ugly head, yet again. I put up with it all through high school. Every time I'd be talking to a guy, he'd find a way to stop it. Kind of makes it hard for a girl to get a date. I don't want to dwell on it today, though. I'm choosing to be happy and put it behind me because it's my birthday. It's going to be a great day.

I'll quickly text Blake now:

Elena: Last night was weird, hey. I've missed hanging out with you this week, and after all the crazy, I didn't get to catch you last night. You better be coming to my party tonight! Indie will be there, I'm sure you will have a good time...

Blake: Sorry. This week has been super busy at work. I'll be there tonight. Save me a drink with the birthday girl. Indie who?

Elena: I'll make it truth serum lol then I'll get to the bottom of what's going on with you two.

I wait but nothing bounces back. Avoidance will get you nowhere, Blake, I'm on to you.

Fi and I get home and continue the party set-up. It's going to look so pretty. I've got Drew putting the fairy lights in the trees while Fiona, Indie, and I set up the table, rugs, and cushions for everyone to sit on. It has kind of a Moroccan theme. Mum's been in the kitchen all day making the food, luckily for all of us kids. She's an amazing cook, and when it comes to birthday parties, she really goes over the top. I'd say we'll have enough food to have leftovers for a week. But with Drew in the house, that's probably a good thing. That boy can eat.

Fraser

I pull up to the house I spent so much of my childhood in and park in the driveway. The Walker's were my home away from home. Anne and Jim were the parents I needed when my family fell apart. It wasn't my dad's fault Mum left, and he did his best to support us. He was working super long hours to make that happen. This family, this house, was my refuge from all the shit in my own family and dealing with an alcoholic mother who only cared about herself. I've been avoiding coming here since I got back. I'm not sure why. I guess for the same reason I can't drive down my old street. There are just too many memories. At least most of the ones in this house are good ones.

I'm going to have to get used to it with our project starting soon. I'll need to be here a bit to check on things when I'm helping Blake project manage. The house looks so different with all the renovations that have been done. It's obvious the amount of time Jim spends working on the perfectly manicured gardens.

"You all right, mate?" Blake asks. I don't know how he does it, but he reads me so well.

"Yeah, all good. Let's go in." I take a deep breath and knock on the yellow front door. I'm greeted almost immediately with a tipsy Drew.

"Thought you weren't supposed to be drinking too much while you're training," I tease.

"It's my birthday, man. You got to have fun on your birthday," he slurs.

"You'll regret it when your alarm goes off in the morning!" Since I've known Drew, which is forever, he's had his alarm set at 5am so he can get in an early surf.

"What happened to you, man? Is that the black eye from last night, or did you piss off someone else?" he laughs at me.

"You're funny. That fucker didn't do a thing last night. Just from rugby this arvo. Copped an elbow."

"Are you still playing?"

"Yeah, haven't stopped. It's great to be back on the Byron team this year."

Elly comes running through from the backyard all excited. "You guys made it," she calls excitedly, kissing us both on the cheek. She looks gorgeous as usual with her hair out and wearing a short black dress.

"Happy birthday, Elly," we say in unison.

"Thank you. I'm so glad you boys are here. After last night, I thought you might not show." She takes Blake's hand and pulls him with her. "You need to meet my friend Indie. I was going to introduce you last night, but it all got so crazy." She waves goodbye to me and Drew, leaving us to chat.

Jealousy pings in my chest, I want that to be my hand she is holding. But it's hopeless. I needed to pull her aside and talk to her about last night. It didn't happen how I wanted it to. She just makes me so crazy that I lose control.

"Wow, man, your parents' house looks amazing." They have certainly done a lot of renovating since I was here last. The house looks like it's straight out of a magazine, with pricy-looking polished timber floors and fresh white paint on the walls. They have redone the kitchen too.

"Yeah, every time I come home to visit there's something different. I think the house is done now. It's mostly Elly's doing. You know how she always loves a makeover."

"Yeah, I do," I laugh as a memory pops into my head. "Remember when she wanted a sister so bad that she talked you into a makeover? I arrived here that afternoon to see the two of you, in the back garden having a tea party, you in a big frilly dress and makeup. Wish I took a photo. I'm sure all your surfing buddies would love to see that one."

"That never happened. You're making it up," he grumbles.

"Um, it did. Why don't we go ask Elly about it now? I'm sure she remembers."

"No, no, we don't need to bring it up."

"I thought so. Fucking hilarious." I laugh again.

We wander through the house to the backyard and I'm immediately wrapped in a warm hug from the twins' mum, Anne.

"We've missed you, Fraser. It's nice to have you home."

"Thanks, Anne, I've missed you all too. The house is looking amazing."

Jim shakes my hand. "Good to see you again, son."

Anne always throws the best birthday parties. There's finger food in abundance, being passed around on platters, and her cooking is amazing. I'm sure everything will be delicious.

"Would you like a drink, son?"

"I'll grab a soft drink if you've got one, Jim."

"I'll get one, Dad," adds Drew.

Jim heads inside to grab Drew's drink and hands them out to us. We clink bottles. "To having all of us in one place again. It's been a while."

"Yeah, it's nice to be back here with this crazy family."

The yard is sparkling with every tree lit up with fairy lights. There's a long table down the centre of the yard lit with candles in little jars and cushions to sit on. It's obviously been well planned out and styled by Elly.

Drew and I set ourselves up on the back deck. We spend most of the night catching up on old times and hearing his crazy stories of the shit he gets himself into while travelling the world surfing. I don't know anyone who can get into as much trouble with the ladies as him, without even trying. Lucky for him his cheeky smile seems to get him out of trouble just as easily.

Blake has been sitting down the back with Elly and Indie since he got here, and I'm trying my best not to let the jealousy take over again. I've been keeping an eye on them but I'm not going to say anything. Tonight's her birthday and I don't want to ruin it, plus what she said last night has sat with me all day. She's right, I need to grow up and trust her to make her own decisions. I can't help but watch her, though. She's glowing tonight and looks like she's having a fun night with her friends, spending most of their time laughing. I want to go and talk to her, but I'll have to wait till the timing is right, with so much of her family around.

Anne brings out the twins' cake. Some massive triple-layer thing. Looks like black forest cake, and I bet it is, it's Elly's favourite. Everyone gathers to sing Happy Birthday. After the cake is cut, everyone separates back to where they were sitting to eat their cake. I look down to where they were sitting. She's not there anymore, it's just Blake and Indie. I wonder where she went. She's been avoiding me all night. Understandable after last night, but now might be a good time to find her and straighten things out. I don't want things to be weird between us, especially now that she's working with me.

I scan the yard and catch sight of her by herself, down on the old swing, under the mango tree. Not the first time I've seen her sitting there alone with her thoughts. I need to talk to her without pissing her off again, but everything that comes out of my mouth is wrong. Just don't be a jealous dick and you'll be fine. My stomach twists with a feeling I'm not familiar with. Is this what it feels like to be nervous? I really wouldn't know, I never get nervous.

"Hey. I was wondering where you got to," I call out to her. She jumps and looks up, surprised to see me.

"Yeah, I just needed a minute to myself." She places her empty paper plate on the ground. "Did you have some cake? It's from the Hill Top Café where I'm working. Their cakes are amazing."

"Yeah, it was good. I can leave you if you want to be alone?" I offer, but it's the last thing I want.

"It's okay, you can stay. It's just being home. It's bringing up so many memories that I thought I buried long ago, you know." She pushes off the ground and starts to swing.

"You down here talking to the fairies, like you used to?"

Her face lights up. "Did I tell you about them?" She laughs.

"No. I spent a lot of time with you in this backyard. I know you used to talk to your fairy friends when you were on the swing."

"They used to have all the answers, but I think my life's a little too complicated for them now," she says with a small smile.

"26 now! You guys are old like me. I guess we have to figure our shit out by ourselves now."

"Yeah, I guess." She puts her head down as if trying to contemplate what she needs to say. "You acted like a total jerk last night, Fray. Why did you punch that guy just because he was dancing with me? He didn't do anything wrong. I'm never going to get a date in this town if you go around beating up every guy that even looks at me."

"He was asking for it, with his hands all over you."

"They weren't, Fraser. You were totally overreacting. I felt sorry for that girl you were with. How would she have felt?"

"Well, we're not together anymore so it doesn't matter."

"Oh shame. Lucky for you. I'm sure you have a line-up of girls waiting to take her place like you always used to."

"Is that right, hey, Elly? You think you know everything about me, don't you? You want to know why I punched that guy? I can't stop thinking about you. I thought I was over you years ago, after you left, but since seeing you in my office on Monday, it's brought everything back, I can't get you out of my head. You make me crazy. I couldn't stand to see someone else's hands on you."

"I wasn't good enough for you back in high school, so what would be different now, Fraser?"

"Why are you being such a bitch? You're the one that walked out on me that night."

She hops off the swing, her eyes burning through me, pushing me on the chest. "I'm a bitch, am I? You got what you wanted from me that night! You knew what it meant to me. You weren't ever going to be mine, you said so yourself. So how am I supposed to be about it?"

I grab her wrists and slowly start to back her towards the fence behind us. It's dark down here and out of view of the rest of the party. "Now that's not true and you know it. You were everything to me in high school. That night meant as much to me as it did you. We just couldn't be together like that because of Drew. You knew that."

"Do you have any idea how hard it was for me? Having

to watch you with a new girl every week, knowing that no matter how much I wanted you, you would never be mine."

"It wasn't easy for me either. Why do you think I went through so many girlfriends? No one compared to you. You're perfect, Elly, and I have spent my life trying to find someone who makes me feel like you do, but that person doesn't exist." I pin her against the fence with my hips, our bodies so close, I'm sure she can feel my hard cock through the thin fabric of her dress.

"But you act like you don't want me. You always acted like I wasn't good enough or something." Her eyes are glassy.

"Gorgeous, I want you more than anything." I push a stray hair out of her eyes. "I can't fight this anymore."

"Fraser, I can't do this again. You broke my heart last—" Before she can say anything else, I pull her mouth into mine. Our lips collide with such desperation and want, after so much time. I run my hands down her body, lifting the sides of her dress to gain access to her bare arse. Her skin feels so good under my touch. Our kiss turns desperate. She parts her lips and gives my tongue access to her mouth.

I wrap my hands under her arse and lift her up with my hands and lean her against the fence. She wraps her legs around my waist, running her fingers through my hair, as our kiss becomes possessive and desperate. "Fuck, I've missed you, Elly."

"I've missed you too." Her hands are in my hair and she pulls me back to her, kissing me again.

I have wanted her for so long and now I'm finally kissing her. I want more. I don't care that we're standing in her parents' backyard and one of them could walk in on us at any time. I just want her to be mine.

I hear someone clear their throat. Elly's eyes go wide.

We have been caught. We pull back from each other and I put her down as we look over to see Theo staring at us. He looks pissed. "Elly, I came to find you to say goodbye. You two are lucky it's me, not Drew."

"Theo, uh yeah, let me walk you out. I'll be back in a sec, Fray." I watch her as she walks away with Theo and Fi.

I take a seat to wait for her. That was not how I wanted this to happen. I wanted things to be different this time. No sneaking around. I need to talk to her, sort it out, before her whole family is on my case. My phone rings; it's an unknown number, that's weird.

"Hello," I say.

"Fraser, it's Mum." Mum, what the fuck does she want?

CHAPTER SEVEN

FRASER

THE EARLY MORNING SUN IS PEEKING THROUGH THE gap in my blinds. Grr, it's too early to be awake for a Sunday. Why can't I sleep? I pull my pillow over my head, trying to block out the sunlight, but it's no use. I'm awake. After the twins' party last night, I just want to sleep, but I can't. The events of last night keep playing through my head. I hear Blake walk down the hall and I jump up.

"You running this morning, man?" I call out to him.

"Yeah, you going to join me?" he laughs.

"Give me a minute." He gives me a surprised look. I return a couple of minutes later in shorts and a T-shirt, with socks and runners in hand. "Ready when you are."

"Okay, just getting my shoes on." We lace our shoes then I follow Blake out for a run.

"Everything okay, man? I've lived with you for years and you never join me on a Sunday run."

"Yeah, I'm fine!" I snap a little more harshly than I mean to.

He takes off in a full jog. We jog for a bit to warm up. I know out of anyone I can talk to Blake. He knows the ins and outs of my shitty past. He knows what my mother's like. "I'm not fine," I huff. "I was finally getting somewhere with Elly last night. She went to say goodbye to Theo and Fiona, and while they were gone, my mother rang."

He looks over at me, eyebrows raised. "Your mum?"

"I hung up on her the first time. I was shocked she was even ringing me. But she kept ringing, so I left the party to take the call. She's been dumped by her latest fling and is asking me for money! Can you believe that after everything she put me and Dad through she now wants money from me. She said she's heard I've started a business and I'm doing all right. I could afford to help her out in her time of need. She only needs enough to get started again. Maybe $10,000."

"Are you fucking serious!" he spits.

"Yeah, I couldn't believe it. I have spent years wondering where she was, with not a single word from her since the night she left us when I was 14. Not a thing. Then she calls, out of the blue, expecting money. Didn't ask how I was or anything." I shake my head, still in disbelief.

"I'm sorry, man. I know she's your mum, but that's low. What are you going to do?"

"I hung up on her and blocked her number. She's not my problem, just like I wasn't hers when I was a teenager."

"Aren't you worried about her?"

"Not at all! She deserves everything she gets after what she did to us." We both put our heads down and pick up the pace. I need to run this out of my system. I'm so fuming mad with her. It's brought everything back. All the shit I buried years ago, the feelings of inadequacy from being abandoned by my mother. All the unanswered questions are pumping through my brain. I'm sure I wouldn't want the answers to them anyway, but they're circulating again.

When she took off with that other guy, leaving us forever, my dad was a mess. I was 14 and trying to support him emotionally. He was working his arse off so we could keep our house. She had emptied out their joint bank account, so Dad had to take on extra work over the weekends to get us back on track, looking after us both.

I was so angry with her. Even if things weren't good between her and Dad, how could she just take all our money and leave us to fall apart? I was her little boy. How could she not care what happened to me? Dad explained to me years later that she was an alcoholic and it had taken over her life. She no longer cared about anyone else, just that she had enough money for her next bottle of booze. That's what most of their fights were over. He had been trying to get her help, but she refused.

The Walker family were our support and they helped however they could. Jim and my dad were really close and Anne was amazing, cooking us warm meals, running me to weekend sports and helping me take care of the house, while Dad was working. I owe that family so much, and that's why I have tried so hard to stay away from Elly. But with her coming home again, all grown up, I just can't resist. She has this new air of confidence about her and her body is fucking perfection. But it's more than just a physical attraction. It's that feeling that was there years ago, a connection I have never had with anyone else, and now it's only gotten stronger. If we start this, I know I'm not going to want to let her go ever again.

We run six blocks at full speed. I'll never admit it to Blake, but he's bloody fast. I'm out of breath and can't keep up. I have to slow down and catch my breath. Blake realises I've slowed down and comes back for me still jogging.

"Can't keep up, hey?"

"I'm just not crazy fit like you. I've had enough." We both slow down to a walk. "Sorry, man, I shouldn't unload all my shit on you. It's not fair."

"Let's just jog then, pussy," he teases, with a smug smile.

I just glare at him but I'm too tired to take him on again, so I start to jog.

"It's fine, that's what mates are for. You know all my shit and I know yours. Did you work out what's going on with Elly last night?"

"Not really. We were getting somewhere, then I took off once Mum called. I was too angry to go back so I'm sure she's going to be pissed with me again. Probably for the best. Us getting involved is only going to cause trouble anyway… Theo walked in on us mid-kiss."

"Oh shit. What did he say?" He laughs at my pain.

"Not a lot, but if looks could kill, I'd be dead!"

"I'm not surprised, man, you were mauling his sister. It explains why Elly's mood changed so suddenly after you left. She took herself off to bed. She said she didn't feel like partying anymore."

"Now I feel bad. That was the last thing I wanted to do, ruin her birthday."

"I'm sure she'll forgive you. She's been in love with you since high school. I'm sure you leaving a party early won't change that."

I whip my head over to look at him. "What do you mean, in love with me since high school? Did she tell you that?"

"Yeah, when we were drunk the other night before she knew I was your friend. I probably shouldn't be telling you. But It's kind of obvious when you two are around each other anyway. I don't know how her family haven't worked it out yet, man."

"That's the problem. Her family was my family in high school. They helped Dad and me out when Mum left. Jim and Anne were like second parents to me. When Theo tells them what happened, they're going to kill me. God, if they knew what happened before Elly left for Sydney, they would really kill me."

"You're both consenting adults and they seem like cool people. I'm sure they will be happy for you."

"Somehow I doubt that." We arrive back home and it's only 7.30am. Why did I get up so early? Today is going to be fucking long. "I'm going back to bed, man. I'll see you later."

"Yeah, good idea. Sleep off your shitty mood!"

Elena

I don't even know how I got through today. I tried to sleep for most of it. My head was still pounding every time I opened my eyes, and I blame Indie and Blake for that. But it's Sunday family dinner day, and when 4pm rolled around, I knew I was expected to be at the family dinner, massive hangover or not.

And tonight, it was agony! Not only was I still feeling awfully sick, but I had Theo on my case the whole time, trying to get me to fess up to Drew what happened last night. He thinks there should be no secrets in our family and he can't be held accountable for accidentlly saying something in truth. But I'm not ready to tell Drew yet. I don't even know what's going on between Fraser and me.

I haven't heard from Fraser today at all, so it looks like it's up to me to work this out. Typical, he lights the flame by kissing me and I get stuck putting out spot fires with my family. Once we were interrupted by Theo last night, I walked my brother and Fiona out as quickly as I could so he wouldn't blab to Drew, and when I came back to the party, Fraser was gone. Nowhere to be seen. The coward took off so he didn't have to face the music.

Once everyone had finished dinner tonight, they decided to stay and watch a movie together. I took it as my cue to get out of the house for a bit. I told Mum I needed to go for a walk to clear my head after dinner. That was the plan. But, as I start walking, there's only one direction I'm going and that's straight to Fraser's place. I remember Blake saying they're only a couple of streets over from me, so I send him a quick text for the address as I walk in the general direction.

Elena: What's your address?
Blake: Why? You sending me flowers?
Elena: Oh, you just ruined the surprise! Address!
Blake: 24 Palm St??

I'll leave him guessing. I type the address into my phone GPS and start heading in the direction it tells me. I had so much fun with Blake and Indie last night. Everything was like it was the first few times Blake and I hung out together, and he gets on so well with Indie. I knew they would. I'm pretty sure I could see sparks flying between them. There was definitely something and I do love playing matchmaker.

We spent the night drinking tequila, playing games, and telling funny stories about our childhoods. He's a bad influence when it comes to alcohol, especially when I try to keep up with him.

I arrive out the front of the house the GPS has taken me to. Their house is nothing special, just a normal suburban brick house. It's probably all they could get as a rental at short notice when they first moved back. I know Blake has big plans of designing and building his special place here in Byron as soon as he's saved enough money. Which won't be long with the way their business is going. I wonder if Fraser is thinking of doing the same? Probably not. I can't see him settling down anytime soon, and a house seems way too permanent for him.

Now that I'm standing in his driveway, I have lost my nerve. I'm not sure what I'm going to say. What if last night was just a one-off mistake for him and he's not feeling what I am? Maybe that's why he did a runner. But I'm sure he must feel it too. There's something between us, something I forgot existed until I was in his presence again. It's not something I can explain, but I know I've never felt this, whatever it is, with anyone else. I have to at least find out where his head's at.

I walk up the pebble driveway to the front door. Why am I here again? Maybe this is a bad idea. No, I need to know what this is. Just take a deep breath, you can do this. It's just Fraser. I knock on the front door. It's green. I wonder if that's a coincidence or if that's why they called their business The Green Door.

Blake answers the door a little too quickly. "Were you expecting someone?" I say cheekily.

"No, but you did just ask for our address, so I was assuming you were on your way," he says, closing the door behind me as I make my way inside their house.

You can tell it's two boys that live here. I mean, they have done a nice job and clearly have good taste, but the whole place smells of leather and masculinity. It's dark and moody with brown leather lounges, a couple of large plants in pots, and what looks like recycled timber crates instead of a coffee table. The walls are slate grey, and it looks like the inside of an expensive night club, not a relaxing lounge room.

"You know me too well already, Blakie!"

He makes a face at the nickname I have given him. "You're here to see Fraser?" He motions for me to come further into the house. I realise I'm still standing in the front entry like I'm scared to walk another step.

"Yeah, is he around or is he still hiding out from me?"

"I'm not hiding from anyone!" Fraser's loud voice carries through the house as we see him walking out of the kitchen with his arms crossed. He's all dark and moody tonight, his hair messy, his face serious. Not the fun-loving man that kissed me at my party last night.

"I'll leave you two to it." Blake gives me a little sympathetic smile then heads down the hall. He knows how difficult Fraser is. We had a bit of a talk about it all last night. He's a really good friend to Fraser. I'm not sure Fraser deserves it after the way he acts sometimes, but the way Blake sees it, they're family, and they have each other's backs no matter what.

"Did I stir something in you last night, Elly, and you've come looking for more?" He's walking towards me slowly like a lion stalking his prey.

"No, Fraser, I'm not here for whatever you're suggesting. I want to know why you took off last night. Thought we better get it sorted before we have to work together tomorrow. You know, the meeting with the real estate agent? I thought we were finally getting somewhere, then I came back to the party to find you had left."

"I didn't want to cause a scene on your birthday," he says, with his eyes on my lips. I'm not sure if he's even listening to what I'm saying.

I can't help but bite my lip. He's making it hard to

concentrate on the fact that I'm mad at him for taking off last night. The way he's looking at me, like he wants to eat me, has my stomach filled with butterflies. I try to shake it off. *You're here for answers, Elena, nothing else.* "And you didn't think it might be a good idea to message me at some stage last night or today to let me know that?"

"Sorry," he shrugs. "I was just assuming you would have guessed when I wasn't there." His face is close to mine and he places his arms on my shoulders.

I shrug him off. "You're such a jerk, Fraser. You only think about yourself. You didn't want to come off like a bad friend to Drew so you ran scared. Well, you don't need to worry, Drew doesn't know anything, and I won't be telling him. I don't know what I was even thinking, letting you kiss me last night." I turn towards the door. I'm out of here. He's more of a selfish jerk than I remember. He beats me to the door and closes it before I can take off.

"Elly, wait." He has me pinned against the door with his arms on either side of my waist. His eyes ablaze, with I think... desire.

"What, Fraser?" His lips are on mine before I know what's going on. His kiss is passionate, and I'm overwhelmed with how good he smells. It's so comforting. Like coming home. I melt into him. I couldn't fight this even if I tried. When it comes to Fraser, my body's instincts take over. I've wanted him for too long. I wrap my arms around his neck as he picks me up by the waist. I wrap my legs around him for support, my back up against the cold wall, and it cools my skin which now feels like it's on fire. Our kiss is long and passionate, neither of us wanting to stop to take a breath.

He breaks it first. "No more talking, Elly. If we talk, we

just fight, and I don't want to fight with you anymore. Okay?"

"Okay, Fraser." I cradle my head in his neck as he carries me down the hall to his bedroom, my legs still wrapped around his waist. Then he throws me down on his bed. I sigh at how strong he is. The look in his beautiful grey eyes is pure sin, and I get a cold shiver running down my body from the anticipation. Something tells me this isn't going to be like my first time with him when he was gentle and caring. He smiles down at me. God, I'm such a pushover when it comes to him and he knows it. One kiss and I'm in his bed.

The sheets underneath me are so soft they must be Egyptian cotton or something fancy. I scramble up the bed as he crawls over me, straddling my waist, locking me in place so I can't move. His lips are back on mine, swiping his tongue, nipping at my bottom lip. Kissing me with everything he's got. As we kiss, his hands roam up my body, lifting my top over my head. Cupping my breast through my lace bra, he places little kisses down my clavicle. Pulling the lace fabric of my bra down, exposing my nipples. The air is cold on my skin and my nipples harden as he takes his time sucking and teasing them one at a time. I moan, unable to help it, his touch feels so good. And I have waited so long.

Pulling back from me smiling, he knows what he does to me. He reaches behind my back to unclasp my bra, growling with appreciation as my breasts are freed and the bra falls away. "So fucking hot," he groans, as he pushes me back down to the bed. His lips are on me again, placing kisses from my neck down my chest. The stubble from his unshaven jaw scratches my skin but it feels so good to finally have his lips on me that I don't care. I want his shirt off. I reach down to touch his chiselled chest, feeling the warmth radiating off his skin.

He stops at my breasts, taking my hardened nipple in his mouth and sucking hard as his hand goes to my other breast and he pinches my nipple at the same time. It's sweet torture. I moan again. Fuck, this feels so good. My back arches off the bed, wanting everything he has to give me.

"Last time I went easy on you because it was your first time, but tonight, gorgeous, you're going to feel what it's really like to be fucked by me."

I hold my finger up to his lips. "You said no talking."

"You're such a smartarse. My bedroom, my rules. You're going to pay for that comment."

"Oh, I'm so scared, Fraser. Hurt me," I laugh at him. He grabs my nipples in each hand, twisting a little harder and biting down on my neck as he does. "Ouch!"

"You still want to be a smartarse with me?" I shake my head and I'm rewarded with a slow gentle kiss. He then slowly trails kisses down my chest and stomach till he gets to where my denim shorts sit. He undoes the stud and zipper, slowly dragging them down my legs and throwing them off the bed.

He's back placing light kisses up my inner thigh. His thumb swipes my pussy through the thin lace fabric of my panties. "So fucking wet already." He hooks his thumbs into the sides of my panties, dragging them off.

Then he's back between my legs, his eyes looking over me. "God, you're gorgeous, Elly. I can't even tell you how many times I have thought about doing this to you again."

My back is arching off the bed, dying for contact from him. He's going so slow. I just want him to touch me. "Is there something you want from me, gorgeous?"

"Touch me, Fraser, you're killing me here."

He offers a seductive smile, and with my request, his mouth is straight on my pussy, tasting me. His tongue swirling circles around my clit as he pushes two thick fingers into me. I cry out in appreciation of his touch.

I reach my hands down and run them through his long hair, watching him as he continues to circle my clit with his tongue and slowly pump me with his fingers. His eyes are on mine as he works me with his mouth. The way he looks at me is almost too intimate. I have to cover my face because watching him is just too much. I rock back and forth on his fingers, loving everything he's giving me, as my orgasm builds so quickly, I can feel I'm on the edge already.

"Fuck, Fraser," I cry out as I let go, my body convulsing under his touch. My whole body is shaking in the aftermath of the unbelievable orgasm he pulled from me.

"You like that, gorgeous?"

"Fraser, I've never... how did you... I don't even have words."

As I come down from my orgasm and look up at him, I realise he's still got all of his clothes on. I suddenly feel very vulnerable lying on his bed completely naked and exposed to him.

"You have too many clothes on."

I push him back up to standing and sit up on the side of the bed. As I pull his T-shirt over his head, he drags his pants and boxers down his legs. Wow, he's fucking ripped and his upper chest is covered in intricate tattoos. Why are tattoos so sexy on men? The boy I knew in high school is long gone. This Fraser Davis is fucking hot as hell and he's all man.

I watch him walk over to his bedside table and grab a condom, ripping the packet and rolling it on. I feel a chill run through my body as I watch him. He's so hot standing in front of me, totally naked. I can't help but stare at him.

This is the body of a guy you would expect to see on the cover of a men's fitness magazine or something. Chiselled-muscle gorgeousness all the way.

He climbs over me, kissing me with such passion, forcing me to lie down again under his weight. I feel small and fragile under his large muscular frame. It feels so good to finally be consumed by his body. I run my hands over his back, feeling his muscular torso. God, he feels as good as he looks. His hands are running down my thighs, spreading my legs as wide as they will go. Every move he makes is slow and thought out. He's driving me crazy with need for him and he knows it. He positions himself at my entrance, and in one quick move, he slides deep inside me. Fuck, he's big. He slowly moves in and out of me, giving me time to adjust to his size.

"Are you okay, gorgeous?"

I don't need long. I'm so fucking ready for him. "Yes, fuck me, Fraser. I can't wait anymore."

Then his lips are back on mine and his thrusts are hard and fast as he loses all control. I rock my hips back and forth to meet him, moving with him as he fills me. He pulls back from my lips and his eyes are fixed on mine again. I don't know how he's doing it but he's fucking me like an animal and looking straight into my soul at the same time. I want to look away under his steely stare, but this time I don't. This is so much more than I'm ready for right now, but when it comes to Fraser, I want it all.

We move together like our bodies were made for each other, and he continues the hard and fast rhythm. I don't think I can take much more. I can feel my arousal building again and my body is beginning to quiver already. Our lips meet again, and I feel him jolt forward, as we hit our peak at the same time. His body collapses on mine.

His hands cradle my head, lacing his fingers through my hair, as his forehead rests on mine. We lie like this for what feels like forever. It's total bliss. I can feel his heart beating fast in his chest. This feeling of closeness with him is like nothing I have experienced before.

Fraser rolls onto his side, hugging me into his chest and finally breaking the silence. "When you left me last time, you ruined me. Don't ever leave me again." He pulls back, looking into my eyes again. His grey eyes are sad now, looking every bit of the lost boy I left all those years ago.

"I'm not going anywhere, Fraser. I'm here for good this time." He gives me a soft smile, but I can tell by the look in his eyes that he doesn't believe me.

"Fraser, we need to sort all this out," I whisper to him, still breathless.

"Not tonight, gorgeous. Let's not ruin this. We can talk tomorrow." He pulls me into his chest, stroking my hair. The sound of his heart beating under my head is so comforting. I could easily fall asleep here, with his safe arms wrapped around me, but I can't. Not tonight.

I lie quietly trying to control my erratic breathing. My teenage self can hardly believe I'm lying in Fraser Davis's bed after having the most mind-blowing sex of my life. Fuck, I didn't know it could be that good. I've been missing out. I mean, sex with Jessie was okay, but it was more about what *he* wanted. Other than losing my virginity to Fraser, I haven't been with anyone else, so I don't have a lot to go off, but now that I know it can be this good, my life will never be the same again.

His breathing has slowed right down. I think he's asleep. I'd better get home. Mum and Dad, not to mention Drew, are going to be wondering where I got to. It's after 11pm and I left for a walk hours ago. Yet another reason I need out of my parents' place. Tomorrow I start the search for my own place. As much as I love my parents, and living with them is easy and cheap, I need my own space.

I quietly roll out of Fraser's bed and find my scattered clothes, pulling them on, and tiptoeing out, closing the door quietly behind me. I hope I didn't wake him. I don't want to fight again. I know he'll be pissed I'm leaving, but I'm not ready to tell my family what's going on here. Not till I know myself what this is. I creep down the hallway to the lounge room and there is a light still on, Blake turns to see me. Damn, I was hoping to get out of here unnoticed. He smirks but says nothing, turning back to the TV show he's watching. How embarrassing.

CHAPTER EIGHT

FRASER

I CAN FEEL THE WARMTH OF THE SUN SHINING INTO MY room. I must have slept all night, that was the best sleep I've had in a long time.

I roll over and reach my arm out for my girl, but her side's cold, she's gone. I scrub my face with my hands trying to wake up properly. Why did she go without saying anything? Last night was fucking hot. I finally thought I had her eating out of the palm of my hand. Why would she just up and leave in the middle of the night?

Well, she won't be able to avoid me for long, we have the appointment with the real estate agent today. I check my phone. Our appointment's at 11am, so I've got plenty of time to get ready, then drop into the office before I drive out to the new townhouses in Broken Point for the inspection.

I chuck on some clothes and make my way out to the kitchen. Blake is up and dressed already for work. He likes to get a gym workout in before work every day. It's his way of being in control of his life, something I know he struggles with, and if that's what works for him, I'm happy he's found it. I just can't get out of bed that early, I find it easier to run or work out at the end of the day, and I have rugby training two nights a week so that's about all I need.

"Morning." He looks up from his coffee and paper with a sideways grin.

"Who even reads the paper anymore? Can't you just get the news on the internet like the rest of us? You're such an old man already," I mock.

"It's not the same thing! This way I can see it all properly."

"Like an old man?"

He ignores my comment and goes back to reading the paper. "So, you and Elly all good then?"

"No idea, she left before we could talk." I pour myself a coffee and sit opposite him, stealing the sports section from the pile of paper sections he has neatly stacked in front of him.

"I'm sure you guys will eventually work your shit out."

I just shrug. "I have no idea why it's become so difficult to talk to her without fighting, everything I say and do is wrong."

"Chicks, hey!" he mumbles into his coffee.

I roll my eyes. "I think I've got the rest of them figured out pretty well. It's just Elly, she's different, and I think she likes to make my life difficult."

"Funny, she says the same about you!"

"Does she now." I go back to reading the sports section. "So, what's on for today?"

"I'll be at city council this morning submitting plans. I've got a meeting with one of the planners about that new development near the beach, apparently some of the locals aren't so happy about it. It's going to be tricky to get passed, but if we focus in on the environmentally friendly aspect we're going for, hopefully they will change their minds.

"Then I'll be doing site checks all afternoon, so I probably won't be in the office much today. What about you?" he says, putting his plate and coffee mug in the sink.

"No worries, Elly and I have that appointment with Shea from the real estate at 11."

"Good luck with that, man. Shea will eat Elly alive. Have you told her she's a total ball breaker that's obsessed with you? I would have organised someone new for this job."

"She is not! Elly will be fine. Shea is the best real estate agent in the area, and Ash has been on my case to get the best price, so we need the best. That's why Elly's styling them for us."

"Well, it's your funeral. Glad I'm not going to be around to see the cat fight."

"You're so funny, man, it's all going to be fine."

He grabs his phone and keys. "You really have no idea about chicks at all. See you later, man," he cautions, shaking his head at me.

I just nod. I wasn't worried about this meeting, but maybe I should be. He might have a point. Shea is pretty over-the-top flirty, and up until now I have kind of just let her go. I never really needed to worry about it before.

I PULL UP AT THE OFFICE AND ELLY'S SITTING IN HER little red car, talking on her phone. I wonder who she's talking to? Her face lights up as she speaks and laughs with whoever she is chatting to. I had forgotten we organised to go over together. Her eyes rise to see me. As I walk past her car, she offers a wave, then keeps talking, so I continue walking past, opening up the office for the day.

Dumping my stuff on my desk and heading to make

another coffee, I'm not sure how to handle this situation without coming off like a dick, but I'll try my best. Because whatever this is between us, I want more of it.

Elly waltzes through the office front doors looking gorgeous as ever in a black blouse and fitted animal-print pencil skirt with sexy-as-fuck black pumps. It's the first time I've seen her in heels, and her legs look fucking amazing, so long and toned. I get an image of them around my neck as I eat her out like I did last night. Fuck, yeah, I'll be doing that again with those heels on.

She hasn't seen me standing in the break room and heads straight for my office. I sneak up behind her and whisper in her ear as I walk past, "So we're playing kiss and run, are we?"

She turns slowly, eyes twinkling with excitement, and I know she's feeling every bit as infatuated as me. "I thought you were going to be pissed with me. I'm sorry I had to leave. I told Mum I was going for a walk and I was gone for hours, and I didn't want her to worry." She pauses for a moment, fiddling with her hair. "And I'm not ready to tell them about... whatever this is." She gestures between us, looking a little unsure.

"What is this, Elly?" I push, wanting her to say what she wants from me, she's so bloody hard to read.

"I don't know, Fraser, what is it to you?" Our faces are close, eyes locked on one another in a standoff. Like we're each waiting for the other to make the first move so we know where we stand. The energy between us is intense, magnetic, even. I'm so drawn to her, but it's not something I can explain yet.

"I'd say we're exploring a mutual attraction that's been here a long time. Let's not put a label on whatever that is just yet, hey."

She seems pleased with that answer. "Good idea, and that's why I'm not telling the family. It's just going to cause unnecessary drama when we don't even know what this is."

I wrap my arms around her waist, pulling her into me. "Next time come up with an excuse for not going home. This is your only warning. I won't be so understanding if you leave me in the middle of the night again."

I lean in to kiss her and she pulls away. "You'll wreck my lipstick. I'm ready for our meeting, you know. I'm told I need to be prepared for this bitch, so I've got my power red lippy on."

"Who told you she's a bitch?" I question, then realise the answer. "Blake!" we say in unison.

Of course he did. "I'm not sure I'm happy about you two being besties."

"Why, you jealous, Fraser?" she says, biting her lip I'm sure to tease me.

"Don't push me, Elly. I'm trying to tolerate your friendship because I trust you both, but it doesn't mean I'm happy about it." I wrap my hand around the back of her neck and pull her into me again. "You can fix your lipstick later." Our lips smash together, and I swipe my tongue through her open mouth. Claiming her, letting her know she's mine, and she always has been.

We pull away and I realise we need to get going or we'll be late. I pat her on the arse. "Get yourself sorted, we need to go in five minutes."

She rolls her eyes at me. "This is your fault, you know. If you could just control yourself, we wouldn't be running late."

. . .

Twenty minutes later we arrive at the five townhouses in Broken Point, and I can see Shea waiting out the front of the first one for us. She's not unattractive. She's in her early 30's with bleached-blonde hair, pouty lips that have been injected with something, and a hot body; she obviously works out. She's also got a great set of fake tits, that are always on display. That's just it, you can tell she's fake all over, not just on the outside. She makes her way through life by getting what she wants in whatever way she can, not my type at all. I go along with the flirting because she's good at her job. She is ruthless at getting the best price every time.

On the car ride over, I filled Elly in with what to expect. She didn't seem worried. We walk up the concrete driveway over to Shea and she gives Elly a look up and down. She holds out her hand for Elly to shake. "You must be the stylist," she says in a condescending manner. This is going to go to shit, I can feel it already.

"Elena. You must be Shea, our wonderful real estate agent. Fraser has told me what an amazing job you do for them every time. It's so nice to meet you," she says with a fake smile.

"You too, Elena." She holds her hand out for me. "And Fraser, it's always a pleasure," she purrs.

"Shea." I open the door to the first townhouse, and we all walk in. The room smells like fresh paint. I love this smell; something about it feels like success to me, I guess because it's the final stage of the project completed. "The painters have only just been this week, so Elena's furniture won't arrive until Friday for the photos. If we can slot the photographer in for early next week that would be best."

Shea makes a note in her iPad, "Of course, I will talk to him and work it all out for you."

We walk through each room, both girls taking notes as we go. This is all going to be fine. Blake was worried for nothing.

"Wow, the main bathrooms are beautiful. Nice touch with the big baths. You could fit two adults in here, Fraser," Shea says, running her hands along the edge of the bath.

"That was the idea."

"What do you say we take this beautiful big bath for a test run before we sell? You know, just to make sure everything is up to company standards," Shea purrs seductively.

Elly's just outside the bathroom, but she would have been in earshot. I turn to see her reaction and she offers me another very fake smile.

"That won't be necessary, Shea. Fraser and I have already test-run the bath and the waterfall shower. Everything is working perfectly." Elly winks at me and smiles sweetly. Joining us in the bathroom, she's not going to play nice at all. That's my girl.

"Oh, nice try, Elena, I doubt Fraser would be interested in someone like you. He's a man of fine taste and needs a woman that can keep up with him. Isn't that right, Fraser?" Shea's eyes are on me and she runs her hand up my arm as if trying to persuade me over to her side. This isn't going to end well. I need to direct the conversion back to business.

"Oh, so somehow an expensive plastic surgeon equals fine taste, does it!" Elly argues.

"Okay, ladies, let's keep looking through the house, keep this professional, shall we," I interrupt the cat fight, walking out into the hall trying to continue the tour without an all-out war erupting.

"Good idea, Fraser, we better get out of here quickly before the stench of desperation sets in and no one wants to buy the place." Looks like Elly's got her nails out and is ready to fight for what's hers. It's kind of cute if it wasn't going to cause drama with the business. I need to defuse this quickly.

"Fraser, you need to control your new stylist or she's not going to last long in this industry," Shea barks, storming past the two of us.

"Oh, honey, no one controls me! If you're worried about anyone's name in this town it should be yours. You have quite the reputation for 'getting what you want,'" she calls back, showing the air quotes.

By the look on Shea's face, I can see Elly's hit a nerve and I need to shut this down. "Elly," I say with a raised brow.

"Oh, fine. I think I have all I need here anyway. I'll wait for you out the front, Fraser." She struts out of the house swaying her arse for my benefit and looking fucking incredible. There's nothing sexier than women that won't put up with any shit, especially from a bitch like Shea.

"Are you really sleeping with that slut, Fraser?" Shea asks.

"That's none of your business, Shea. Elly is going to be working with us from now on as our stylist so you two are going to have to get along. You will not disrespect her, is that clear?"

"As long as she watches her mouth around me."

"Let's just agree to be professional and all get along so we can work together."

Elena

I wait out the front of the townhouses leaning up against Fraser's car. Flicking furiously through my phone to try to take my mind off what just happened. After what the boys told me she was like, I promised myself I wouldn't let her get to me. My heart is still thumping in my chest. I hate confrontation, but I'm not putting up with that shit. If Fraser won't put her in her place, I will.

I'd love to just leave, but Fraser's my lift back to my car at the office, so I'm stuck here waiting for him to return. I know Blake had warned me about her, but she's awful. Even if she gets them more money, it couldn't be worth having to deal with her, could it?

The two of them return through the front door and he shakes her hand. She looks over to me and I smile sweetly and wave. Like I'm her best friend. Oh honey, you don't intimidate me one bit. Good luck trying to get your hands on Fraser now, he's all mine.

We jump in the car and take off back to the office.

"You cooled down a bit, Elly?"

"Cool as a cucumber, Fraser, why wouldn't I be?"

He shakes his head at me. "Can you try not to piss off our best realtor, please? We need her, Ash won't be happy if I fuck up the sale."

"Well, hopefully from now on she'll keep her hands to herself and do her job. I don't understand why you can't just get someone else for the job, a male, maybe?"

"Look at you getting all jealous. You know it's harmless, right? You don't have anything to worry about with Shea."

"I'm not jealous, Fraser. I just don't appreciate fake sluts hitting on you, that's all."

"It's kind of cute that you're so jealous," he laughs at me. "Now you know how I feel when guys put their hands on you."

I roll my eyes at him and look out the window. He's starting to piss me off now, I just want to get out of here.

He pulls into the office car park and parks his car.

"You coming in for a bit?"

"I've got to be at the café at 2 for the afternoon shift, I better not."

"Just come in for a sec, I need to show you something important."

"Okay, just a sec, though, or I'll be late." I throw my sketch pad in my car then follow Fraser through the building to his office. He makes himself comfortable sitting on the edge of his desk with a sexy smile on his face. Man, I can't resist his sexy smile and he knows it.

"What have you got to show me, Fraser? I really am going to be late for work at the café."

He reaches his hands out to me and I hesitate for a second. I know where this is going to lead. Why can't I just walk away? I groan a little, frustrated with myself for giving in so easily, but when I look into his stormy grey eyes, I melt every damn time and he knows it. I put my hands in his. He pulls me in, holding me in place with his strong arms around my waist and softly planting a kiss on my lips.

"I like this," he compliments, running his hands down my skirt. "And the heels are so fucking sexy." He kisses me again, more aggressively this time, and I run my hands through his hair, playing with the longer bits at the back.

I pull away from him to give myself some space. "Did you bring me here under false pretences, Mr Davis," I ask, biting my lip for effect.

"Maybe I just wanted to see what you would look like spread out over my desk, your long legs wrapped around my neck, in those sexy-as-fuck heels." His eyes are intense, and his lips turn up at the side in that sexy smirk of his.

I don't know why, but the way he says it has my lady parts throbbing with need. What the fuck is wrong with me? Where's the strong independent woman I'm supposed to be who would be mortified at such a comment? All Fraser has to do is talk dirty to me and I'm ready to follow his every instruction. Looks like I'm going to be late for work.

"When are the other boys coming in?" I ask, trying to sound more confident than I am.

"They're not today." He walks towards me, closing the gap between us, wrapping his arms around me and pulling me in for a kiss. Our mouths meet with force, the desperate need we have for each other too strong to resist. I know I shouldn't be doing this in his office, someone could drop in at any time. But as soon as he kisses me, my body softens into him and all logic is gone. I don't care about the consequences. I want him to do bad things to me, wherever and whenever he wants to.

My hands wrap around his waist and roam up his back, feeling the strong muscles through the fabric of his shirt. His hands slide down my back and stop when they get to my arse. He digs his fingers in, kissing me harder. Cupping my arse, lifting me, and turning me round so we're leaning up against his desk. I can feel how much he needs me, and it's a massive turn-on. I'm dripping wet already, waiting for his next move.

He pulls back slightly, clearing a path on his desk. Then his lips are on my neck, I moan softly as he places kisses down my throat, sucking and nipping at my skin as he goes. At this point, I'm so turned on from him, I'm sure I could come from this alone. His hands roam up under my skirt, and it bunches around my waist as he places a hand on my stomach and lays me back on his desk. I prop up onto my elbows so I can see him. He's so sexy like this between my legs, looking down at me like I'm a delicious meal he's about to devour. My head spins with anticipation.

His smile is wicked. "You try to act like such a good girl, Elly, but I know for me, you're anything but." He runs his finger over my sensitive spot. "You're so fucking wet for me, aren't you, gorgeous."

"Yes," I whimper.

"He hooks his finger in the side of my panties, dragging them down my legs, then places them in his pocket. "These are now mine." His eyes twinkle with cheeky delight.

Is he kidding, he's going to keep my panties? Before I have time to protest, he lowers to his knees, pushing my legs wider on the table. He lifts one of my legs, placing kisses from my knee down my thigh. His fingers dig into my flesh as he goes. He runs a finger through my dripping wet pussy and my back arches off the table with need. I want everything he has to give me, and I don't have to wait long before he buries his face in my pussy, circling his tongue around my clit, then sucking me, licking me. He's devouring me, eating me up, and it's almost more than I can handle.

"Oh God, this feels amazing," I moan. My hands go to the back of his head and I lace my fingers through his hair. I'm greedy for more as my hips have a mind of their own and rise to meet his rhythm.

He pulls back and pushes in a finger, then another, circling it round, stretching me. I'm already on the edge as I try to dig my nails into his desk. I feel him lower his lips to me again and sucking on my clit harder this time, as he pumps his thick fingers in and out of me. My body rises to meet his thrusts. My eyes roll back in pure pleasure. There is a loud bang and what sounds like the front door opening. I go to jump up, but he places his hand on my stomach and goes harder with the other hand, tipping me over the edge. I cover my mouth as the orgasm ripples through me and he continues to lap me up, every last little bit of me. My eyes glance over to look at the door to his office. It's open! Shit! Blake or Ash are going to walk in at any moment.

He stands and pulls me up to him. I straighten out my now very crumpled-up skirt and try to fix my hair before Blake walks in on us in this compromising position. Why didn't I even close the door? Luckily it sounds like Blake has gone straight to his own office first. I grab my bag and head for the door, but Fraser catches my wrist in his hand.

"Gorgeous, that was fucking unbelievable," he says, cupping my face and fixing my lipstick with his thumb. I must look an absolute mess.

I try to pull out of his hands, feeling awkward about what we just did. In his office of all places. "I've got to go, Fraser, I'm going to be late for work."

Blake knocks at the door and we both look over to him. "Hey, guys, how did the meeting go this morning?"

"I'll let Fraser fill you in, I'm late for work," I say, pulling out of Fraser's grip on my wrist and rushing out of the office. I can feel my face is flushed. How embarrassing! It's going to be obvious what we were doing. My red power lipstick is probably smeared all over my face. Blake's going to think I'm a complete slut.

"See you later, Elly, thanks for taking a look at that project for me. So good to have you around the office," the smug bastard says with a massive smile on his face. He could care less if Blake had walked in on us. It was probably his plan all along.

I feel so naughty and dirty, I have never done anything like that before in an office, much less out of the bedroom at all. But I kind of like it, I feel exhilarated at the same time. And it was about me, not him. A girl could get used to that kind of special attention. Just maybe not in his office next time.

I drive home as quickly as I can, my heart still thumping in my chest, and run in the door to my room to change into my jeans and work T-shirt, and to find some new underwear. I was hoping to have time for lunch but there's no way now. I don't want to be late on my second week of working there. I'm already a complete disaster on the coffee machine. I fix up my makeup and run out the door.

I make my way up the street as fast as I can. "So sorry, Indie, I got held up at the office with Fraser," I say, almost out of breath.

"Hey, chickee, don't worry about it." She checks her watch. "You're here on time and we're not busy anyway. You okay, though? You look kinda stressed."

I throw on my apron and start my shift helping Indie, wiping down tables and packing the dishwasher after the lunch rush. "Yeah, all good, just a rush to get here."

"Wasn't that you were fooling around with Fraser? It's so obvious something is going on with you two!" she questions, raising her eyebrow at me.

I slap my face, covering my eyes dramatically. "Is it that obvious?" I know I'm smiling like a total goof, but I can't help it.

"It's totally obvious, chick!"

"I don't even know, Indie. What am I doing? When I'm around him I'm not thinking straight. I know we shouldn't... you know, because of his friendship with Drew, but there's always this fucking hot chemistry between us. I can't help myself."

"It was obvious you guys were into each other back in high school. It doesn't surprise me at all now that you're home and you're both single that you're wanting something more."

"Well, what am I supposed to do about Drew? He'd kill us if he ever found out."

"Drew's a big boy. We've all grown up now, I'm sure he'll be fine." She waves it off like it's nothing.

"I don't know about that. When we were younger it was the one pact we had—best friends were off-limits. I didn't stick to that back then either. Swear you won't tell anyone what I'm about to tell you."

"I swear." She crosses her heart.

"After the graduation party, Fraser and I had a fight and somehow I ended up back at his place." I look up at her with my hands over my eyes again, I can barely say it.

"And?" she questions.

"We both had a moment of weakness and we ended up, well, you know."

"Having sex! I can't believe you still can't say it out loud, Elly, how old are you?" She laughs at me. "Stop stressing about it. It's not as big of a deal as you're making it out to be."

"It was a big deal. He was my first, you know, it was a big deal for me anyway. But straight afterwards we had a massive fight and that was when I decided to move to Sydney. I didn't see him again until last week."

"I always wondered why you took off so quickly and didn't spend the summer here with the rest of us. Now it all makes sense. Honestly though, Elly, I think you're just being a drama queen. It's going to be totally fine. Maybe just don't tell Drew that part; it's in the past, he doesn't need to know."

"Oh thanks, now I feel heaps better. I'm just a drama queen," I say, rolling my eyes at her as I wipe the tables with more force.

Indie's phone rings and she walks out the front to take the call.

Am I just being overly dramatic? Maybe Drew would be okay with me seeing Fraser. It's not like they're as close as they used to be, and we are adults now. There is also the weirdness of telling my parents.

Indie comes back into the café all excited.

"Guess what."

"What?" I say.

"Is what you said the other day about wanting to move out of your parents' place still true?"

"Yeah, it's definitely time. You got a plan?"

She claps her hands together in excitement. "Do I have a plan. You know how I have been wanting to have my own art gallery for a while now? Well, the current tenant of the gallery in the Main Street of Broken Point has just finished up their lease and they're offering it to me! I won't be able to afford to rent the gallery and my apartment, so I was wondering if you wanted to move into the gallery with me? It's got a two-bedroom apartment at the back."

"Let me think about that for a minute. Hell yeah! That sounds awesome. When can we move in?"

"Really? You're really keen?"

"Um, yeah. This is exactly what I need. Freedom! Let's do it."

She claps her hands with excitement again. "Oh, Elly, this is going to be so much fun! We can get the keys next week if that's not too soon."

"Definitely not. This is going to be awesome." We hug in excitement.

CHAPTER NINE

FRASER

I've been trying for hours to draft up the plans for a new development we're working on. Ash is on my case and wants the plans in to council by the end of the month, but I feel like I'm getting nowhere. It's nearly 4pm, and every time I get started, I'm interrupted by another call. We have taken on so many new clients since opening up last year. I think our business is almost at the point where we need to hire someone to take care of the office, with all the day-to-day running of the business and answering calls, so I can get on with the designs and Blake can be on site more with his building crew.

I throw my pencil down, frustrated. I need a break. I'll go annoy Blake, see what he thinks. He's back in the office after the morning on site fixing up some last-minute problems with the Broken Point townhouses. They should now be ready for Elly to go and style on Friday.

I knock on his office door then walk right in; he's busy on his computer with something. "How did you go this morning at Broken Point?" I ask.

"Plumbers have fixed the problem and I ran the final inspection so they're ready to sell."

"Great, what's wrong with your computer?"

"Just trying to fix the invoicing for this job but this program is a pain in the arse. I don't have time for this today!" He looks up at me over his computer. "We need an office manager."

"I was just thinking the same thing. I'll leave it to you to find the right person then?"

"Like I haven't got enough to do," he grumbles.

"I'll find someone then?" I suggest.

"No, I'll do it. You'll hire some busty bimbo so you have someone pretty to look at. We need someone that can run the office, take calls, invoice, do all the jobs we don't have time to do."

Dodged a bullet there, I can't think of anything worse than having to run interviews. It's much more Blake's department. He's better with people.

"Okay, thanks, man. I know you'll find the right person for the job. I'm just heading over to the Walkers' to check on a few of the finishing details for the holiday rentals before we start on them. I'll see you back at home later."

"Yeah right, that's what you're checking over, nothing to do with Elly," he mutters under his breath.

He's right, checking on the samples just gives me a good excuse to see her. Elly hasn't bothered to get in contact since she ran out of here on Monday, and I think it's time I paid her a little visit. She thinks she's playing hard to get but I know her better than that. She's trying to run because she's scared. She just needs a reminder of what she is missing out on by avoiding me.

I knock on the door at the Walker house and Drew answers. "Hey, man," I greet him, "your sister around? I need to check out the new samples she's found for the holiday villa bathrooms."

"She's still up at the café, but she should be home soon. I think her shift finished at 4.30. Can you hang around for a drink?"

"Sounds good, I'll just have a soft drink. I've still got work to do tonight." He grabs two Cokes from the fridge and I follow him out to the back deck.

"Where did you take off to Saturday night? We were all wondering where you were."

"Sorry, yeah, I got an important call, and it was too late by the time I finished so didn't come back."

"What important call?" he questions.

"Mum."

"Oh." His face falls.

He knows not to ask any more questions about that. He was there through all of the shit with her in my teenage years, and unlike Blake who knows the whole story, Drew and I deal with our problems in the best way we know how. Ignoring them!

It looks like Anne has just arrived home from work. She's carrying piles of folders as she pushes through the front door and dumps them down on the dining room table. She looks up and notices we're out the back and walks out to us on the deck.

"Afternoon, boys. Do you get to slack off when you run your own business, Fraser?" she says with a warm smile.

"Nice to see you too, Anne," I say sarcastically.

She laughs. "Oh, you know what I mean."

"I came to talk to Elly about the samples for your accommodation. She's not back from work yet so we're just catching up while we wait. But yeah, it's pretty nice working your own hours."

"Well, I'll leave you boys to it. You should stay for dinner, though, make the most of it while Drew's home."

"That would be nice, thanks, Anne, think I will." Staying for dinner sounds like a great idea. Make Elly squirm a bit, that will teach her to avoid me.

The only problem is it's a little more awkward than I thought it would be hanging with Drew. I don't like lying to my mate. It doesn't sit well with me. I just want to fess up, tell him how I feel about his sister. It's one of the reasons that we didn't stay as close as I thought we would have after high school. I felt so guilty about what happened after our graduation. It's not that I didn't want it to have happened. I just didn't like lying to him about it. So we kind of drifted apart.

"You should come down and watch the rugby this weekend," I offer. "We're playing the Dolphins at home, and there's always some sort of a brawl. It should be entertaining to watch, and I know the other guys from school would want to catch up with you. Most of them are still the same as the last team we played in before you got famous and left us."

"I'm not famous, yet." He laughs, "Yeah, I'm in, it should be fun. You want another?" He holds up his drink.

"Nah, I'm good, thanks." Drew heads inside to get another drink, and as he does, the front door swings open a little too quickly, with Elly making a dramatic entrance. Always the drama queen. Looking a little dishevelled, her ponytail half falling out. She's cute in her café uniform with her signature tight jeans. Her eyes find me, and she gives me a little smirk as she mouths, "What are you doing here?"

"Hey, sis, you want something to drink?" Drew yells to her from the kitchen.

"Please, make it alcoholic," she calls back. He hands her

a beer and she follows him out to the deck where I'm sitting. Kicking off her ballet flats, she jumps in the egg chair and sits cross-legged as it swings back and forth.

"You look like you've had a long day, Elly, you okay?" Drew asks her.

"You have no idea, Drew!" She rolls her eyes in an over-the-top way.

"Sounds like we're about to get the full dramatic story," he grumbles.

"Well, you asked, so shut up and listen. First, this morning we had some sort of mothers' group with six screaming toddlers that were allowed to run amuck; you really think they would have taken them to a park or something. I'm sure small children don't want to be at a café. Anyway, then, would you believe it, we had three spilled milkshakes during the lunchtime rush, and to top it off, some kid projectile vomited all over one of our outdoor tables."

"Eww," we both say.

"So yeah, it has been a long day!" She sighs. "What have you boys been up to?"

"Fraser's here to see you," announces Drew.

"Oh, what for Fraser?" she says as her eyes widen and she looks a little scared.

"Just about the samples for the holiday villas, but that can wait till later. Your mum's asked me to stay for dinner, so I'll be here for a while," I say with a cheeky smile.

"Oh, okay." I can see the relief wash over her as she realises I'm not here to out us just yet. She skulls her beer. "I'll leave you boys to it then. I'm going to take a shower, wash this bad day off me." She jumps out of the chair, leaving it swinging, and heads inside.

Elena

Kill me now. Could this day get any worse? Not only have I had a shitty day at the café, but now I come home to chill out and Fraser's here looking sexy as fuck when I'm trying not to think about him. Flashing me that cheeky smile of his. He's up to no good, I just know it. Oh, and getting an invitation for dinner, how convenient. This is going to be so awkward. How am I supposed to act like a normal person around him, knowing we're hooking up behind everyone's backs?

There's no knowing what I will do when he's close to me. I can't control myself around him. The last week has proven that!

Steam fills the air of the bathroom as the hot water hits my back. Oh, it feels so good. This is what I needed. I can feel my body coming back to life again. Maybe I'll just stay in here all night, where I'm safe and warm. But I want to see him. I've been avoiding him since Monday because of what we did in his office. We nearly got caught by Blake, and he was prepared to let that happen! So he could prove to Blake that I'm his or something. I don't know, but it's had my head scrambled ever since. What was that? I've never been so angry and turned on at the same time.

I guess I better get out, I have been in here for a while.

I turn off the shower and realise I haven't grabbed any clothes. Damn! That's so annoying! I'm so tired from my crazy day at work, I'm not thinking straight. I crack open the door. I can't see anyone, so I creep out in my towel. Luckily my room is just across the hallway from the bathroom, so no one sees. I walk straight to my wardrobe, opening the door, and stand there trying to work out what I should wear.

Something casual but sexy enough to get his attention. "Ah ha," I say out loud to myself. I've got just the thing. I pull my white cotton dress out of the wardrobe. It's low-cut and kind of short but still casual. I drop my towel and hold the dress up, ready to put it on.

"Nice choice," comes a familiar voice from behind me.

I jump and grab my dress, covering my naked body. "W-what are you doing in here?"

Fraser is sprawled out on my bed, hands behind his head looking way too comfortable. A massive smile crosses his face at the peep show he's been watching. "Well, I wasn't expecting you to come in wearing only your towel, but it was a nice surprise." He jumps up off my bed and closes the gap between us.

"You know what I mean, why are you in my room? Do you want to get caught?" I whisper.

"You were gone for too long and Drew's ducked out to get some milk for your mum. I was bored waiting for you. You have the longest showers ever. What are you doing in there that takes so long?" He wraps his arms around me, touching the bare skin of my back with his hands.

"Girly things, it takes a long time to look this good."

"Sure you weren't just excited to see me and had to take care of yourself?" he says, smirking at me.

"Does your mind always have to go there?" I roll my eyes at him.

"Around you it does." His hands are now on my bare arse.

"I need to get dressed, Fraser. We can't get caught like this." I try to push him away so I can get dressed but he won't budge. He's a wall of muscle. I don't even know why I tried, he's so much stronger than me.

"Would it be that bad? Then it would all be out in the

open. No secrets from your family." His eyes are serious now. I can see how important it is to him that we tell them, but I'm not ready yet.

"I don't want to keep secrets from them either, but don't you want to see what this is between us first? Cause it's going to go one of two ways if they find out. They'll be pissed or marrying us off within the year, and neither of those options works for me!"

"The second option's not so bad, is it?" he says, lightly placing kisses down my neck.

"Fraser, what are you talking about? You don't even have long-term girlfriends. You don't want to marry me."

"Maybe I was just waiting for the right girl." His grey eyes are staring straight into mine, pulling me under his spell again as he slides my dress out of my hands, dropping it to the floor. I can't help myself. I reach up and kiss him. My hands going to the back of his head as I pull his mouth to mine. How can it feel so good? His stubble scratches my face, but his big full lips are so soft and feel so good.

I jump back when I hear a car door slam out the front; that must be Drew. "You need to get out of here quick, before he gets in the house."

"We're not finished here," he whispers in my ear as he walks over to the door.

I just nod as he closes it, his eyes still glued on me. I quickly pick up my dress and throw it over my head. I finish getting dressed and do my makeup and hair. Tonight is going to be hard. I'm so worked up from kissing him like that. I have no idea how I'm going to get through dinner.

I wander into the kitchen, trying to play it cool even though I'm anything but. "Do you need help with anything, Mum?"

"You took your time." She raises a questioning brow at me. "You can help with the salad if you like."

"It was a long day, so I needed a long shower to wash it away." I start to chop up all the veggies she has lined up on the chopping board. Trying to distract myself.

"You look nice, honey, you've gone to a lot of trouble just for dinner."

"It's just a dress, Mum, not a big deal. So, Mum." I stop to take a breath and think about how I say this. "It looks like Indie has found a new place to live where she can have an art gallery as well in Broken Point, and she's looking for a roomie, so I'm going to move in with her."

She looks up from the food she's preparing. "We only just got you back home. You don't have to waste money on rent, stay here a bit longer."

"Mum, as lovely as it's been living with you guys again, I'm 26. I need to take care of myself and do my own thing. The rent isn't too much, for this place either, so I'll be able to afford it easily."

"Did you hear that, Jim?" she calls out to my dad on the deck, probably thinking he will be able to change my mind. "Elly's moving out with Indie." Dad walks into the kitchen with a plate of cooked steak. He's been out the back cooking the BBQ with the boys.

"You sure, honey? You're welcome to stay here as long as you need to."

"Yes, Dad, I'm sure, I need to do this for me."

"Well, that's good news then. I'm excited for you. Just let me know when you're moving and I will clear my schedule so I can help."

"Thanks, Dad," I say, kissing him on the cheek.

"What's going on?" Drew calls out from the deck. He's got bloody big ears, you can't have a conversation around here without him hearing what's going on. Drew and Fraser come in from the back.

"Nothing's going on, Dumbo, I'm just moving in with Indie next week, nothing for you to worry about."

Fraser has a massive smile on his face, looks like he's happy about that. He's probably thinking it's so I can fuck him without the family finding out, and that might be half of it. But mostly it's because I feel like last time, I went straight from living with my family to living with Jessie. It was only a month of staying on friends' couches in between, then I moved in with him. I haven't had time on my own to do my own thing.

We sit down to eat dinner and Fraser conveniently sits across from me. The look in his eyes is pure sin. I can feel my face heating up just from the way he's looking at me. His eyes roam up and down my body, then he licks his lips. I hope no one else notices the way he's looking at me, but it must be hard to miss. I can feel my face heating up under his gaze. It's doing things to me, things I shouldn't be feeling at this very inappropriate time. I look down at my food, moving it around on my plate. I have no idea what the conversation is going on around us, my brain is totally scrambled.

"Are you all right, Elly? You're very quiet tonight," Dad asks, looking concerned.

"Yeah, just got lots going through my head, you know, with the move. That's all, Dad."

"So, when do you think they will start on the building of the holiday accommodation, Fraser?" Dad asks.

"We're just waiting for final approval from the council. It won't be long, and as soon as we get the go-ahead, they will get started. I'd say within the month."

"So, how is the new business going anyway?" Dad asks.

"Really well, we need to hire an office manager because we can't keep up with the work on our own."

"That's fantastic, good on you boys for giving it a go, it's so nice to see young hardworking people have success."

"It was the best decision we could have made. We've been nominated for an award as well, for 'Best Eco-Friendly Design' from a new company. It's for the new library building we did when we first got back to Byron."

"Congratulations, love, that's fantastic news." My mum is up clearing the table and stops to hug Fraser.

"We're both proud of everything you have achieved," beams Dad.

"What about me?" Drew whines. As we all roll our eyes.

"You're making a fortune travelling the world, of course everyone's proud of you, Drew," I tease. "Not everything's about you." He's such a brat, always has to be in the limelight.

"I just wanted to remind you all how awesome I am."

I punch him in the arm as I walk past, helping Mum clear the table. He's pissing me off tonight. It's probably not his fault, but he's the biggest reason Fraser and I can't really be together, so he deserves that punch even if he doesn't know why.

Being a twin is hard sometimes. When we were kids, I always felt like he got all the special treatment, like my parents could see he was going to be special and I was just some regular kid, so he got all the attention. As teenagers, Theo and I were left to our own devices most of the time. Mum would be off taking Drew to surf lessons in the mornings before she had work, and the afternoons were the same. She would finish up work and be down at the pool with him for swim squad. We spent all of our family holiday time going to his surf comps. It was always about him. I'm super proud of where he is now, doing so well. But I think he forgets the sacrifices the rest of us made so he could follow his dream.

I help Mum stack the dishwasher and Fraser joins us in the kitchen. "Thanks for dinner, Anne, it was delicious."

"No worries, love. It's so nice to have you kids all home together. Did you want to stay for dessert?"

"I better not, I've got an early start tomorrow and work to finish tonight. Elly, you want to show me those samples before I go?"

"Yeah, I'll just go get them, they're in the study."

"That's all right, I'll come with you on my way out. Bye, Anne."

I walk into the study and reach up to pull down my sample board from the top shelf and his arms are on my sides. I turn in his arms and our eyes are locked on each other again.

"I thought I would never get you alone again tonight," he whispers in my ear. "God, you're a tease in that dress with no bra on. I've been rock hard since you sat down in front of me, your tits almost popping out of your dress, your hard nipples showing through."

"It wasn't easy for me either." I can feel my face flushing again at the mention of how hard he is. Why does he have to say things like that to me?

"I'm glad you're moving into your own place, no family around to catch us when we're up to no good," he says, lifting my hair off my neck and placing small kisses down to my chest.

"Fraser, this is Dad's office, he could walk in at any minute."

"Fine," he says, pulling back. "When can I have you all to myself again?"

"I don't know. But you haven't tried that hard. If you want me to yourself, you could always ask me out on a date or something," I offer, playing with my hair. Who am I around him? A girl who stares up at her high school crush. Batting her eyelashes and playing with her hair trying to be all cute. It's kinda sickening. I have to laugh at the image of myself.

His eyes sparkle with delight now. "So, you want a date with me? When are you free?" he asks, closing the gap between us again.

"Saturday, I guess." I'm looking up at him, talking in almost a whisper, trying to get the words out before I'm consumed by his presence, his sexy smile, the way he smells so masculine.

"Saturday it is. Meet me at my place, say 3, so we still have time to do something before it gets dark, and I'll take you on a date. Better tell your parents you're staying the night at Indie's or something, because you're not coming home." He cups my face in his hands.

"Is that right? What if I'm bored by the end of the night and want to come home?" I tease.

"You won't be." He bites my bottom lip and I groan. Then he smashes his lips into mine.

I'm done, all coherent thoughts gone. This man, the magnetic pull he has on me, so much more than when we were younger. I already know it's going to destroy me if we fall apart, but the pull is too strong, and I have to see what this is.

CHAPTER TEN

FRASER

I quickly jump out of the shower. I didn't mean to be running this late, but our footy match went into overtime with a massive brawl just before half-time, so I only just got home. I quickly chuck on a T-shirt and my boardies. Elly must've arrived while I was in the shower. I can hear her talking to her best buddy Blake. I don't know what the go is with the two of them, but they seem like they have known each other for years, not weeks. I better get out there before he takes her out again instead of me.

I walk into the living room to see her sitting on the lounge cross-legged. She flicks some of her hair out of her eyes as she talks to Blake. She looks gorgeous, as always, with her long hair down framing her pretty features.

She jumps up as soon as she sees me, like she has been caught doing the wrong thing, twisting her hands in front of her. If I didn't know better, I'd say she looks nervous. Not like the normal Elly I know, the one who's always so confident and in control. She's wearing little short shorts and an expensive-looking white singlet top. She always has the fanciest clothes. Some designer labels, for sure. I remember in high school, she would be working every shift she could at the café so she could save up enough to get the latest designer bag or shoes that she just had to have. Everything had to be a designer. I'm not sure why she bothers because she's stunning and would look good in a paper bag. I hope she remembered her bikini. It would be a shame to get her little designer outfit wet, and I intend to go for a swim once we get to our destination.

"Are you ready to go, Elly?" I'm not sure why, but this feels so awkward, like a real first date. Maybe that's why she looks nervous, she feels weird about it too.

"Yeah, I'm good to go. See you later, Blake. Don't have too much fun tonight without us."

"Ha, not likely. You know me, just probably watching Netflix or something. See you guys when you get back later."

We walk down to my car, keeping our distance from each other as we jump in. Why is this feeling so weird?

"Where are you taking me?" she asks, looking over to me. Her eyes are hypnotising. The blue-green pools of the irises, like the ocean on a warm summer's day. They call my name. I have to pull my gaze away from her so I can concentrate on driving or we're going to have an accident.

"It's a surprise. You'll just have to wait and see," I tease. "Did you bring your swimmers like I asked you to?"

"Sure did. Are we going to the beach or something?"

I just shrug my shoulders at her, keeping my eyes on the road.

"Just tell me, Fraser! You know I don't like surprises." She glares at me over her sunnies.

"Yeah, I remember, learned that one the hard way. But you'll like this, I promise." I probably shouldn't be surprising her after last time. It was her 16th birthday and I had spent the whole day with Drew, but I wanted to make sure she knew I hadn't forgotten about her as well. So that night when I heard her and her mum come home, I waited in her room for her with her present. Leaving the light off was probably my first mistake. Saying surprise before she had turned on the light, my second.

She must have been carrying her Doc Martins in her hands, because as soon as I said it, she hurled them at me, whacking me straight in the face. I ended up with a bleeding nose and a black eye. You think that would deter me today, but it doesn't. I know she will like this surprise.

"Okay, fine, I'll wait, but it better be good," she huffs.

"You'll like it, so stop being such a cry baby. How did you go with the styling set-up yesterday? The photos you sent through looked great. The furniture you chose reflected the look we're going for exactly. You make a perfect addition to our team."

"Thanks. I had a bit of trouble getting some of the items I wanted in time, but once I build up my inventory with my own styling props, it'll be easier."

"Where did you get the art from? I haven't seen any of those paintings before. Is it an artist I would know?"

She laughs at me. "They were Indie's paintings. She's a really good artist, hey?"

"Yeah. We'll have to use her paintings again."

"She would like that. She's trying to get her name out and noticed. That's why she needed the gallery, to build up her brand. She said people trust you better if you have some sort of a studio or gallery where they can see your work on display."

"Let her know, Blake and I will do whatever we can to help as well."

"I will. She would really appreciate that. The whole

day ran smoothly, the furniture rental company I used delivered all the furniture on time, and it was all perfect. But it was a long day by myself. I forgot how physical lugging furniture around can be. My body is killing me today."

"You're definitely going to like where we're going then."

"Are you taking me for a massage?"

"No, but I wish I thought of that. I could use one myself after the game this arvo."

"I can't believe you're still playing. Drew said it was a crazy game! Aren't you getting too old for team sports?"

"Who are you calling old? I'll still be playing when I'm in the retirement home."

She laughs at me. "Of course you will."

We have nearly arrived at the surprise location, and I look over to watch her reaction when she sees where we are.

She's looking out the window and her face breaks into a massive smile. "Oh my God, Fraser." She hits me on the arm in excitement. "You brought me to Ti Tree Lakes. I love this place. Remember when you first got your licence and I begged you to get me out of town? That crazy bitch Audrey had been giving me a hard time and you brought me here to get away from it all. It's so magical and peaceful. I had totally forgotten about this place."

I pull into the car park and stop the engine. "I knew you would love it. See? I told you to trust me. I know you better than you know yourself. I remembered how much you loved it last time we came here. I didn't hear the end of it for weeks. You went on and on about how nice your skin and hair were after swimming here. Plus, I thought we might be able to get a little privacy away from the town gossips and all the usual places we could bump into your family."

"It's a perfect first date, thank you." She looks over to me with the most beautiful smile. She's finally relaxing.

I grab the beach towels out of my car boot, and we walk down the winding dirt track that takes us to the lake. "Looks like we have the place to ourselves. You ready to go for a swim?"

"Sure am." She's already wiggling off her shorts and singlet to reveal the cutest pale pink bikini with pineapples all over it.

"Pineapples, hey?" Fuck, she's hot! My dick is instantly hard at the sight of her in that tiny bikini. There's not much to it. I can see her every curve, with her tits on full display. It makes me want to take her right here on a towel down by the lake. There's no one around to see us. We could… But I know Elly, and that won't go down well. I'm going to have to control myself around her and try to take it slow until later.

"What's wrong with the pineapples? They're meant to be good luck, and I thought I might need it with you today," she says with a cheeky smile, giving me a little shimmy.

"There's nothing wrong with them. You look fucking hot!"

"Thanks, thought you might like this one." She flicks her hair over her shoulder. "Beat you in." She's already running down to the water before I've had a chance to remove my T-shirt. I learnt long ago not to bother entering into any competition with her, or Drew, because they want to win at everything, and they will do whatever it takes to make it happen. It's easier not to compete.

I remove my shirt and make my way down to the water, trying to adjust myself so the effect she's having on me isn't so obvious. She's swum right out into the middle of the lake. I dive under to catch up to her. Man, the water feels good as it hits my sore muscles. It's warmer than I thought it would be for this time of year. This is just what I needed this afternoon. Time alone with my girl.

"What took you so long, slowcoach?" she taunts, bobbing around in the water. She's only in up to her shoulders and splashes me playfully as I swim towards her.

"I was just enjoying the view. It's fucking amazing."

"It's so beautiful here, hey?" She's looking around, taking it all in.

I pull her closer to me, wrapping my wet arms around her. "I was talking about you." I run my hands through her long hair and bend down, my lips meeting with hers, breaking the uncomfortable tension that's been there since she got to my place this afternoon. "I like this," I say, flicking the side of her bikini bottoms as I run my hands down her sides and under her arse.

"Thought you would." She blushes, dropping her head, getting all shy with me.

I bring my hand to her chin, bringing her face up so our eyes meet. I run my thumb across her lips and they part. She wraps her arms around my shoulders, and I pull her in close to me, as if I'm going to kiss her, but then pull her under the water with me instead. We make it to the surface of the water, and she hits me and splashes me. I can't help but laugh. She's now soaking wet with hair dripping around her face.

"What did you do that for?" she scolds, trying to look angry with me.

"The water's good for your hair. I was helping you get it wet," I laugh, flashing her my best cheeky grin.

She splashes me again, pretending to pout, and I pull her in for a kiss. "You can't stay mad at me, I'm your ride home."

"I guess. Just no more wetting my hair."

I pull her into me and wrap my arms around her. "Okay. No more wetting your hair."

We swim for a bit longer, just relaxing and enjoying the quiet and calm a place like this brings. The sounds of birds chirping in the trees. "Come on, let's go get dry. The sun will be going down soon and I'm taking you for fish and chips at the beach. Hopefully, there'll be a nice sunset."

"Look at you, Fraser, getting all romantic. Who would have thought."

"Well, I have no idea what I'm doing, but for you, gorgeous, I'm trying." She splashes me again and I throw her a warning look. "You don't want to start that again, do you?"

"No, no, no," she screams as I splash her back, and she runs up the side of the lake and out of the water to where we left our towels.

We dry off and pack up our belongings and head back up the winding trail to the car. The beach is just a short drive around the corner, and we can pick up dinner on the way.

We've been sitting on the beach with our fish and chips watching the sun set for the last hour. I know this is only our first official date, but this is exactly how I imagined dating Elly would be. She might dress all fancy and put on the facade of someone who's confident, but when you hang out with her, she's super chill and down to earth.

Being around her again is just like it was when we were kids, only now, I can't deny the way I feel about her. Every time I see her the feelings get stronger. She's like my drug and I can't get enough. This time things have to work out for us. I can't afford to lose her again.

I see her shivering. I wrap my arm around her trying to

warm her up. "What do you say we head back to my place? It's getting cold now the sun's down."

"That sounds good, I'm dying for a shower." She smiles sweetly.

"You're always dying for a shower."

"It's my happy place. Don't you think, no matter what type of day you have had, life just feels better once you're in the shower surrounded by warm water?"

"Yeah, I guess. Maybe if you're in there with me it would feel like that."

She offers a shy smile. "That's not quite what I meant."

"When you start talking about you in the shower, that's all I'm imagining."

"Of course that's where your dirty mind goes," she teases.

I shake the sand off the towels. I reach my hand out, lacing my fingers through hers, as we walk hand in hand back up the beach to where we parked my car.

Elly sits looking out the window as we drive home. She hasn't said a word since we got in the car. "You okay?" I ask.

"I had forgotten how beautiful this area is. I really missed it when I was in Sydney, amongst other things."

"Why did you run away to Sydney anyway, Elly? We could have worked things out if you'd stayed."

"No, we couldn't. Look at us now. It's eight years later and we're sneaking around so we can see each other. Anyway, I left for Sydney because you said we couldn't ever be together. Remember, those were your exact words. I will never forget them. And I wasn't sticking round to watch you date every other girl in town under my nose."

"Harsh, Elena!"

"Well, the truth hurts, Fraser! You keep saying I ran away from you, but I didn't run. I just moved on because you didn't want to be with me. I knew I had to start my own life, where I couldn't be hurt by watching you with other girls." She's getting all feisty now. I probably shouldn't have said anything. I have no comeback for what she just said. She's probably right. At the time, I really couldn't see how we could make it work.

"I'm sorry things ended the way they did that day. I felt like you were running away from me. Just like Mum did. Because I wasn't worth fighting for."

"Fraser, I wasn't running away from you. I just couldn't be around you anymore, and it wasn't because I didn't care about you. I was in love with you and couldn't do anything about it. Being around you and not with you was torture."

"Being away from you was harder, Elly. I completely lost it when you left. I felt like a part of me was missing. Then I found out from Drew you'd moved in with that guy only a month after you left. That fucking hurt, Elly."

"I'm sorry, Fraser, I didn't know you cared that much. You didn't tell me any of this at the time. I felt like Drew was the most important one to you. You wouldn't do anything to risk his friendship."

"He was important to me, your whole family is, that's why I didn't want to stuff it all up. But you're the one I can't live without. I know it's only been a few weeks since we reconnected, but the feelings I have for you haven't ever gone away, and I want to see what this is. This time, no running!"

"So do I, Fraser, I'm just not ready to tell the family yet. So, can we just see what this is for a bit, then tell them when we're ready?"

"Yeah, okay, but I don't want to wait too long." I stare out to the road, trying not to cause an argument over this or push her too much.

Elena

We pull up at his house after the lovely date he planned. Shame he had to ruin it by bringing up the past, or maybe I did. I can't remember. But whoever did, it's put me in a bad mood now. "I need a shower, can I grab a towel?" I ask, standing with hands folded, waiting for him to open his front door.

"Go get in. I'll bring one in to you."

"What about Blake?"

"He's not joining us in the shower, Elly."

"Not what I meant. Won't he be around, you know?"

He opens the front door and walks in the house. "Looks like he's not here. His car wasn't out the front, so we don't need to worry about him. Go run the shower, I'll be there in a sec."

Shit, is he planning on showering with me? He's so comfortable with himself. He doesn't care who sees him doing what! I guess it's because he's so experienced. He's probably had thousands of showers with other girls, probably in this shower. *Elly, don't let your mind go there.* Now I'm imagining him with other girls in all sorts of positions. Damn it! Stop, thought train, before you derail me.

Why am I so insecure when it comes to him? I guess I've only been with him and Jessie. And Jessie was kind of vanilla when it came to sex. We would never take a shower together, or do anything outside of the bed, for that matter. With Jessie, it was straight-up vanilla sex. Four different positions, that was it, and very rarely oral sex. I mean, he would expect me to give him head occasionally, but sex with him was all about him. Normally, when he felt like it. If I'm honest, I didn't have much of a sex drive with him at all, so I just kind of did it when he wanted to shut him up. To keep him happy. It was never anything great, so why would I want to go back regularly. Probably explains why he cheated on me in the end.

Fraser and Blake's bathroom is modern, probably been updated recently. With large polished concrete-look grey tiles on the floor and up the walls. It's dark and moody. The shower is one of those modern ones with just the panel of glass partitioning it off from the rest of the room with a massive waterfall showerhead. I turn on the faucet and hop under the warm water as steam fills the air. The water hitting my back slowly warms me up. It feels so good. I need one of these showerheads in my life. It's amazing.

I start to lather up the soap and wash my body. Fraser walks in the room, completely naked, holding two towels that he drops on the countertop, and walks straight into the shower. Like he's done this routine a hundred times before. I'm so new at this. I don't even know where to stand. With his massive frame, there's no way we'll both fit in here. I mean, it's a biggish shower, but how do you shower at the same time as someone else?

"I'm done. I can get out if you like so you can shower?" I offer.

"That seems like a bad idea, gorgeous. I was hoping you might like to show me what you like to do in one of these long showers you take."

"You mean you want me to...?" I can't even say it out loud. Does he want me to touch myself?

"You know what I want, Elly, for you to show me how you get yourself off. I want to watch you."

Oh my god, he's serious. I can feel my face blushing just at the thought of what he is asking me to do. Okay, Elly, pull yourself together, you can do this. It's not like I don't pleasure myself sometimes, I just haven't had an audience before.

I lean up against the cold tile wall and slowly run my hand down my tummy, over my landing strip to my clit, and start to circle. As I run my other hand up to my breast, slowly teasing my nipple. I'm rewarded with a low growl of appreciation from Fraser. He's watching my every move, his eyes dark and seductive with the promise of a naughty night to come. I feel a tingle of excitement at the thought.

"Good girl. Fuck, you look hot playing with yourself, Elly. I could watch you do this all day." He grips his hard cock in his hand and slowly strokes as he watches me. His body is insane. I can see every ripple of muscle on his six-pack up to his broad shoulders. He has an intricate tattoo that crosses from one shoulder to the other.

This is the hottest thing I have ever done. I can't believe how turned on I am watching him watch me. I can feel how wet I am with my arousal practically running down my leg. So I move my hand between my legs, pushing two fingers in. Finger fucking myself as he continues to stroke his cock more aggressively now. I'm so sensitive after being on edge all week wanting him. I'm sure my body is going to explode at any second just from his gaze and my fingers sliding in and out.

"Fraser, this is so fucking hot." His eyes are fixed on me, watching my every move, and I can feel my climax building. I press my thumb back on my clit as it builds. I have to hold myself up against the shower wall to stop my legs from buckling beneath me as my orgasm rips through me and my body feels weak.

Fraser's eyes are still on me. He edges closer and I can tell he's nearly there. His hand moving back and forth with hard and fast strokes until he lets go all over my stomach.

The hot sticky liquid running down my front. His smile is pure satisfaction as he wraps his arms around me, pulling me into him. "That was so fucking hot, Elly. I knew you weren't the good little girl you pretend to be."

"Maybe you just bring out my naughty side," I purr.

"That's the aim, gorgeous, and there's going to be a lot more to still explore." He takes the body wash off the shelf, lathering it in his hands, washing himself. His hands run over his chiselled chest and arms. His body is seriously ridiculous. I could watch this all day.

"Your turn." He squeezes more of the body wash in his hands, lathering up again. "Turn around." I do what he says, and his hands roam down my shoulders and back, massaging as he goes. It feels so good on my sore muscles. His hands move around to my front, over my breasts and stomach, cleansing and massaging every part of me as I lie my head back on his shoulder, relaxing into him. I don't want him to stop. It feels so good on my sore muscles from yesterday.

"I guess I can see the appeal in your long showers now," he says.

I giggle. "They're not normally that exciting," I say sleepily, as he shuts off the water.

We hop out of the shower and dry off. "Bed now," he says, wrapping me in a massive fluffy towel. I hope Blake isn't home. This is going to get weird if he is. I make my way quickly down the hall to Fraser's bedroom with my towel tucked tightly to my chest. Fraser's close behind me, totally nude, without a care in the world. As soon as we're in his room, he takes my towel, drops it to the floor, and wraps his arms around me. He pushes me back onto his bed. As his lips meet mine, he kisses me roughly, swiping his tongue through my open mouth and biting my lip. He's different tonight, like a wild animal possessed.

"That, in the shower, Elly, was too much. I need more of you now."

"How are you ready to go again?"

"Always ready when you're around." He kisses down my neck, roughly grabbing my breasts in his hands. "On all fours, gorgeous. I want to see that arse when I fuck you this time."

I roll over and he slaps me on the arse. "Ouch, what did you do that for?"

"Because I felt like it. Your arse looks hot up in the air like that." He slaps me again, then slides two thick fingers into my waiting pussy. I moan and dig my fingers into the sheets. It feels so good. What is he doing to me? This feels fucking amazing. He pumps his fingers slowly in and out, warming me up for him. He pulls out his fingers and I can hear him tear the foil packet.

His hand is back on my hip, steadying me, as he pushes into me in one move. He reaches his hand around to grip my breast as he slams into me again.

"Are you okay, gorgeous?"

"Yes, don't stop," is all I can get out as he pumps into me again and the outside world fades away. All I can focus on is his hard, fast thrusts as he fucks me from behind. It's rough, but I fucking love it. I feel alive in a way I have never felt before, leaving my whole body tingling with the anticipation of the next time he thrusts into me. His fingers dig into my hips, and I grip onto the sheets, trying to stop myself from collapsing under his weight.

"Fuck, Elly, I'm going to come."

I nod my head as I feel one last pump as he bites down on my shoulder. I let go completely as he rips the most incredible orgasm from me. It feels like an out-of-body experience to someplace I have never been before. I'm shaking and I collapse into him as he pulls me close to his chest and rolls us over. He cuddles into me from behind, pulling my body as closely into him, placing kisses on my shoulder as he strokes my hair.

"Oh my god, Fraser, that was fucking insane! You're insane."

"Are you okay?" he asks, stroking my hair. "I just lost control. I was worried I hurt you."

"No, you didn't—well, not in a bad way. I just never experienced anything like that before. I think walking is going to be an issue tomorrow," I say with a little laugh.

"Good, I've done my job then. You won't go anywhere else if you know you can get the best from me."

"You know I'm not going anywhere else," I mumble sleepily, hugging his arms closer into me. I close my eyes as blissful sleep takes hold.

I wake up a couple of hours later to a ping. I check my phone and it's not me. It must be Fraser's phone. I sneak out to use the bathroom, and on my way back, I hear another message ping on Fraser's phone. I can't help but glance over to see who'd be messaging him at this time of night. It's that bitch Shea. Of course it is! What could she want? I can only see the first part of the message. "Hey, sexy, looking forward to seeing you on..." before it cuts off and I would need his pin code to see more.

Damn! When is she seeing him? It's probably just work-related, but why would she message at this time of night, with "hey sexy" if it's work-related? Grrr, there's no way I'm going to be able to go back to sleep now!

CHAPTER ELEVEN

FRASER

Elly is still fast asleep. She looks so angelic with her hair fanned out on the pillow around her. I could wake her and go for round three, but she looks so peaceful. I'll leave her a bit longer and attempt to make breakfast before she wakes up. We don't have much in the way of breakfast food. But I've got sourdough and avo, I'm sure that will be all right. I'm really not very good at this kind of thing.

Normally I don't let girls hang around for breakfast. If you let them stay that long, they get all clingy and want a second date. But Elly's not any girl. She can stay as long as she wants.

I pour coffee for each of us and look up to see her wandering out of my bedroom. She's wearing my T-shirt from yesterday, looking cute as ever, still half asleep.

"I was going to bring you breakfast in bed, so you didn't have to get up yet."

"Oh, that's all right, I'm up now. What have you made me? I'm starving." She sits at the dining room table, combing her long hair with her fingers, then swirling it up into a messy bun on top of her head.

"I bet you are! Sorry it's nothing exciting." I place the toast and coffee down in front of her.

"Thank you, this looks delicious," she smiles.

"Got to look after you," I say, pulling her in for a kiss. "So, what's your plans for today, gorgeous?"

"Probably just packing, getting ready for the move next Sunday. It's mostly just clothes, but I don't want to leave it to the last minute. I've got too much on with work this week."

"Blake, Drew, and I'll help you move. So you don't need to stress about anything. We'll have it done in no time. Spend the day with me." Now I'm the one sounding all clingy.

"Thank you, that would be great. I didn't want Dad to do it all. I think there's something going on with him at the moment."

"Do you think he's sick or something?"

"I don't know. He's had lots of appointments lately. He just worries me. He never takes it easy, always puts everyone else first. He forgets he's nearly sixty."

"Don't worry about him. Jim's as strong as they come. You know that, and I'm sure he would tell you if there's something to worry about."

"Yeah, I guess." She smells her coffee. "Smells so good."

"You always do that."

"What?"

"Smell your coffee before you drink it."

She laughs at me. "Do I? I like the way it smells, I guess that's why."

"You didn't answer my question earlier, spend the day with me?"

"I'll stay a little longer, but then I really do have a list of jobs to get done today."

"Hope Indie's ready to have my ugly face around. I plan on having lots of sleepovers at this new place of yours and actually getting some time with you."

"Is that right, hey? What if I've decided, after last night, this isn't for me?" she teases cheekily.

"You're just asking for trouble, missy! Do I need to come over there and remind you how good I am?"

"No. I remember," she laughs. "And now I need food so I'm ready for round three."

"Is that right?"

"Yeah, I guess," she shrugs, shoving more toast in her mouth.

We sit for a while eating our breakfast. She looks lost in thought.

"Hey, Fraser?"

"Yeah?"

"Last night, when I was coming back from the bathroom, I saw the message on your phone from Shea. Is something going on with you two I should know about? Cause if we're doing this, I'm not sharing you!"

"There's nothing to worry about, Elly. She was just confirming our appointment with the photographer for Monday."

"Late on a Saturday night?" she raises her eyebrow at me.

"Yeah, I can see how it looks. I'll talk to her to make it clear I'm taken and she needs to be professional."

"You better, or I'll hunt her down and make it clear for her!" She glares at me with her best death stare so I know she's serious.

"You're scary when you're jealous. I wouldn't want to be another girl."

"I'm not jealous. She just needs to make sure she stays away from you. Simple."

We both turn toward the front door when we hear the noise of a key turning. In walks a sheepish-looking Blake. I was wondering why he wasn't up yet. He's always up early. Thought maybe he was off on a run, but by his attire, I would say that's very unlikely.

"Big night out, hey, man?" I tease.

"Must have been," Elly says, raising a suspicious eyebrow. "He's still in the same clothes as last night. Walk of shame. What did you get up to, Blakie?" she pushes him for answers.

"Nothing. Just drank too much and crashed at a friend's place. Thought I was being nice giving you two some space. Won't bother next time if I'm going to get one hundred questions when I get home," he grumbles.

"I'm not convinced. You look like you've been up to no good to me!" taunts Elly.

"You can think whatever you want, Elly. I'm going to take a shower."

Elly turns to look at me all wide-eyed. "How interesting. I bet there's more to that."

"It's none of our business, Elly, stay out of it."

She rolls her eyes at me as she collects her plate and cup and heads for the kitchen. "Since when do I do what you tell me?" she mumbles under her breath.

"That's it. I heard that!" I jump up and run into the kitchen behind her, picking her up and throwing her over my shoulder.

"Fraser," she squeals. "What are you doing? Put me down!" She slaps my back, laughing.

"Not a chance, missy, you're going to pay for that comment!" I march into my bedroom and throw her down on the bed.

Two hours later, we were still in my bed wrapped around each other. "Fraser, I need to get going. As much as I'm enjoying lazing about in bed all day with you, I really do have to get my stuff packed up today. I won't have time with work this week."

"Okay, guess I'll let you go home." I kiss her again. "Do you have time to drop past the office this week? I've got another styling job for you."

"You're not just trying to trick me, are you? Luring me into your office under false pretences again?"

"That was fun. But this time I do really have some work to show you."

"I've got the morning shift at the café on Wednesday, so I'll drop in about two, if that works?" She kisses me goodbye as she rushes off.

Elly has just left when a message pings on my phone:

Drew: Wanna go for a surf this arvo? I'm bored!

Fraser: Yeah. All right. Going to be pretty rusty, though. Been a while.

Drew: I'll pick you up at two. We'll go to Watego's.

Fraser: See you then.

I strap my board onto Drew's jeep and jump in. I feel so guilty. I'm seeing his sister behind his back, but she's not ready to tell him, so I have to respect that.

"Hey, man, what's going on?" I ask.

"Not a lot, just needed to get out of the house."

"Elly driving you nuts like she used to?"

"The opposite, actually. She's avoiding me. There's something going on with her, she's been acting weird since our party. You don't know anything about it, do you?" Drew asks, raising a questioning brow at me. I get the feeling that he knows more than he's telling me.

"No, why would I?" I say, trying to play it cool. Shit, what does he know?

"Just cause you've been working with her lately, I guess. Thought you might know what's going on. Are Elly and Blake dating? She's always on the phone texting him."

My heart starts to beat faster, and I can feel my hands clenching. She better not be talking to him that much. "Is she? No, I think they're just friends."

"Well, she's talking to someone with the goofy smile on her face." I can breathe now, it's probably just when she's messaging me. Drew has no idea what's going on.

"She's probably just talking to Indie or checking Facebook or something," I say, with a shrug. "Probably just distracting herself so she can get over her ex."

"Yeah, I guess that could be it. Doesn't explain why she's avoiding me, though. Don't know what she saw in him anyway. The guy was a total dick! And why would you want to get married at this age. We're way too young for all that, right, mate? Too many chicks to bang."

"Hah, yeah, that's right." I need to change the subject, this is too weird. "When do you go back on the circuit?"

"Two weeks. I can't wait. I always want to come home when I'm away, but when I get here, I just want to be out there again competing."

"Yeah, I bet, you lucky bastard. You're living the life."

"Have you seen your dad lately?" he asks.

"No, not since last Christmas. He's off travelling with his new wife. They have one of those converted combies and have been travelling around Australia for a couple of years. They come check in every now and then."

"Good for him. I'm glad he's doing so well."

"Yeah, it's nice to see him so happy. I just hope she sticks around, for his sake."

"I'm sure she will, man."

We pull up at the beach and hop out, undoing our boards from the roof racks.

"Race you to the water," he calls, already running down the beach, board under his arm.

"What's wrong with you Walker kids? You have to compete over everything," I call back. He probably can't even hear me. He's halfway down the beach already. Why do I feel like there was more to that conversation? Is he on to us?

CHAPTER TWELVE
ELENA

THIS WEEK HAS FLOWN BY, BETWEEN WORKING AT THE café, starting on the next styling job the boys have given me, and packing for the big move tomorrow. I've hardly seen Fraser at all.

We have been texting every day, and on Wednesday, when I met him at the office, he wouldn't let me go, so I told Mum I was at Indie's again and spent the night with him. Not ideal when you're in your mid-twenties. I'm glad I'll be in my own place tomorrow, so I don't have to sneak around anymore. It's kind of ridiculous.

Drew is being an even larger pain in my arse than normal and keeps questioning where I'm going every time I leave the house. He's acting all clingy and needs to be back on the surf tour. He's too bored sitting around the house so he's pestering me.

It's now Saturday afternoon and Indie and Blake have met up with me and Drew to walk up the street to our local rugby field. Fraser has a home game. We thought we would make an afternoon of it, watch him play, then go for drinks and dinner.

"Remind me why we're going to a football game again?" Indie complains, bumping shoulders with me as we walk.

"Drew's idea, blame him!" I say, loud enough so he can hear.

"Isn't it every single girl's dream to be watching sweaty men run around on the footy field, tackling each other?"

"What on earth gave you that idea, Drew! We have much better things we could be doing with our time than watching a bunch of meatheads running around a footy field," Indie replies back, as we both shake our heads at him. I can't say I agree with her, though; I've been looking forward to this all week. Any chance to perve on my man and his ridiculously hot body and I'm there.

"True, I'm sure you would prefer watching me surf some waves, half naked, hey, Indie?" Drew brags, as he wraps his arm around her. She shrugs him off with a smile.

"Eww gross, Drew," I whine. "Can you not flirt with my friend in front of me?"

"Calm down, Elly. Just joking."

"Don't you two have that pact anyway?" grumbles Blake. I don't think he likes Drew's arm on Indie.

I glare at him for reminding Drew of the pact and throwing me under the bus at the same time.

"Yeah, I still remember our pact as teenagers. Best friends are off-limits. Sorry, Indie, we could have been amazing together," he laughs.

"It's okay, Drew, really," she assures him.

I get that sudden uneasy ping of guilt in my chest. If only he knew about me and Fraser. I'm such a hypocrite.

"Ha, yeah, that pact, I had forgotten about that. It was so long ago."

I'm getting sideways glances from Indie and Blake. They know I'm in big trouble when the truth comes out. I already know that, I'm not stupid, that's why I don't want to tell Drew. I know he hangs on to things. As a kid he would always make us go through with any bet we made. There was no backing out no matter how bad it was.

Maybe I'll just wait till he's back overseas and tell him over the phone, so I don't have to deal with the tantrum. But I can't bear him not talking to me for weeks when he's away. Like last time we fought. He's a pain in the arse, but I also like to know I can check in with him whenever I need to. I hate people being annoyed with me. I think that's why this situation is getting to me. I hate feeling like I'm doing the wrong thing for the people I love, especially my family.

We arrive at the field. The same field where we used to play sports as kids. It's still exactly the same. Indie and I make a beeline for some spare seats at the back before they're all gone, while the boys go line up to get us a drink.

"Drew's going to be so pissed when he finds out you're dating Fraser," she warns.

"Yeah, tell me something I don't know! Maybe tonight we need to find Drew someone of his own. So he's all happy and loved up, that way he'll be more understanding," I suggest.

"You're talking about your brother, right? There's no way he's going to be loved up with anyone, he's the biggest man-whore I know!"

"Yeah, you're right, scrap that plan. Maybe whatever this thing is with Fraser will fizzle out in a few weeks and I will never need to tell him."

"Yeah, maybe. All I'm saying is good luck if he ever finds out," she whispers as the boys arrive back with our beer as the players run onto the field and the game kicks off.

"What number is Fraser, Drew?" asks Indie.

"Four, he's the lock," he answers.

I had already worked out where he was as soon as he ran on the field. He spotted me and gave me a cheeky wink. I have no idea what the lock is supposed to do in the game, sports are not my thing, but I really hope I'm not going to see him get smashed up today.

We're ten minutes in and I'm bored already. Watching sports, playing sports, or talking sports, just not my thing. The boys are totally preoccupied with the game and won't let me talk to them because they're concentrating, and Indie's on her phone. Least I get to watch Fraser running around; he's a god, so hot to watch.

"What are you looking at? You've been on your phone since we got here," I ask Indie.

"Sorry, I'm trying to work out how to sell my art on Etsy, but I'm so crap with computers. I can't get anything to work."

"You should show it to Blake. He's good with computers, he'll be able to help you out."

"Yeah, okay, I'll ask him later. I dare not disrupt the game and get yelled at like you," she whispers.

"I know, right? Men and sports," I say, rolling my eyes.

The whistle is blown for half-time and the players gather on the sidelines for a drinks break. I nudge Blake so it's not obvious to Drew. "What's the go with the groupies?" I recognise Shea, the real estate agent from the townhouse. She and a bunch of her slutty friends have gathered on the sidelines, talking to our team. I wouldn't normally call other girls slutty. Cause I think we should be able to wear whatever we like and not be judged for it. But in this case, we're at a football game and they're in next to nothing. This week it's turned cold as it's the start of winter. I'm in jeans and a jacket and I'm still cold. They must be freezing. Of course Shea's focused on Fraser, touching him playfully on the arm and laughing with him. He was supposed to have talked to her this week, but clearly that hasn't happened. He's like a magnet for slutty girls. They love him, and it looks like he loves the attention back just the same.

"Don't worry about her, Elly, it's you he's into. You know that," he whispers back.

"If that's the case, he doesn't have to look so interested in her," I complain.

"He's not, she just throws herself at him. Trust me, if you know Shea, she's like that with everyone."

Fraser looks over to us, knowing I'm watching the whole show between the two of them. He doesn't look worried, though, even though I'm giving him an evil stare. He just smiles at me and carries on. I want to get all possessive, go over there, slap her fake face, and show her who he belongs to, but I can't with Drew here.

He's infuriating. Either he's stupid or he just doesn't care! I don't normally get so jealous. I don't even know why I'm letting her bother me so much. With Jessie, I didn't care who he was talking to. Maybe that's why this is bothering me. Look how that ended up, and he was supposed to love me and want to spend the rest of his life with me. He was cheating on me right under my nose! How can I possibly trust anyone else? Or maybe it's because Fraser has never had a real relationship before?

Yeah, he's dated plenty of girls, but he's never stayed with one for longer than a couple of weeks. He's never had to think about anyone else. He tells me it's because of me. I'm the reason he's never stayed with anyone. But how can I trust he's not just fucking me out of his system because it's new? Then he'll get bored and be looking for someone more exciting in a few weeks.

I sit feeling pissed-off for the entire second half of the

game. I really just want to go home, but I can't make a scene or it will be obvious something's going on. I don't know why I even came to watch. I have no idea about this game, and now that I know it's where the town skanks hang out, parading around in their little outfits, with their fake tits on display for all to see, I hate it even more.

The game ends with our team winning and the players make their way over to the sheds.

"Thank god that's over," says Indie.

"You girls going to come over and say hi?" calls Drew, already walking off to where the players are congregating at the sheds.

"You boys go, we'll catch up with you all at the pub," I say. There's no way I want to talk to Fraser right now.

"You okay, Elly? You've gone all quiet," Indie asks, putting her arm around me as we make our way out of the grounds.

"I don't know, Indie. I have no idea what I'm doing, starting something up with Fraser. Is this a really big mistake?"

"You can't help who you fall for, Elly. It's been obvious there was something between the two of you since you guys were teenagers. I think you owe it to yourself to give it a go, see how it plays out, no regrets. Plus, my life's so boring at the moment, if you are a total train wreck at least I'll have something to entertain me," she laughs.

"Oh, thanks, good to know I'm your entertainment! There's just so many reasons not to, you know?"

"Elly, you can always find reasons not to do something, but if it's what your heart wants, follow it. You'll work the rest out later." We walk into the pub and go straight to the bar. Indie orders two beers.

"How did you get so smart, Indie girl?"

"Guess not taking my own advice. Living too many mistakes," she laughs. "But you know what? That's not me anymore. I'm going to do the same from now on. Getting the art gallery and moving somewhere new with you feels like the fresh start I need. I'm going to start living my life again and stop pining after what I thought my future would look like."

"That sounds like a great plan. To new beginnings," I chant, clinking my glass with hers.

We search the pub for a table. It's still pretty empty at this time of the day, so we can take our pick. We find a big table at the front, looking out over the street, and take a seat.

Half an hour and three beers later, the boys finally arrive. Fraser's sporting a fat lip from one of the game's tackles. I have no idea why he likes playing such a violent sport. The boys all grab a drink and pull up seats at our table. Fraser sits opposite me. He smiles his cheeky-as-fuck smile, but I turn my head so I can ignore him. I'm still pissed from the events I witnessed during half-time.

"You girls having a party without us?" Drew says, looking at the table of empty glasses.

"Well, you took your time, and we're celebrating moving in together. From now on, our lives are going to be so exciting and fun, hey, Indie?" She clinks her glass with mine as we both giggle.

"I think you two need some dinner before I'm walking your drunk arses home again," scoffs Blake.

"Thanks, Dad, glad we brought you," jokes Indie.

"We can always rely on you to look after us, Blakie," I tease, as Indie giggles at me again and Blake rolls his eyes.

"Good idea. I'm starving," says Drew. "Let's go order."

We head up to the counter to order, and 20 minutes later our food arrives.

As I'm about to cut into my steak a text pings on my phone. I look down to see it's from Fraser.

Fraser: What's your problem?

Elly: Oh, sorry, Fraser, am I supposed to be all over you with my tits out like every other slut in Byron?

Fraser: You're talking about Shea? Stop being silly, I've already told you there's nothing there, she's just a massive flirt.

Elly: Really? You looked pretty cosy with her this afternoon!

I start eating my food, ignoring his texts, and he glares at me across the table. I can see how annoyed he's getting, but I don't care. His double standard fucking pisses me off.

I purposely turn my head and try to concentrate on the story Drew entertains us with. Something about the latest girl he picked up at last night's bucks party for Ash. Fraser and Blake were there as well. They all went to the Pink Flamingo, our local strip club.

I have no idea how Drew gets himself into these situations. We couldn't possibly have shared a womb for nine months, we're so different. Indie's right, he's a total manwhore. From what I can gather, he got friendly with one of the dancers and she lost a bet or something and he got to take her home for the night. Story doesn't make any sense to me, I guess you had to be there. I can't think of anything worse. Fraser was very sketchy on the details of what actually took place, and after I saw what he was like today with another girl when I'm around, I don't really want to know what he got up to at that club last night.

I look down at my phone again because I can't help myself:

Fraser: You're being ridiculous and acting like a child.

I can see he's still watching me and knows I have just checked my phone. Is he serious!

Elly: Maybe? So I guess you're saying, if some guy was all over me flirting, you'd be fine with that?

Fraser: That's not what I said.

Elly: Sounds like it to me.

"You want another drink, Indie? Let's go to the bar." I grab her arm and pull her with me.

"What's going on with you, you're acting crazy?" she calls, as I drag her through the now-crowded bar.

"Fraser's being a dick!"

She looks back at him then to me. "You guys haven't even talked to each other since he got here, I'm confused."

"He's texting me with his double standards."

"Oh. Total dick."

We line up at the bar and wait to be served.

"Hey, I know you girls. You're from the café on the hill?" a man says, tall, dark and handsome. I do recognise him and his friend from the café, the two of them come in every morning.

"Oh yeah, you're flat white, no sugar, Americano," laughs Indie.

"Yeah, how do you remember?" says the one with the blond hair.

"You come in every morning," says Indie.

"I have no idea how you do it, Indie. I've still got no idea. What are your names? So I can remember them at least. I'm Elena and the lady with the good memory is Indie."

"I'm Tristan," says the one with the dark hair.

"Luca," says the one with the long blond hair in a man bun.

These boys are cute. Tonight just got a lot more interesting.

"Nice to meet you guys properly. You want to play some pool? The tables are free." I can see Fraser watching me, but I don't care. Who the fuck does he think he is being all possessive. We make our way over to the pool tables and start the first round.

Half an hour later, us girls are up three. These guys suck at playing pool, but they're super nice. I almost feel bad for kicking their arses so badly, almost, but I do like to win at all cost.

Another message pops up on my phone:

Fraser: What do you think you're doing?

I look over to him and shrug my shoulders. He knows what I'm doing, proving my point.

Looks like Drew has found a new lady friend. He's heading our way with his arm draped over some girl. She's very young, with long super-straight brown hair, and I'm not surprised she's gorgeous, his women always are. "I'm going to get going, sis, I'll see you tomorrow for the big move."

"Thanks, bro," I say, mocking him. "Don't be late. We need you home at nine, okay?"

"Might not have slept, but I'll be there." He gives the girl a wink and they walk off.

"Gross, I don't want to know what he's getting up to."

"You girls want to mix things up?" asks Tristan.

"Sure, you boys sick of getting smashed by two girls?" Indie laughs.

Fraser

She's making me crazy. She knows what happens when she makes me jealous. I can feel my hand clenching under the table and my heart starting to race as the adrenaline starts taking over.

Blake is watching me. He knows I'm about to lose my shit. "Calm down, Fraser, you know she's just trying to get back at you. She spent the whole second half of the game fuming because Shea touched you on the arm," he says.

"Is it that obvious?" He raises an eyebrow at me. "Why can't she just talk to me like a normal person?"

"I'd say she's trying to prove a point. Drew has gone now, try being the bigger person. Just go over there and ask her to talk without causing a fight."

As he says it, one of the fuckers wraps his arms around her while she's bent over the pool table to help her line up the pool cue. I'm not watching this shit anymore.

"Yeah, sorry, mate, I can't do that." I slide my chair back and stalk over to the pool tables where she's playing.

"Fraser, just talk to her," Blake calls out to me as he follows behind me.

"Fraser, you boys coming to play with us?" she laughs. She's drunk and thinks this is a big joke.

"We need to talk." I grab her arm and pull her outside with me.

"What are you doing? I was having fun, those boys are nice," she cries.

"I know what you were doing, Elly, and I'm trying not to cause another scene." We're out the front, leaning on the wall of the building near the street.

"What?" she says, batting her eyelashes at me trying to be cute.

"You have proved your point. I won't let Shea flirt with me anymore."

"Really?"

"Yes, no other fucker is putting his hands on you again." I pull her face to mine, kissing her possessively. "You're mine, you understand?"

"Just like you're mine. It goes both ways, Fraser." She runs her hands up my arms, placing them on my neck, playing with my hair as she kisses me back. "You need to learn how to be in a relationship. All this possessive shit if some guy looks in my direction, but you're allowed slutty girls hanging off you and I'm supposed to just ignore it? I'm not some pushover that will just do whatever you want to keep you happy. My last relationship ended with him cheating. So yeah, I've got some insecurities when it comes to trust, but when you let girls flirt with you like you do, it makes me feel like I mean nothing to you, and I'm going to let you know about it."

"I'm sorry, gorgeous, I'm not used to this relationship stuff. But you have to talk to me next time I stuff up, not shut me out."

"Okay." She touches my lip. "It looks sore."

"It's fine." I kiss her again to prove the point. "Let's go back inside with the others and play some pool."

"Okay, but be nice, those guys we were playing with are our regular customers at the café. They're nice guys, don't give them a hard time."

"As long as they keep their hands to themselves."

We walk back in with my arm around her waist so they know to back off. The other boys are gone, it's just Indie and Blake. Good.

"You two look cosy. What's going on here?" Elly questions.

"Nothing. We're not cosy." They pull apart from where they were standing as Indie says it.

"Just playing pool, waiting for you two to sort out your shit," Blake says, getting all defensive.

"Okay, chill out, man, let's play, Elly and me versus you two."

"Oh, I don't want to play Blake," says Elly.

"You worried I'll kick your arse again?" Blake says with a smirk.

"Maybe," says Elly, crossing her arms.

"Tough! They're the teams, Elly, you're stuck with me." I wrap my arms around her and kiss her cheek.

"Okay. But you better bring your A-game tonight, Fraser. I'm not losing to them."

"Terms: losing team has to strip off at the beach and do a nudie run into the water," Blake adds.

"Done!" I agree. This is going to be funny.

"Hey, I didn't agree to these terms! Don't I get a say? It will be freezing!" Elly complains.

"No," both Blake and I say, laughing at her stomping her feet like a toddler having a tantrum. Indie's laughing at her friend's pain. I'd say she'd be up for anything and could care less about a nudie run.

We lose the first round, and Elly talks them into a best of three. Then we win the second round so it all comes down to the third. Elly's her usual competitive self, but she's had way too much to drink so she's a little all over the place. I'm half tempted to throw the game so she has to do the run so I can see her naked tonight, but then I remember, that means Blake would too. That's not going to work! I'd better make sure we win.

I sink our last ball but miss getting the black in. So it's Indie's turn. She lines up the shot and sinks their last ball but also misses the black. It's down to both teams to sink the black and it's Elly's turn. I go around behind her to give her some advice.

"Get away, Fraser. You're going to stuff me up. I know what I'm doing, I don't need your help," she says, swatting me away, all serious.

"Okay, Miss Know-it-all. But you'd better get it cause you know Blake will and that will leave you running nude up the beach."

"I'm not going to miss it."

She lines up the ball, slightly bent over the table, leaning on one leg to get the perfect shot. Then, in her drunken state, she loses her balance, shooting the cue forward and hitting the white ball. It bounces off the table, completely missing the black, as she falls to the floor. We all erupt into a fit of laughter.

She sits sulking at her misfortune. Indie's laughing so hard she has tears running down her face, then Elly starts laughing as well. She must realise how silly it looks.

"You're a mess, Elly," I say, holding out my hands to help her up. "Come on, a swim will do you some good, sober you up a bit."

She's shaking her head. "I'm not doing the nudie run, you can't make me," she protests, still laughing at herself, making it hard for me to get her upright.

Blake sinks the winning shot, and the game is over.

"We lost because of you, miss. I can't do the nudie run all by myself. I'm pretty sure you're doing it with me!" I say, picking her up over my shoulder and heading out through the front doors of the building. The other two follow behind me still in hysterics.

We get over to the beach with her struggling in my arms and winging the whole way. I put her down on the sand.

"Indie, don't make me do it. You know I can't get nude in front of people," she begs at Indie's feet.

"Come on, Elly. You're the one who said you want to start living your life, what better way!" Elly is still looking up at Indie with pouty lips, begging her. "Well, how about just your bra and undies then. But you still have to run into the water," Indie offers, still laughing at her friend's misfortune.

"Fine. You guys are big meanies."

She's going to do it, I never thought she would. She is so shy about this type of thing. She's got her boots off and stands pulling her dress over her head. She's just in a black lace bra and G-string and she looks fucking hot. I pull my shirt over my head and drop my jeans down as she takes off down the beach to the water. "No looking, Blake," she pleads.

"What? I wasn't." He's still laughing with Indie, the two of them now sitting on the sand taking off their shoes.

I whip off my briefs and take off down the beach butt naked after Elly to make sure she doesn't drown in her drunken state. She's knee-deep in the water when I get there.

"Come on in, the water's fine," she says, laughing to herself.

I wrap my arms around her, crash tackling her into the water. As we come up, our mouths meet, and she wraps her body around mine. "You look so hot in just your bra and panties. How am I supposed to walk back up the beach with this?" I say, thrusting my hips forward so she can feel how hard I am.

"I thought the cool water would've fixed that."

"Not when you're around, gorgeous." We kiss again and I can feel her shivering. "Come on, let's get you out and dry, you're cold. The other two are now in the water as well, swimming a bit further up, so we can get out without them seeing."

"You worried about Blake seeing me?"

"Of course I am. No man could resist seeing you like this, and you two are already too close for my liking."

"It's not like that with him, Fraser. Seriously, you have nothing to worry about, we're just friends."

We walk up the beach, collecting our clothes, as the others come out of the water joining us.

"We're going to get a kebab on the walk home, you guys in?" calls Indie.

"I'm going to take Elly home. She's freezing. We'll see you guys in the morning."

"Okay, see you then," they both say.

We make our way back up the beach towards Elly's house. As we get close to her street, she turns to walk towards her parents' house, but I grab her hand and steer her in the direction of my place.

"I've got to stay at home tonight, Fraser. We're moving in the morning, remember?"

"Don't care. You're coming home with me. You can't leave me like this till tomorrow." I place her hand on my rock-hard dick. "You can go home in the morning. Just say you stayed at Indie's."

"You're so bossy when you're being controlled by your dick," she laughs at me and cuddles in under my arm for warmth as we make our way to my place.

CHAPTER THIRTEEN

ELENA

I can feel the warmth of the sun shining into the room and Fraser's arms snaked around my body. I could get used to this feeling, waking up with his sexy naked body wrapped around me. I wonder what time it is. I reach over to the bedside table to check my phone. 8.45, that's not too bad, I close my eyes and snuggle in again. Wait, 8.45, shit! We're supposed to be moving this morning. Everyone at home will be wondering where I am.

"Wake up, Fraser, it's 8.45!" I shake his arm, and he rolls over and pulls me back to him.

"Stay for a bit longer, gorgeous," he mumbles sleepily. I push my way out of his arms. "Oh, you're no fun."

"Come on, we need to get up now! I'll go over to the house first so they don't suspect anything. We can have fun later, when I'm in my own place."

I jump up and start to throw my clothes on and lace up my boots. Grrr, why did I drink so much last night? I can't even think straight this morning. I have total brain fog.

"See ya in ten." I kiss him goodbye then rush out the door as quick as I can.

I run through the front door at home and meet eyes with Drew sitting at the breakfast table. Damn, I was hoping to avoid this conversation today.

"Where have you been, sis?"

"Where's the girl from last night, bro?" I ask, as I grab one of his pieces of toast and bite into it, sitting down next to him at the breakfast bar.

"Hey, you can make me some more now for that!"

"Sorry, I don't have time, I need to pack, everyone will be here soon, but thanks for this piece," I smile sweetly at him.

"Typical," he grumbles, getting up to make himself some more.

"So, where's your friend?"

"Back at her place. Where have you been anyway? I thought you would've been up early organising everything for the move."

"I went home with Indie. We had a little too much to drink so I wanted to make sure she got home safe."

"Oh, that's nice of you, sissy. Why don't I believe your story, though?"

I shrug. "I don't know, little brother, maybe cause you're sneakier than me. And you would be up to no good!"

"Hmm maybe... What's going on with you lately, Elly? You've been avoiding me since the party. I thought this trip home would be like old times with us hanging out together. But you're always out. Is there something going on or are you just avoiding me? Are you okay?"

"I'm fine. Anyway, you took off early last night with the girl when you could have hung with your awesome sister, so you're just as bad! And since when do you worry about me so much?"

"Since always. It's a big bad world out there and it's my

job to look out for you. Fraser thinks you're just trying to get over Jessie. Is that what it is?"

"Does he! Wait. You talked to Fraser about me? Why would you do that?"

"I'm worried about you, Elly." His forehead creases in concern, and now I feel even worse. I probably should just tell him and get it out in the open. What am I supposed to say to him? *Yeah, everything's fine, I'm just screwing your best friend from high school and it's messing with my head.* I'm sure that's going to go down well! *Oh, and by the way, we fucked back in high school too, no big deal.* He's going to flip his lid! Or maybe he won't? We're all adults now, he probably won't care at all. There's only one way to find out, I need to just tell him straight up what's going on. Do it fast like ripping off a band-aid.

"What if there was something I needed to talk to you about? I can tell you anything and you won't get mad with me, right?"

"Anything. What is it, Elly?"

"Well, you know how..."

Mum walks through the front door with Blake, Indie, and Fraser. "Look who I found out the front, the moving crew."

I jump up from where I am sitting. "Oh, good. We can get started. The boxes are in my room." The others head for my bedroom.

Drew puts his hand on mine. "What is it, Elly?"

"Doesn't matter now, I'll tell you about it another time."

He still has the same worried look on his face, but now's not the time. I don't know what I was thinking. I follow after the others as quickly as I can. Probably best we don't talk about this today anyway.

Four hours and two trips later, we've packed Blake's ute

and our various cars with all the boxes and furniture from Indie's place and mine, and delivered it to the new apartment. Luckily there's only one flight of stairs at this new place.

As soon as I saw this place I was in love. It's so cute. I'm assuming it's art deco style. Probably built in the 1920's judging by the facade. There's a shop frontage downstairs at the front of the building, then you follow the long hallway to the stairs at the back. Our apartment and the art gallery, where Indie will be able to display her work, are up there. I love 1920's anything, the fashion, the furniture, but especially the architecture. I could hardly believe my luck when Indie brought me here last week to have a quick look.

"I'm so excited, Elly. I can't believe we're roomies." Indie hugs me as we stand in the living room to our new apartment.

Fraser walks in with the last box. "Nice place, I'm impressed."

"I knew you would like it. It's like stepping back in time, hey? How good is this beautiful dark timber floor?" When I first checked out this place with Indie, the floor was the first thing I noticed. "Did you see the beautiful geometric patterned cornice on the ceilings in every room? The owners must have had everything restored perfectly for it to look this good, hey?"

"Yeah, I'd say so, they have done a nice job."

"Go check out the massive balcony off the front that looks over the main street, you can nearly see the beach." The boys go to look over the balcony, then come back in.

"Yeah, this place is sweet, Elly, and I'll be able to crash here after a big night at the pub," suggests Drew, as usual thinking with his dick.

"Is that right? You won't be able to bring any of your

girlfriends back here! Isn't getting pussy the only reason you go out? I'm sure those are the words I've heard you say."

He gives me his cheeky grin. "I'm sure I've said nothing like that, Elly. I love women, all of them. I would never disrespect them like that."

"Yeah, sure, whatever you say, Drew."

"Can we be let off our moving duties to go for lunch? I'm starving!" grumbles Drew.

"Yeah, okay. Where do you guys want to go? My shout for you guys helping."

"There's a sushi place downstairs that will be quick and easy," offers Indie.

"Good idea, Indie. Here's my credit card, Drew. Can you get what everyone wants and bring me back a tuna and avo?"

"Yeah, no worries. You're not coming?"

"Nah, I want to get started setting up my room." Fraser's eyes look over to me excitedly.

"I think I'll stay and help. You won't be able to put the bed back together by yourself. Get me the same as Elly, will you, Drew." Drew nods and leaves with the others.

"Thanks, Fraser, but you didn't have to stay."

He follows me into my new room and closes the door behind me, "I finally have you to myself. Let's christen your room." He wraps his arms around me, pulling me in for a kiss.

"I knew you had an ulterior motive for staying. But this place is a total mess. Even if I was thinking the same thing, it's hardly possible at the moment. How about you help me put the bed together as you said, and I might let you stay tonight."

"I'm definitely staying tonight, that's not even a question, and we don't need a bed put together to have a little fun right now, Elly. I thought I had taught you that already, but maybe you need some more lessons in less-vanilla sex." He walks us back towards the wall, his hands going straight to my arse. "We could use the shower again, or I could bend you over that cute retro bench top in the kitchen? Or what about the balcony, looking out over the street below?"

"Fraser," I cry, slapping him across the chest. "The others will be back soon. We can't leave this room or we'll get caught." As much as I try to fight it, his words do things to me. My body is already wet with arousal hearing him list off all the places he wants to have sex.

"I've been trying my best to keep my hands off you all day, and now they're all gone, I'm not waiting any longer."

He has me pinned up against the wall with his hips. He grabs my wrists in one of his hands and places them above my head. I can feel his rock-hard cock pushing into me. As our lips meet with passionate persuasion, he has me all but begging for him in a matter of seconds.

I'm not sure how I keep getting myself into this same predicament with him. But I love it. His body pinning me right where he wants me. His lips are on mine, and I can't help but soften into his kiss. Whatever he wants, I want to give it to him, whenever he wants it. He makes me feel naughty in a good way. As soon as our lips meet, my body is his and my brain loses all rational thought. There are no rules anymore, just want for the pleasure he's about to provide.

His free hand tugs my shirt up and over my hands. He then uses my shirt to tie my hands in place as he turns me around to face the wall, leaning my bound hands on the wall for support. His hands move up my body to my breasts, cupping them as he pulls the delicate lace fabric down, exposing my nipples to the cold air. He twists my nipples in his fingers. Just this small movement does all sorts of things to my insides, and I moan with pleasure, pushing my arse back into his hard erection, greedy for more. He trails kisses and small nips from my neck across my shoulder as he cups my breasts, gently massaging them.

"Fuck, you have the best tits," he almost growls. His lips are now on my neck, kissing up to my ear before softly biting down, sending a wave of goosebumps through my body. "I'm going to fuck you just like this, my naughty girl, hard and fast from behind."

We both jump when we hear a knock at the door. "Shit, get me untied, Fraser! That could be my parents."

He starts laughing at my predicament. "What if I go get the door and get rid of whoever it is. I'm not finished with you yet. I like the way you look like this. Way too much to untie you right now."

"No way," I'm stomping my feet at him being such a smartarse at a time like this. "I'm not staying here like this. Untie me now!" The person at the door knocks again. "I'm coming," I yell, in the direction of the door, as Fraser leans over and unties my hands. He's still laughing at the situation and how panicked I am. "It's not funny," I whimper, nudging him off me. I pull up my bra, tug my crumpled-up T-shirt down, and try to flatten it out as I run into the living room to answer the door.

"Theo," I can feel how flushed my face is. I must look like a beetroot. "Hey, big brother, what are you doing here? Thought you had to work today."

"I did but my shift is finished, and Fiona has sent me over to help. You okay? You look a bit flushed, Elly, everything okay?"

"Yeah. Just moving heavy furniture, I'm not fit for it, that's all. Are you still driving Fi nuts with all the pregnancy stuff?" I ask, trying to deflect from the colour of my face and my crumpled-up T-shirt.

"How did you know about that?"

"Girls talk, Theo. Leave her alone. She knows what she can handle. She's a big girl and the strongest woman I know. She doesn't need you bossing her around, being all protective."

"Of course you're on her side. I'm not bossing her around. Can't blame a man for trying to keep the woman he loves safe!"

"Just saying, give her some space, so she still wants your ugly face around, that's all."

"Ha ha, you're so funny, little sis. Where's the rest of the moving crew?"

"They went for lunch, it's just me and Fraser here. We're setting up my bedroom."

"Hmm, that explains the red face then."

"Theo," I smack him on the arm.

"Have you told Drew yet? You need to tell him before he finds out like I did. He could have walked back in now, then what?"

"We're being careful. It would have been fine because we weren't doing anything," I say, giving him a filthy look. His goody-two-shoes attitude is starting to piss me off. You can tell he's a cop, he knows too much.

Fraser finally walks out of the bedroom. "We'll tell him when we're ready, Theo. This isn't your problem to worry about."

"You know keeping secrets never goes well, especially from Drew. You two know him better than anyone. This isn't going to go down well."

"Stop lecturing us. You're not working right now, and we don't need you being the family cop. Come and help.

That's what you're here for." I start pushing him down the hallway into the bedroom to help us with the set-up.

Theo's right, though, Drew hates secrets as much as I do. We're so screwed when we do tell him.

A few hours later, with everyone's help, we have all the furniture in place and have set up the kitchen, lounge room, and both bedrooms. Blake took it upon himself to set up anything electrical, so everything is almost done. Drew and Theo left an hour ago for the Walker family dinner at my parents' house, so it's just the four of us now.

I collapse onto the sofa. "I'm exhausted. I can't do any more unpacking today."

"Me either. We're pretty much done anyway." Indie joins me, slumping down next to me, placing her head on my lap.

"What do you ladies want to do for dinner then?" Blake asks.

Food is the last thing on my mind. I'm so tired my eyes are nearly closing just sitting here. "I don't care. Anything where I don't have to move to make it happen."

Blake grabs his phone and stands to leave. "I'll order a pizza then."

Fraser grabs his keys. "I'll come with you, man, and grab a bottle of wine to celebrate."

Indie and I are still curled up on the lounge. I can't move. So glad the boys are here to take care of dinner, because if they weren't, I'd probably just have toast for dinner tonight, or nothing, which would have been fine too.

I feel Indie's weight shift on the lounge. "Hey, Elly."

"Yeah, Indie," I mutter, with my eyes closed.

She's come to stand right in front of me. "Open your eyes. I've got an idea."

My eyes flicker open and I slowly sit up to look at my friend. "This sounds dangerous! What's the big idea?"

Indie's twisting her large hoop earrings around. She must be nervous. I've noticed she does this when she's worried about something. "Hear me out. You know how you've been trying to start up your own business and now we have this massive space, well, it's too big for just an art gallery, and there's an underground storage space too."

I'm sitting up a little further now, giving her my full attention.

"I'm thinking, why don't we join forces somehow, my art, your styling? We could start collecting some of our own special furnishings and styling pieces, which we can store downstairs, to go with what you can get from that hire place you use. If we join our experience and money together, it will be a lot easier to get it off the ground. We can start small with the jobs we can get from the boys. Then Blake can set us up a website so people can find us, and, if we do it together, we will always have someone to bounce ideas off."

"Are you serious about this? You won't get sick of me? You know I'm a pain in the bum and you're already living with me."

"Yeah, of course I'm serious, otherwise I wouldn't be saying it. We will organise it so we have our own roles so we are not on top of each other."

"Sounds like you have already given this a lot of thought. Why not, hey? This is a fantastic idea. I've been too scared to take the leap by myself, but if we do it together, we have each other." We jump up hugging each other as the boys walk back in the apartment with the pizza.

Blake puts the pizza boxes down on the dining room

table. "What's going on? You two were half dead when we left, now you're jumping around smiling."

"We're starting a business together," we both scream excitedly.

Fraser's looking at Blake with his eyebrow raised. "How long were we gone for?"

"I'll get some glasses," I call out from the kitchen as I try and reach the top shelf where the wine glasses are. "We have even more to celebrate now, you boys want wine too?"

Blake calls out first, "Definitely."

Then Fraser. "Nah, I'm good. I don't like wine."

I walk back in with three glasses. "Why didn't you get yourself some beer then?"

"It's a school night. I'm trying to be a good boy."

"Since when do you care about being a good boy? You're bad to the core, Fraser Davis."

"You two need to get a room, I'm sick of the overshare already," Indie laughs, trying to look disgusted in us.

"We've got one, and you might want to put earphones in tonight. It's going to get loud," says Fraser excitedly.

"Fraser," I cry, slapping him as Indie and Blake just laugh at us. He's so embarrassing.

Indie fills the three glasses. "To us and our new beginnings."

The three of us clink glasses. "To new beginnings."

I'm standing on the stage in front of my whole year group, trying to plead my case. I'm holding some palm cards in front of me, but I can't see what they say, and no matter how hard I try, I can't get any words to come out of my mouth.

I take a deep breath and try again, but as I go to talk, I look down and realise I'm completely naked and that bitch, Angela Cook, is in the front row of the hall laughing at me. Everyone else joins in. I should run off the stage, but my feet won't let me. It's like I'm glued to the floor. Why can't I move or talk?

I can feel my body start to drip with sweat as my heart hammers in my chest and the laughing gets louder. So loud it's deafening. Then my mum is there, at the side of the stage. She must be here to help me. I try to call out to her, but I can't. She just mouths the word "disappointed" then disappears.

What's going on? Why is no one helping me? What's happening? Then I see Drew. Maybe he can help, he always helps me. He walks up to the front of the room and starts knocking on the stage. Why is he doing that? Why isn't he helping me?... knock... knock... knock... it's getting louder... knock

I roll over and realise I was dreaming or having a nightmare. What was that? Phew, I'm glad that was just some weird dream. The banging is real, though, and it's still happening. It's coming from the front door. I check my phone. It's only 7.15am. Who's here at this time? I throw on my bed shirt and PJ pants and head to the front door, leaving Fraser all snuggled up in my bed still fast asleep.

I open the door.

"Mum," I almost yell, "what a lovely surprise!"

CHAPTER FOURTEEN

ELENA

It's way too early in the morning to deal with another one of these awkward family situations. I bet Theo told her to come and check on me, trying to get me caught out, or maybe she's worked it out herself. My mum has always had a sixth sense when it comes to me lying.

My beautiful mother stands in the doorway. She must have been up at 5am to look as good as she does. Her long hair is pulled into a neat bun and she's wearing a fitted floral mid-calf-length dress. For someone in her late fifties, she is stunning and every bit the perfect school principal.

She stands in the doorway with a basket of food. "I thought you and Indie might need some food to get you started, and since I didn't have a chance to drop by here yesterday, I wanted to see the new place before I started work today. I hope I didn't wake you up?"

"Oh, of course. No, it's fine. My body's a bit stiff from moving all that furniture yesterday. I just couldn't get out of bed, but I needed to anyway. I've got a shift at the café at ten."

"Can I come in then, honey?" I hadn't realised but I'm still standing in the doorway holding the front door open.

"Yeah, of course, silly me, sorry, Mum. Come on in."

"Thank you, honey. Wow, this place is lovely. You guys did well finding it."

"I know, I'm in love with how vintage it is. Why don't you go take a look at the kitchen," I point in the direction of the kitchen, "and I'll just grab my dressing gown and be right with you."

"Of course. We can have some breakfast, then I want the full tour before I have to get to work."

I hurry to my room. Shit, how do we handle this one. I've got to get rid of Fraser before she sees him.

He's lying in my bed with his hands resting behind his head, chest exposed, and looking fucking hot with the sheets just covering his cock. How can he look so relaxed? He must have heard that conversation.

"What's Anne doing here?" he whispers.

"Here for breakfast. You know how she likes to fuss about making sure we eat well. Quick, get dressed." I throw his shirt and jeans over to him. "You're going to have to sneak out while she's in the kitchen," I whisper back.

He doesn't budge from his relaxed position. He's got that cheeky smile on his face, the one I know means trouble. "I'm not going anywhere, Elly, think I'll just stay where I am. One of your mum's home-cooked breakfasts sounds delicious."

"Fraser," I threaten with my best serious face, so he knows I mean business.

"I think it's time we tell your mum anyway. What better time than now? I'm not hiding away from everyone anymore."

"No, not happening today, you need to go." I go over to

where he's sitting and grab hold of his arm, trying to get him up. "Come on, Fraser. Please. I don't want to tell her you're my boyfriend like this. Just another thing to add to her list of Elly fuck-ups."

He looks hurt, and I realise what I just said. "So, I'm just a fuck-up now?"

"I'm sorry, that's not what I meant. I just want to do this right." I lean down and kiss him on the lips.

"Okay, but I'm not happy about it! What am I supposed to do, shimmy down the drainpipe? I'm pretty big, you know, and this building is old. It's not going to go well."

He's up pulling on his clothes, still looking very unimpressed with me.

"I'm sorry, I'll make it up to you tonight, I promise," I offer, fluttering my eyelashes at him, trying to be cute.

"You better," he mumbles under his breath, not impressed with the whole situation.

"I'll keep her busy in the kitchen while you sneak out the front door." I kiss him goodbye. "Have a good day at work." I rush back to the kitchen.

"Wow, breakfast smells delicious, Mum, but you didn't have to do this." She's found her way around our kitchen no problems and made scrambled eggs with bacon and all the trimmings. Everything is laid out beautifully, she's even made fresh coffee, I don't know how she does it.

"It's the least I could do, honey. I know how well you look after yourself when I'm not around. That's why you're so skinny, you need some decent food."

The front door creaks as it closes and we both look to the hall. "Old places, they're so noisy," I shrug, and she nods in agreement. Phew. We got away with that one. He's gone. I take my first full breath since Mum got here, now I can relax. I feel so bad kicking Fraser out like that and about what I said, but I know in her eyes, it will just be another thing I haven't done perfectly like my brothers.

"What's that delicious smell?" Indie walks in rubbing her eyes.

"Mum's here with breakfast for us." Her eyes are wide at me and I can tell exactly what she's thinking.

"Wow, thanks, Anne, this looks amazing. We'll have to get you over every morning if I can wake up to this."

"It's my pleasure, Indie love, but it's just a one-off. I'm pretty sure Elly moved out so she can have her own space. She doesn't want me cramping her style, especially at this time of the morning. You never know who you might run into in the hallway." She raises an eyebrow at me.

I bury my head in my hands. Great, she knows, and she's just waiting for me to tell her. Whenever I was lying to Mum as a kid, she would pretend she didn't know a thing, then she'd do something nice for me like take me shopping or to a movie. I'd feel so guilty I would fess up every time! That's what this is. She knows for sure, and she's waiting for me to say something. This time I'm keeping my mouth shut. I'm not ready to burst my happy bubble with family drama just yet.

Fraser

This will not be happening again, sneaking out before one of her family members sees me. What are we, 16? It's getting ridiculous. She'd better tell Drew soon or I'm going to have to tell him myself. Fuck the consequences!

I arrive at the office after a quick detour home to shower and get ready for the day. This is a big week for us, with our business being nominated for an award, and we're going away to the Gold Coast for the awards ceremony on Saturday night. We also have our new staff member starting in the office, Claudia, our new office manager. Elly's mum, Anne, found her for us. When she heard we were looking for someone, she knew just the right person. Claudia's kids go to Anne's school, and she's had a bit of bad luck lately with her husband leaving her and the kids and needed a job and fast. With years of experience in office managing before she had her kids, I'm sure she will be the perfect person for the job.

Blake has organised a meeting for us this morning so we can get to know each other and work out what her exact role will be. As usual, it looks like I'm late. The boys and Claudia are both in his office already, oops.

"Morning, Ash, Blake, Claudia." I reach out to shake her hand. "Sorry I'm late, it's been an interesting morning already." Claudia looks to be in her mid-thirties with long dark hair which she wears pinned back. She looks very professional in her navy-blue jacket and skirt.

Blake is giving me a death stare for being late, but he's trying to be polite in front of our new staff member. "It's okay. We were just going through a few things until you got here."

I pull up a seat next to Blake.

Ash smiles.

"Now, Claudia is going to be working school hours. She will finish up for the day at 2.45pm so she can collect her kids from school," says Blake.

She's fiddling with her hands and looks so nervous. "I hope that's going to work with you guys? It's so hard to find something that fits around school hours, and I don't have any family around to help out with the kids."

"I can't see why it won't," I offer, trying to reassure her.

"This is a new role for us, so any help we can get to organise this place the better. It's going to be better than what we had before." This is obviously a big deal for her. I guess it must be hard having kids, especially on your own. I never really thought about how you would manage all that before, but it's what it would have been like for my dad when Mum left, so if I can help someone in the same situation, I'm going to do what I can to make it work for her.

"Thank you all for the opportunity. Since Anne told me about your company, I have looked into your past work and I love what you're all doing. I think it's amazing how you're trying to work as many eco-friendly aspects into your designs as possible. I'm very passionate about protecting the environment myself."

Blake looks impressed. "Well, I think you will fit in here perfectly then."

"You will be a great addition to our team," adds Ash.

I nod in agreement.

My phone is buzzing in my pocket. I pull it out to turn it off but it's Dad's name that lights up the screen. I haven't talked to him for weeks, and he can be really hard to get hold of depending on where they are in the country.

"Sorry, guys, I better take this. Claudia, I'll leave you in Blake and Ash's capable hands. Anything you need, though, I'll be in my office all day so just come and grab me."

"Thank you, Fraser, nice to meet you." I give her a wave and head to my office to answer my phone.

"Dad, how's things?"

"Great, son. We've spent the last three weeks slowly making our way from Sydney to Melbourne along the Great Ocean Road. You would love it here, it's beautiful."

"How's Janice?"

"Perfect, son, your old dad's a lucky man."

I can hear him smiling through the phone, and I'm so happy for him. After everything he went through with my mum, he deserves all the happiness in life.

"That's great, Dad. So glad you're enjoying yourselves. When will you be home next? I need a proper catch-up."

"Missing your old dad, are you? We're looking at coming home at the end of next month. Is everything all right, son? You don't quite sound yourself."

"I guess. The business is going well. We have hired an office manager to give us a hand around here because we're so busy. We've also been nominated for an award for the library rebuild we did here in Byron."

"I'm happy for you, son. You deserve to be doing well, you boys have worked so hard on this business. I knew it would be a success."

"Thanks, Dad. I appreciate it."

"There's still something playing on you, though, I can tell. What's up?"

"It's nothing... It's Elly, she's back in town, and we've kind of started dating."

"Well, that's great news, isn't it?"

"Yeah, it's just she hasn't told her family yet. She's worried about a silly pact she had with Drew when they were kids. She's scared if she tells them, it will hurt her close relationship with him. But I'm starting to feel she just thinks I'm not good enough for her. You know what the Walkers are like, they're all so close. They're the perfect family. Maybe she's worried about telling them because I'm not the man she wants to bring home to them.

"Son, you know that's not true. That girl has been in love with you since you were teens. It was obvious to all around you, and trust me, that includes Jim and Anne as well. We just thought you two hadn't figured it out yet!

Now you have, you need to hang on to her and work out how you make it all work. Her brother will come round, might just take him a while to see it from your perspective."

"Thanks, Dad, that was exactly what I needed to hear. Was it that obvious?"

"Blind Freddy could have seen it. Got to go, son, Janice has just walked in, ready for her daily workout, if you get my drift."

"Too much information, Dad!"

"Sorry, son," he laughs, "talk soon."

"Bye, Dad."

It doesn't matter how old I get, I still feel better when I run things past my dad. Somehow, he has all the answers and knows just the right thing to say. It makes me wish he was still living here. Elly doesn't know how lucky she is having such a close family. What I wouldn't have given to have her family growing up, parents who loved each other, siblings always there looking out for you. That's why I spent so much time with them, it was the closest I was going to get to normal, even if they were someone else's family.

I feel like I've gotten nowhere today. I'm reworking these latest drawings trying to work out how on earth we keep to Ash's budget and still include some of the eco options Blake and I have come up with. This project is going to be huge and will really put our company on the map. It's a four-storey apartment building with shop fronts below. We've been working on this design for months now. Ash is really excited about it, but he's a pain in the arse to keep happy. He's our numbers man and will let Blake and I pretty much do whatever design we want as long as it's not going to cost too much and will make our company big money in the end. I can't really complain; he's the reason we had this opportunity in the first place and he's bloody good at what he does, that's why we're doing so well.

If we get this next job right, I will have enough money to be able to build my own place here. That's the dream, anyway. Somewhere close to the beach. I've been playing with design ideas for it, but it will all come down to finding the perfect block of land. First, we need to get this contract, and if that means jumping through a few hoops to keep Ash happy, it will all be worth it.

There's a knock on my door and I look up to see Claudia. She smiles softly.

"Blake's out for the afternoon, so I'm just letting you know I'm about to finish up for the day. All the accounts are filed. Let me know tomorrow if you can't understand my new system, but it's pretty self-explanatory, and I've set the phone to an answering machine for the afternoon, so if you're too busy to take the calls, you can just check the messages later. I hope that helps."

"That all sounds amazing. What did we do without you?" I smile back. Why didn't we think of setting the phone to a message? I've been answering it like a sucker.

"Thanks for all your work today, Claudia, see you tomorrow."

She gives a smile and waves, then she's gone.

Today has flown by, it's 2.45 already. I think Claudia is going to fit in perfectly here. If today is anything to go by, she's very efficient, and within the first day has us starting to catch up already.

I just get back into my design when Blake arrives back from his site checks and pops his head around my office door to check in.

"Hey, man, how did you go at the new site?" I ask. "And what's with the smirk? Did you finally get laid?" I rib.

"Good, it's all on track for starting next week, and no smirk, just having a good day. How did Claudia go?"

"I think we have the perfect fit there. Go check out the new filing system she's put in place. We could never have done this ourselves."

"Great. Have you worked out what you're doing for the awards ceremony on Saturday night?" Blake asks.

"We have six tickets, Ash and Chloe obviously, and I was thinking we should take Elly and Indie. We can stay at the hotel and make a weekend of it. What do you think?"

"I think that's a great idea. We can introduce them to some industry people as well. Might help with their business."

"Perfect. I'll call Indie. I have a favour to ask anyway, unless you want to?" I question, raising my eyebrow at him. I'm positive something's going on between them, even if he won't admit to it yet.

"No. Why would I?"

"No reason." He leaves for his own office, and I try Indie's number. She answers straight away.

"Hey, Indie, it's Fraser. I've got a little favour to ask."

"Really, what can I help you with?"

"We have this award ceremony this weekend on the Gold Coast. Blake and I are wondering if you and Elly want to join us. Ash and his fiancée will be there. It's a great opportunity for you both, and it means a weekend away, all expenses on us. What do you think?"

"Sounds good. Why is that a favour? Sounds like I'm going to owe you guys."

"Well, in that case, I'll take my IOU now! I need help to find a dress for Elly. I want to surprise her with something beautiful, and I've got no idea where to start. You're good at that kind of thing, aren't you?"

"Of course I am, Fraser, but you know how much she hates surprises. Is this a good idea?"

"Yes, she only thinks she hates surprises, she'll love this one."

"Okay, but if she hates it, I had nothing to do with it, it's on you."

"I'm a big boy. I can take the blame."

She laughs, "Okay then, I'm free Wednesday arvo. We can meet up and work it all out then."

"Can you make sure she has the weekend off at the café too, without it being obvious? And don't tell her a thing. Let's keep all this between us until Thursday. Thanks, Indie, you're the best, see you then."

Now I just have to convince Elly to come along with us, but I'm sure Indie can help with that.

CHAPTER FIFTEEN

ELENA

I'VE JUST FINISHED MY SHIFT AT THE CAFÉ. I WALK through the front door and dump my bag and keys on the buffet in the lounge room and make my way down the hallway to my bedroom. I stop in my tracks. What is this?

Hanging in my doorway is the most beautiful wine-red silk gown I have ever seen. I look around trying to work out why it's here hanging in my doorway. It's simply stunning, with a plunging neckline and a low back. The silk is so smooth it looks like liquid flowing from the hanger. I look over the gown again and notice there's a little note pinned to the coat hanger.

Gorgeous, I need you by my side at the award ceremony Saturday night, and I knew you'd say no because you had nothing to wear. So now there are no excuses. There's shoes and a bag on your bed, all designer, of course.

Fraser x

Wow, this dress is stunning. I can hardly believe Fraser picked it out. He wouldn't know the first thing about fashion. I take a quick look at the label. OMG, it's a Clara

Ashton! It must have cost him a fortune. No one has ever bought something so beautiful for me.

Indie pops her head out of her room. "I see you've found your present. He did all right, hey?"

"Um, yeah. I can hardly believe he bought it himself!" I reach out and touch the silky fabric. It's divine.

"He might've had a little help. He has no idea about fashion," she laughs.

"I knew it! Thank you, Indie. It's beautiful."

"So, are you going to go with them then?"

"I guess I've no excuses now."

"Good, because I wouldn't want this to go to waste and I'm not going without you." She pulls out a gorgeous black lace gown with a low back.

"Oh my," I squeal. "Are you coming too?" We're both jumping up and down like excited little kids.

"Fraser invited me. He's got someone he wants me to meet and thinks they might like my art. We're staying at the Palazzo Versace Gold Coast."

"Indie, that makes this even more exciting. I told you our luck is going to change. This is our year!"

I grab my phone out of my bag and send a quick message to Fraser.

Elly: Thank you, baby. The dress is stunning and of course I'll come with you xx

Fraser: Can't wait to see it on you... and take it off you... Glad you're coming, it wouldn't have been the same without you.

Elly: You've no idea how excited I am. I've never been to anything like this before. Thank you for inviting Indie too.

Fraser: It'll be a fun weekend for all of us.

. . .

We arrived at our hotel, The Palazzo Versace Gold Coast. This place is unbelievable, and Indie and I spend the afternoon in the hotel spa getting pampered like never before. We have a massage and our hair and makeup done. This is "the life". It must be what it feels like to be famous, getting ready for the Golden Globes or something.

I look the best I've ever looked. Indie's just headed back to her room to get dressed. She's staying down the hall in a room with Blake. I've no idea where the boys have been all afternoon. They said something about catching the game on the TV, in the hotel bar, but that was hours ago. They really should be back by now. We have to leave in 20 minutes. Typical Fraser, he's always late.

I keep looking at my dress hanging on the doorframe. It's so beautiful. I've been putting off getting dressed. I'm scared to put it on. What if I spill something down the front of it as soon as I put it on, or wipe my makeup all over it?

I've never worn anything so extravagant before. I don't want to wreck it. At least not before Fraser sees me in it. Where is he? I check the time again. We should be heading downstairs. I guess I better put it on. We have to go really soon.

I pull my dress off the hanger and carefully slip it on and do up the zipper. The fabric feels amazing on my skin, so smooth and silky.

I stand and admire myself in the full-length mirror. I almost don't believe my own reflection, I look seriously amazing. My long hair is in big Hollywood curls swept over to one side with a clip. My eyes are smoky, and the look's complete with wine-red lips to match the colour of my gown.

I hear the door open and turn slowly, trying not to make any sudden movement that might destroy the dress. Fraser stands in the door and the look on his face tells me he's impressed with the changes I made today.

"Wow, Elly, you're stunning! More like the Elly I used to know with the change of hair."

He comes up behind me, wrapping his arms around me, spinning me and standing back so he can see me from the front as well. His eyes roam up my body and his face breaks into a broad smile.

"Yeah, the blue wasn't going to work with this dress, so boring blonde it is, for now anyway," I say, smoothing out the fabric of my dress.

The look in his eyes says it all. He likes what he sees. "Well, you look a million dollars, gorgeous."

"I feel it! Stop wasting your time admiring me, we're going to be late. You need to get ready." He places a soft kiss on my neck. Then unhooks his suit from the hanger and starts to undress in front of me. He knows what he's doing.

"Like what you see, gorgeous? Maybe we should just stay here tonight and have fun on our own. What do you say I peel you out of that dress so you're wearing as little as me."

"You getting nervous, baby? Trying to avoid all the people downstairs?" He shakes his head, giving me a look like he wants to devour me. "Well, if it's not nerves, I didn't go to all this trouble to just stay in and get naked with you, so we're going. You better get a move on."

I walk into the bathroom to top up my lippy before we leave, and he's fully dressed in his suit by the time I get back. Seeing him in a suit does things to me. He looks unbelievably hot. I can see why he was a little tempted to stay in tonight. Seeing him dressed up, I'm taken back to the first time I ever saw him in a suit, the night of our school formal. He looked so good that night.

I sit in the limo with Indie, Drew, and his date, just outside the hall, and I take one more look at my makeup in the compact mirror from my purse.

Indie and I are both so excited to get dressed up for the first time. I'm in a long pale blue gown. I saved up for months to be able to afford it. We've both had a spray tan and our hair and makeup done. I don't think Drew could care less what we're doing. He's been pashing his date, Chelsea, since we picked her up. Totally gross!

"I'm so excited I feel like I'm going to be sick," I whisper to Indie, as we make our way up to the school hall.

"Not in that dress you're not! I know how much you paid for it. You'll be fine. Just relax and have fun, that's what tonight's supposed to be about." She takes my hand, and we walk in together.

The hall looks amazing. The decorating team has gone above and beyond this time. There are silver sparkly streamers everywhere.

As I look around, I can't help but scan the room for Fraser. I know I shouldn't but he's under my skin. I've been obsessed with him for years, and wherever we are, I look for him. I know his schedule at school and where he's playing sports on the weekend. Kind of stalkerish but I don't care, he's just as bad with me. And in the last few months, something has shifted between us, we're closer than ever. I didn't accept any other invitations for dates tonight. It just didn't seem right knowing how I felt about Fraser. He's the only one I want to be here with, but that was never an option because of Drew. So Indie and I decided to come together, especially as her boyfriend is two years older than her, so he wasn't allowed to come.

Fraser's probably not here yet. He's always late, but as I scan the room, I'm surprised to see him on the dance floor in the arms of Angela Cook, the bitch who made my high school life a total nightmare! He hates dancing and he knows how awful she is. Why is he dancing with her?

I can feel my heart beating faster as the anger and adrenaline start to pump through my body. Two can play at this game, Fraser Davis! My eyes go straight to the large group of guys standing down the back and I see who I'm looking for, Adam Silver, Fraser's biggest enemy.

Adam has been asking me out for months, but out of respect for my friendship with Fraser and whatever else is going on between us, I kept turning him down. Well, not tonight, buddy. I'm not missing out on another thing because of selfish Fraser.

Fraser and Adam have been involved in some sort of rivalry since Adam beat him in a one-hundred-metre running race in year seven, and since then, they've been competing over everything. I know dancing with Adam will piss Fraser off majorly. They compete at everything, and Adam always is just that little bit better. But what do I care now, seeing him with bitch-face Angela.

I walk right up to Adam and ask him to dance. He looks surprised but happy to be asked by me. He takes my hand and leads me to the dance floor. He then wraps his arms around me as we start to dance. I feel kind of bad for what I'm doing. I don't really have any interest in Adam, but he's a nice enough guy, and if Fraser can go out with whoever he wants, then so can I.

"I was wondering how long it would take you to come to your senses and finally agree to date me," Adam whispers in my ear.

"Let's just start with a dance, hey, see how this goes?"

"Oh, baby, one dance with me and you won't be able to turn me down."

Cocky bastard! We'll see. We're two dances in when I notice Fraser look up from Angela, laughing at something she's said, and his face changes instantly when his eyes meet mine. I smile sweetly and give him a little wave just to make sure I'm rubbing it in. I can see the anger in his eyes as he cracks his knuckles, stalking over to us.

"What do you think you're doing, Elena?"

"Dancing, Fraser, just like you. Fun, isn't it? Why don't you head back to your date? She's starting to look annoyed," I taunt, with my arms still wrapped around Adam's shoulders.

"Nope, not going to happen. I'm not leaving you here with him. This guy is trouble, Elly, you don't know him like I do."

We stop dancing as it's clear Fraser's not going to let this go on. Adam pulls back from me a little, still with one hand on my back.

"Oh please," I snap, "you're hardly worried about me, Fraser. If you were, I wouldn't have walked in here to see you dancing with bitch-face over there. Go enjoy your night so I can enjoy mine."

"What's your problem, man? You need to back off before I make you," Adam challenges, infuriating Fraser further.

"You're my problem. Get your hands off her," Fraser hisses, nudging Adam's shoulder so he's forced to drop my waist, and it's on. Adam throws the first punch, getting Fraser square in the jaw, followed by Fraser thumping Adam on the nose. Two of our teachers jump in and hold them back from each other. I've seen enough, I'm out of here.

"You're such a selfish prick, Fraser, it's always got to be about you," I yell, running out the front doors of the hall, tears now streaming down my face.

. . .

"Earth to Elly, where did you go?" Fraser's standing right in front of me.

"Sorry, I was just thinking about the last time I saw you in a suit, our formal."

"Hope only the good parts of that night, not the bad!"

I stand in front of him and fix his bow tie. "What, like 'Jealous Fraser'? He was in full force that night."

"You did bait me on purpose, though, dancing with Adam."

"Maybe, but you deserved it, dancing with Angela!"

"Maybe, and I don't regret any of it. Without fighting with that dick Adam, I wouldn't have had to chase after you when you ran off. And what happened when I found you was worth it all," he says, drawing me in closer to his body. "After years of having to scare off every guy that even looked your way, I finally got to be the one holding you in his arms, kissing your tears away."

I can feel the tears welling in my eyes at his admission and I blink them away. I can't cry right now, I'll wreck my makeup. "I wish I knew how you felt back then."

"I know, we were only young, but I knew that night no one would ever compare to you. The way I felt about you when our lips first met..." He rests his forehead on mine, both of us remembering the moment that's etched into our brains forever.

I smile up at him remembering, wishing somehow things hadn't gone down the way they did. We've wasted so much time.

He kisses my forehead. "I know I can't kiss your lips because of the lippy," he smiles.

I laugh at him for breaking the moment with a stupid

comment like that. "No, you're right, I don't have time to fix it, we're already late. Come on, let's get going." I slip my hand into his and we walk out the door.

Ash and Chloe are in the hall waiting for us; they aren't staying the night at this hotel so don't have a room. We walk past Blake and Indie's room, collecting them on our way to the elevator. Luckily, we don't have to go far. The awards ceremony is being held downstairs in the hotel ballroom.

Tonight's going to be a good night. I can feel it.

The six of us enter the ballroom and I can hardly believe my eyes. This place is insane. It's so extravagant. Everything here screams opulence, from the oversized chandeliers hanging from the ceiling to the detailing on the walls. The tables are set with pillar candles and fragrant flowers running along the centres of the tables.

"Wow, this place is insane," Indie whispers, grabbing my hand. "Don't leave me. I feel so out of place here. They'll probably think I'm gate crashing and kick me out."

"Me too, Indie girl. This is like a whole other world! But you don't look out of place, you look stunning in that dress."

"So do you, chickee. Can you believe this night?"

Fraser has found our table and motions for us to join him.

Fraser

We've done the rounds, meeting all the important people Ash wanted us to meet, and we're now sitting at our table listening to the awards being presented. The night is dragging on. We've had our entrée and mains served already as the awards are announced. Our category will be up soon.

But right now, this is the last thing I want to be doing.

Since I walked into our hotel room to see Elly in that sexy red dress, all I've wanted to do is unwrap her from it.

She's not helping either. She's sitting by my side, her hand resting on my lap, and every now and then she runs her hand up and down my leg, her perfect red nails digging in slightly as she goes.

She has no idea what she's doing to me. She's driving me crazy, and I have to just sit here in a stuffy tux, smiling along, as the awards ceremony goes on. Why couldn't we have been up first? Then this would be over, and we could be back in our room fucking. I hope we don't win because I'm not going to be able to get up and accept the award if we do, not in this condition. Think unsexy thoughts, think unsexy thoughts.

It's one of those nights I wish I could have a drink to help me relax a bit, but it's best I don't. Alcohol and I don't mix well. I take after my mother in that way, and I can't stop at just one so it's best not to start. I learnt that the hard way when I was younger.

This is not my idea of fun. I'm only here because Ash talked me into it with his speech about it being such good exposure in our industry, and since we're still so new, he thinks it's a really good idea. I'm lucky to be in business with him, he has such a good brain for this kind of thing.

Our category is announced, "Best Eco-Friendly Design."

There are four other companies in the running for this award. As their designs flash up on the screen, I know there is no hope we will have won, they all look incredible. And I know for a fact that some of these companies are really big names in the eco-friendly community. It would have to be a miracle for us to win. But I still want it, this award is a big deal. As the announcer shows our images of the Byron Bay

Library, I can feel my stomach twist with nerves. Don't know if we deserve it, but let it be us.

"The winner is 'The Green Door' for its eco-friendly design for the Byron Bay town library."

We all look at each other in disbelief. I can't believe we're winning this type of award our first year in! We make our way up to the podium together, accepting our award. Luckily there are no speeches.

As I make my way back to our table, my focus is on Elly. She's beaming with excitement for us. I feel like the luckiest man in the world, with my business being so successful, and the most beautiful girl in the room who only has eyes for me. How life can do a complete 360 in the matter of a few years.

I'm done with this awards ceremony. I'm taking my girl back upstairs to bed.

Why is my phone ringing? What's the time? It feels like we only just got to bed. Who could be ringing me at this hour? I roll over, feeling around for my phone in the dark. I answer without even opening my eyes.

"Hello."

"It's Theo. Are you with Elly?" I sit straight up. Why is Theo ringing at this time?

"Yes, do you want me to put her on?"

"No, it's fine I just couldn't get hold of her, she must have her phone on silent or something."

"What's wrong, Theo?" Something in my voice has Elly sitting up now, her eyes opening wide.

"You need to get her home. It's Dad. He's collapsed and hit his head on his morning run. We're lucky someone found him. He's still unconscious. I'm following the ambulance into Byron Hospital now."

"What's going on?" Elly mouths to me.

"Shit. Theo. We're on our way, but we're on the Gold Coast so we'll be two hours. Keep us posted with how he's going."

"Will do. Drive safe. We don't need anyone else in hospital today." I'm still looking at my phone. Shit. What should I do first?

"What's going on, Fraser?" Elly has tears already welling in her eyes. She knows this isn't going to be good.

"That was Theo. It's your dad."

"Dad! What's happened?"

"Elly, he has collapsed on his morning run. Theo's following him to the hospital and your mum's with him in the ambulance. We need to get home as soon as we can. They have no idea how bad he is yet."

Elly's hands are covering her face as she gives in to the tears. "Oh my god, we need to go now." I wrap my arms around her as she sobs. "He's got to be all right, Fraser. I don't know what I'd do without my dad."

"It's all going to be fine, Elly. We're not going to have to find out. I'm sure he's going to be okay. He's a tough guy. By the time we get home, he'll probably be sitting up in his hospital bed laughing the whole thing off. Pack my bag for me. I'll get the others sorted so we can leave straight away."

She nods, and as if on autopilot, starts throwing things in bags. I run down the hall to tell the others.

CHAPTER SIXTEEN
ELENA

I run through the front doors of the hospital, straight to the reception desk. "My dad, Jim Walker, was brought in two hours ago by ambulance. Do you know what room he's in?"

The young woman on the front desk looks me up and down then types something into her computer. Why is she taking so long? Damn me for being two hours away when something bad happens. I should have been here with him already. God, I hope he's all right.

The car ride felt like one of those bad dreams where you're in a rush to get somewhere and you just can't get there. Two hours felt like ten. Fraser drove as fast as he could, but it didn't feel quick enough and the others were fussing over me the whole time. I just wanted to get to the hospital and be with my family. My chest feels so tight and I can feel my heart still racing. Please just let him be okay.

"What was your name?"

"Elena Walker."

She walks out from behind her desk. "Come with me, Elena. I'll take you through to where the rest of your family is waiting for your dad." She takes my hands in hers. "Now, I'm not sure if your family has kept you up to date with your dad's condition."

"We've been driving. They probably didn't want to worry me while we drove from the Gold Coast."

"Well, at the moment he's in surgery. He's had a bleed on the brain from the fall he had this morning. He's very lucky someone found him when they did. We have one of our best surgeons in with him now so he's in good hands." She lets go of my hands and starts to walk down the hall.

Oh no, my poor dad. Now the tears start. I can't hold them back any longer. I just want to see him and know he's all right. Please let him be okay, I silently pray to whoever will listen to me.

I look up to see the nurse is halfway down the hall already. I'm so scared I feel numb and realise I haven't started moving to follow her. Then I feel Fraser's arm wrap around my shoulder, leading me in the direction the nurse is taking us.

"It's going to be fine, Elly. He's a strong man. I'm sure he's going to be okay. I'll come with you." He walks with his arm wrapped around me, moving me forward to the waiting room.

As we enter the waiting room, where my family sits huddled together, they all look up. Theo sits with his arm wrapped around Fiona and Drew sits with Mum holding her hand. Their eyes rise to meet ours. These people mean everything to me, and up until now, our family has been so blessed to never have to deal with something so scary. I can see that even Theo, who is always the strong one, has been crying.

"Elly," Mum cries, as she rushes over to me, pulling me into a hug.

"What's going on, Mum?"

"We don't know. He's in surgery at the moment. We haven't heard anything since they took him in." She has tears welling in her eyes, but I can tell she's trying to hold it together for us.

"He'll be okay, Mum. I'm sure of it. He has to be, right?"

"I hope so, honey. Come on, sit down with us." I go and sit next to Drew and he wraps his arms around me.

"I should go," says Fraser.

Mum grabs Fraser's hand. "No, stay and wait with us, Fraser. You're family too, you should be here. Thank you for bringing Elly back so quickly." She walks him over to where she was sitting. He doesn't say a word, just nods his head, and sits holding her hand. He's been around my family for so long they do see him as one of us.

I hug into Drew's chest. "You're shaking, sis, are you all right?"

"I'm just worried. What if he's not... what if he."

He cuts me off before I can say it. "He will be."

"I guess it's that moment when you realise, just because someone is your parent and they have been there your whole life, that doesn't make them invincible. They won't be here forever. But I'm just praying it will be for a long time to come."

"He will be." We sit in each other's arms for a bit, then he pulls back to look at me. "Where were you two this morning, sis, you and Fraser?"

I drop my head. I don't want to have this conversation here and now. "You know the awards ceremony for The Green Door was last night. We stayed on the Gold Coast with Blake and Indie after it."

"You and Fraser are seeing each other, aren't you?"

He's whispering so the others don't hear. "That's what you were trying to tell me the other day before you moved." I look at his face. I can't tell if he's mad or just worried about Dad.

"How did you work it out?" I sigh, feeling a weight being lifted off my shoulders.

"The two of you have been acting weird around each other since our birthday party, and then, when we couldn't get a hold of you this morning and Theo called Fraser, I put two and two together."

"Do you hate me?" I bury my head in my hands. "I'm sorry I didn't tell you. I could never find the right time, and I didn't want you to be mad at me because of the pact we had as kids."

He lets out a little laugh. "Elly, we're not kids anymore. I'm hardly going to hold you to a pact we made when we were like 14. Yeah, it's going to be weird seeing you together, but I love Fraser. He's always been part of our family, and if he makes you happy, then that's all that matters. Especially after what's happened today. Family is everything."

I almost can't believe what I'm hearing. All this time I've been so worried about what the family was going to think, and they love Fraser as much as I do.

"Thank you for saying that, Drew. You don't know what it means to me." The tears start again. "You know you have always been my favourite brother."

"I know, sis, and I always will be. Don't keep secrets from me, though. You can tell me anything, you know that. Whatever it is, we will always work it out."

We all sit in silence for what feels like forever. Why haven't they come out to tell us what's going on? I mean, I have no idea how long this type of surgery is supposed to take, but this seems like it's taking way too long. Maybe something's gone wrong and they can't fix it.

As if they were reading my mind, a younger-looking doctor comes through the swinging doors and we all sit up, waiting for the news.

"I'm Dr Cove, I was taking care of Jim's surgery today. It was a complete success and we have stopped the bleed. He's resting in recovery, but he's still a bit groggy, so I think it's best just a couple of you go in at a time, so you don't overwhelm him. Mrs Walker, can I talk to you for a second before you go in?"

He's going to be all right, thank God! Drew hugs me again. I can see Fraser over his shoulder, walking with Mum over to the doctor. I wonder what he wants. Dad's okay, though, so I feel like I can breathe for the first time since we had that phone call this morning.

Mum comes back from talking to the doctor, with fresh tears. "Mum, what's going on? I thought everything was okay?"

"Yeah, there's a few other complications. I just need to go and talk to your dad. How about you guys go down to the cafeteria and get some lunch, then you might be able to see him."

Fraser

We all make our way down to the cafeteria and line up in the queue. Theo's up front with Elly, talking to her and Fiona about the baby.

Drew bumps arms with me. I tell him, "That was a crazy scare this morning, man. I'm glad Jim's going to be okay."

"Yeah, me too. I'm not so sure about you, though, after what I just found out." Oh shit! He knows. Theo must have told him.

"What do you mean?" I say, backing up slightly. Is he about to thump me?

"It's cool, man, I'm just joking. So, you and Elly, hey? She told me about you guys. I'm happy for you. It was kind of obvious something was going on."

"It's not going to change anything between us?" I ask.

"As long as you look after her, or I'll have to track you down and kill you." He gives his best death stare, but Drew is the least scary person I know. He couldn't hurt a fly. I don't think, in all the time I have known him, he's ever been in a fight.

"That makes two of us," Theo pipes up. Theo on the other hand has connections and scares the shit out of me.

I put my hands up in defence. I knew they would both be super protective of her. She's had the three of us looking after her for most of her life. "I'm not stupid. I'm not going to do anything to hurt her. She's safe with me."

Elly turns to give us a look. "You guys can stop talking about me like I'm not here. I can hear everything you're saying, and I don't need anyone looking after me or killing anyone for me. I can look after myself, thank you very much!" she demands, with her hands on her hips, standing her ground.

Fiona gives her a high five. "You go, girl, tell 'em how it is."

"No one's going to take that away from you," I insist. "We all know you're 'Little Miss Independent'." I wrap my arms around her and kiss her on the cheek.

"Don't call me that. But good, I'm not some damsel in

distress that needs a hero." She reaches up and kisses me on the lips.

We get a disgusted look from Drew. "Gross, guess this is going to take a bit of getting used to. Can you two love birds try and control yourselves around me, please?"

We all laugh. It's hardly the time for all of this, but it's helping to ease the tension of worrying. Maybe this little secret coming out today was the perfect timing after all. I love this family and I would do anything for them. The way they have always looked out for me and my dad. I just hope Jim's going to be back to normal before we know it, because we'll all be lost without him if he's not.

We gather at the cafeteria dining room and eat our lunch. There wasn't much to choose from so it's ham-and-cheese sandwiches on white bread. You'd think a hospital cafeteria would be all about healthy eating, but clearly not this one. Elly's scoffed hers down. She must have been hungry. We both missed breakfast in our rush to get here so it's understandable.

"Do you want anything else to eat? You ate that pretty fast."

"We did miss breakfast, you know! I'm good now, I just want to get back up to see Dad. I want to know what's going on. Mum said something about complications. What would that mean?"

"I don't know. Let's head back now and see what we can find out." I do know. I was standing with her mum when the doctor said it, but Anne wanted to see Jim and find out from him what's going on before we tell the others.

"We're going to head back up and see if we can get in to see Jim. We'll see you guys back up at the waiting room," I say, as I take Elly's hand. She looks so different today, so fragile. I know I would be a mess if it were my dad, and she's really close to Jim. She's always been daddy's little girl. Everyone knows that, so she's taking this pretty hard. But for the first time since knowing her, I can really be here for her the way I want, and her family is okay with it.

Anne is walking back through the swinging doors to the waiting room as we make our way closer. It's obvious she's been crying.

Elly lets go of my hand and runs to her. "Mum, what is it, what's going on?" She wraps her arms around her mum.

"What's happened, Anne? Come and sit down, you look exhausted." We all take a seat together.

"It was more than just a fall. He had a heart attack this morning. That's what caused him to collapse and that's why his surgery took so long. They needed to work on his heart as well. They've had to put in a stint."

"But he's going to come through this and be fine, though, right?" Elly asks.

"Time will tell, honey, but it looks like they have been able to get to it in time, and with a few changes to his diet and helping him avoid stress, he should make a full recovery."

Elly looks so scared as she wraps her arms around her mum. "It's going to be okay, Mum. He's strong and he's had the surgery now. He's going to be back to normal before we know it."

The others are now making their way back up and she's going to need to tell them. I suggest to Anne, "Can we go in and see him now? That way you can talk to the others about it."

"Yes, good idea, Fraser. Just remember, he's still a bit out of it."

We walk in to see Jim lying in his hospital bed, his head wrapped in a bandage and his arm hooked up to a drip. It's only been a couple of days since I saw him last, but he looks so frail, not like the big strong father of this family I know so well.

Elly knew something was going on with him. She has been worried about him for weeks but just didn't know what was wrong. She goes over to his side and holds his hand. He opens his eyes, realising who it is.

"Elly," he smiles weakly up at her. "Fraser, thanks for rushing back to see me. I'm sorry your weekend away got cut short."

"Don't worry about that now, Dad. We just want to see you all better." She smiles sadly at her dad. She's really worried.

"How are you feeling, Jim?"

"Yeah, not too bad, mate. They've got me on the good stuff until I recover from the surgery, so not in too much pain."

"How long do they think you'll be in here for, Dad?"

"Probably just a week or two, while I recover, honey."

Elly squeezes his hand, "Is there anything we can get you from home to make you more comfortable?"

"Thank you, Anne's taking care of all of that. It's just nice to see your faces. Make sure you visit this week. I'm going to get bored sitting in this bed with nothing to do."

Elly kisses him on the forehead. "Of course we will. You're going to go nuts in here. I don't think I've ever seen you sit still before," she laughs.

"I'm sure you'll be up fixing something in the hospital, annoying the nurses, before we know it, Jim."

"Let's hope so." He gives a little smile, but I can tell he's worried and probably in a lot more pain than he's letting on.

"Come on, Elly, I think the others will be wanting to come in now and your dad needs to rest."

She kisses him on the forehead again. "I love you, Dad, get better." She rubs his hand and gives it a squeeze.

"Thanks for coming to visit, you two. Fraser, you look after my baby girl."

I nod, and he gives me a knowing smile. Well, it looks like the whole family knows. Now we can just relax and be together.

"I'll be back tomorrow, Dad."

"See you then, Elly."

We say our goodbyes to the others and head home. Elly hasn't said a word the whole drive back to her apartment from the hospital, and I have no idea how to talk about this. "I might just swing past my place and grab some clothes so I can stay with you tonight. I don't want you to be alone."

She gives me a small smile. "Thanks, Fraser. I'm sorry today was so crazy. We were supposed to be celebrating your win."

"There's nothing to be sorry for. Family is the most important thing. Your dad's going to need a lot of support over the next few months, but we have each other now, so anything you need, I'm here for you." I rub my hand up her leg and she looks over to me with a small smile. "You can always help me celebrate later anyway."

"Fraser!" she says, as she slaps me on the leg. "Do you always have to go there?"

"What, round you I do." She laughs at me. "Why don't you go have a shower, gorgeous, and I'll fix you up something for dinner."

Elly nods and heads to her room. Poor thing looks exhausted.

Now to work out her kitchen. I open the fridge and there's next to nothing in there. I look up to see Indie.

"Hey, Fraser. Sorry we didn't get to the shops this weekend. We might have to order in."

"Pizza it is then," I suggest.

"How is Jim? What's going on?"

"He's in recovery from the operation he had to stop the bleeding from the fall. I'll let Elly fill you in on the rest when she's ready, but it looks like he's going to be fine."

"I'm so glad, we have been so worried all day. You look tired. Why don't you go join your girl and I'll organise the dinner."

"Thank you, Indie."

I head down the hall and I can hear Elly crying through the door to the bathroom. I don't know if I should go in or leave her alone. Maybe she needs this time to herself. Fuck it. I want to be there to make her feel better. I can't hear her crying and leave her alone.

I push open the door and find her sitting on the floor in the shower, legs crossed, head in her hands. "It's okay, Elly, I'm coming." I strip off as fast as I can and get in as she stands up. I wrap my arms around her as she cries into my chest. "Let it all go, gorgeous. I'm here for you."

"I'm sorry, Fraser, today was just too much. I'm so scared for him."

"Don't be sorry. You're allowed to cry after what's happened today. It's scary seeing someone you love going through something like this. You don't always have to be so strong. I'm here for you when you need to let it all go."

"Thank you, baby. You've been so amazing today. I don't know how I would've got through it without you."

We stand together for quite some time, with the hot water running over us. "Come on, I think we better get out. Our pizza's probably here."

"I'm not ready to let go yet," she says, as she nuzzles her

head into my chest again. I hear her stomach rumble. "I guess I am hungry. Let's go."

We eat our dinner in almost silence with both me and Indie not quite knowing what to say.

"I'm sorry, guys," Elly says, "I'm going to bed. I think I just need to sleep." I watch her walk down the hall then look back to Indie. I feel bad to leave her with the mess to clean up.

"Don't worry about this, Fraser. Go with her, she needs you. I've got it."

"Thank you."

I jump into bed behind Elly and wrap my arms around her, pulling her into me. Before long I can hear her even breathing. She must be asleep.

CHAPTER SEVENTEEN

ELENA

This week has been a juggling act, between my shifts at the café, styling work with the boys, and trying to be at the hospital as much as I can for Dad. I haven't had a second to think.

Dad says he's fine at the hospital by himself, but I know he's not. He's bored out of his brain and he needs someone to keep him company and to keep an eye on him.

He was up this morning trying to help one of the nurses and lost his balance and fell again. He doesn't know how to take it easy, and he's going to end up hurting himself. He's lucky he just ended up with a few bruises this time.

He's not used to being the one who needs help, and he's not coping with it. But he'd better get used to it. With months of recovery ahead of him, it's going to be a while before he's back to his normal self and up and going.

Fraser's been amazing this week, so supportive, and the family has adjusted to us being together so it's not as weird anymore. Well, kind of, anyway. Drew freaks out every time we kiss in front of him, but he's just going to have to get over that.

Today I've been at the hospital most of the day and it's now 4pm. Fraser will be here soon to pick me up so we can head out and do a site inspection on a property near the beach. They're just having some minor interior renovations done, and he's asked for my advice on the colour palette. I'm picking up more and more work with them as people see the photos of the townhouses and can see how much of a big difference it makes.

My laptop has become my best friend. I would've been screwed this week without it, but being able to work while I'm here with Dad has certainly helped me do it all.

There's a knock at the door to Dad's hospital room and we both look over to see the same smiling face that's been looking after Dad all week, Dr Cove. He's lovely and is doing a wonderful job taking care of Dad and reassuring him when he has questions.

"Jim, Elena. Sorry to interrupt. Just here to do my rounds."

I smile up at him from my computer. "All good, you're not interrupting."

"Jim, how are you feeling today? I heard you had a bit of a fall this morning."

"Yeah, but I'm better now, doc."

"Don't worry," I ensure the doctor, "I'm keeping an eye on him now. He won't get up to no good on my watch."

"I bet. You're a good girl, Elena. You've been here with him all week," he says, with his sexy-as-fuck smile. If I didn't know better, I'd say he's flirting with me. Right in front of my dad too. Ballsy.

"Hey, can you two stop talking about me like I'm not here? I may be old but I'm not deaf."

"Sorry, Dad."

"Let's check your stats then, hey, Jim."

Dr Cove goes about doing his normal checks on Dad and then writes in his chart.

"Hey, Elena, can I see you out the front quickly before I go?"

I make my way out the door of Dad's hospital room and stand in the hall. I wonder what he wants. Dr Cove follows me out. He is tall. I have to crane my neck up to him. "Is everything okay with Dad?"

"Yes, sorry to worry you. He's doing well. This isn't about him. I was just wondering, once your dad is discharged and not my patient anymore, if there is any chance we could go out sometime?" he asks with that same sexy smile.

"Like, on a date?"

"Yes, like a date. What do you say, Elena?" His beautiful eyes meet mine. He's definitely handsome, and in another lifetime, he would have been perfect, but he's not Fraser.

"I'm so sorry if I gave you the wrong impression. I have a boyfriend."

"Fraser Davis, just here to pick up Elly." Fraser holds out his hand to shake Dr Cove's. Right on cue! Typical he had to walk in on the doctor asking me out. "Is there a problem with Elly's dad? This little chat looks serious." Fraser's eyes are fixed on Dr Cove who takes a step back from me, putting a little more distance between us.

"Everything's fine with Jim. Nice to meet you, Fraser," he says, shaking Fraser's hand.

"Hey, baby, how was your day?" I say, waiting for the reaction or overreaction that I know is coming. I wonder how much he heard of that little chat with Dr Cove.

He wraps his arms around me, kissing me straight in front of Dr Cove. "It was good, gorgeous. But we'd better get going quickly if we're going to see that house. Better finish up with the doctor while I go say hi to your dad. He walks into the room, "Jim, how are you today?" his loud voice bellows.

I turn to Dr Cove. "I'm so sorry about that. Thank you, I'm flattered, but as you can see, I have a boyfriend. Thank you so much for everything you are doing for Dad. We appreciate it," I offer with a smile.

"That's what I'm here for, Elena. Sorry I overstepped the mark. I shouldn't have asked you. I'll see you tomorrow on my rounds."

"It's fine, really. See you then."

I walk back in the room and I can feel how red my face is. That was so embarrassing.

"Fraser, why did you do that?"

"What, Elly? I thought I was very controlled. I didn't get into a fistfight with the good doctor, just made sure he was aware you're taken."

Dad starts to laugh. "You two remind me of your mother and me when we were young. She had all the boys after her too. You'd better get used to it, Fraser. It's what happens when you fall for the best-looking girl around. That's why I married your mother as quick as she would let me, to put a stop to it. Good luck to you, Fraser."

"Thanks, Jim."

"Don't go putting ideas in his head, Dad. Come on, Fraser. We'd better get going." I lean down and kiss Dad goodbye.

"Behave until I'm back tomorrow. No more helping the nurses. You're here to rest." Dad squeezes my hand and smiles up at me, and even if I'm smothering him with my overprotectiveness, I know he appreciates it.

I take Fraser's hand in mine and we walk out to the car.

He whispers in my ear, "You're going to pay for that tonight."

"What? I didn't do anything."

"Being so irresistible that men constantly want you."

"I can't help being irresistible," I say, batting my eyelashes at him.

"You'd better try." He swats me on the arse playfully, and I yelp, jumping into his car as fast as I can so he can't do it again. Maybe he's growing up. That all went down better than it would have a few months ago.

Fraser

After inspecting the house near the beach, we make our way back to Elly's apartment. I follow her up the stairs, watching her arse in those tight jeans she wears. At this point I'm not sure we're going to make it inside before my dick takes over and I have to fuck her right here in the stairwell.

Instinctively, she knows what I'm thinking and takes the stairs two at a time in a race to the top. She opens the front door and peers inside.

"The coast's clear. No Indie in sight." Before she has a chance to argue, I pick her up and throw her over my shoulder.

"What are you doing, Fraser? Put me down," she says, laughing and trying to wiggle free.

"Not a chance. I need to remind you why you're with me." I carry her to her room, throwing her down on the bed.

"You going all caveman on me, Fraser, claiming your woman before the other Neanderthals can?" she laughs.

I'm sitting on her, pinning her arms to the bed. "Damn

straight! You're my girl, Elly, and the world needs to know it. But for now, I'll make sure you remember, so you don't go getting any ideas about the doctor, or anyone else for that matter."

"Fraser, you know you're the only one I want. You can stop carrying on." She wiggles beneath me, trying to push me off her.

"Well, if you think I'm carrying on like a caveman, I might have to fuck you like one tonight."

"And how would that even go?"

"I don't know. Rough? Take what's mine. Wrap your hair around my hand and pull it tight as I fuck you from behind. Bite you as you come, screaming my name. Something like that."

"Sounds like a normal night with you then!" she teases, still laughing at me.

I smile down at her. She's perfect like this, laughing, trying to tease me. "Well, what did you have in mind then?"

"What if I want to fuck you this time, claim you? Show you that you have nothing to worry about. I'm all yours."

I let go of her hands and roll onto the bed beside her. "That sounds fucking hot. I'm all yours, gorgeous, show me what you've got."

She has a naughty twinkle in her eyes that I'm enjoying seeing more and more lately as she's becoming more adventurous with me.

She stands up to the side of the bed and removes her jeans and T-shirt, standing in front of me wearing only a pale pink lacy bra and G-string. Peeking through the thin lace fabric, I can see her pink nipples of her perfectly rounded, perky breasts, which are just begging me to touch them. But I remember this is her show, so I behave, and wait for what she has in mind.

She climbs over me, tugging at my T-shirt and pulling it over my head. She then moves her way down my chest, running her fingers over my abs as she arrives at my waistline where my jeans start. Her delicate fingers are making quick work unbuckling my belt and sliding down the zipper of my fly, wiggling my jeans down my legs and tossing them on the timber floor.

She turns back to me with a sexy smile as she hooks her thumbs into the sides of my boxer briefs, biting her lip as she slides them down, watching my cock jump free. I like this side of Elly, she's playful and sexy as fuck.

My eyes are begging her to touch me, ease the tension that's been building since I saw her talking to that doctor. The need to claim her so strong. But instead, she straddles me, as she runs her hands up the sides of my chest until our faces meet. She looks straight into my eyes, teasing me with her wicked smile. She knows what she's doing all right.

She brings her lips to mine, slowly kissing me. Then her touch is gone and she's placing small kisses down my chest, down my happy trail until she makes it to my cock. She takes me in her hands and licks from the bottom to the top, sending a shiver down my spine. She's driving me crazy and I'm finding it hard to just watch her.

She makes her way back up again, swirling her tongue around the tip and tasting the pre-cum that's leaking out. Fuck, if it's not the hottest thing I've ever seen. Then she takes me in her mouth. My hands go instinctively to the back of her head, lacing through her hair, as she takes me deeper in her mouth.

"Fuck, Elly, that feels so good."

I take over the pace, gripping her hair tighter and moving her head back and forth so I'm fucking her mouth. She pulls back. "Thought I was in charge here."

"You are, but you're driving me fucking crazy. I need to fuck you now."

She lifts her head, smiling at me as she removes her bra, dropping one strap at a time seductively like she's giving me a strip show, then unclipping the back as it falls to the bed beneath her. Her hands move to her panties as she locks her fingers in the sides of the lace, slowly sliding them down her toned legs. She knows what she's doing to me and she's in no hurry to give me what I want. My eyes are glued to her, watching her every move.

She moves slowly back between my legs, but this time she spreads her legs, straddling me. My throbbing cock can feel the warmth from her arousal as she grinds on me, leaning her body forward and placing a small kiss on my lips. She moves over to her bedside drawer, pulling out a condom. Her hands are back on my cock, rolling it on. With no restraint left, I run my cock down the glistening slit of her entrance and push myself in as she lowers down onto my cock. She lets out a little gasp as I slide in balls deep.

Her hips start to roll in small circles, getting used to my size, and I pull her down to me so I can kiss her again. As my hands roam down her body, feeling her silky-smooth skin, until they stop on her curvy arse. I dig my fingers into the flesh of her hips, as I pump my throbbing cock into her harder, and we start to move together.

She breaks the kiss and rises so she's sitting all the way upright, giving me a full view of her amazing body. Her tits bounce as she rocks her hips back and forth, picking up the pace, really giving it to me. She's a fucking goddess. Her perfect body riding me, taking what she needs.

I reach up and cup her tits in my hands, rolling her hardened nipples between my fingers as she continues to rock back and forth on my cock.

Holding myself up, I suck on the right nipple while still holding the other, rolling it between my fingers.

She throws her head back, "Yes, yes, yes!" she screams.

And I can feel the muscles of her pussy tighten and contract as she completely loses control. "Fuck, Fraser."

"That's it, gorgeous, come all over my cock."

She lowers her head to mine as I move slowly inside of her, filling her up with my own release.

"Fuck, Elly! If that was you showing me I'm yours, I believe you! That was fucking amazing. You were like a woman possessed."

She smiles, all shy now, her face flushed with little beads of sweat forming on her hairline. She looks sated and relaxed as she slides off me, rolling onto her side and placing her head in the crook of my arm. "See? You have nothing to worry about. I'm all yours," she mutters sleepily.

I NEVER THOUGHT I WOULD BE IN THIS POSITION, BUT the connection I feel with Elly is overwhelming, in a good way. I don't want to leave her side. I've been staying at her place most nights since her dad got sick, and our connection is getting stronger every day. When I'm with her, I forget all the shit from my past, and all I can see is our future.

Today, even though it's a Sunday, I've been at the office finishing off some work for this week. Elly had a busy day of shopping planned with Indie, for their styling business, so I took the opportunity to catch up while I could.

Before I head back to Elly's tonight, I need a change of clothes for tomorrow, and I'd better check in with Blake. It's been two weeks since Jim had the heart attack, and his recovery is going really well. Some days are better than others, but the family are all staying positive and getting on with what needs to be done. He's back at home now and Elly has been taking him to his appointments and looking after him as best she can so Anne can still work. It was hard for her to get time off at such short notice.

Hopefully, I can get in and out of here quickly then be back with Elly in time for dinner. I wouldn't admit this out loud, but I've missed her today. It's amazing how fast things are moving with us now that her family finally knows what's going on. I can see our whole life playing out in front of us, and for once, I'm not scared of what the future holds. I want it all with her. Marriage, kids, the perfect house with the white picket fence, just like the family she grew up in. My chance for a real family.

I pull up at our house and have to park on the curb. I wonder who owns that red sedan parked in the driveway. Maybe Blake has got himself some pussy after all. Good for him.

As I walk in the front door, I can hear Blake talking to a female. He sounds serious but that's standard Blake. He would be like that with a date as well, I imagine. But as I look to see where the voices are coming from, I see him sitting at the dining table, and my eyes widen in fear when I see who he is with. My mum! I can feel the colour draining from my face. I'm not ready for a face-to-face confrontation with her. I thought hanging up on her the other week was clue enough that I didn't want to see her. What the fuck is she doing here?

CHAPTER EIGHTEEN

FRASER

"Why are you in my house?" I know I'm being rude, but what the fuck is she doing here? I'm not giving her money just because she turned up at my house. Is she fucking kidding?

"I'm here to see you, my boy. It's been way too long. Come and give your old mum a hug."

Blake stands up. "I'll give you some space to chat." He walks down the hall to his room, and I'm silently begging him, with my eyes, not to leave me alone with her. I'm not sure what to do. I want to run back out the front door, but I know, now that she's here, I'm going to have to deal with her.

"Come on, son, come sit with me. I'm sorry I haven't been around much. We have lots to talk about and catch up on."

I don't move from where I'm standing in the doorway. I don't want to go anywhere near her. She's not my mum, she's some stranger. Her face is the same, but she's aged a lot! Her hair now grey and her eyes sunken, she looks thin and tired, but I can tell she's the same woman I knew. She's here for one thing and one thing only. This is all an act to manipulate me so she can get what she wants. My bet, that money she was after on the phone call.

"I know you're not here to see me. You couldn't care less about me and catching up on lost time. So, I'll ask again, why are you here?"

She smiles sweetly. "Son, of course I care about you. Come sit with me and tell me what's going on in your life. Your friend tells me you're doing really well with your business."

I have no words. The anger is radiating off me. How dare she sit here and pretend to be my long-lost family that actually cares about each other and wants to be involved in each other's lives. I can feel the adrenaline pumping through my body, she makes me so fucking mad.

"Is your girlfriend's father all right? Your friend said he had a fall and is sick. I've come around a few times this week and you haven't been here. Come, tell me about your girl. It's nice you have found yourself a girlfriend."

"Elly's none of your business. Stop asking me questions, trying to pretend you care, when I know you don't. If you did, you wouldn't have left me when I was 14. What kind of a mother just walks out on her own kid?"

She stands up from the table and walks over to me. She goes to touch my arm, but I pull away. "I can see I'm not going to get anywhere with you today. It's obviously been a long day for you, but I'm your mother and I want to be part of your life now. I'll come back tomorrow when you're not so tired."

"No, don't, I don't want anything to do with you. You destroyed Dad and me when you left, and you never looked back. It was all about you. It's always all about you. You abandoned us. I don't even know what would have happened to us if it wasn't for the Walkers. They took us in and helped Dad get back on his feet. They're my family, not you. A woman that walks away and doesn't look back on her child, her family, can't call herself my mother and expect to be a part of my life in any way."

"I had my reasons, Fraser. Now that you're older I thought I might be able to talk to you so you can understand my side."

"I will never understand your side. It doesn't matter what you have to say. You didn't just leave Dad, you left me, and I didn't hear a thing from you until last month."

She looks angry now and that's the face I remember, my mum drunk with a fight to pick, normally with my dad. He never earned enough money, or didn't do enough around the house, or it was his fault she had to look elsewhere for companionship because he worked too much.

"You know you will never really be a part of that picture-perfect family. They just feel sorry for you. You're like a stray dog. They'll take you in and look after you, but you'll never be one of them. They're not your real family. You come from a family of fuck-ups and alcoholics, and it's surprising you're doing so well. But I'm sure it's only a matter of time before you'll fuck up your own life," she sneers, with a murderous look in her eyes.

"There's the woman I know! I knew you couldn't put on this nice act for too long. Your true colours had to shine through eventually."

"Well, I'm the only real family you will ever have."

"That's not true. I've got Dad. He's the only real family that I will ever have, not you!"

Her face breaks into a sarcastic smile. "Yeah, the man you call Dad. Except he's not your blood!"

With those words, I feel a chill run through my entire body. "What do you mean?" I spit at her.

"It's a long story, Fraser, and you're obviously too tired to talk tonight, so maybe another time."

My heart is pounding so fast I can hear it in my ears. What in the actual fuck is she on about? Is this her feral attempt to get under my skin, spinning some lies?

"Well, you clearly came here to tell me, so go on!"

"Your dad and I had been married for five years and trying for a baby since we got married. It just wasn't happening. I saw a doctor and had some tests done, and I knew it wasn't me causing the problem. Your dad, being the stubborn man he was, refused to get the tests done. He said it would happen when the timing was right.

"But I couldn't wait and hope that it might just happen by some miracle when there was clearly a problem with him. So, I took things into my own hands before I got too old and couldn't conceive at all. I waited until the timing was right. As luck would have it, your dad was away on a business trip for the weekend, so I went to a bar and found a guy I thought looked all right, and nine months later you were born. Your father was stupid enough to believe you were the miracle we had been waiting for. He never worked it out."

"You're lying. Why would you wait until now to tell me? There's no way this is true."

"Haven't you ever wondered why you look nothing like your dad?" she scoffs sarcastically.

What is happening here? The room is spinning and I feel like I can't breathe. The anger is pulsing through my body. I can't believe what I'm hearing.

"So you're saying I'm the result of a drunken, one-night stand with some stranger. You fucking bitch. How could you do that to Dad. He loved you. Even though you were horrible to him and treated him like shit, he still worshipped you, and when you left, he fell apart and prayed you would come back. But truth be told, we were both better off without you and your poison. Get the fuck out of my house."

"You have to understand. I wanted a baby before it got too late in life. Sometimes you do crazy things. It's because I wanted you so badly."

"No, I don't understand. None of this makes any sense. If you love someone you don't do that to them... and if you wanted a baby so badly, how could you walk out on me when I was only 14? Did I turn out to be such a disappointment that you just left me behind? What the fuck is that?"

"It wasn't you that I left, it was your dad. We couldn't stop fighting. I had to leave."

"More lies. You need to leave Dad out of this. I know for a fact you left with another man, I saw you leave. I'm not stupid! You're such a liar. I don't believe anything you say. You need to get the fuck out now!" I open the front door. "Don't ever contact me again."

"Get a paternity test. You'll see I'm not lying."

I slam the door in her face. Her fucking lies. There's no way he's not my dad. I might not look that much like him but we're so similar in other ways. He's my dad. I know it.

I don't even know how to process what she told me. It's too much. I need to message Elly. I can't go around there tonight. I need to think this over and try and process what my mum said.

Fraser: Gorgeous, I'm going to stay at home tonight.
Elly: No worries, baby, hope everything is okay?
Fraser: Yeah, just need a quiet night. Sweet dreams x
Elly: You too xx

Elena

It's only 6am but I'm sitting up in bed doodling in my ideas book for the business I'm starting with Indie. I've been having so much trouble sleeping the last few weeks with everything that's going on, with Dad being sick, and us starting our new business.

With so much extra time on my hands, I've been using it to work out ideas for the business. So, in the last week, we have worked out our budgets for our styling furniture and a price list so we know how much to charge our clients. We still need a name and logo so we can organise our marketing side of things, and nothing seems right yet. Hopefully Indie has some better ideas than me. As the artist, I'm sure she will come up with something amazing. My phone lights up the screen with Fraser's name. It's early for him.

"Morning, gorgeous."

"Morning, baby, I missed you last night."

"Yeah, sorry about that, you're not going to like this then."

"What is it?"

"I've had to book a trip down to see Dad. He's in Victoria at the moment and there's just some stuff I need to talk to him about in person. I'm on my way to the airport now."

"Is he okay, Fraser?"

"Yeah, he's fine. Just some family stuff that needs to be sorted out. Nothing to worry about. Sorry I couldn't see you before I left, it was all really last-minute, and this early flight this morning was the only flight I could get today."

"That's fine, I'll miss you, though. When will you be back?"

"Should be back on Sunday, just see how I go. The reception probably won't be very good where we are staying, so don't be surprised if you can't get hold of me while I'm gone."

"Okay, Fraser. Well, good luck with it all. Let me know when you get in."

"I will, gorgeous. See you later."

"I hope you work it out, bye."

Wow. What was that? It must be something pretty major going on with his dad for him to just take off like that. Not even time to come and say goodbye. I try to think back over the last few days, and everything was completely normal, no red flags pointing to him having to take off. If his dad's health is okay, why the urgency? Doesn't make any sense. Did I do something wrong yesterday? This is all so strange. I try to shake it off, but all of a sudden, I have an uneasy feeling washing over me, a strange sinking feeling; something's not right, I just know it.

Well, I guess I'm going to have a whole lot of time to work this week. We haven't even been together that long, but already I'm not sure what to do without him around. Exactly what I promised myself I wouldn't do again after what happened with Jessie. Rely on a guy to rule my world instead of mapping it out for myself. So much for "Miss Independent". I'm going to spend the week pining over him, I just know I will, and he didn't even care enough to drop in and say goodbye before he left.

CHAPTER NINETEEN

FRASER

I PULL MY BAG OFF THE BAGGAGE CAROUSEL AND WHEEL it through the airport to the front entrance. As the doors slide open, I'm hit with the cold winter air. Victoria is freezing this time of year and the wind hits my face with an icy chill.

I see him before he sees me. There's the man that raised me. His smiling face lights up as soon as he sees me walking out of the airport terminal. I hope he is my dad. How could he not be? We have always had a close relationship. We get each other without having to say a word, and where most teens fight with their parents, I never did with him. We have always been close. I had to come and find out for sure. I didn't sleep at all last night. The words my mum said are eating me up inside, and I have no idea what he knows. It's not the kind of conversation you have over the phone. So a quick trip to Victoria was the only solution.

"Hey, Dad."

"Son." He wraps his arms around me, bringing me in for a hug, his head coming up to my shoulder. I'm a head taller than him and it never bothered me before this moment. We really are nothing alike in the looks department. His hair, although thinning now, is a sandy blond, his complexion is fair. My hair is dark brown, almost black, and thick with a bit of a curl to it, and my skin is olive. We're nothing alike. I always just thought, growing up, that I must have taken after Mum's side in the looks department. But maybe what she said is true.

We make our way to his car parked in the lot. "So, what brings you all this way to see your old dad?"

"Can't a boy just miss his father? It's been too long and talking over the phone's just not the same."

"You can, but somehow I get the feeling this impromptu visit has more to it. Is everything okay with Elena and her dad?"

"Yeah, she's fine. Jim's doing much better than two weeks ago. Still not out of the woods yet but improving every day."

"I'm sure, knowing Jim, he will be back on his feet before we know it. Janice and I will make a trip home next month and we might stay awhile so I can visit him. He was always there for me, and I want to be able to do something for him in his time of need."

"That would be nice, Dad. It would be good to have you around. You can come in and see our new office. I've missed you."

He wraps his arm around my shoulder. "Come on, let's get you back to the caravan park and get you settled for the night before dinner. You're going to love it there. It's set in bushland which also has a jetty looking out over the water. It was a good idea for you to book a cabin in the park we're staying in. There's not much room in the van, and you know what Janice and I are like!" He laughs at me with a wink.

"Dad, too much information! I'm glad I booked the cabin now! I don't need to be scarred for life."

"What can I say, I'm a lucky man."

He opens the boot on his four-wheel drive SUV, and I throw my bag in and I jump in. He smiles across at me. "I'm glad you're here, son." He smiles as he drives out of the airport car park. "How long are you staying for?"

"Just until Sunday. I can't take any more time off work. We are so busy at the moment. I feel bad leaving the boys with the extra work but hopefully our new office manager will be able to pick up some of the slack for them. I'm going to have to do a bit of work while I'm here, but we should manage to have some time to relax as well. Do you have your fishing stuff with you?"

"Sure do. We will definitely be going fishing. Janice isn't so keen, so I've been going alone. It'll be great to have you with me."

On the drive back to the caravan park we're both quiet, wrapped up in our own thoughts. I have no idea how to bring up what Mum said. I don't want to hurt him, but if I'm not his son, I need to know, and he has the right to know, after all this time, what she did to him. I think I'll leave it till tomorrow so I can have one last night pretending the only good part of my family was actually real.

THEY SAY TIME FLIES WHEN YOU'RE HAVING FUN, AND the last 24 hours with my dad and Janice have gone really fast. It's like the old days with Dad. Every summer he would take a week off work and we would go camping near the beach. We'd spend days swimming and catching fresh fish for dinner. I hadn't even realised how much I'd missed those times we had together. Once I finished school and went off to uni, life got so busy that we just stopped going. This trip is long overdue.

It's been nice to get to know Janice. I haven't spent much time with her before, but I can see why Dad likes her. She's warm and caring and she adores him, which is exactly what he deserves. Janice said she never had kids because she didn't find the right person in time. It's a shame they met later in life. You can see they would have made wonderful parents together and what I'd have given to have a mother like her. It's so nice to see him finally happy which makes what I have to do tonight even harder.

I feel bad for the way I left, not saying goodbye to Elly properly, but I just couldn't face her yesterday. I messaged her when I got in, so she knew I was safe. I know I should call her today but I'm having trouble bringing myself to. I don't know what to say to her. She wouldn't understand this situation. It's so far from the family she grew up with, and I feel so inferior to her. She just wouldn't understand what I'm going through. I mean, how could she? My head has been a total mess since Mum said those words, and everything I thought I wanted, I'm not so sure of anymore.

Janice has gone into town to get some groceries for dinner while Dad and I sit at the end of the dock fishing, just like we used to do when I was a kid. So now's the perfect time to bring it up, while it's just the two of us. But what do I say?

"Dad... have you heard from Mum at all lately?"

He raises a brow. "Lately? That's a bit left-field, son. I haven't heard anything since she walked out on us all those years ago. Why do you ask?"

"She rang a couple of months ago asking for money."

I can see his whole face change. I never bring Mum up.

I know how much it upsets him and he looks really mad now.

"She rang you asking for money!"

"Yeah, she did. It was really strange. She said things weren't going so well. She had been dumped or something and heard I've started a business and am doing all right, so could I give her $10,000, to help get her back on her feet."

"She's got to be fucking kidding. Don't give her a cent, son!"

"I didn't, I hung up on her, but last Sunday she turned up at my house."

He runs his hands through his hair. "She what? What was she expecting? She just turns up after all this time and you would feel sorry for her and give her money?"

"I have no idea what she was expecting. She tried to play happy family, then when I wouldn't play along, she got mad and told me a whole heap of shit which I hope to god isn't true."

"Like what?" He looks over to me, waiting for my answer.

"She said you're not my real father. But that couldn't be true, could it?"

His head drops and he looks down at the water below. "It might be?" His eyes rise to meet mine again.

"What do you mean? Did you know this all along?"

"No, I didn't, and I didn't know for sure."

I'm up now pacing. He knew. What the fuck! None of this is making sense. If he knew, why would he have raised me if he didn't have to?

"I can't believe this! How could it be true? I wanted you to tell me there's no way and it's all lies."

"Sit down, son, stop pacing. I'll tell you what I know."

I sit back down beside him, but I'm so agitated it's hard

to sit still, my heart is pounding and fists clenched. I feel like I'm about to lose control. This shit isn't happening.

"About six months after your mother left us, I finally decided to clean out the stuff she left behind. She wasn't coming back, and I needed it gone so I could move on.

"As I was sorting through her things, I found an old diary of hers. It was in a little blue box with some of your baby things. At the time I thought it was strange, as there were no other diaries in her things, and I couldn't remember her ever writing in one, so I started to read it. It was a diary of her pregnancy with you, starting at conception. The diary explained how she felt about the fact that I couldn't give her the baby she so desperately wanted. So, she took it into her own hands before she was too old to have one."

This is too much. I feel like my head is spinning. How is this true? Who am I even? The son of a fucking alcoholic, lying cheating bitch, and some stranger. This is fucking unbelievable.

I look over to him and I can see the tears in his eyes and the pain on his face. This is bringing it all back again for both of us.

"But, if it's true, and you're not my biological dad, why did you keep me when Mum left? I wasn't your problem. You didn't have to take care of me, so why would you?"

The tears roll down his face now and shift my anger towards my mum into sadness for him. "You were my son regardless of whether I was your biological father. I raised you and loved you from the moment you were born. I don't care if I'm your biological father or not, I'm still your dad." He reaches out for my hand. "I will always be your dad, this doesn't change that." He pulls me in for a hug, and I can't help it. Something has snapped inside of me; tears I have been holding in since she left start to trickle down my face.

We sit for an extended period looking out to sea. This is all too much.

"Why didn't you tell me at the time, when you found it?"

"I didn't know anything for sure, and you were a 14-year-old boy who had just lost his mother. How would you have coped with that as well? When I read that diary, it crushed me worse than when she left. You're everything to me, son. I made the decision then that, no matter what I had read in that diary, it didn't change how I felt about you and what you are to me. You will always be my boy."

"Don't you need to know for sure, Dad, like having a paternity test?"

He shakes his head. "If you need to, son, but it changes nothing for me."

"I think I need to go for a walk and clear my head."

"Okay, son. I'll be waiting here for you when you get back."

As I walk, all I can think about is how could she do this to him, to us! I'm half of a man I don't even know and have no chance of finding, and somewhere out there is a man that has no idea I'm his child. I can't help but wonder what he's like. Would I look like him?

Not knowing where I came from makes me feel sick to my stomach, and as much as I know I shouldn't, I need something to take the pain away from this heavy feeling in my chest. I can handle it this time, I just need a couple of drinks to take the edge off.

CHAPTER TWENTY

FRASER

DAD DIDN'T BRING UP THE WHOLE PATERNITY THING again for the rest of the week. We just spent quality time together as we would have on any normal holiday. But it's not normal. My family is fucked up! I always knew we weren't a picture-perfect family, but it's so much worse than I ever thought. It's not Dad's fault, so I would never take it out on him. What he did for me, bringing me up alone when he knew I wasn't his blood, took so much strength and courage. He's a better man than me. I don't know if I would be able to do the same thing if I were in his shoes.

I flew home today and now I'm sitting in the pub, just around the corner from Elly's apartment, and having a drink to calm my nerves before I go to see her. I know I probably shouldn't be drinking, but I just need something to take the edge off, something to take away the pain that's been lodged in my chest since I saw my mother a week ago.

The scotch goes down so well. I didn't even realise how much I've missed it until this past week. But it's the only way I can relax and calm all the thoughts in my head. I have no idea how I'm supposed to move past this and get on with my life. I feel broken and completely lost. I have no idea who my biological dad is and no way of finding out, even if I wanted to. The thought is messing with my head. I'm not even me anymore. I don't know who I am. I'm fucking messed up. How do I move on with my life when I have no fucking idea who I am? I wish I could go back to before she said it, or un-hear what she said, and just go back to not knowing.

Two drinks later, feeling a little more in control, I make my way out of the pub up to Elly's apartment. Hopefully she's home, I need to see her.

Elena

Drew is leaving early tomorrow. He's got a big surf comp next week in Brazil, so Mum's throwing a special Sunday-night dinner. Indie and Blake are joining us as well. I don't even care if Fraser gets all jealous about it. I haven't heard from him since he landed at the airport in Victoria on Monday to go and visit his dad.

I've messaged and called a few times but haven't gotten anything back. He said before he left that reception might be a problem, so hopefully that's all it is. He does have me a little worried, though. Our conversation on Monday morning before he left was so strange and I have had a feeling of unease ever since. If he really wanted to talk to me, he would have found a way, bad reception or not. In this day and age, there is always a way to contact someone if you want to.

Dad's in bed resting. I want to see him before everyone else gets here. "Hey, Dad. How are you feeling today?"

"Elly, what a nice surprise." He pats the bed for me to

come and sit with him. "I'm feeling good today, just a bit tired. I went on a bit of a walk this morning and it's taken it out of me. How's your week been?"

I sit next to him and kiss him on the forehead. "I don't know, kinda odd," I say, raising my eyebrows.

"Why's that, honey? What's going on?"

"Fraser has been away with some family thing. I haven't talked to him all week. It's just a bit unusual for him, we normally talk every day. Maybe it's a good thing. Things were moving kind of fast with us. I don't know, maybe he's changed his mind."

"His family is pretty complicated, honey. Maybe he just needed a bit of space to deal with some stuff. I'm sure, once he gets back, everything will be fine. We can all see how much he adores you."

"I hope you're right, Dad," I smile at him sadly, squeezing his hand.

We can hear chatter coming from the lounge room. "Sounds like the others have arrived, honey. You better get out there and enjoy the special dinner your mum's organised."

"Can't I just hide out in here with you all night? I don't feel like socialising."

"No. Your mother would kill you. She's gone to a lot of trouble for this dinner," he laughs. "Go on, go have a good night with your brother before he leaves us again. I'll come out a bit later."

I walk into the living room and everyone's already sitting out the back on the deck with drinks in hand. I get a fresh drink from the fridge and make my way out to them, pulling up a seat next to Drew.

"Wish you didn't have to leave so soon, baby brother."

"Yeah, me either, this time. I don't want to leave while

Dad's still not one hundred percent, but if I don't, I'll lose my place on the tour. Mum assures me she'll let me know if I need to come home for anything. But, if she doesn't, you will, won't you? You know what she's like. She'll probably let me stay away too long. I want to know if anything happens." He looks so worried, it must be hard having to leave at the moment.

"Of course, I'll keep you up to date daily. He's going to be fine, though. Look at him today, he's looking so much better already. You won't need to come home, go and be the superstar we all know you are."

He gives me a lopsided smile. "Superstar, hey. I knew you were my biggest fan!"

"Ha ha, not likely, but I'm going to miss you, little brother."

"You'll be fine. You've got Fraser now. You don't need me anymore."

"I'll always need you! And I'm not so sure how well I've got Fraser. I haven't even heard from him at all this week, since he went to see his dad in Victoria."

"Really? You should talk to Blake, he seems to know what's going on with him. But you know how Fraser can be. I'm sure there's nothing to worry about."

"Hey, Blakie, come talk to me," I pat the seat next to me. He makes his way over and sits down. "So, tell me, have you heard from Fraser this week?"

"Only a couple of times. I think his reception is pretty bad."

"But you have heard from him?"

He looks surprised. "Hasn't he called you?"

"Nope, or answered any of my messages. Nothing," I sigh, with a shrug.

"I shouldn't be telling you this, Elly, and I don't want

you to worry, but he's just going through some family stuff. He probably just needs a little space to process."

"Stuff he can talk to you about but not me?"

"Elly, I don't want to get in the middle of you two. He'll talk to you when he's ready. I'm sure he'll ring first thing when he gets back."

"I hope you're right. Something feels really off." He offers me a small smile. He'd better be right. I'm not feeling good about this situation at all.

Mum fusses over us all at dinner, and it's nice as always, although on the healthier side, because she's on a health kick with Dad, since he had the heart attack. So it's all salads with grilled chicken, salmon steaks and lentils. I'm not complaining, it's still delicious.

Dad made an appearance to eat a little but was too tired to stay for long, so he's back in bed now. He's such a big presence in our family normally. It's strange when he's not here. Mum's overcompensating majorly and has made a ridiculous amount of food. I think Indie and I are going to have enough leftovers for the week. Mum's lined the Tupperware containers up on the kitchen bench and we have been instructed to take it with us.

I've said my goodbyes to Drew. We won't see him again until Christmas now unless Dad gets worse and he needs to come home. I grab my leftovers and head for the car. Indie's going to stay out for a bit, she has a date or something.

No sooner have I walked in the front door and dumped my bag and keys, than there's a knock at the door. I open the door and I see Fraser's handsome face staring back at me, his hair all messy and his eyes ablaze with desire.

"Fraser," I jump into his arms, wrapping my legs around his waist. "I've missed you," I say into his lips as I kiss him.

He tastes like scotch and his lips feel so good on mine. All the worry I had earlier disappearing.

"I've missed you too, gorgeous." He kisses me with desperation, running his fingers through my hair.

I pull back from him and look into his grey eyes. He looks different somehow. There are dark circles under his eyes, he looks like he hasn't slept all week. His stubble is longer than normal and starting to form a thick dark beard. "Why didn't you call me? Is everything okay? I was getting worried."

"Let's talk later, I've missed you." With my legs still hooked around his waist, he wraps his arms around me, hugging me into his chest, and carries me to my room.

He places me on my bed and climbs over me, removing my top over my head. His lips are back on mine, slowly kissing me now like he's savouring every little bit.

I should close my eyes, but they're fixed on his and his with mine. This is so intimate. He's so intense, but his grey eyes are so pale and look sad. He slowly removes my jeans, dropping them to the floor, then kisses back up my body, spreading my legs. He lets out a growl as he makes it between my legs, pulling my panties to the side, licking me, tasting me, while all the time his eyes are on mine.

He strips off his clothes while I remove my panties and bra. We're lying in my bed completely naked, just kissing. Our bodies are intertwined with each other, not able to get enough, but not wanting to break apart either.

This is heaven. It's so nice to have him back. I was starting to worry he might be done with me. Our lips remain locked as our tongues dance and our kiss becomes more aggressive, more hurried and desperate. I need him in me, to feel the connection we have when our bodies are one. His hand makes its way down my tummy to my hip, leaving a trail of goosebumps in its path. I'm so turned on I can barely stand it. All the time we've had apart has me needy and desperate for him to fill me up.

He lines himself up with my entrance and slowly pushes inside me. There's no warm-up tonight. I can feel his desperation in everything he does. He's missed me too. My back arches off the bed, needing him to move, but he hesitates and pulls back. His eyes stare into mine like he's looking into my soul, questioning me, but I don't know what the answer is. All I know is, I love this man with everything I have, and I never want to be away from him again.

His eyes close as he slowly starts moving inside me. It's slow and intimate, so different to every other time I've been with him. This is something out of this world, a connection like no other. My body shudders as we reach our climax together, our foreheads pressed against one another. That was so intimate, I have tears welling in my eyes, and I can't even explain why it was just so much more. I pull back to look at him; his eyes are sad, he looks lost, like a lost little boy. I remember when I've seen those sad eyes before; this was like our first time. My heart starts to race in panic. This was different for a reason, something is wrong.

"What's wrong, Fraser? Why are you looking at me like you just lost your puppy?" He rolls off me and I feel the sudden urge to cover myself up, so I sit up and pull the sheets up over my chest.

"I'm sorry, Elly, I can't be who you want me to be. I'm not the right man for you."

"What are you talking about?"

He's sitting on the side of the bed looking at the floor. He can't even look at me now. "Play happy-ever-after, pretend like this will all work out perfectly, that's not how things work out for me."

"What are you talking about? Did something happen when you visited your dad?"

He gets up and starts to dress, and I sit in silence, trying to wrap my head around the words he's saying. What the fuck is going on? One minute he can't get enough of me, now he's telling me he can't do this.

He turns to look at me, his face now hardened and serious. "I'm sorry, but I'm not the man for you. You need someone who can treat you the way you deserve to be treated. Someone you can create a life with, and that's not me."

I sit up on the bed silently pleading with him with my eyes. "Where is all this coming from? Don't you think I should be the judge of that?"

"No, I'm making this call. I want you to be happy, have a happy life. I can't hold you back from that anymore because I'm jealous. I'm letting you go."

"You make me happy, Fraser. What are you talking about?"

"Yeah, but I won't, that's the thing. I'm not the man you want, I can't be him."

Now I'm fuming fucking mad. He came here knowing he was going to end it, and he still fucked me. What a fucking arsehole. I don't even know who this man is.

"Seems like your mind is made up then. You're done with me just like that. I had heard the rumours, you get what you want then dump 'em when you're bored. I should've known it was too good to be true and that I wouldn't be any different."

"Yeah, you're right. I'm not the kind to settle down, that's what I'm trying to say."

"Wow! What the fuck was this then! One more fuck for the road? You came here tonight to break up with me and you thought you'd get in one last screw before you left me forever? I don't know what I ever saw in you. I should've known better."

"Elly, it's not like that with you. I'm sorry, I'm a selfish arsehole, I know. I just had to have you one last time, you have to understand, I just needed to say goodbye to you."

"Well, you got everything you came for, so goodbye, Fraser, nice fucking knowing you. You can get the fuck out of my life now." I lie back down, turning my back to him. He may have just ripped my heart out but he's not going to see my tears.

He lets out a sigh and I hear him walk out of the room. I hear the front door open and shut. He's really gone. That's it, the man I have loved since I was 16, and now he is gone forever. It's over.

I pull my pillow into my chest as the tears I've been holding in break free. My chest hurts so much I feel like I could die from the pain. I never thought someone I loved so much could hurt me like this, especially not him. I sob into my pillow until I have nothing left.

My eyes are dry, and I stare at the ceiling in the dark. I should go and take a shower, wash the pain away like I normally do, but I can't.

His smell still lingers on me and in my sheets. I can't let that go, not yet. Even if he is a cold-hearted bastard who clearly never cared about me in the way I did him, I'll just hang on to it for tonight. I hug my pillow into my chest tighter, and close my eyes, letting sleep take me away from the pain.

CHAPTER TWENTY-ONE

ELENA

It's been three weeks since Fraser walked out on me, and I haven't seen or heard from him since. Any work The Green Door boys need me to do comes through either Blake or their new office manager. We always said, right from the start, it won't affect our working relationship, and it won't as long as we don't have to be in the same room together. If I never have to see him again, it will be too soon.

I still have no idea what he was talking about that night. It's got something to do with his family but that's all I know. Guess it's not my problem now.

Except I can't stop thinking about him. Why is he so far under my skin that I'm still worried about him? Even after the way he treated me. That night he was acting so strange. I've never seen him like that before. At first, I was hurt, thinking I was the stupid one for thinking I could change him somehow and that he would settle down with me. I felt stupid for believing we were falling in love.

Now that I've had time to process, though, I know there's got to be more to all of this. Blake just keeps telling me to be patient and give Fraser time to deal with it. But what's he dealing with and why can't we just talk about it? I hate all the secrets and it sucks because I feel like I'm losing Blake too. They're just so close and he would never say a bad word about Fraser. No matter what he does, Blake always has an excuse to cover for him. I don't know what it is between the two of them. There's got to be more to their past than either of them let on.

I look up from my spot on the cash register to see Tristan and Luca walk into the café. Today has been nonstop busy so I'm taking orders and Indie's just churning out coffees as fast as she can.

"Hey, guys, to what do we owe the pleasure? You don't normally come in on a Saturday. Just after the usual?" I ask.

"Yeah, we were just in the area and thought we would drop in and see our favourite baristas. What are you ladies doing when you finish your shift today?" asks Tristan.

"Don't know about Elly, but I'm free," Indie calls out over my shoulder from her spot on the coffee machine.

"Sorry, guys, would have loved to, maybe another time. I've got a baby shower for my sister-in-law straight after this."

"Sounds exciting!" Tristan teases.

"Yeah, I know! Just what I feel like doing with my Saturday, but Mum would kill me if I didn't turn up, sorry."

"Well, what about I give you my number and you and Indie work out when you're free, and the four of us can do something more fun then." He writes their numbers down on a napkin and Indie puts it in her apron.

I hand them their drinks. "See you guys on Monday."

"See you then, ladies," Luca says with a wink as they walk out of the café.

"You're no fun, Elly," Indie grumbles, throwing a marshmallow at me.

"Hey!" I turn and give her a filthy look. "What! I do have a shower this afternoon."

"Yeah, I know, but you're never going to call them anyway, are you?"

"You don't know that." I pout.

"Fraser's gone, Elly. I know you're sad it's over, but he was the one that ended it. I'm sure he's out there having his own fun. We need a night out and those boys are fun. You know it would be a good night, we get on with them both so well. Do it for me, I need this," she begs.

I roll my eyes at her dramatics. "You're probably right, but I'm just not ready, I'm sorry, Indie."

Indie smiles at me sympathetically and goes back to cleaning the coffee machine. I think the crazy rush is finally over, thankfully. I just want to get out of here today. "I'm going to wipe the tables down."

"No worries, chick."

On top of Fraser leaving me out of the blue, I'm so stressed. I'm having trouble sleeping and stomaching food, neither of which has ever been a problem for me in the past. I usually love to eat. I've lost so much weight my clothes are all falling off me and I'm considering a shopping trip this week so I can get something that will fit.

It just feels like everything has got on top of me all at once with Dad being sick. It's hard to see the man who has always been my family's strength recovering from his surgery. Instead of being my big, strong dad, he still looks so thin and frail.

Mum's still in total overkill mode. She's like an Energizer bunny running from work to doctors' appointments with Dad, then cooking meals like a crazy woman. She has been delivering food to us for some reason. I think it's the only way she knows how to cope.

She literally hasn't stopped since Dad collapsed that day. I'm getting worried that it's all going to hit her and she's going to crash.

I haven't told any of them about me and Fraser. I'm sure they're wondering why he's not around, but for now, they don't need to know what happened. It's just something else for Mum to worry about and she doesn't need that. She's got enough on her plate.

Indie has been great, having not long ago been through a break-up with someone she was in love with for a long time. She's been trying to distract me as best she can and keep me laughing. I'm not sure what I would do without her. I'm so glad I decided to move in with her because she's the best friend a girl could ask for.

Blake is also in contact every couple of days, checking in on me and on Dad's progress. I'm not sure if Fraser is putting him up to it, probably not, but I just can't believe he could stop caring completely. It just doesn't make sense. Even if he's done with me, this family was a massive part of his life.

I'm done with the tables and it's 1pm, so my shift is over.

"I'm out of here, Indie, see you at home later," I call as I throw my apron on the hook and grab my bag.

"Yeah, I'll be there, sitting around the house bored, not on some fun date with a sexy guy, like I should be."

"Sorry, maybe soon, Indie." She rolls her eyes at me.

I make my way down the road to Mum and Dad's house. Mum's hosting Fiona's baby shower. It's hard to believe she's halfway already, 20 weeks along. It's probably a bit early to have the shower now, but Mum insisted we all needed something to cheer us up. Apparently, an afternoon of tiny finger food and looking at baby stuff is supposed to make all our problems go away.

Fi is looking fantastic in her active wear. She's got that pregnancy glow you hear about, with just a little baby bump. If you didn't know she was pregnant, you would just think she had a big lunch. I wouldn't expect anything less from her. She's a total health nut. She works out five days a week and eats the healthiest diet of anyone I know. She'll be one of those types to pop out the baby and be at the gym the following Monday, I'm sure.

The shower is a collection of her work friends, besties from school, her sister and mum, my mum, and me. Her sister is nothing like her. She's a total princess dressed in some fancy sundress, and I can see she drives Fi nuts. It's really funny to watch them interact. I wonder how they could have grown up in the same house and turned out so completely different.

We get a moment, after all the present unwrapping is done, and Fi gives me the 'please save me' look and I'm on to it.

"Fi, can I get some help out the front with something?"

"Thank you for saving me, Elly. I don't know whose idea it was for this shower, but it's not my thing at all. Do you think we could just escape for the rest of the afternoon and no one would notice?"

I let out a little laugh at how dramatic she's being. "That's pretty obvious, thanks for doing this for Mum, though. I think she needed it to take her mind off everything."

"That's okay, I think we all did," she says, rubbing her belly. "It helps to make it all feel more real for me too."

"I bet. I have no idea how you process bringing a child into the world. You're a braver woman than me. Just the idea of it scares the shit out of me!"

"Well, I'll let you in on a little secret... it scares me too, but don't tell Theo."

"I would never, us girls have to stick together."

"Speaking of that, how are you holding up? You don't look yourself lately, Elly."

"I'm just tired. There's so much going on."

"Nothing to do with you and Fraser breaking up?" She raises a knowing brow at me.

"How did you know?"

"It's my job to notice what's going on around me, that's why I'll make a good detective one day."

"Now you sound like Theo, and yes, you will."

"Oh, I do, don't I?" she laughs. "I spend a lot of time with him. Don't you tell him I said that! But really, how are you?"

"I don't know. Confused. I don't even know what happened."

"I'm sure you two will work it out. There are just some people who are meant to be together, and you two are meant to be, I just know it," she smiles.

I shrug. "I don't know about that anymore. I don't think I could ever even talk to him again after the way he ended it. And besides, he's probably on to the next girl by now, knowing him."

"You know you weren't just another girl, Elly. Something must have happened for him to end it."

I shrug. I'm over talking about him, it's just depressing. I need to change the subject.

"Has Theo stopped micromanaging you?" I ask.

"No, he's been worse than ever. He's been in the boss's ear too. I've only got three more weeks as his partner, then I've been given light duties in the office."

"I bet that went down well when you found out!"

"Right! He's still in the doghouse. I know his heart is in the right place, but I'm a big girl and I can look after myself. I know what I can handle."

"I'm sure you do. You're scary as fuck. I wouldn't mess with you!" I nudge her arm. She just laughs at me.

"Guess I better go back in, plaster a fake smile on my face, and pretend like I'm having fun."

"You better, it's all for you. I might sneak out, though, before Mum starts on me. I'll see you tomorrow night at dinner." She hugs me and wanders back inside.

Fraser

It's Saturday night, and after a massive home game I'm out with the rugby lads. Blake refused to come, had something better to do in Sydney or something. He said he's not watching me self-destruct everything I've worked so hard for. Ash is with his fiancée so he's no good to me.

So I'm on my own. Some mate he is. Blake's being kind of a dick lately. But I don't care, that's his loss tonight. I'm out to have some fun with the boys, and after a couple of drinks, I'm starting to feel at peace with the world again. With a drink in hand, all my fucked-up thoughts are a thing of the past.

Shea has just walked into the bar and spots me, her face lighting up as she offers a little wave. I'm sitting at the bar, and her eyes don't lose contact with mine as she talks to her friend. I know what's coming next; she's not the kind of woman that gives up easily, which is why she's such a good real estate agent.

She walks over to me swaying her hips as she goes. The term cougar would suit her perfectly. She's in a tight black dress which is cut low in the front, showing off her fake tits, and wearing massive heels, showing off her long legs. She's really not my type. She's a little too manufactured. But the only girl who is my type, I've completely fucked up with. So now this is the life I'm destined to live. No one will compare to Elly. But that's okay, I don't plan on settling down with anyone, so it doesn't matter. A quick fuck is all I'm up for, someone to take my mind off my fucked-up life.

"Well, look who it is, out on his own. Did the girlfriend let you out for the night, Fraser?" she teases, running her hand across my shoulder.

"No girlfriend!"

"What happened, Fraser? You realise she was too stuck up and you needed someone a little more fun like me?" she says, biting her lip.

"Maybe... why don't you join me, Shea, and we'll see how much fun you can be."

"Sounds good to me, baby, I'm glad you've finally come around. What you drinking? I'll top you up."

"Scotch."

We spend the next three hours talking and laughing with each other. Every time she touches me, I feel guilty. I don't know why, it's not like I'm still with Elly. I broke it off, so I shouldn't feel so guilty for hanging out with Shea. But breaking up with Elly doesn't change the way I feel about her. Nothing will ever change that, no matter how much I drink.

But I know it's better this way, for her anyway. The drunker I get, the better this idea looks. Most of the other boys have made their way home so I guess it's time I do too. Maybe one last drink...

Shea's all over me now. She's been trying all night, but

now she's ramped up the sluttiness. "Come on, baby, let's go back to your place, keep this night going."

Even in my drunken state, I know this is a bad idea, but I no longer care. I can't make things any worse. I have already fucked up my chances with Elly beyond repair. So why not just go back to the single life, have fun, don't worry about the consequences.

"Fuck it, why not?" I wrap my arm around Shea's shoulders, and we walk out of the pub and up the street, towards my place. I'm a little drunker than I originally thought. I may need her to hold me up as we walk.

Opening the front door, I can't see a fucking thing, the lights are all off. I fumble around trying to find the light switch and manage to knock over a lamp in the process. It crashes to the ground. "Oops." I can't help but laugh. I'm not sure who's more drunk, Shea or me, but everything she's doing is fucking hilarious and I can't stop laughing.

I can hear Blake coming down the hall. He finds the light switch and flicks it on. "Fraser, what the fuck are you doing? It's 1am." Blake's "Mr Serious", as normal. Maybe he's my dad cause he sure acts like it. I laugh at the thought. Fuck, I'm really drunk, laughing at my own jokes.

"Lighten up, man, come join us and have a little fun like last time we got drunk together. I'm sure Shea's up for it." I look at Shea, giving her a wink.

"I'm up for anything, baby, you know that. Come on, Blake, come have some fun."

"Have you lost your mind? Are you trying to completely fuck up your chances with Elly? Because this will do it. If she finds out about this, you're done for good, man."

"He's not worried about her. He's come to his senses and wants a real woman, not that whining little bitch."

"It's done with her anyway, man. I fucked that one up

already, so what's it matter?" Blake looks so pissed. It's not his life so why does he care so much? "Anyway, why do you care so much about Elly? You fucking in love with her or something? I see you, man, messaging her to check on her."

"You need to watch yourself, Fraser. I'm the one friend standing by you at the moment, and with comments like that, I might just give up caring altogether like you clearly have."

Blake turns to Shea. "Shea, you need to back off, Fraser's going through some stuff and you are not what he needs."

"What do you know about what I need?" I slur. "No one knows what I need but me." Words are starting to not even make sense to me. I think I need to sleep this off. I'm way too drunk to keep on talking.

Shea scoffs. "He's a big boy, Blake. You need to back off, let him have his fun."

"Nah, I can't. I'm doing this for Elly, man. I know you're hurting, but you need to get the fuck over yourself and start thinking about the rest of us again. She doesn't deserve this. It's time for you to go, Shea." Blake shows her the door, making sure she leaves. "Now, Shea!"

"Wow," I snarl, "I've never hit you, Blake, but you're fucking pissing me off tonight."

"Fuck this," Shea screams. "You're not worth it, Fraser. See you later," and she takes off out of the house.

Blake's, staring right through me. He's so close he's all blurry. I don't think I've ever seen him this angry before. "You're pushing me, Fraser. Someone's got to look out for you before you fuck up your whole life."

That's it. Who the fuck does he think he is, telling me what to do. "Fuck up my whole life! It's already done, Mum made sure of that!" I spit at him. I'm so angry now. Who does he think he is, "Mr Fucking Perfect"?

"You need to sleep this off, Fraser, before someone gets hurt." He's up in my face and I see red. As I swing to punch him, he gets me first. The last thing I remember is my cheek fucking stinging as his fist connects with it, and I go down like a sack of potatoes, hitting the hard timber floor below.

CHAPTER TWENTY-TWO

FRASER

"Get up, Fraser."

I squint trying to see where the noise is coming from. Blake's standing over me. Fuck, he looks mad.

"Why are you in my room? Leave me alone, I need to sleep." I cover my eyes to hide the light. It makes the thumping sound in my head worse.

"You're on the living room floor, where you passed out last night."

"What?" That would explain why my back is killing me. I sit upright and regret it immediately when my head starts to spin, the living room a blur. "What the fuck happened last night? Why is my head so fucking sore?"

"We got into a fight, after you brought Shea back here."

I run my hands down my face. "Shea?" My head is really spinning now. "Why did I do that?"

"Don't know. You're trying to self-destruct is my guess, but right now you need to get up. Your dad's going to be here in an hour, and I don't want him to see you like this. It's not a pretty sight."

"Why is he coming? Did you call him?"

His expression is stern; he's really pissed with me. "Go have a shower and get your shit together, Fraser."

What the fuck is going on? I don't even know if I can stand up right now. My head is thumping so hard. I touch my face—ouch—now I can feel the lump on my cheek where Blake must have hit me. How much did I drink?

I drag my sore tired body off to the shower and wait till the room fills with steam before I get in. This shower is going to need to be hot, steaming hot. The hot water hits my back and brings some life back to me. My head's still thumping like a bitch. I'm going to need a painkiller to get through this. Why is my dad on his way?

I try to remember the events of the last 24 hours. Rugby, then drinks with the boys. Oh yeah, then Shea was at the pub. Shit, did we kiss? I can't remember. I don't think we did, but why would I bring her back here? Blake's right, I'm sabotaging my own life, and I don't even know how to stop it. I'm not even sure if I want to know what happened. What's the point?

I pull myself together and finish my shower. Why is my dad coming today? Was I supposed to know that already? I don't remember him saying anything last time we talked.

I dress in a T-shirt and track pants and head out to the kitchen to hunt down some painkillers and some water.

Less than an hour later, I'm sitting in my living room with Dad, Janice, Blake, and a psychologist. I think her name was Cherie.

They're all talking about me like I'm not here. Truth be told, I'm not. I'm in a world of pain and just want to reach for another drink to numb it. It's been working so well the past three weeks. This is like some fucking intervention or something.

"Why are you all talking about me like I'm not here? This is my life, isn't it? Don't I get a say in what's going on?"

My dad's warm eyes meet mine, and I can see how concerned he is. I don't want to scare him. "Son, we're all really worried about you. I know you've found out some pretty heavy stuff lately, and we just want to give you some other options to help you through. Maybe the way you've been coping isn't ideal."

"Why don't you and I just have a chat, Fraser?" says whatever her name is. "Maybe everyone else can go get some lunch or something." I just nod. I've got nothing else left in me. What am I supposed to say to her?

She's very formal for a Sunday. She's in an emerald green blouse and fitted skirt with white framed glasses resting on the end of her nose.

"Why don't we start with what happened when your mum came to visit four weeks ago? It sounds like this all started then." She watches me, pushing her glasses a little further up her nose.

"I don't really want to talk about my mum. She's a manipulative bitch."

"Fraser, I know this is going to be uncomfortable for you, and you're not in the best frame of mind right now, but those three people care about you, and I think you owe it to them to give this a go."

I lower my head to look at the floor. I can't look at her while I say this, it's still too hard to say out loud. "She said the man I thought was my father my whole life, isn't. She slept with someone else while Dad was on a work trip."

The sweat is pouring off my face. I can't do this today. What was Blake thinking?

She pulls out a notepad and paper and starts to jot down something. "How did that make you feel?"

My hands are clenched into fists again at the thought, and I crack my knuckles to relieve the tension. It's not working. Just hearing those words again makes me fuming mad. "What do you think? Fucking angry! How would you feel? You go your whole life thinking someone is your dad and it turns out your life has been a lie."

"I'd say anger is fair. How have the last few weeks been since you found out?"

Is she for real? A fucking walk in the park. What is she expecting me to say? "Awful, but you already know that, or they wouldn't have called you."

"I want to hear in your own words how the last few weeks have been for you."

"A total blur. I let Elly go because I knew I couldn't give her the life she deserves. I knew I was slipping into a dark place again. I didn't want her to see this, to have to deal with me like this. I can barely remember what day of the week it is. I have no idea what I'm doing. I just want to drink, it numbs the pain."

"Why is that?"

"Because I'm too fucked up, my mum made sure of that. She waits till my life is back on track, then she comes back to fuck it all up again."

"You have a lot of anger directed towards your mum."

"She deserves it. She left me and dad when I was 14, to go off with some boyfriend of hers. She's selfish. Everything needs to revolve around her, and I hate that she's the only living relative I have."

"Are you worried you will be like her?" Her questioning eyes burn right through me, making me feel ten years old in the principal's office.

"I am like her!" I shout, louder than I intended to. "How could I turn out any other way? She's a lying, alcoholic slut, and look at me. As soon as things get hard, I'm straight back to the alcohol again, just like last time Elly left. That's why I knew I had to let Elly go, before I hurt her like how my mum hurt us, me and Dad."

"Is this the girlfriend you talked about earlier?"

"Yes, she was my friend when we were kids, but she left me, just like my mum."

"So you're worried she might leave you again, so this time you got in first so she couldn't?"

"No, I just knew... I knew I was losing control again. I didn't want her to be around to see what I'm really like."

I bury my head in my hands. My head is throbbing. This is too much. I can feel beads of sweat dripping down my forehead. This room is so hot. She keeps looking at me with that same understanding smile. How is she reading me so well?

"And yes, why wouldn't she leave me again if she knew how fucked up I am? I know I couldn't be what she needs. How could I? I feel like I'm only half a man. I have no idea where I come from. How can I love her and give her all of me when I'm so fucked up? She deserves so much better than me."

"It sounds like you didn't allow her to decide for herself. Did you tell her about your dad?"

"No, she's got enough going on with her own family. Her dad's been sick, and she's worried about him. She doesn't need to have me to worry about as well."

"Sounds like she probably needs you more than ever then." Her judging gaze pierces me, and I know she's right. That's why I feel so guilty, but I'm a mess. I can't be who she needs me to be.

"I can't help her, I can't even help myself. I told you, I'm too fucked up."

"Fraser, that sounds like the story you're telling yourself. Just because you've had some major revelations about your upbringing, and who your father is, doesn't mean you're going to turn out like your mother. It also doesn't mean that you're too fucked up for someone who loves you to help you through a hard time, even if her dad is sick. She needs you as much as you need her."

"It's not a story. It's the truth."

"Why don't we try a different story? One of a wonderful father who raised you your whole life, knowing for half of it that you weren't his biological child, but not caring because he loved you so much. One where your girl-friend," she checks her notepad again, "Elly, loves you so much, she wants to help you with all the challenges in life, as well as be there for all the good times. One where your best friend cares so much about you, he's paying for me to be here on a Sunday, because he can't watch you self-destruct for another day. Sometimes family is not the blood you share, but the one you make with the people who choose to share their life with you," she smiles sympathetically.

I feel so sick, my head is spinning. Not only with this horrendous hangover but the words she is saying. 'Family is not the blood you share but the people you choose.' I want to believe her, but... oh fuck, I think I'm going to be sick. I jump up and make a run for the toilet.

Fuck, I don't ever remember feeling this sick. I just want to curl up in a ball and die.

I know she's here to help me, and she's right about it. All this isn't the life I want. I don't want to be anything like my mother. I wash my face with renewed purpose and slowly make my way back down the hallway to where she's sitting. I slump back down where I was on the lounge.

"Fraser, none of the issues we have talked about today are quick fixes. You have a long way to go, with years of anger and resentment, and it's going to take time to work through it all. But, if you're willing to give it a go, I have lots of tools in my tool kit that can help. I'm sure we can work through this all together."

I nod my head. I have no more words.

"I have the information for the local Alcoholics Anonymous group, or the one the next town over if you would prefer. I think that's going to be a good place to start. You can meet some others going through a similar situation and get a support team around you.

"You can also talk to your GP about some medications that can help with withdrawals. The good thing is, you have done this process before and been on top of it, so you know you can. This was a relapse, but I'm sure, with the support of your friends and family, you will be on top of it in no time.

"Here's my number. If you want to book in to see me again, we can work out a plan moving forward."

I take the card from her. "Thanks," I say, defeated.

"I'll see myself out. Hope to see you again soon, Fraser. Good luck in the next few days."

As soon as she's gone, I drag myself back to bed. I've gone cold turkey before, so I know I can do it again. And if I want to get my life back on track and stop blaming my mum, I need to get my shit together. The next few days are going to be hell.

Elena

I'm nearly finished displaying the flowers in the new

vases Indie found at some art auction last week. The vases are stunning, handmade and glazed in the most beautiful teal colour. Her taste is impeccable, and they work perfectly with the fresh modern vibe we are going for with these townhouses.

Whenever I finish a styling job on a home that's for sale, I do a final walkthrough at the end just to look for anything I've missed. As I do, I always make up a little story in my head about the kind of people who will live in the place. What jobs might they have, will they have screaming kids who will be running through the halls out to the backyard, if they're happy or not?

These townhouses look to me like they're going to be happy spaces. I get the feeling that they're going to symbolise fresh beginnings for the people who will live here. These people are all running from something, and these homes will be their sanctuary. They're a safe place to start a new life. With that happy feeling, I better get out of here before the others start to arrive. I would like to avoid running into Fraser. I make my way back to the kitchen to grab the wrapping from the flowers.

"Didn't think you would show up for this," a shrill voice calls.

I jump and turn round to see Shea and her resting bitch face. What does she want?

"Why? I'm the stylist. The Green Door boys wanted everything perfect for the auction today, and I wanted the flowers to be fresh so the rooms smelt nice. Of course I'm going to be here."

"I just thought, since Fraser and I are kind of a thing now, you wouldn't want anything to do with him, that's all. It's kind of embarrassing for you, since he dumped you and all."

Wow! Low blow, even for a bitch like Shea. Luckily I had lots of experience dealing with girls like her in high school.

"I doubt very much that you and Fraser are a thing. You're delusional, Shea. And besides, even if that were true, I'm still a professional, unlike some. I'm not going to let anyone down."

"Oh really? Just ask anyone who was at the pub Saturday night if we're a thing. He spent the night with his tongue down my throat."

With that imagery, I have a sudden urge to be sick. She can't be fucking serious. There's no way. Even though things have turned to shit with us, he wouldn't have hooked up with her, would he? He might have, I feel like I don't know him at all anymore.

"You've gone quiet. Guess it must hurt to know 'Little Miss Perfect' doesn't always get the guy and the happily ever after."

"I'm just shocked that you could make up such blatant lies, just to hurt someone else. What kind of a cold-hearted bitch are you?" I'm sure she must feel the chill from my death stare, but it has no impact on her, her face is unchanged.

"The kind that's got your guy. No need for me to tell lies, baby, it happened. Just ask Fraser when he gets here." With that, she walks away with a smug look on her face, her heels clicking on the floor as she leaves.

I want to hit her in her perfect fake face, split that fucking silicone-injected lip right open. See how she would go doing the auction today with a bleeding lip, that would be funny. I'd stay around to watch that. But I won't. I take a deep breath. Be the bigger person, Elly. She's not worth it. I'm sure she's lying to get at me, but there's this nagging feeling that maybe it's true. I haven't seen Fraser since that night he broke it off, so who knows what sluts he's been sleeping with.

I take one last look at the room and put good vibes into the home for its new owners. I think everything is where it's supposed to be. I'm so proud of this set-up. It looks amazing, and Indie's art on the walls makes the place something special. I hope she sells some of them. I've found, in the past, that the new owners often like the art so much, they buy it for their new house. Looks like I'm finished, so I'm out of here before anyone else turns up.

I pack the extra flowers I brought in my boot, along with my tool kit, and turn to see Blake across the street with the developer Ash. I wave and offer a smile. I miss Blake. It's all so weird between us at the moment, so I haven't seen him since Fraser broke it off, just the occasional message.

He makes his way across the street. "Hey, Elly, how're you getting on? How's your dad this week?"

"Yeah, all right, I guess. Dad's doing well, back on his feet."

"That's good to hear."

"The townhouses are looking perfect for today. I'll get out of your hair," I mutter, my voice barely a whisper. I open my door to jump in my car. As much as I miss him, I don't want to stand here making small talk after what Shea just said. I'm so close to tears, I just want to get in the car and go home.

"You making sure you don't cross paths with Fraser? You don't have to worry, he's sick so he's not coming today."

"That's not good he's sick, but it's probably for the best that we don't see each other, don't you think? I'm sure he's not keen to see me either, especially after what Shea just said."

"What did she say?" He looks pissed now.

"Fraser and her are a thing. Apparently the whole pub saw it?"

"You need to talk to Fraser, Elly, don't let her poison your mind. She's just a jealous bitch. There's so much more to what Fraser's going through. He loves you, Elly, he has since you were kids. Don't give up on him, just give him time to work through it."

"Well, there's my answer then. I didn't believe it, but I guess it's true if you can't tell me for sure it's not."

"There's so much more to all of this than you know. Talk to him. He won't admit it, but he needs you."

"See you later, Blake." I close the door and start my engine. I can feel the tears starting and I don't want to cry in front of him. I have no idea what's going on. Nothing makes sense anymore. Who do I even believe? I just want to go home and have a shower, wash away this shitty way I feel. Then I'm messaging Tristan from the café. If Fraser gets to move on, so do I!

I'm done with fucking Fraser Davis.

CHAPTER TWENTY-THREE

ELENA

"Come on, Elly, hurry up, we're going to be late," Indie calls out from her room.

I stand in my bedroom looking in the mirror. I look awful. So tired and drained. Even the makeup isn't covering it tonight. Maybe I should just cancel. I don't want to go anyway. I've lost the courage I had at the beginning of the week when I was pissed with Fraser for sleeping with Shea. I don't even know for sure if he did, but she sure made out that that's what happened, and trying to move on and go on a date seemed like a good idea then.

"All right, hold on." I make my way out into the hall. "Do I look okay?" I ask, as I straighten out the layers of my dress. This dress is super cute and normally puts me in the best mood. It's a creamy colour with little tiny polka-dots all over it. It's short with a low V neck, but with a layered frill skirt, so it's not over-the-top sexy, and the long sleeves are perfect for this time of year when the evenings are still cold. Tonight, though, nothing's working. I just feel like jumping into my PJ's and heading back to bed.

"You look stunning, chick. Now come on, let's go," Indie says, as she grabs my hand and drags me down the hallway. We're meeting the guys in the bar just around the corner then heading for dinner.

"Okay, Indie, you can stop dragging me now. I'm not going to run."

She gives me a sideways look. "That's what someone who's about to run says to convince their captor to let her go, so she can run."

"How crazy do you think I've become?"

"I don't know, chick, you haven't left the house much lately, and I've been hearing you talk to yourself a lot. Don't know if you're ready for the straitjacket yet, but you're heading there," she laughs at her own joke.

"Ha ha, you're so funny, I'm not turning into a crazy person."

"I know, but I got you to stop worrying and smile, so we can walk in looking like we want to be here. I need this, chickee, I really do," she begs, plastering on her best smile and linking arms with me.

The guys are already at the bar, sitting at a table down the back, and they both look up and smile when they see us. I plaster my best fake smile on my face and pretend like I'm happy to be here. You can do this, Elena, it's not that hard; just make polite conversation, eat some yummy food, then go home to your cosy PJ's and bed.

We make our way over and take a seat. I can't help but admire how seriously good-looking these boys are, and if I've got to be out, at least I've got something good to look at. Tristan is your traditional tall, dark, and handsome, with green eyes. He would normally be just my type, and Luca is slightly shorter with longish blond hair, which he has in a man bun. He's unshaven and a little edgy-looking with tattoos up his arms, just like Indie. They make the perfect pair.

We take our seats and make polite small talk. Both guys seem nice. Since that night when we played pool, they've been making an effort to come into the café at a time when we're not busy, so they can chat, but I still feel like I know nothing about them.

"What are you girls drinking?" asks Tristan.

"I'll just have a white wine, please," I reply.

"Me too," smiles Indie.

I don't even feel like drinking, which is not like me, but I feel like I need to keep my head straight tonight. We don't really know these guys, and I'm so uncomfortable being on a date. I'm glad Indie's here.

The boys return from the bar and we make small talk about their jobs.

"So, what do you guys do for work that you can drop in so regularly for coffees? Or are we just so irresistible you come across town just so you can talk to us," asks Indie.

"Well, there is that. But we work for the council in environmental services. Our office is just around the corner from the café, so it's pretty easy too."

I think Indie is crushing hard on Luca. She's leaning her elbows on the table, with her head resting on her hands, and she hasn't taken her eyes off him since we sat down.

"Are you into bushwalking and camping, Indie?" asks Luca.

"Oh, I love the great outdoors," Indie almost yells, all excited. She's hanging onto his every word.

"What about you?" Tristan asks me.

"Sorry, not really. I love the beach. Spend most of my spare time there. Are you big on camping?"

"Not really, but when Luca started asking Indie questions, I realised I know practically nothing about you except that you work at the café. Just thought I'd ask. What do you do with your time besides working at the café and going to the beach?" He smiles, flashing his perfect teeth.

"I'm an interior stylist. Indie and I have just started our own business. She is an artist, and we're working together to style houses when people want to sell."

"That's really cool that you have your own business."

"Yeah, it is. It's only early days at the moment, but it's doing well. We're quite busy already, so I don't know how much longer you'll be seeing us around the café."

"Oh, that will be a shame for us, but amazing for you guys."

Oh, I hate small talk! It's so awkward, the whole getting-to-know-you stage. It's when you realise how boring your life is.

"Do you want to go for dinner?" asks Tristan, looking as awkward about all of this as me.

"Sounds good. Let's do it," I say, and the others follow our lead.

We head upstairs to the best seafood restaurant in town, Ocean View. This place is fancy. I've only been here a couple of times, when we've had an extra-special event. The last time was for Mum and Dad's 35th wedding anniversary.

We wait at the front as Tristan talks to the waitress.

"Follow me," she says, smiling and leading us through the restaurant. My eyes widen at the sight of the other tables full of delicious-looking seafood dishes. Some have tiered platters packed with lobsters, prawns, oysters, and various other seafood. They look amazing and must cost an absolute fortune. We arrive at our reserved table and the others take a seat.

I fake a smile as I sit down, trying to be happy to be here. My body is here but my mind is back with Fraser, still trying to work out what went wrong. I feel too sad to be out trying to pretend like I'm moving on. It just doesn't feel right.

I can see how much of an effort Tristan is trying to make, he seems like such a nice guy, and he's fucking hot. What is wrong with me? Why am I still hung up on the arsehole who fucked me then dumped me?

The waiter comes to take our order, and Luca orders another bottle of wine for the table.

I ordered seafood linguini, normally my favourite from Ocean View restaurant, but tonight I'm not so sure. The boys both ordered beef and lobster and Indie ordered the Barramundi.

Twenty minutes of awkward small talk later, our food arrives. Thank God it was quick, I'm all but out of things to talk about. I dig in. It's delicious, and I'm glad I ordered the linguini, but like I have been over the last few weeks, I'm full after a few mouthfuls and can't eat anymore. Kind of a shame when it costs so much.

"You done with yours already, Elly?" asks Tristan.

"Yeah, you want to finish it off? Don't want it to go to waste." I push my plate over to him.

"Hell yeah, it looks amazing." He digs straight in after already polishing off his whole meal.

I look around the table and the rest of them are having a good time; why can't I even try, what's wrong with me? There is no way Fraser would be thinking about me as much as I am about him. Tristan has finished the rest of my meal and is watching me and I'm sure he is thinking, *Why did I bother asking this sad sack out?*

"Elly, you're very quiet. Is everything okay?" Tristan says, as he grabs my hand across the table.

"Sorry, yeah, I'm just feeling a bit off. I might go out on the balcony for a bit to get some fresh air," I smile over at him. He really is a nice guy. I feel so bad that I'm such a downer of a date.

"Okay, I'll join you." He slides his chair back and holds out his hand for me. I take it reluctantly. Why does this feel so weird? I've been on dates before, held guys' hands, but this just doesn't feel right.

"We make our way out to the front balcony, which looks over the ocean, and take a seat. It's so beautiful here, looking out over the beach with that fresh ocean smell. There's a nice breeze tonight, so every so often little droplets of ocean spray land on our faces.

Tristan is looking at me and frowning.

"I'm so sorry, Tristan, you're such a lovely guy. I'm just not in a good place at the moment."

"It's okay, Elly, I shouldn't have pushed you for a date. I just haven't stopped thinking about you since that night at the bar. But that's the problem, isn't it? You're still hung up on the guy you were with then?"

"I'm sorry. I am. I don't know why he dumped me, it's over. But we have known each other since we were kids. It's just going to take a while to move on. You know?"

"Yeah, I get it. I've been there too. I nearly got married last year, but she left me at the altar. It's taken a while to move past it. We had our whole lives mapped out, and then the rug was ripped out from under me."

I cover my mouth with my hand. "Oh, Tristan, that's awful. Did you find out why?"

"No, we haven't spoken since. There was a note, but it just said she was sorry, nothing else."

"Wow, that's so harsh. I can't believe someone would do that. How long were you together for?"

"Five years."

"Wow, yeah, that's just crazy. You know what, though? This is what I keep telling myself: it's all for a reason, we just don't know what it is yet. Someone awesome will be just around the corner for you, I'm sure of it."

"Thanks, Elly, hopefully. I hope you get your situation sorted out as well. And, while we're sorting out our shit from the past, we can still have fun tonight, right?" He smiles a warm caring smile that makes me feel so comfortable with him. He's totally right. I can still have a good time with him as a friend.

"Of course, that sounds nice," I smile back.

"You know, we could just fuck him out of your system. I'm sure we would both feel better for it," he jokes with a cheeky grin, but I'm not sure if he's joking or serious.

"Probably," I laugh, "but I'm not the kind of girl who has one-night stands, and we both know this can't go anywhere right now, so you're stuck with the boring friends version."

He gives me a sideways smile. "Thought so, but you're beautiful, Elly, you can't blame a guy for trying."

"Thanks, Tristan, you're not bad-looking yourself. If I was in a better place, then maybe this could be something." I offer a smile. "Let's go check on the others."

We make our way back inside just in time. Indie's getting drunk, I can tell by that look in her eyes.

"Hey, they're back. We're going to get tattoos," Indie calls out, way too loudly for the fancy restaurant we're in.

I look back at Tristan. "How long were we gone for? She's trashed!"

"Not long enough for that."

"She is a lightweight. We need to get her out of here before she gets any louder," I whisper, so only Tristan can hear. "Are you trashed, Indie girl? Hey, why don't we pay for our dinner then go for a bit of a walk? You can work out what you're getting while we walk."

"Sounds good, chickee. Hey, I've got an awesome idea. You should get one too. It'll be so much fun. It'll make you feel better too, I promise."

Now I know she's really drunk. She knows how afraid I am of needles. She must be completely smashed if she thinks that's even likely.

Tristan and I go up to pay for the others. They're both off-their-faces drunk, in total hysterics. "Looks like we're the responsible adults tonight," I whisper to Tristan.

"Looks like it. I'm okay with it if it means I get to spend some more time with you. We might find something to cheer you up." He bumps arms with me, and I offer a smile in return. He's really nice and talking to him is helping me forget how awful I've been feeling.

We make our way up the street. The other two are walking in front of us with their arms linked, or should I say, stumbling around in front of us.

It's a beautiful night for this time of year, and the walk is actually making me feel better.

"Everything okay, Elly? You keep checking your phone."

"Yeah, sorry. It's just that since my dad got sick, I'm worried I will miss an important call about him. It's become a bad habit."

"Your dad's sick?"

"Yeah, he's getting better, though. He had a heart attack just over a month ago, so he's improving but I can't stop worrying about him."

"That must have been scary."

"Yeah, it was. He's doing well now, and the doctor said, with some lifestyle changes, he will be his normal self before long, but I just can't stop worrying. I've never really had anxiety before, but now I just feel worried all the time, and I can't sleep."

"You're having trouble eating too?"

"Yeah, how did you know? I'm sorry, I'm telling you way too much. You were after a fun date and you got a nut job."

He laughs. "A cute nut job."

I smile up at him. "Thank you, you weren't supposed to agree with me."

"I don't think you're a nut job. I know exactly what you're going through. I've had anxiety for years, I know how debilitating it can be. Have you talked to someone? You know it's normal to feel the way you do. You have a lot going on, Elly, don't give yourself a hard time."

"Woo hoo, I'm going in," we hear Indie call out excitedly.

"Oh God, what now?" We look over to see her run into the tattoo studio.

"We better stop them before Luca's got a permanent reminder of this night etched on his skin," I warn.

"I'm sure he wouldn't even notice in amongst all the others. Have you seen his arms?"

"Yeah, I did notice. You got any?"

"A couple," he says. "I'd show you later, but you have friend-zoned me, and they're hidden."

"Is that right, hey?"

We rush in after the drunken duo and find them already flicking through the design books on the counter.

"Elly, I've found the perfect one for us," Indie calls to

me, shoving the book in my face. I pull it back a bit so I can see the image. It's a photo of two friends with tiny little coffee mugs on their wrists. "It's perfect, right? Coffee besties, like us," she calls, grinning up at me. She's totally serious about this.

They are kind of cute, these little coffee mugs. How much could it really hurt? I kind of feel like I need to do something crazy to take me out of the crazy thought spiral I'm in.

"Okay, Indie, I'll do it with you."

"Yesss," she squeals. "Are you serious?"

I nod and she grabs my hands and screams excitedly.

"I thought we were supposed to be the sensible ones talking them out of it," says Tristan.

"I know, right, but I'm sick of being the sensible one, aren't you?"

"Yeah, I'm in too."

The boys both pick a design. It's a tree that looks like a pine tree in a diamond and triangle. They're going to get it on their arm. They get set up first.

"Do you want me to hold your hand in case it hurts?" I ask Tristan.

"You're quite the smartarse now, Miss Elly. Just wait until your turn comes."

"Oh, I'm definitely going to need you to hold my hand. There's a very likely possibility I'll pass out doing this." He laughs at me, but I'm serious. I'm suddenly feeling very nervous. I'm not sure if I can go through with this, but I want to. In half an hour, the boys are both done and look happy with their new permanent arm art. Now it's our turn.

"Don't you let go of my hand, Indie."

"I won't, chick, I've got you, you can do this."

We sit next to each other holding hands as our other hands rest on the table, getting the transfer of the little coffee cup drawn on.

"I love you, Elly, I'm so glad you moved home." She smiles at me and it makes me feel so much better. She's been such a special friend to me, especially over the last few months, and I've been so fixated on Fraser that I've forgotten that all the other things I came to Byron to do are falling into place. We have created this amazing business together, and it's now starting to take off. I have the best friend and roommate a girl could ask for.

"I love you too, Indie." She smiles back at me. As they start the tattoo, shit, it hurts. Indie doesn't look bothered at all. I'm just going to keep looking at her. I don't want to see them do it or I'll faint for sure.

Twenty long minutes later, the sound of the tattoo gun stops.

"All done, girls." What? It's done! I look down at my arm and see the tiny tattoo and small dots of blood, and that's the last thing I remember, until I feel Tristan picking me up.

"You okay, Elly?" His brow is furrowed, and he looks worried. I pull out of his hold on me.

"Ha, yeah, I'm fine. I look down at my arm and it's bandaged up now. "Told you I'm a fainter." Oh, why did I do that? I'm so embarrassed.

Indie and Luca are killing themselves laughing at me. "Now I've got a new Elly-fainting story to tell," Indie giggles.

"There's more?" Tristan questions.

I nod my head, embarrassed. "Come on, let's head home."

The boys come back to our place for coffee, and before we've even walked in the door, Indie and Luca are all over each other. They disappear down the hall. "I think I'm going to need earphones tonight," I laugh.

"I'd say so. We could make our own noise, so you don't notice," he teases, with a cheeky smile.

"I'm sorry, Tristan, I just can't."

"It's okay, Elly, I was just joking. How about we have that coffee?"

I head into the kitchen to make the drinks, feeling guilty. He really is very nice and so considerate. I should be making more of an effort to get to know him. But I just can't do any more than friends right now, not while I'm still so confused about Fraser. I walk back into the lounge room and place the coffee down in front of Tristan.

"I'm sorry tonight didn't end up the way you planned."

"You know what, Elly? It's okay. I had fun tonight, and I've made a new friend. It's all good," he smiles.

"Looks like Luca's going to be staying tonight. I can set you up on the lounge if you like?"

"That would be good, thanks."

I bring in some blankets and a pillow to set him up on the couch.

"Night, Tristan."

"Night, Elly. If you get cold and need someone to cuddle, you know where I am," he offers with that same cheeky smile. He doesn't give up easily.

"Night, Tristan," I say with a smile, as I walk down the hall. It's late, past 1am. I feel bad for just leaving him on the couch, but I'm so exhausted, and it's just not going to happen between us.

Fraser

It's been five very long days since Cherie, the psychologist, left our house, and I spent most of the day in bed. I have no idea how I got so lucky with my business partners, but they have been taking care of everything at the office. Ash has even been working from the office instead of home, they must really be worried about me. Dad and Janice have set their van up in our driveway and have been helping me in any way they can.

I still feel terrible, but I'm better than I was yesterday, and I want to get out of the house. I need to visit Jim to see how he is.

"Hey, Jim. Sorry I haven't been around much lately. How're you feeling?"

"Getting there, son. It's not been easy. I'm still a bit dizzy but I'm nearly over the worst of it. They say I can start exercising again next week, and I can't wait. Being stuck in bed's just not my style."

"No, I'm surprised they have had you in bed this long. It's good to hear you're feeling better."

"Your dad came to visit yesterday. It was good to see him again. It's been a while. Janice is lovely. It's so nice to see how happy he is."

"Yeah, he's in town for a bit, it's nice to have him back home."

"He said you stuffed up with Elly. What happened, son?"

"I don't know why he told you that, but I'm sure you have heard it all from her anyway."

"No, she hasn't said a word. I could tell something was wrong with her, but we don't know what it is. What's going on, son? It's obvious you're crazy about each other. How could you have stuffed up that badly?"

"There's so much she doesn't know. It's all too complicated."

"You're talking about your dad not being your biological dad? That was sure a surprise, wasn't it!"

"Did Dad tell you everything? Man, he's got a big mouth!"

"He's worried about you, Fraser. He just needed someone to talk to who knows this situation, but I'm glad he did. If you keep it all bottled up, and no one knows you're in pain, they can't help you. We're all here for you, son, but you need to talk to Elly. She's a mess. She's keeping it all to herself, trying not to burden us with it, but I can see it's eating her up. I don't like to see my baby girl hurting so much."

"I'm so sorry, Jim. I want to fix it. I just don't know where to start with her. I stuffed up this time. There's no way she'll see me."

"Just tell her the truth. Tell her what's going on, then it's up to her to decide what she'll do with the information you tell her. We all make mistakes, especially when we're not thinking straight."

"I bet you never made mistakes with Anne. You're the perfect couple."

He laughs at me. "I was young and dumb like you once, Fraser. No one's perfect, and you would be surprised how majorly I fucked up at times with Anne. I was lucky Anne's a good woman and forgave me. You just have to be open and honest with Elly."

"Thanks, Jim. It's good to see how well you're doing. I'll come and visit again later in the week." I shake his hand. He's so frail and looking a lot older than he was before all this happened. It's taken a toll on him. I just hope that, once he's back on his feet again, he will be the same old Jim we know and love.

I now feel even worse, knowing I left Elly to go through this alone. She's right, I'm a selfish pig.

CHAPTER TWENTY-FOUR

ELENA

I walk down the street kicking the dirt with my boots because I don't have the energy to pick up my feet. That was a long shift at the café. We were unusually quiet, and it dragged on. I'm tired, so fucking tired, but I want to see Dad before I go home. It's become my routine after I finish at the café, I drop in to see him to make sure he's okay.

The house is quiet, and Mum must still be at work. I pop my head around their bedroom door to see if he's awake. Looks like he might be asleep. I better leave him. I slowly close the door, when I hear him.

"Hey, honey, come to sit with me?" He pats the bed beside him.

I go over and kiss him on the cheek, taking a seat next to him. "Sorry, Dad. Did I wake you?"

"No, I'm just resting, still a bit dizzy. Come tell me about your day." He sits up.

"Not much to tell. Working at the café was a pretty slow day."

"How's the business coming along with Indie?"

"Actually, better than expected. We got a new client today, a really big one. Might even mean we can both quit the café. They're the furniture hire company I have been using for The Green Door jobs. Their in-house designer quit last week, and they were looking for a new one and offered it to me. I turned them down, and instead, offered to freelance for them under our business name. It's going to mean consistent work which is amazing."

He smiles at me softly, his eyes full of concern. "Why aren't you smiling then? This is the break you've been working towards since you moved home."

"I don't know. It just doesn't feel the same, you know, with everything that's happened lately."

"Oh, honey, I know you're worried about me, but you know I'm getting better. I'm going to be just fine. Your dad might be getting old, but I can see this is more than just what's going on with me. This is about Fraser, isn't it?"

"No, why would it be?"

"I know, honey. He came to see me today and told me what he did. He's not in a good way."

"He came to see you? Why would he do that?"

"He wanted to see how I was getting along and apologise for not being here while I was recovering. He was checking up on you too."

"Why would he do that? He was the one that ended it."

"He's got a lot going on, things that you can't understand unless you have been there. He didn't have the kind of childhood you did, with a supportive family around him, and he's got some issues to work through. He needs a bit of time to find himself. You're just going to have to be patient with him."

"That's what Blake keeps saying. Even if you're going

through some stuff, that doesn't excuse treating other people badly."

"No, I agree, but maybe just wait till he's ready and at least hear him out."

What on earth is going on? And why do I feel like the only one he can't talk to when I should be the first one? "Okay, I'm not some pushover, though. Whatever his story is, it better be bloody good. How are you doing anyway, Dad? You look really good today, you've got that sparkle in your eyes again."

"I'm having a good day and I'm excited. Did you see they've started to excavate the backyard? After all the planning, it's all finally happening!"

"Yes, I did. It's very exciting, and I'm so glad you'll have this project to concentrate on. Means you have to stick around."

He takes my hand in his. "I'm not going anywhere, honey, stop worrying about me. You're stuck with your old man for a long time to come."

"You better not leave me, I need you around." I kiss him on his forehead. "See you tomorrow."

He reaches out for me and pulls me into a hug. "Things will get better, honey, it's just a bump in the road. Give him the time he needs, and you'll understand."

Maybe. Bet Fraser didn't tell my father everything! And if he thinks it's going to be as simple as explaining to me that he's got some shit going on, he's got another thing coming. After what he has put me through the last few weeks, it's going to take a hell of a lot for me to forgive him.

As soon as I walk inside our apartment, I can smell something amazing, Indie must be cooking dinner. I find her in the kitchen stirring the pot on the stove.

"Hey." I smile over to her, dumping my bag on the lounge.

She looks up and smiles over to me. "Hey, chick."

"I'm so lucky to have you in my life, Indie. This dinner smells delicious." She smiles, pleased with herself. But I'm not just saying she's an amazing cook, though it's lucky she is, because I definitely don't take after my mother in that department. She serves the dinner into two bowls and places them on the table.

I inhale the scent. "Yum, my favourite." It's beef stroganoff; I love this dish, and normally, I'd be woofing it down, but I'm still struggling with my queasy tummy.

Indie eyes me up and down. "You need to eat up, Elly, you're fading away! I've made plenty so you can have seconds if you want."

"Yeah, I know. I don't know what's wrong with me. I just feel kind of sick all the time."

"It's just the stress from everything. You need to eat more, and you'll be fine."

I sit, moving my food around in my bowl and know I should be eating. It smells amazing, but I just can't stomach it. I'm full after a couple of mouthfuls.

Indie looks up from her finished plate of food with a sympathetic smile. "You okay, chick? You look miserable."

"Same old shit! Why are all men such arseholes?"

"What's he done now?"

"I don't even know if it's true, but possibly slept with that slut Shea."

She gasps and covers her mouth. "He wouldn't have done that, would he?"

"I don't know. According to her they did! But then, get this, he went to see Dad today. They had a big chat and Dad said the same as Blake, I need to trust him. He's working through some big stuff, just hang on and everything will be okay."

"Cryptic! I don't know, chick. I reckon he's had time. Why does he go to everyone else to talk about all this and not you?"

"I know, right? That's what I don't get as well. If he would just talk to me then I could be the judge, I could work it out with him, whatever it is."

She grabs my arm. "Come on. I'm taking you to do something fun tonight, we need to take your mind off him."

A short drive into the hinterlands and we walk into the large art studio Indie has taken me to. I cover my mouth so my laugh doesn't escape. "You brought me to a life drawing class?" I whisper. There are easels set up around the room with people drawing in different mediums. At the front of the room there's a small stage, with a man posing, completely butt naked.

"Sure did! And the smile on your face now is priceless." I'm sure she's right. I can't help but smile, I'm so awkward with stuff like this. "I'm not mature enough to be here. You know I'm going to laugh and ruin it for everyone else."

"No, you won't! And don't worry if you do. I know these guys won't care, they're used to people being a bit awkward when they first start drawing." Her emerald-green eyes flash with excitement. This is Indie in her element, and these are her people.

"You know these guys? Why did I even ask, of course you do!"

She smiles back at me. "You ever wonder where I am on a Tuesday night?" she raises her brow at me. "I work here," she laughs. "I have for years."

"Oh my God, Indie, I knew you were comfortable with what you've got," I say, gesturing to her bits, "but I can't believe you strip off and let people draw you! So much for shy little Indie."

"I'm only shy meeting new people, and I don't have to talk to anyone up there, so it's easy," she shrugs. "It's really not a big deal, you should try it, Elly. It's totally liberating, and the money is awesome."

"You're full of surprises, Indie."

We take a set toward the back so we can get started on our masterpieces. I'm giggling and I can't stop. This guy is unbelievable, muscular and toned, and he's just standing there like some statue of a Greek god with it all hanging out. I can't stop staring at his junk. It's just hanging there. I have no idea how people do this as a job.

"Elly," she bumps arms with me, distracting me from the view. I have to check myself to make sure my mouth isn't hanging open. "What do you want to draw with?" She holds out different types of pencils for me to choose from. "And close your mouth."

"Oh my, Indie, you know this guy? Are they all as hot as him?"

She rolls her eyes. "Yeah, Elton, he's a friend of mine. They're all different, lots of shapes and sizes to keep it interesting for the artists."

"Charcoals, I think." I grab the long stick of charcoal from her and stare at the blank page. "What do I even do? I don't know where to start."

"You've done art classes before. Just draw what you see," she says, hitting me on the arm, "and try to stop giggling, people are staring." She's giggling back at me, trying to stop herself, but every time she looks at my face, she starts again. Hope they don't kick us out.

Two hours later, we have seen various models. Not all the best-looking people but all of them so confident. I've been trying to contain my laughter, but some of the poses, wow!

Indie's drawings are, of course, unbelievable. She's such an amazing artist. Mine are okay. They're probably too funny to be classified as art, but Indie is encouraging me to keep going, and she was right, it's making me feel better. I haven't laughed this much in weeks.

"We so should frame these and put them up in the apartment!" she says.

"Well, maybe yours, they're beautiful, Indie. Mine are more..." I try to think of the correct word, "abstract." I laugh, pulling a crazy face to accentuate my point.

"There she is, the Elly I know and love. We definitely need to do this weekly if I'm going to get you back."

"What, Elly the crazy person?"

"Yeah, she's the one I like," she laughs, and I crack up laughing back at her. Tonight has been so much fun.

CHAPTER TWENTY-FIVE

FRASER

I stare at Elly's front door with no idea what to say to her. I hope she doesn't slam the door in my face. It's what I deserve, but I hope she will hear me out. Deep breath. Fraser, you can do this. Make it right with her.

I'm sweating so much I feel like I've just done a session at the gym. I wipe my hands down my jeans and try to get my shit together. Just coming here is so much harder than I thought it was going to be. I'm not good at admitting when I'm wrong. But I know I've fucked up majorly with Elly and I want to make it right, whatever way I can.

I knock and wait. Maybe she's not home? I wait a bit longer... She must be out or something. I'll come back another time. I turn to leave when I hear the door open and a small voice.

"Fraser, what are you doing here?" I turn back to see her, my Elly. She looks tired and so thin in a pair of skinny jeans and a T-shirt. Her dad was right, and I feel sick that it's because of me. What the fuck was I thinking? I don't even know.

"Can I come in? We need to talk."

She nods and opens the door.

"Is Indie around?"

"No, she's working," she sighs and leads me over to the lounge, and we both sit in awkward silence. I guess she's waiting to hear what I've got to say for myself, but I'm not sure where to begin.

"Do you want anything to drink?" She's so calm. I thought she would be yelling abuse at me. But she patiently sits legs crossed, hands resting in her lap, waiting for me to talk.

"No, I'm fine, thank you." My mind is racing. What do I say to her? I just want everything to be okay between us, but I don't know how to make it right. I crack my knuckles to try and ease the tension I'm feeling. "Are you okay, Elly?"

"What do you think, Fraser?" She raises her head to look at me and I can see how angry she really is. "How could I be? You left me with no explanation. Everyone keeps telling me to wait for you. That you're going through some family stuff. It's pretty hard when I haven't heard from you in weeks."

"I'm so sorry, Elly, I've been a selfish arsehole! I know I have. I'm so sorry, things just got so complicated so fast. I didn't know how to process it all." I reach for her hand and she tugs it away. That magnetic pull I feel towards her is still there, and I want so badly to touch her, take comfort in the warmth of her skin on mine, have her lips pressed to mine, taking away my pain. But I know that's not what I deserve. I deserve for her to reject me.

"I don't want your apology now, Fraser, it's too late... but I want to know why? Why on earth did you do that to me?"

I run my sweating palms down my jeans again. Why am I sweating so much? Seeing how angry she is, it's making me nervous. Maybe this is it. I went too far this time and she's not going to forgive me. This is the end.

"I was messed up! There's no real excuse." I shake my head. "I know my behaviour is unacceptable, and I understand if you don't want my apology or to ever see me again, but I need to explain where my head was at when I left that night. So you know it wasn't you. I'm so sorry I left you to worry, this was nothing to do with you. You're perfect."

"Okay, explain." Her eyes are now a sad blue-green colour, like deep ocean pools, cloudy after a storm. The way she looks at me, it's breaking my heart to see her like this and know it was me that caused it.

I take a deep breath, trying to clear my mind so I can explain. "That Sunday night before I left to go and see my dad, my mum turned up at my house. She was there when I got home and wanted to talk."

Her eyes widen. "Your mum, I thought you weren't in contact."

"We're not! I hadn't seen her since the night she left when I was 14. She thought she could just show up after all this time and I'd give her money to help her out of the current mess she's in. When I didn't, she turned on me like she always used to. This time it was something that cut me so deep. I'm still not sure how to process it."

"What did she say?" Her face is softening, her eyes showing a hint of the warmth she normally holds for me.

"She said when she was younger, a few years after she and my dad were married, they were trying to fall pregnant and they were having problems. Apparently, it was Dad, not her, so she took it upon herself to find someone that could give her the child she so desperately wanted."

Elly gasps as she connects the dots. Her eyes are wide as she hangs on my every word.

I take another deep breath trying to get the words out. "She waited until Dad was away on one of his business trips, went to a bar, and found some guy she thought would be a suitable sperm donor, and that was that. The man I had believed to be my dad my whole life... isn't my blood. That's why I took off to go and see him that next day. I had to know if it was true."

"Is it true?" she gasps, her hands over her mouth.

"Yeah, we had the paternity test done a few weeks ago. He's not my biological father." I sob. The tears I have been holding back for weeks are now rolling down my cheeks. Telling her makes it all feel so real. This is my fucked-up life now.

Elly's eyes are now welling with tears. "Oh, Fraser, that's... I don't know what to say, that's so awful. Did your dad know all that time as well?" She sobs, reaching out for my hand. Her touch feels so good, so comforting.

"No, not the whole time. She never told him. He worked it out for himself after Mum left. He didn't tell me, because in his eyes, I was his son no matter what. It didn't change the way he felt about me. He had hoped I would never need to know. It's a lot to deal with, but we're working through it together with my psychologist. Dad and Janice arrived last week and he's in town for a while."

"You have a psychologist?"

"Yeah, Blake organised her for me."

"He's so good to you, Fraser. I don't know what you did to deserve such a good friend, but you're lucky you have him."

"You don't even know half of it. This is the second time he's saved me when I've hit rock bottom. I can't even tell you how much I owe him."

"When was the first time?" she asks, looking puzzled,

and I realise we have never talked about what happened after she moved away all those years ago.

"When you left me, after our graduation."

"I didn't leave you, you wouldn't be with me. I chose to move on with my life when I knew it wasn't going to work with you." She pulls her hand back, annoyed with me again.

"Ahh," I run my hands through my hair, frustrated with myself. "What I meant was, when I fucked up with you the first time. I started drinking heavily. That summer I was a complete mess, and by the time Blake and I met at uni, I was in a bad way. He was the one that worked out I had a problem and talked me into getting help.

"Drinking was the only way I could block out the empty feeling I had inside. The ache my body was feeling because you weren't around. You had been in my life for such a long time and then you were gone without another word. Just like my mum. I feel so lost when I'm not around you, like you complete me, and when you're not around, there's a darkness that takes over. I've been using alcohol to fill the void. You always wonder why Blake and I are so close. He thinks I saved him from his awful family, and he saved me from myself... Twice."

"I still don't understand," Elly says. "Why you couldn't just come and talk to me about all this. Why was it all a secret? I could have been the one to save you this time, that's what I'm supposed to be here for."

"I was lost, Elly, and I know what I'm like when I go to that dark place. I didn't want to put you through that. I didn't even know who I was anymore. I have no idea who my biological dad is, and I'll never know. We have no way of working it out now. It was eating me up inside. All I kept on thinking is, I'm just like my mum, a drunk that's no good for anyone. That week I was away, I started drinking again. I didn't want to drag you into my awful life. Why would you want to stay, knowing how messed up I was?"

"Fraser, I didn't want to be with you because I thought you were perfect. I have known you a long time and no one is perfect. I wanted to be with you because you were you. My hero in school, scaring off all my bullies, the sad boy when his mother left that needed me to help distract him from the pain by skipping class and going for a swim in the middle of the school day, my brother's best friend who would gang up on me driving me nuts but then follow it up by doing something sweet like leaving a bar of chocolate or a flower from the garden on my pillow, the one that could light up my face with his cheeky smile just by being him. I didn't need you to be anything other than you." She sobs, fresh tears rolling down her cheeks.

"I didn't know that's how you felt, Elly. Since Mum left, I have felt like I wasn't enough for anyone. How could I be? When the one woman that's supposed to love me unconditionally left me without a word. She didn't even say goodbye that night. The last thing she said to me was, 'go do your homework, you little shit, so you don't end up stupid like your dad'. I saw her get into that guy's car and she was gone. That was it."

Elena

I can't believe what he's telling me. This is something that you read about in some trashy magazine, not the story of someone you care about. How could his mother do that to them? His poor dad, with everything he's been through. First her taking off with some other guy, only to then find out his son wasn't his. You never would have known, he worked his arse off to do all he could for Fraser. I remember how hard he used to work. He didn't want Fraser to go without anything, he adored him. I wipe away the tears that have escaped down my face.

"What your mother did to you and your dad is just awful, Fraser. I'm so glad you're seeing someone to work through it all. I wouldn't even know where to start if I had found out something like that about my family. You're a good man, and you deserve a good life. I hope you can get some clarity working with her."

His sad eyes rise to meet mine, "But?"

"But I don't understand why you didn't come to see me. I would have been right by your side to help, in any way you needed."

"I don't know, Elly, I was embarrassed. Look at your perfect family, then look at mine. I didn't know how to process it all myself, let alone tell you about it. The best part of my family was my dad, and I'm not even related to him."

"Yeah, but he raised you and you take after him more than you know."

"Elly, I know this is asking a lot of you after what I did, but do you think we can try again? I miss you. Not having you in my life is torture. I don't know how to do this without you." He wraps his arms around me, pulling me into a hug, and the tears are back. I rest my head in the crook of his neck where it fits so perfectly, and we cry.

I don't know how much time passes. After a while I pull back. I'm so sad for him but still so angry as well.

"I have missed you too. I mean, look at me, I'm a mess without you. But I don't think you know how awful this was for me. I'm going through shit too. I've been so worried about my dad, and I needed you. We're supposed to be in this together. How can I ever trust you not to just up and leave when times get hard? And don't even get me started on Shea."

He snaps his head back to me. The look on his face says it all. Something happened there.

"What about Shea?"

"She told me at the auction you two were sleeping together!"

"She said what?" He's up pacing back and forth now, running his fingers through his hair. I can tell he's agitated. "We're not, Elly, we didn't... you can ask Blake, it didn't happen. I didn't even kiss her." He's dropped his head now, deep in thought. "If I'm being completely honest, I could have... I was really drunk that night and I had given up all hope that I could fix things between us. It could have happened, but Blake stopped me."

"Wow, Blake saves the day again. You really do owe him!" Is he kidding; he could have slept with her? I mean, I know we had broken up but that fucking hurts.

"Yeah, I know! I'm sorry, Elly, I wasn't thinking straight, and I was very drunk. I knew I had already fucked up with you, I thought I couldn't make it any worse."

"You were thinking with your dick! I don't know what to say, Fraser. I think the hurt runs too deep. I love you, I always have, but how do we come back from this?"

He walks back over to the lounge and sits right in front of me, holding both my hands. I don't pull away. I want his touch, not giving in to him is killing me as much as it is him. All I want to do is take him back and kiss those irresistible lips of his. But I'm not some pushover that will just jump when he says so. Just because he is ready. I need time to process all of this and work out what I want. Work out how I want my life to look.

"You just need time and so do I. I've stopped drinking completely, and I'm going to keep working with my psychologist. I'm not turning out like my mum. But if you give me time to work this all out, I promise I can be the man you deserve."

"Let's just go back to being friends and see how we go. I can't make any promises for anything else, but I want you as part of my life, Fraser."

He smiles up at me, "Okay." He kisses me on the cheek. "I'll give you as much time as you need." He pulls away and walks to the door, before stopping to turn back to me. "This time I'll wait for you, though, Elly, no fucking around. There will never be anyone else for me but you, and I'll be waiting for you when you're ready."

He walks out the door, and I burst into tears again. This is too much to process. I'm still so angry with him for the way he handled it, but my heart hurts for him and what he's going through. I have loved him for a long time. Those feelings don't just go away because you're angry.

CHAPTER TWENTY-SIX

FRASER

THE RAIN IS REALLY COMING DOWN OUT THERE TODAY. It's one of those dark and gloomy days where it feels like it should be time to go home already, but it's only noon. My office is so dark I have the pendant light on and the lamp over my desk. I've been staring out the window for a while, going over my conversation with Elly last night. Getting any actual work done seems impossible today.

It stung that she didn't take me back and wants to just be friends for now, but I understand where she's coming from. She needs time, and I'm going to give her all the time she needs, but she'd better understand I'm not going to give up on her. She will be mine again. One of the things she brought up stuck with me: Shea. I have been avoiding dealing with her since we came home drunk, but there's no avoiding dealing with her any longer.

I need to talk to Shea and she's not going to like what I have to say! Finding out that she's been spreading rumours, especially to Elly, is the last straw. Elly's my priority now.

I messaged Shea first thing this morning to book a meeting, she should be here shortly. Blake has offered to sit in on the meeting, just to make sure she doesn't pull any stunts. I need this to run smoothly. We don't want to make an enemy out of her, but she needs to know where I stand.

I hear Claudia greet her at the front desk, "Good afternoon, welcome to The Green Door. Can I help you?"

"No, I'm here to see Fraser, he knows I'm coming," Shea barks, rudely dismissing her. I can hear her power walking down the hall with her heels tapping along our floorboards. She walks everywhere like she's on a mission.

"Fraser, you wanted to see me?" She walks into my office, standing her umbrella by the door, and takes a seat. She's dressed in a short body-fitting dress with her tits on full display. You can tell she means business, and I'm not talking about anything to do with real estate.

"Yes, thanks for coming. Sorry for the late notice. I'll just grab Blake so he can join us for this meeting."

"I'm sure we can work whatever this is out ourselves, you don't need to bother Blake."

"That's okay, it's not a bother to him, and it's a business matter so he wanted to be included."

I walk into his office, "Shea's here for the meeting."

"No worries, I'll be right there." He follows me in and takes a seat beside me.

"So, what's all this about then, boys?" she says. Sitting tall in her chair, one leg crossed over the other, her hands resting on her lap tapping her long red nails impatiently. Her eyes look between me and Blake.

"Shea, we both appreciate the wonderful job you do for us every time we need a property sold, and the past 12 months have been a pleasure working with you, but going forward, we have decided to go in a different direction for all of our sales. We feel it's best for the company."

She stiffens in her chair and her eyes go straight to me.

"What? What are you talking about? You know I'm the best agent around. How could anyone else be better for the job than me?" Now she looks pissed, and I'm sure if it weren't for all the Botox injections in her forehead it would be wrinkled with concern.

"That you are, the way you work and get the best price every time is nothing short of impressive. I'm sure you will be very busy with the upcoming spring season, but at this time, we have decided it's just best for the company to go another way moving forward."

"Nothing to do with what happened the other week then?" she sneers. Her eyes are still fixed on mine. She's furious. You can practically see the steam coming from her ears.

"Let's keep this professional, hey," cautions Blake.

She whips her head over to look at Blake. "Blake, I think it's time for you to leave. This is clearly more than just business, and I need to talk to Fraser in private. Close the door on your way out."

He looks back to me and I nod. "Okay, I'll be in my office if you need me." He gets up and walks back into his office, leaving the door open.

Shea gets up from her seat and makes her way over to me, sitting on my desk and crossing one leg over the other. The way she moves is very calculated. This woman is used to getting what she wants, and she's happy to use her body to make that happen. She leans over, giving me a full view down her top. "So, what's really going on with you, Fraser?" she says, placing her hand on my arm. "You bring me back to your place the other week, I thought we were having a good time until Blake put a stop to it. Is he into you or something?"

"That's a definite no!"

"I thought we were finally getting somewhere. It's been clear how into me you are, and after the last year flirting with each other, I knew it was only a matter of time before we ended up together. Then you don't respond to my messages, and now this! Trying to block me out completely. What's going on?" She looks really upset. I didn't even see it from her perspective before.

"I'm sorry, Shea, it was never going to happen with us. I'm in love with someone else. I was in a really bad place that night, and I'm sorry it went as far as it did. I didn't mean for you to get caught up in my mess. One of the reasons I just don't think we should work together anymore. Lines have been blurred, and we can't keep it professional anymore, don't you think?"

She removes her hand from my arm like I have just burnt her. "I think I see pretty clearly how it is, Fraser... what, you're back with little miss goody two-shoes and she's told you not to work with me anymore? Is that what's going on here?"

"No, Shea, it's just what I said, simple as that. Now, unless there is anything business-related to discuss, I think this meeting is done. Don't you?"

She's mad, I can tell, but she hops off my desk, smooths out her dress, and turns to me with a glare I have never seen from her before. "You will regret this decision, Fraser. No one dismisses me like this. It doesn't work like that in this town." She grabs her umbrella and struts out of my office as fast as she can.

What the fuck was that look? Now I believe the rumours. She's a total bitch when she doesn't get her own way. I mean, what could she actually do, anyway? I have as much pull in this town as she does. She's just all talk, and other than a couple of loose ends we need to tie up with the Broken Point townhouses, I shouldn't have to deal with her again, and hopefully, that will be the end of it.

Elena

Indie and I ceremonially hang up our aprons and give each other a high five as Rachel closes the front door. Today is our last shift at the café. We have officially resigned, with more work than we can handle coming our way in our styling business. It was time, and I can honestly say I will not miss this place.

Well, maybe some of the customers. Tristan and I have become quite good friends and seeing his smiling face as he walks through the café makes my day. He's back in the dating game and has been coming into the café regularly to give me updates on his terrible dates. He has worse luck than me! The rest of it, like the bloody coffee machine that hates me and that mothers' group that insists on coming in every Wednesday morning with screaming toddlers, I will not miss one bit.

Rachel, the café owner, has organised a bit of a party for us after we closed today. We make our way to the courtyard out the back to see a golden 'Good Luck' sign, hanging from two branches on the old tree.

"Girls, I'm going to miss you, this place will not be the same without your smiling faces. No new staff will compare. I have no idea what I'm going to do without you."

We both hug her. "Good luck with your new business," she tells us, "don't forget about us when you get rich and famous."

We laugh. "I'm pretty sure we're not going to get rich

and famous. Keep our positions open, we might be back within the month," I laugh.

Indie bumps me with her hip. "Not this time, Elly, we've got this."

"I'm sure you two will be amazing." Rachel smiles warmly. "Now let's celebrate with some cake."

I'm pretty sure her speech was aimed at Indie. She's been here a lot longer than me and she was Rachel's right-hand gal. She's going to be lost without her. She's also made the most delicious black forest cake, like the one she did for my birthday. I'm secretly hoping there'll be some left after the party so we can take it home with us. It's the first thing I have eaten in weeks that hasn't made me feel sick.

Indie is chatting to Luca, and Tristan has come along with him. They have just arrived. Tristan's eyes go straight to me. He mutters something to Luca then walks through the party over to where I'm sitting, with that same cheeky smile on his face.

"Hey, Elly." He smiles warmly.

"Hey, Tris," I say, throwing my arms around him in a hug. "Thought you would have something better to do with your Saturday afternoon than come to our farewell party, like a ridiculously bad date to be on or something."

"What's the point when I won't have my favourite barista to tell the story to on Monday?"

"True, you'll have to make friends with the new girls, but they won't be as much fun."

His dark eyes are locked with mine. He's really intense today. Why do I get the feeling something is different with him? "Or as beautiful, I'm sure." I blush instantly at his kind words. Shit, something has changed, we're back on this.

"I'm sure they will be better at making coffee, that machine can't hate them as much as it does me!" I laugh, trying to break the tension he's creating. What's going on with him today? Ever since that double date we had, it's been just friendship, nothing else.

"Why do you do that, Elly? Deflect the compliment I give you by putting yourself down?"

"I don't know, I guess I don't really know what to say when you give me a compliment like that."

"Say thank you. Do you even know what you do to me?" He runs his hands through his hair in frustration, his eyes are back fixed on me. "Let me take you out again."

"You're asking me out again?" I gasp in surprise.

"Why not? It's been enough time for you to get over your ex, and we clearly have fun when we're together. There's more than just friendship here, Elly, I know you can feel it too," he says, picking up my hands and pulling me closer to him. I can see the hunger in his eyes, but I can't do this with him. I take a step back, dropping his hands.

"I'm sorry if I've led you on, Tris, but this is just friendship for me. I can't do anything more than that."

He now looks pissed, "So it's true then? You're back with him?"

"No, where did you hear that?"

"It's a small town, people talk, and that's what they're saying."

"I'm not, but we're trying to work things out. We have a lot of history, it's complicated."

"I can't be friends with you anymore, Elly," he says sadly.

"I'm sorry, Tris, that's all I can do." I really am sorry. I like him, just not the way he wants me to.

"Guess I'll see you around then, Elly." He turns with a deflated smile.

"I'm sorry, Tris," I call after him.

He walks away and I feel so bad, but it's just not going to happen between us. I'm in love with someone else.

I need more cake. I cut another slice and move to sit at the table under the big fig tree. The cake will make me feel less guilty. I've gone from feeling completely alone, wondering what's wrong with me, to fighting them off when I just want to be alone. "How did we get here, Elly, how did it all get so complicated?" I mutter to myself.

I laugh to myself at how fucked up the timing in life can be sometimes. Then I realise I'm in public. Indie's probably right, I must be ready for that straitjacket. I'm not just talking to myself but laughing out loud. I must look completely crazy.

I don't know what Tristan's heard and who from, but we're not back together yet. I know it's what Fraser wants, and after what he told me the other day, I can't stop thinking about it. All my heart hurts for him.

I feel bad I haven't reached out to him. What he's going through is heavy and he and his dad have a lot to work through. I'm just not ready to go back to what we were just yet. I know it's selfish, but I need this time to sort out my own life, just like he needs time to work through his past.

Now's my time to work out my life by myself. I need to know I can do this on my own, not have to always rely on a guy to follow through life. When I'm ready, if Fraser's still interested, I will give it another go with him, but only on my terms.

But starting something up with someone else, even if he's as good-looking and nice as Tristan, is a bad idea when I know my heart lies with Fraser, it always has. It makes me sad that I can't keep Tristan as a friend, but I also understand sometimes it's just too hard.

Indie leaves Luca's side and comes to sit next to me.

"You okay, chick? We saw Tristan take off, what happened?"

"He wanted more than just friendship. I can't give him that, I was just being honest with him. Now I feel terrible."

"You did the right thing, you can't lead him on if you're not interested."

"Was I leading him on?"

"No, not at all. I just meant, it's best to let him know now. He's a big boy, he'll be fine." She pats me on the leg, "Come on, this is a happy day. We're celebrating moving onto bigger and better things."

"I'm happy," I mutter, faking a smile.

"Nice try." She gives me her best smile back.

"I'm going to get going. Looks like the party's wrapping up anyway." I say my goodbyes, leaving Indie chatting to Rachel, and start the short walk to Mum and Dad's for the afternoon. I wish Drew was around. It's times like this I need him. Our phone conversation yesterday wasn't much help. He sounded distracted. When he's back competing, he can be vague. He puts everything he's got into working out and doing what he can to be at his best. Guess my silly boyfriend problems aren't really that important when you're trying to be the number one surfer in the world.

CHAPTER TWENTY-SEVEN

ELENA

I AM WOKEN TO A SUDDEN THUMP ON THE BED NEXT TO me and roll over to see a smiling Indie, all bouncing and excited.

"What are you doing? It's early Sunday morning, my sleep-in day," I grumble, slapping her away. She rolls out of my bed, pushing back the curtains, blinding me with daylight. I shield my eyes with my hands, but there's no chance I'll go back to sleep now.

"Not today. We're going to the beach. It's going to be a beautiful day. See? Look how stunning it is out there. We can't just lie about all day in bed, and besides, Blake and I have decided we need to get you out of the house. Get some colour on that skin of yours," she teases. She's way too enthusiastic for this time of the morning, and on a Sunday, I would prefer lazing about feeling sorry for myself.

"Sorry I'm not tanned year-round like you! Why does Blake care, anyway?"

"He misses you, Elly. Come on, we need fun Elly back." She's pouting her lips at me now and giving me the sad puppy-dog eyes.

I push the covers back, defeated. "Okay, you win, I'll come, but why do we have to leave so early?"

"To get a good spot. It's school holidays. It's going to be packed down there with all the tourists. Come on, get up, we're spending the day down there. I've packed lunch already, and Theo and Fi will meet us down there."

"Grr, give me time to wake up and have a shower."

"Atta girl, you might even have fun," she says with a wink, leaving me to get ready.

After a shower I'm feeling much more enthusiastic for a beach day. Maybe Indie's peppiness is rubbing off on me. I think it's just what I need. Maybe Indie's right, it is a beautiful day, and I can feel the warmth of the sun calling my name from my room. I wonder where my swimmers and hat are. I haven't had to use them since the move. I rummage through my wardrobe and find my floppy straw hat and pineapple bikini. This will have to do. I throw my bikini on with a simple white cotton dress over the top. Some lip gloss and waterproof mascara to finish the look. No makeup today; what's the point if I'm going to have to cover it in sunscreen as soon as we get down there?

Indie and I walk down to the beach, passing all the cute touristy shops on our way. Luckily we live so close with the amount of items Indie's bringing with us. I feel like a packhorse. We've got a picnic basket she tells me is full of food for the whole day (she must be forgetting how much Theo eats), an umbrella, some sort of ball game, towels, and sunscreen. She really has thought of it all.

As we walk closer, I can make out the shadowy figures of Theo, Fi, and Blake, and one other, Fraser. I knew there was more to this little day at the beach than she originally let on. She just loves playing matchmaker and this is right up her alley. I'm surprised she hadn't tried something like this sooner.

"Forget to mention Fraser would be here, did you? I would hit you, but my hands are full," I say, glaring at her. She has a smug smile on her face.

"Did I? I thought I told you that. Sorry, too late to back out now, though, they've seen us," she says, raising the arm with the umbrella in it to wave.

"Hmm, convenient, Indie. I will remember this."

"What! Don't give me a hard time, Elly. It's time you two got your shit together. He's been the perfect gentleman for weeks now, trying his best to win you back. Don't you think it's time you forgave him so you two can get on with your happy lives together? Plus, I want to be a bridesmaid at your wedding, so you need to work it out before I'm old and ugly," she says, batting her eyelashes at me.

"What are you on about, there's no wedding. You do remember what he did, don't you? You were the one saying I needed to get over him, he wasn't worth it, now you're team Fraser all of a sudden."

"Yeah, but we didn't have all the facts then, did we? Now we do. I kind of get why he acted that way, don't you?"

"Yeah, but I don't want him to think I'm some weak little pushover who'll allow him to treat me badly."

"I'm pretty sure he doesn't think that. You scare the shit out of us when you're mad! He's done his time, Elly. He knows he fucked up, and from what Blake tells me, he's been through hell with this psychologist over the past month working through all his past traumas. He needs you. Do you still want to be with him?"

"Of course I do. How could you even ask that?"

"Don't you think it's time then?"

"Maybe," I shrug. She is right. It's been two weeks since

he came and told me about his family situation. I really do need to see him and work this all out.

Fraser sees us coming and his eyes are fixed on me as I make my way down the beach. All of a sudden, I'm feeling very self-conscious of my lack of makeup. Why didn't I take a bit longer to get ready? I should have known Indie was up to something. Fraser's lying on his towel, shirt off, his broad chest on full display. I'd almost forgotten how hot he was with his shirt off. Man, today's going to be hard.

We finally arrive in the middle of the beach where they've set up camp for the day. It felt like an eternity dragging all this stuff with us. The boys jump up to help us get everything set up.

"Hey, you guys are finally here," calls Fiona excitedly.

"Sorry, I couldn't get Elly out of bed," Indie says, and I throw her a death stare.

"It's a Sunday. How are you lot so happy about being up so early?"

"Wow, you girls brought the whole set-up," grumbles Blake, trying to work out the umbrella.

"It pays to be prepared, Blake, you'll thank me later when you need something," explains Indie, taking over with the umbrella, showing him how it's done.

"You know you live around the corner and could go home at any time if you need something, right?"

"Yes, but I would prefer not to," Indie bites back, laying out her towel. I think they've been spending too much time together, they're starting to sound like an old married couple.

Fraser's standing behind me, after laying my towel out on the sand for me. He whispers in my ear, "Elly, you look gorgeous as always." His words leaving a scattering of goosebumps down my arms. He still has the same effect on me.

This is why I have been avoiding him. I have no idea how he does it, but my body is on high alert whenever he's around me. My skin tingling, my lips waiting for his—ah, what am I saying? Stop daydreaming like it's old times! It's not, this is the same dick that broke your heart not that long ago.

"Thank you," I smile.

"Come for a walk with me, I want to show you something."

"Okay. You going to put a shirt on?" My eyes can't help but roam over his chest, remembering how he felt under my touch.

He raises a brow at me, "Why, you getting excited?"

"No, just worried you might get sunburnt, it's pretty hot today," I tease with a little smirk.

"That's not what your eyes are saying. Are you offering to help me out and rub sunscreen on for me?"

I shake my head. The last thing I need to do is touch him right now, I'm already not thinking straight.

"Think I'll leave it off. Take my chances with the sun then." He grins back at me; he knows what he's doing, he doesn't play fair.

I swallow the lump forming in my throat. Well, this is going to make it hard to concentrate on what he wants to talk about. Already all I can think about is how his muscular chest would feel under my hands.

We walk up the beach a little.

"How's your dad going?" he asks.

"Really well, starting to look like his old self again. But you already knew that cause you've been going to visit him every couple of days."

"Yeah, I have. Still, just checking. I didn't see him yesterday."

"How's your dad, Fraser? Is he still staying here?" So,

we're doing awkward small talk. I'm not sure what else to say. I want to jump into his arms, run my hands through his hair, while he kisses me.

"They left last week for a new adventure up the coast."

"It must be nice to be able to pack up and leave, just go wherever you feel like, whenever you like."

"Yeah, it suits them perfectly. It was nice to have him home for a while, though, I needed it more than I knew."

"Yeah, I bet. I'm glad you had that time with them. Are you guys good with each other after everything that happened?"

We have stopped walking now and stand side by side looking out over the water. If I make eye contact with him, I'm gone, I just know it.

"Yeah, we've talked it all through. We're as good as we can be. It's never going to be perfect, but I'm lucky to have someone who cares about me so much. He's such a good man. I only hope I can be as good a dad as he is one day when I have kids."

I look over to him; is he serious? "Fraser Davis thinking about having a family one day. Who is this psychologist? And what has she done with the boy I once knew?"

His eyes come back to mine and his face softens a little. "It's time to grow up, Elly. The last month has been really hard, but it's what I needed, and now I've got a really clear vision of what I want for my life." He offers me a smile. He's looking like his old self again.

He sits down on the sand and pats the spot next to him for me to sit with him.

"I've got something I want to show you. I hope you're as excited about it as me. I'm nervous to show you in case you're not."

"Nervous? You're never nervous about anything. What is it?"

"Yeah, but this is something I really want to work." He pulls out his phone and starts scrolling through. "It's this." On the screen of his phone is a photo of an empty block of land.

"What is this?"

"You know how much you loved the town of Broken Point when we were working on the townhouses there? Well, a couple of weeks ago, I saw this come up for sale. It's a couple of blocks back from the beach and on a massive plot of land, it's perfect." He looks up at me, his grey eyes melting the walls I've put up.

"It looks great! Are you boys doing a new development there?" I say excitedly.

"I bought it," he smiles sheepishly.

"Are you serious? This looks amazing, I'm so happy for you, Fraser, this is exciting. So I guess you will be designing your place to put on there? I knew Blake wanted to build his own home, but I didn't know you were looking to settle in one place."

"I'll be designing our own place to put on the block. I bought it for us, Elly. I've been saving for quite a while, and now I have someone I want to do this with. We can build a home for us to live in. I know I said I would wait, and I will wait as long as you need, but you're the only one I see in my future, and I'm kind of hoping this will be the start of a new life for us. A life where we work together so we can both be happy. So, I'll do the architectural designs, but I want you to do the interiors so we can design it together."

"For us? I don't know what to say. I'm in absolute shock!" I take the phone from him and look at the block again. He bought this for us?

"The block can sit there as long as we need, we don't need to rush into anything if you're not ready for it."

I have no idea how to process this. I sit looking at the photo of the block on his phone again. Is he serious, a block of land for us to build our dream home on? I should be angry with him for making this decision without me, but I'm not. This is the sweetest thing anyone has ever done for me, not buying the block, but making the commitment to our future together, and he did it knowing I could reject him. I can't help it, my face breaks into a massive smile.

"So I take it, by the smile, you're happy? I did the right thing?" He looks so nervous, still waiting for me to reply.

"Yes." I wrap my arms around his neck and bring our faces together. "Yes, good decision." Our lips meet, and our kiss is perfection. God, I have missed him. His stubble brushes my face as my hands roam through his hair. He swipes his tongue into my waiting mouth. I hear a couple of kids laughing, and I'm suddenly aware that I'm now straddling him, in the middle of the beach, on a Sunday morning. A bit too much for the poor passers-by. I shift away and stand up, pulling him with me. "Come on, we should get back to the others."

"Elly, what's this?" He runs his finger over my wrist.

"Oh, that, um, it's a little coffee cup."

"Why do you have a tattoo of a little coffee cup on your wrist?"

"It's a long story, but Indie's got one too. It's kind of a bestie thing."

He raises his eyebrow at me. "That surprises me less because she's covered in tattoos. I can't believe you got one, even if it is small, the way you are with needles."

"It wasn't a pretty sight! But luckily it was over quickly. I was very brave," I say, laughing.

He runs his finger over it again. "I feel like I've missed so much over the last couple of months. I'm so sorry, Elly."

"It is what it is. It's all done now, so let's just concentrate on the future. Come on, we better get back to the rest of them." I try to pull him along, but he stands still.

"Oh, I just want you all to myself a bit longer." His lips are on mine again, pulling me into his body for another kiss. Then down onto the sand with him. The rest of the world disappears as we kiss in a tangled mess. All I can think of is him, his hands on my skin, the feel of his bare chest pressing against mine, and the hardness I feel pushing into me. He's missed me all right. Right now, I can feel how much.

He pulls away this time, looking into my eyes. "We're in this together now, Elly, I won't run again."

"I know, Fraser. This is it now." He looks happy with that answer and gives me one more small kiss.

"Okay, let's get back to them then. We have some exciting news to tell." The smile on his face is priceless. I think this is the happiest I have ever seen him.

"Fraser, before we do, let's get a few things straight. I will be paying half the mortgage. I don't need you to take care of me. If we're in this together, I want to be equal."

"Let's work out the details later and just enjoy the moment, hey, 'Miss Independent'."

"You can't start calling me that too, you've been talking to my dad too much." He just laughs at me.

We walk back up the beach to the others, hand in hand.

"Finally." Indie jumps up all excited and comes over to hug us. "Nice to see you two have worked things out."

"Calm down, Indie," I say with a smile.

"We're heading in for a swim. You two coming?" calls Blake.

It's been such a beautiful sunny day. It's only

September, but you can tell winter is over and we're going into my favourite time of year, where the days are longer and warmer. And after our chat this morning, it feels like everything's about to get a whole lot better.

WE'VE BEEN FOR A SWIM, THEN ATTEMPTED TO PLAY the beach volleyball game that Indie brought, but it got too competitive, so we pulled the pin. The lunch Indie brought for us is delicious.

The boys have gone back into the water. We finish off our lunch and laze around on our towels.

"Hey, Elly, why aren't you eating like your normal piggy self?" Fiona asks. "If you don't eat it, I'm going to have to. I can't help myself, this baby is a hungry one." She pats her stomach.

"Hey, thanks! I don't eat like a pig!"

"Not today anyway," Fiona and Indie say, both laughing at me.

"I don't know, I just haven't been feeling well lately. Food's hard to stomach."

"Sounds like you're pregnant to me," scoffs Fiona, laughing at her own joke.

Indie hits me on the arm "That's it! Fi's right, it does sound like you're pregnant."

"Really funny, girls."

Her eyes have gone wide and she looks scared. "No, really think about it, Elly, you have felt sick for a couple of months now, you haven't been yourself. I think Fi's onto something here."

"Don't be silly. That's just all the stress worrying about Dad." They're looking between each other, like I'm missing something that they understand completely.

"Stop that."

"Doesn't explain the blockbusters, there's more than stress going on there," Indie adds, pointing to my tits.

"Hey!" I cover myself up. She's right, though, these things will barely fit in my bikini. I was thinking it must have shrunk. "There's no way I'm pregnant. You have to have sex for that to happen, and if you two remember correctly, I've been moping around the house by myself for the last couple of months."

"Yeah, but before that you weren't. You might be a few months along. I didn't work out I was pregnant until I missed my second period. I was busy with work and just hadn't thought about it. By the time I took the test, we were already eight weeks along."

"Yeah, but the last time I had sex was like two and a half months ago. If I was pregnant, I would have known by now. You would be able to tell, right? Plus, we always used protection."

But if I think back to that last night, did we? I don't remember him stopping to grab protection. We missed each other, we were in the moment, and I'm pretty sure he was drunk too. Now that I think back, after everything he said the other day... shit, maybe we didn't. But I'm on the pill so should be fine, yeah, I'm sure it's fine. If I'm fine, though, why are my hands all of a sudden so sweaty?

"You've gone pale, Elly, you okay?" asks Indie. I can tell she's worried.

"I'm on the pill, so even if we didn't use protection, I would've been covered, so I'm not, it's all good." My heart is beating faster, and my hands are all shaky. I don't want kids yet. I'm not, I can't be.

"When was your last period?" asks Fi.

"Um, this sounds bad, but I have no idea. I'm on the

pill. I just take it until I start to spot, then I have a week off for a period. It only happens every three to four months, and now that I think about it, it's been a while. Like, maybe before I started hooking up with Fraser. I don't know when."

"Shit, Elly, we need to get you a test!" says Fi.

"No, I'm fine, it's not that, it can't be. Not now when things are starting to work out. I'm just stressed at the moment, that's all." I shake my hands out, trying to stop them from shaking.

The boys start to make their way out of the water. "Don't either of you say anything of this to them," I say, pointing to the boys. "I know what Theo is like with information. He'll run back to Mum and Dad with it and the whole town will think I'm pregnant by dinner." I give them my best death stare and they signal that their lips are sealed.

Now what do I do? I'm not. I couldn't be, could I? Do I get a test and see or just stop taking my pills to see if my period comes? Why did they have to put this in my head? Here I was thinking my luck was changing and I could just relax, and now I've got something new to worry about. Even worse, if I am pregnant, Fraser is going to freak out. There's no way he's ready for a kid. He's going to run for it again, and I'm going to be left to deal with this alone.

The boys come and stand over us dripping, making us wet. "Hey, what are ya doing?" I scream.

"You girls looked hot, thought we would cool you down," teases Theo, as they all laugh at each other. I should've known this was his idea.

We jump up and dry off.

Fi's packing up. "It's probably time for us to get going, Theo. We have stuff to do this arvo and Elly has just realised she has forgotten to do something important, she better get home and do it."

I look over to her and shake my head. She's so subtle. Not! Bloody Theo will be questioning her all the way home now. "Think I'm going to head home too," I say, starting to pack up.

Fraser wraps his wet arms around me, pulling me into him. "Can I come home with you? I don't want to rush you, but I've missed you."

"I've missed you too. How about you give me time to have a shower and get myself ready. Then I just have to drop in and see Mum and Dad. I'll come round to your place after that so we can do something tonight and celebrate."

"You okay, gorgeous? You don't look right," Fraser asks.

"Yeah, I think so, just too much sun."

"Okay, I'll see you tonight." He kisses me goodbye, and Indie and I head back to our apartment. I need to get a test before tonight. I can't wait any longer. I want to know what I'm dealing with."

CHAPTER TWENTY-EIGHT

FRASER

There's a knock at the door, that'll be Elly. She must be keen to see me again, she's earlier than we agreed.

I open the door. "Well, this is a pleasant surprise, couldn't stay away from me any longer, hey?"

"No, no, it's not... We need to talk, Fraser." She looks sick. She's white as a ghost.

"Okay, what's wrong? You don't look so good." I take her hand and lead her into the house. "Do you need some water or something?"

"It's not good. This is bad, very bad, Fraser. I'm freaking out." She's pacing back and forth and running her hands through her hair.

"What is it, Elly? You're starting to scare me. Has something happened with your dad?"

"No, Dad's fine... Oh my goodness, I can't do this, I can't even tell you." Her breathing is short and sharp. She looks like she's about to have a panic attack. She's really freaking out. She's shaking her head and muttering to herself.

I wrap my arms around her, trying to comfort her. "Hey, hey, come on, Elly, just breathe. I'm not sure what could have happened that's so bad since I saw you a couple of hours ago, but whatever this is, it'll be fine, we can work it out together. Come on, just slow down your breathing or you're going to pass out." I walk her over to the lounge. "Come and sit down. I'll get you some water." I help her sit down then run into the kitchen to fill a glass of water and run back to her. "Here, this will make you feel better."

She shakes her head. Her eyes are big and scared-looking. She slowly drinks some of the water then sits there staring at it. She won't even look at me. "Nothing can make this better, Fraser, nothing."

"Well, Cherie thinks the best thing to do, when something seems all too much, is to talk to someone about it and work out a solution together. Nothing is ever so bad you can't work it out."

"Cherie?"

"My psychologist."

"Oh, well, she's wrong this time. When I tell you, it's going to make you freak out too."

I put a finger under her chin to raise her face to mine. "Come on, look at me, Elly." Her eyes rise to look at me and they're welling with tears. "Just tell me. What is it?"

She opens her handbag and hands over a long pink-and-white stick. "There are two blue lines," is all she can say.

"Is this what I think it is?" She nods her head and bursts into tears.

"It's okay, Elly. Everything's going to be all right." I wrap my arms around her as she cries into my neck. I can't believe that she's pregnant. This is insane!

We sit with our arms wrapped around each other until her tears calm down. I pull her back to look at her again, wiping the last of her tears away with my thumb. "It's going to be okay. We can work this out. Do you know how far along you are?"

"I don't know. The last time I had sex was the night you left. So maybe twelve weeks, according to the Google search I did, but it could be longer?"

"So it's mine?" I half joke with a cheeky smile. But it has been a while since we were together, she could have been with someone else, I guess.

"Of course it is! Who else would it be?" she cries, slapping me across the chest.

"Sorry, I was just joking, trying to lighten the mood." Thank God, I couldn't handle the thought of her with someone else.

"Not funny, Fraser! Why aren't you freaking out, like me?"

"I don't know, Elly. I just don't feel like this is a bad thing. I know I've fucked up royally with you these last couple of months, but I love you. I've loved you for a long time. You're my girl and the only one I could ever imagine having a family with. I know we're still just working things out, but I'm here for you, and I'll be here for our baby too, even if it's just as your friend," I say, grabbing her hand.

"You love me?" Her eyes meet mine. She looks so unsure. How could she not know how I feel about her? It's now I realise how one-sided things have always been. She's right, I've been so selfish. She's so open with me, but I'm so guarded. I never really give her my all, worried I will get hurt myself, but I've hurt her all along instead.

I cup her face with my hands and stare into her beautiful eyes. "I always have, I just have a stupid way of showing it."

"You can say that again! I'm so scared, Fraser. I don't think I can do this. I'm not ready to be a mum."

"Gorgeous, you don't have to do this alone, we're in this together. I'll be here every step of the way. I promise I will never leave you again."

Her beautiful sad eyes stare into mine. Her cheeks have tear stains running down them and her mascara is smeared under her eyes, but she's still the most beautiful woman I have ever seen. And to think she's carrying our baby.

My hands go to the back of her head. I lace my fingers through her long hair as I kiss her slowly. "I love you, Elly." She nods as she kisses me back. I pick her up, pulling her onto my lap. As we continue to kiss, her hair falls around her face. She smells like vanilla and coconut, it smells like her, like coming home. Her soft lips are salty from her tears, and I kiss her again, trying to kiss away the fear she's feeling.

I wrap my arms around her. I want her to feel safe with me. I know I've screwed up in the past, but I want her to feel my arms around her now and know I've got her. I will be here for her through all of this.

She responds by kissing me back, more passionately now, and when she pulls back to look at me, I can see the look in her eyes has changed. There's that hint of naughtiness there.

"I've missed you, Fraser," she whispers into my lips, kissing me.

"I've missed you too, Elly." My hands wrap around her tighter and I pull her into me, kissing her back with intensity. She's in my arms, where she belongs, and I never want to let her go again.

"My body's missed you," she mumbles into my mouth. She slightly grinds herself on me and my cock instantly springs to life, and I suddenly feel like my pants are way too tight.

She kisses down my neck then back to my lips more aggressively, and I match her. It's been far too long. I need to feel her body close to mine. My hands run through her hair as I hold her close to me, as her lips smash with mine desperately. We can't get enough of each other, it's been too long apart.

She slowly stands up, pulling my hands to follow her down the hallway to my room. She removes my shirt over my head as I lift her dress over hers. We stand chest to chest, hugging each other's bodies, feeling the familiar closeness and warmth of our skin to skin.

This is new territory for me. For the first time in my life, I'm not sure what to do in the bedroom. I want to rip off her clothes and fuck her hard, like I normally would, but I'm scared I'll hurt the baby. Is that a thing? Can you hurt the baby? Surely people fuck all the time while they're pregnant, but I'm just wrapping my head around this new information, and I have absolutely no idea. I rest my hand on her belly, rubbing my finger back and forth, and her hand comes to rest on mine. Neither of us say a thing but just feel this moment together and what it means.

She takes the first move, rising on to her tippy toes to kiss me, her hands in my hair as she pulls me in closer to her and our kiss intensifies. I can feel her touch dust over my arms as she makes her way down my body, her fingers making quick work of my belt buckle, and she unzips my pants, dropping them to the floor. I undo her bra, sliding it down her arms and freeing those fantastically round, perky tits of hers. My hands go straight to them, cupping them and massaging. "I've missed your tits."

"Of course you have," she groans, rolling her eyes at me.

"They're fucking huge, Elly."

"I know." She lowers her head, burying it in her hands

like she's embarrassed. I kick the rest of my pants off then slowly navigate her towards my bed, pushing her down onto the mattress. I take her left breast in my mouth, circling her nipple and sucking hard, making her moan in pleasure. Then I take the other and do the same thing. Her body is extra responsive, and every little move I make has her moaning and raising her hips off the bed, looking for more.

I make my way down to her panties, hooking them with my thumbs and dragging them down her long legs, discarding them on the floor. Then I'm back between her legs, spreading them wide. I bury my face in her pussy, tasting her. Man, I've missed this, it's fucking heaven. I lick her, circling my tongue around her clit.

Her hands go to the back of my head as she starts to ride my face, her hips slowly moving back and forth. "Fuck, Fraser, that feels so good, don't stop." She moans, applying more pressure to my head as I slide my fingers into her dripping pussy. Then with my free hand, I reach for her breast, squeezing her nipple while working her clit with my tongue. I pump my fingers in and out as she arches her back off the bed, moaning in pleasure. I can feel her pussy tighten. "Fuck, Fraser, fuck," she cries out as she convulses around my fingers, completely letting go as she rides through her orgasm.

"Mmmm, Fraser, that was so good... more, I want more," she mutters. Running her hand over her body and reaching down for me. "I want to feel you inside me."

I look back at her, not sure what to do. I want to fuck her badly too, but how does this work?

She looks at me, confused. "Fraser, I need you inside me. What are you waiting for, no condom needed this time?"

"Um, I'm just worried about... well, you know, that I'm going to hurt the baby?"

She looks down at me and her face breaks into a huge smile. "Oh, baby, it's so nice you care so much, but right now all you need to worry about is keeping me happy. We're not going to hurt the baby, get up here and fuck me."

She doesn't have to tell me twice. "Spread your legs wider," I command.

She does what I say with the sexiest fucking smile I have ever seen. I lift her legs so they're over mine and run my cock up and down her slick folds, teasing her as I push straight in, balls deep.

She closes her eyes and moans, "Yes, Fraser. Fuck, it feels good to have you inside me again." I dig my fingers into her hips as she rises off the bed to meet my rhythm. Fuck, this is so good, our bodies moving together like they were made for this, for each other. I tease her with every pump, in and out. Her eyes are on mine, silently begging me for more, and as I pick up the pace, her lips go into a perfect O shape as her eyes roll back in her head.

"Elly, you need to come." I can feel my balls tighten as she screams out my name, riding her orgasm. I cover her mouth with mine, swallowing her cries of pleasure in my kiss.

"You're mine, Elly, forever."

CHAPTER TWENTY-NINE

FRASER

Today has been unlike any other. We had the first ultrasound appointment and got to see our baby. The radiologist places Elly at about thirteen weeks along. Seeing that little bean on the screen, and hearing the heart beating, was unlike anything I've ever experienced.

I think this week we've both finally come to terms with the fact that we're going to be parents. And watching Elly's beautiful smiling face as she watched our baby move around on the ultrasound screen tells me she's not freaking out anymore. She wants this as much as I do. We're going to be a family.

From the ultrasound appointment, we went straight to visit Jim and Anne to share our news. They were both surprised but very excited for us. Then we called Dad and Janice. I could hear Janice's excited scream through the phone. She never had any kids of her own, but I can tell this is going to be one spoiled grandbaby.

I almost have to pinch myself at how quickly things have turned around for me. For the first time in my life, I look into the future and can see only good things. My own little family in the beautiful home we built together, full of love and happiness. This may have happened a little earlier than we would have planned, but this baby will know every day how loved they are.

We're back at Elly's apartment now, lying on her bed. She was exhausted after our day and needed an afternoon nap. I look over to her. Her eyes are still closed with her golden locks falling around her face, she looks perfect. As if feeling my gaze, she starts to stir, rolling over. I pull her into my body, resting my hand on her belly. You can't even tell by looking at her that she's pregnant. Other than the massive tits, she looks the same, but after seeing that image on the screen, I feel like putting my hand on her belly so I connect with our baby. She rests her hand on top of mine, and I brush her hair away from her neck so I can kiss her.

"We should go out for dinner tonight. We could meet up with Blake and Indie and tell them our good news," I say.

"I think Indie already knows. It was her and Fi that guessed, that's why I took the test," she mutters sleepily.

"Well, we can go out and officially announce our news and celebrate with them."

"That sounds nice. Can we get Mexican?"

I kiss her neck. "Anything you want, gorgeous."

"Good, because I'm starving, and I've been thinking about tacos all day. I'll message Indie." She sits up, stretching and pulling her hair into a messy bun on top of her head. She grabs her phone off the bedside table, typing the text. "Indie's in," she says, smiling into her phone as she returns it to her bedside.

I roll over and text Blake, a reply bouncing back straight away. "Blake's in. He'll meet us at six. So we'd better get up and get ready."

Elly jumps up, opening her wardrobe. I assume she's searching for the perfect outfit for dinner.

I message Blake back and put my phone down. As soon as I do, another message bounces in, and I see a message from Shea.

Elly looks back to me for the response from Blake. "What's wrong, why are you looking at your phone and frowning?"

"Um, yeah. I'm just not sure what to do?" I say, double-checking my phone to make sure I've read the text correctly.

"About what?" She's back to looking through her wardrobe, grabbing items of clothing and arranging them on the bed.

"Shea has just messaged to say there is some paperwork she needs me to sign tonight. It's for the townhouses, but I can't for the life of me think what it could be. Everything should be all done for them."

She looks up from her outfit arranging, with a soft smile. "It's okay, Fraser. I know it's just business. Go do it, then you're done with her, right? You won't have to deal with her anymore."

"Yeah, true, but I don't even know what it could be."

She gathers the clothes. "I'm just going to have a shower. Go see what it is, then we can go out to dinner to celebrate." She kisses me, heading out of her room in the direction of the shower.

"Oh, not fair, I'd prefer to stay and have one of your famous long showers with you," I call after her, and she waves me off.

I turn up at Shea's place. I haven't been here before. It's nice if you like the ultra-modern look. Just a couple of streets back from the beach, this place is massive and white, with cube-like shapes stacked on more cubes. There's timber screens and massive prickly pear cacti all through the garden. It's what I would expect her to have—sleek, stylish, and a little prickly.

She probably paid next to nothing for it too, knowing her ballbuster negotiation skills. For that reason, it's a shame we won't be working with her anymore, but it was just getting too messy so it's definitely for the best.

I haven't seen her since that day in my office when we decided not to work together anymore. I'm really hoping this isn't going to be too awkward. Just get in, sign the papers, and get out of here and out to dinner with my girl. I knock on the door and Shea opens it in a rush. She must have just got home. She's in her normal business attire, a body-hugging black dress with her tits on full display.

"Hey, Fraser. Sorry to call you out like this on a Friday afternoon. It just couldn't wait. I was supposed to have this paperwork in by 5:30pm today, and I was going over it at the office when I realised your signatures were missing. Come in. Would you like a drink?"

"No, thanks, I'll just sign the papers then be on my way." I follow her into the house. We walk into a massive living room, all in white.

"Of course, you probably have something to get to with Elly?"

Why is she being so nice? There's something weird going on here.

"Yeah, we're going for dinner with friends," I say, trying to keep the conversation short but making sure she knows I'm not hanging around.

She smiles at me and it's the fakest smile I've ever seen. "Oh, how lovely. I'll just get the papers from my study, won't keep you long."

She marches down the hall on a mission, disappearing through a doorway. I turn to look around. This place is like out of a magazine or one of those perfect show homes. Nothing's out of place. It's all so neat and tidy, doesn't even look like someone lives here, not even a cup in the kitchen sink.

How strange. It looks like it's styled for sale. I thought she said it was her place in the text, but it must be one of the addresses she's selling. Guess it makes sense, it's only 5pm, she's probably still working. But I'm sure she said this was her house.

She walks back in the room with the papers from the townhouses. Placing them on the dining room table, she motions for me to sit at the table as she pulls out a chair and takes a seat next to me.

She's flicking through and checking over the papers in her hand. Nodding as she checks off each page. After she has gone through the whole document, she looks up with a sideways smirk on her face.

"I'm so sorry, Fraser, when I checked this afternoon, I was sure we had missed your signature on these, but it's here plain as day now! I have no idea how I didn't see it earlier, silly me. Sorry I wasted your time. Guess I can get these off today after all," she says, pushing her chair back and standing up.

"Okay, I guess we all make mistakes." I stand to leave. "Bye, Shea, see ya later."

"Bye, Fraser. Have a nice evening. Hope it's not too eventful," she taunts, sarcastically grinning at me.

I fake a smile and close the door. This whole thing just feels off. Shea doesn't stuff up. The whole playing dumb act isn't her. She's meticulous about everything. The even stranger thing is, she didn't try anything. The last year I have known her, she always tries something. I just want to get back to Elly and have a nice night with our friends.

Elena

I sit at the dining room table, freshly showered, in the cute outfit I picked for tonight's celebration dinner. I'm wearing a black silk singlet top with a jade-green mini skirt and my sexy knee-high boots. I figure I'd better make the most of wearing all my favourites before I'm too fat to fit in them anymore.

This sandwich looks delicious, fresh whole-grain bread with salad and mayo. Yum, this is my favourite snack this week.

Fraser will be home soon, from signing the papers at Shea's house, and we're going out for dinner with the others. I'm finally hungry again, and now I know I'm eating for two. The doctor we saw this week says I need to really work on eating enough to put back on the weight I lost and then some.

As I sit down and take my first bite, I hear a knock at the door. Oh, how annoying, who could it be?

I contemplate not answering it, we're not expecting anyone. It's probably the guy asking about solar panels again. They come at random times of the day and have been driving us nuts since we moved in. We keep telling them we don't own the place and we can't make these types of decisions. But they just send a new guy the next time and we have to go through the whole sales pitch again.

I look back at my sandwich, contemplating what to do. Ah, I better open it, it might be something important. I open the door to see Tristan leaning up against the hallway wall, hands in his jeans pockets. "Tris, what are you doing here? Are you looking for Luca? I think he and Indie are out somewhere." This is weird. I haven't seen him since the farewell party at the café a month ago. Why would he turn up on my doorstep?

"Oh, nice to see you too, Elly! I'm not looking for Luca, I'm here for you. You could at least look happy to see me."

"I am, I'm just surprised, that's all. Are you missing my awesome coffee making skills already?" I laugh. No one would be missing them.

"Yeah, something like that." He looks off, like he's on edge or something. His eyes keep darting from the stairway to the apartment.

"What's wrong? You don't look like yourself." He's normally really relaxed and carefree, but not tonight.

"Can I come in?" he asks. His dark eyes meet mine, and I feel uncomfortable. I'm not sure if it's just because I know Fraser will be home soon and he'll get jealous if he sees another guy here, or if it's because of how we left things between us. But I decide I better let him in and see what's wrong.

I motion for him to follow me in. "Of course. Do you want a coffee or something? I'm just having something to eat, before we head out for the night."

"Yeah, that would be nice, thanks. I won't stay long, don't want to interrupt your plans."

I walk into the kitchen with Tristan closely behind me, hands still in his pockets. He stands close by, a little too close, invading my personal space. He's leaning on the kitchen counter watching me as I make our drinks. I'm not sure what to say to him. I didn't really think I would see him again after how we left things. But here he is, acting all strange.

I look over to him as I pour the boiling water from the kettle, and his eyes widen as he sees the ultrasound photo on our fridge. It was the first thing Fraser did when we got home from our appointment. He's so excited about this baby, not what I was expecting from him at all.

"So it's true, you're having a baby?" he scoffs, his eyes still glued to the photo on the fridge.

"Um, yeah, it's crazy. I'm still coming to terms with it myself." I hand him his coffee hoping to break the weird tension that's building between us.

He looks at me as he takes his mug of coffee, his eyes still wide in disbelief. "Indie mentioned it, but I wanted to see it for myself. And you're back with your ex?" He looks up over his coffee.

"Yeah, we're working things out. He's really excited about the baby, so am I," I say with a smile.

"That's nice. I'm glad it's all worked out for you both." A text pings on his phone and he smiles as he reads it.

"Some good news?"

"Nah, my sister just texted something funny."

"Oh, okay. What's going on with you, Tris? What brings you here on a Friday night?"

"I was just in the neighbourhood on another bad date. It reminded me of you and our chats at the café. I thought I would check in on you. I don't get to have our daily catch-ups anymore."

"Yeah, I've missed your dating horror stories, they're always good for a laugh. What happened today?"

"Same old stuff. She was nice enough, just no chemistry. You know," he shrugs.

My tummy makes a loud rumbling noise, and I realise I haven't finished my sandwich. I walk back over to where I was sitting earlier at the dining room table, and I continue eating.

"What are the new girls like at the café? Bet they get your order right."

"They're all right, I guess, they're not you." He's looking straight into my eyes. There's a fire there and that feeling of unease washes over me again. Fraser should be home soon, and he's not going to like another guy being in my apartment, especially when he finds out we went on a date. I may have left that little detail out when I told him about how Indie and I got our tattoos. But the feeling is more than just that I can't handle Fraser being jealous, especially when he's got nothing to worry about. It's that there is actually nothing between Tristan and me, at least not on my side.

"Elly, why did you take him back? He sounded like a complete dick from what you told me."

I look up from my sandwich, surprised by his comment. "He was going through some family stuff. When I let him explain it all made sense. Sometimes things aren't what they seem, you know."

"He left you without a word as to why! Hardly sounds like he's going to be the best father for your child, don't you think?"

I hardly told him anything about what happened. How can he have such a strong opinion on the matter? "He had a lot going on at the time. We've sorted everything out now, so it's all good. Why are you so worried?" I'm starting to feel really uncomfortable now, and his questions are kind of pissing me off. Why is he looking at me like that?

He shrugs it off like it was nothing. "Just think you deserve better and you could save yourself a lot of heartache by just walking away from him now. I can take care of you and the baby. I would be good for you, Elly."

I can practically feel my eyes pop out of my head. What the fuck is he going on about, he would take care of us? "What are you talking about, Tris? We're just friends. We have never been anything more than that. Fraser is the baby's dad and the man I love. Why would I walk away from him? We have sorted it all out. I don't understand why you think this is anything more. I think maybe you should go." I go to stand to show him out, but he grabs my wrist, motioning for me to sit back down. His eyes look sad.

"Sorry, Elly, I have overstepped the mark. I just care about you, that's all. I don't want to see you get hurt, and if you stay with Fraser, you're going to get hurt, it's guaranteed."

What is he talking about? He guarantees I'll get hurt by Fraser?

"Why, do you know something I don't? Fraser's not going to hurt me."

"No, I just know guys like him. One way or another you'll end up hurt." As he says it, he knocks over his coffee, with the hot liquid splashing all over his shirt. He pushes his chair back, trying to avoid the hot liquid that is spilling from the table.

I jump up and run to the kitchen to grab some paper towel to mop it up and run back into the dining room to see he's removed his shirt.

I hand him some paper towels and he starts to clean up the hot liquid from his chest, then the table. We mop up the rest on the table then I dump the paper towel in the bin in the kitchen.

"I'm so sorry, Elly, don't know how I did that. I'm so clumsy."

"Are you okay, did it burn you?"

"No, I'm fine. No harm done," he says, brushing off his chest.

"Don't worry about it. Your shirt's probably ruined, though."

He looks down at the crumpled-up shirt in his hand. "Oh well, didn't like that shirt much anyway."

We hear a click in the door. Fraser must be home. This isn't going to look so good. If I know Fraser, and I do, he's going to freak.

Tristan looks between me and the door. "I'm sorry to do this, Elly. You're a nice girl. Things could have been really different between us if you just gave me a chance. But I owe my sister a favour and you kind of pissed her off."

Before I know what's happening, Tristan grabs my wrists in one hand and my head with the other, pinning me against the wall, and smashing his mouth against mine.

CHAPTER THIRTY

ELENA

I try to pull away, but Tristan has me pinned in place, his lips on mine.

"What in the actual fuck is going on here?" Fraser is fuming mad. He's cracking his knuckles and looks like he's going to rip Tristan's head off.

Tristan pulls away from me with the biggest grin of satisfaction on his face.

I push him away, getting distance between us. "What the hell, Tristan! Why did you do that?" This must look so bad, Tristan here with his shirt off, kissing me. I know I would freak out if the roles were reversed.

"You don't have to fight it now, Elly. He's seen us. We can just be together."

"What the fuck is going on, Elly? Who is this dick?" Fraser yells.

"I don't know what's going on, Fraser. It all happened so fast. I didn't want this, Fraser, you have to believe me. We were just friends and he just kissed me out of the blue."

"Likely story, Elly. You two looked very cosy. There's clearly more going on here than just friends."

I start to cry and try to stop the tears of frustration. I know what this must look like. But it's just not true. I had nothing to do with that kiss. He forced himself on me and I couldn't move. I have no idea what's going on or what Tristan is talking about. His sister and me pissing her off? Who is she?

I start to walk towards Fraser. "You have to believe me, Fraser. This isn't what it looked like, I've been set up."

"Why don't you tell him who I am Elly? The guy you were seeing while you two were on a break. You have to wonder, Fraser, whose baby is she carrying anyway?"

I see red and flick my head around at Tristan, glaring at him. What the fuck is going on here? It's like he's setting me up. Am I being pranked or something?

"What the fuck are you saying, Tristan? There is nothing to question, Fraser. I never slept with him, he's making it up."

"How can I believe anything you say when I walk in on this scene? Him with his shirt off, his hands all over you. How stupid do you think I am?" He's so mad you can practically see his nostrils flaring, and I half expect him to march over to Tristan and thump him. This time I wouldn't stop him, he fucking deserves it for what he just did. "I'm fucking out of here."

"No, Fraser, don't go. I need to talk to you, to tell you what actually happened," I plead with him, trying to grab his hand so he will listen to me. I'm desperate now. I don't want him to think I've been cheating on him. I would never do that, even when we were broken up. I couldn't even think about anyone else like that, because it felt like cheating on him, my heart belongs to him. I would never do anything to destroy what we have.

Tristan looks between us and makes his way over to the

door. "Well, I'm out of here. Good luck with cleaning this mess up, Elly. Don't say I didn't warn you about Fraser. Things could've been so different if you just listened to what I was saying," Tristan sneers, as he walks off and out the front door.

My eyes are still focused on Fraser. I'm too scared to take them off him in case he runs. "Fraser, please let me explain," I sob through tears.

"I saw it with my own eyes. There's nothing to explain," he mutters, looking down. He just looks defeated now. "I never thought you could hurt me the way you have tonight, Elly."

"I didn't do it, Fraser, he forced himself on me. I was trying to get away from him. He's setting me up for some reason." I feel like I'm just repeating the same lines over and over again, but I don't know what else to say. How did this night all turn to shit so quickly?

"I've got to go, I can't be near you right now." He turns and takes off out the door.

I run into my room and grab my keys and take off out the front door after him. I can't let him go off thinking I kissed someone else on purpose.

What the fuck was Tristan talking about? I should've listened to his warning and I would have avoided this? I have no idea what's going on.

I slam the front door behind me and run down the hallway and stairs. As I run down the stairs, my foot slips on something and my ankle rolls. I hear a snapping sound and my legs go out from under me. I slide down a few stairs and land with a massive thump on my arse.

The pain throbs through my ankle and it fucking kills. More tears stream down my face. Can this get any worse? My ankle's got to be broken. It hurts so much, but the pain that really worries me the most is the dull cramping pain I have in my lower tummy. I hope the baby's okay.

I try to pull myself up to standing with the stair railing but it's impossible, and in my rush to go after Fraser, I've forgotten my phone so I can't even call anyone. I'm stuck here until someone comes and finds me. I close my eyes and try not to focus on the searing pain radiating through my body, but it's impossible. The pain is taking over my brain and I feel so sick. I don't care about my ankle. "Please let my baby be okay," I silently pray.

I have no idea how much time has passed when I see Indie round the corner with a massive smile on her face, but it soon changes when she sees me. She runs to me.

"Oh my God, Elly, are you okay?"

"No," I cry. I'm in so much pain now.

"Can you stand up?"

"Not by myself, I tried. I think my ankle's broken."

"Come on, I'll help you, we need to get you to the hospital."

She places her arms around me and carefully tries to help me up to standing. As she lifts me, we both see little spots of blood left behind on the stairs where I was sitting. Her eyes widen at me, but she doesn't say anything.

She wraps her arm around me and helps me hobble out to the car park and into her car. I'm shaking from the pain, it's fucking intense. Why did I run after him in these boots? It was never going to end well.

Indie jumps in the car on her side and starts the engine. "Where's Fraser? I thought we were all meeting here for dinner? Should I call him?"

I just shake my head. I'm in too much pain to talk.

"It's okay, chickee, I'll get you to the hospital, you're going to be just fine."

Fraser

I run down the stairs. I've got to get away from here as fast as I can, before I do something I'll regret. What the fuck did I just walk in on? I can hear Elly call my name, but I don't care. I don't want to hear her lies. How could she do this to me? To us, our family?

I start to walk, nearly out of breath from running and the panic of what I just witnessed. Another man's lips on her. That scene will be permanently etched in my brain like a fucking parasite boring a hole straight through my heart, eating me alive. "Fuck!" I scream into the street. Some walkers glance over at me at my outburst but continue on when they realise I'm nothing to worry about.

I need to stop freaking the fuck out, but I can't. My heart is beating so fast I feel like I'm going to have a fucking heart attack. I gasp for breath, trying to calm myself down. I should have punched that fucking pretty-boy arsehole right in his face, that would've made me feel better. Why the fuck didn't I do that?

I need something to take away the pain, stop my head from spinning out of control, and as fate would have it, the pub is less than half a block down the road in front of me.

The only place I know to go when things fall apart. Just one drink and I will feel calmer and in a better position to process what I just witnessed. I walk up to the bar and order a scotch, my drink of choice when shit gets too real. Then take a seat at the bar.

The scotch sits in front of me, taunting me, but I keep hearing Cherie's words: "You're in control of your life and your reactions to what happens." I don't have to drink this, but I know if I do it will numb the pain, for tonight at least.

I'm so fucking mad. What the hell did I walk in on? Some guy with his shirt off, hands all over my girl, his tongue down her throat. Has she been seeing him the whole time? Is it his baby and she's just lying to me? Could fate be so fucking cruel to make me fall for a woman that would fuck me over, just like my mother did to my dad? Could it be true?

None of this makes any sense at all. She looked scared, her eyes wide and upset, not like she was into him. But they were kissing.

Now I remember where I have seen that fucker before. They were playing pool together that night she was trying to make me jealous. What the fuck! Has this been going on since that night? She said at the time that she knew him from the café, where they probably had secret meet-ups while I was at work.

Fuck, my head is playing tricks on me, my imagination's going wild imaging all types of scenarios. But none of them makes sense.

Screw it, there's no point holding myself back. What have I got to be good for anyway? It's actually over with Elly. She's with someone else and I need something to ease the pain.

I lift my glass to my lips, then place it back on the bar. This is a bad idea. It doesn't matter how mad I am about what I just saw, I'm not going to do this to myself again. I need to get out of here. I turn to leave and out of the corner of my eyes I see Shea walk into the pub. What's she doing here? She's the last person I want to see tonight. I drop my head and turn back to the bar, hoping she hasn't spotted me.

But I can hear the tell-tale click of her heels tapping on the hardwood floor as she stalks over to me. I raise my eyes to see her with a massive smile on her face. An over-the-top smile like she's just won the lotto or something. What is it she wants? She stops walking right in front of me.

"What's wrong, Fraser? Why so sad?"

"What do you want, Shea?"

"You've changed your tune since I saw you a couple of hours ago. Did something happen for you to be sitting in a bar all alone?" she taunts me, lowering her bottom lip as if to fake cry.

"Fuck off, Shea," I hiss, dismissing her and turning my head.

She walks round to my other side, placing her hand on my shoulder. I get a shiver down my spine from her touch, my body recoiling from her.

"Oh, I think you know me better than that. I make it my business to know what's going on in this town."

"Well, this is none of your business." I shake her off, lowering my head, reconsidering my drink.

"Let me play the guessing game then, hey." She places her finger to her lip as if contemplating what could be wrong with me. "Tell me if I'm right. Your perfect little lady's not so perfect after all, is she, Fraser?"

I raise my eyes to meet hers. What the fuck does she know. Her smile returns. "Want me to go on? I'm on to something, aren't I? Her eyes are bright and sparkly like she is enjoying every minute of this, knowing I'm in pain. What a masochistic bitch. How could she possibly know what happened tonight?

"Perfect little Elly was convinced I was the slut. Doesn't look like it now, though, would I be right, Fraser?"

What's she on about? How could she know I caught Elly with someone else? Unless... I remember what Elly said back at the house, 'I'm being set up, Fraser.'

"What the fuck did you do?" I raise my head, glaring at her, waiting for her response.

She's a little taken aback at my response and takes a step back, stumbling on her heels. "Nothing, just a little matchmaking. Told you not to fuck with me. Guess now you know how it feels," she says, way too sweetly, as she walks off flicking her hair.

Fuck! I run my hands through my hair. This is a fucking nightmare. What the actual fuck is going on? My head is spinning. Have Elly and that guy been sleeping together? Or has she been set up as she said? For as long as I have known her, she has only ever been up front and honest with me. I know her, don't I? She doesn't have a bad bone in her body, she wouldn't do this, it's not her. I'm such an arsehole for even thinking she would after her taking me back and everything I did to her. I should have trusted her. I need to get out of here and make this right before I fuck this up for good.

I leave my drink on the bar, I don't need it. I need to see Elly and work this shit out. I make my way out the front door and run into Blake.

"Thank fuck you're here, Fraser, I've been looking for you everywhere. Why aren't you answering your phone?"

"I turned it off. What's wrong?"

"Elly needs you, Fraser. She's in the hospital. She's had a fall."

"What? What's happened?"

"She fell down the stairs chasing after you. She hurt her ankle, it might be broken."

"What about the baby?"

"The baby?" he questions, raising an eyebrow.

That's right, we were going to tell him tonight. "She's pregnant."

"Indie didn't say, just that Elly's scared and she needs you."

His ute's parked right out the front of the pub. We jump in and he takes off so fast his tires squeal. I can't believe she fell trying to chase me. I should have just stayed and listened to her, then this wouldn't have happened.

Blake looks over to me and he looks pissed. "What were you doing at the pub by yourself, Fraser?"

"I was going to have a drink, but I didn't."

"What the fuck is going on with you two anyway? Are you fighting again?"

"I don't know what's going on, that's what I'm trying to work out. I walked in on some guy kissing her in her apartment tonight."

His eyes go wide. "What? That doesn't sound like something Elly would do. She loves you, Fraser. Remember how sad she was when you split up last time?"

"Yeah, I know, I wouldn't believe it either, but I saw it with my own eyes! Shea just said the weirdest thing too. Something about her playing matchmaker and now I know how it feels."

"You were here with Shea?"

"No, I ran into her, or she came looking for me, I don't know. But she was all smug like she knew something I didn't, calling Elly a slut. She has something to do with all this."

"Sounds like Shea has set her up. Man, she's a manipulative bitch. This is exactly something she would do when she doesn't get her own way. I told you she was trouble. Elly wouldn't have done this, man, you know she wouldn't. There's got to be some sort of explanation."

CHAPTER THIRTY-ONE

FRASER

Blake pulls up in front of the hospital and we make our way in as fast as we can. I just need to get to her and make sure she's okay. I go to the reception desk.

"Hi, I'm looking for Elena Walker. She was admitted tonight after an accident."

The receptionist looks at her computer. "Yes. Sir, she's in maternity. They're monitoring her while they wait for X-rays on her ankle."

"Okay, can you take me to her?"

"Only family at this time of night. You'll have to come back in the morning."

"I'm her fiancé, the baby's dad. I need to be with her."

She looks me up and down, then writes something down on a piece of paper.

"Take a left then head down the hall until you reach the maternity ward, press the buzzer and tell them who you are. They'll let you in. She points to Blake. "Your friend will have to stay and wait here."

I take the paper with her little map on it. "Okay, thank you." I turn to Blake and he nods his head and takes a seat as

I make my way through the swinging doors to the maternity ward.

I press on the buzzer. "Hi, I'm Fraser Davis, here to see Elena Walker, I'm her fiancé."

"No worries, I'll buzz you through."

The door swings open and I make my way through to the ward. It's really quiet and dark with most of the lights off. There are signs up saying that when the lights are out, it's quiet time.

The lady on reception smiles. "She's in room 12. You can make your way down there now, I'm sure she will be happy to see you," she whispers.

I walk through the door to see Elly in a hospital bed with her leg propped up with an ice pack on it, her eyes closed. Indie's sitting next to her holding her hand. She looks up, surprised to see me. I can see she's been crying with mascara-stained cheeks.

Indie gets up and comes over to me.

"You can only stay if you're not going to fight with her. They're already worried about the baby, and if you stress her more, she could lose it."

"I'm not here to stress her, I just wanted to make sure she's okay. What are they saying?"

"They checked the baby's heartbeat and it's still strong at the moment, but she had a bit of a bleed when she fell, so they want to keep her in to monitor her for the night. Hopefully everything will be okay."

"What about her ankle? Blake said they think it's broken?"

"Yeah, it might be, it looks awful! They haven't X-rayed yet. She's on painkillers so she's a bit out of it."

"How did you get to stay? I had to tell them I was her fiancé just to get up here."

"I think they thought we were a couple," she giggles.

Elly stirs and looks over to us. "Fraser, you came."

I go to sit next to her, holding her hand. "Of course, I came as soon as I heard."

"So you're not angry with me anymore?" she mutters sleepily.

"How about we talk about all of that later, when you're better."

She closes her eyes again and I kiss her hand. "Thank you for coming," she says with a small smile. She must be exhausted. I know I am.

Indie gives me a wave and mouths, "I'm going to find Blake."

Elena

The sunlight is filtering in and I slowly open my eyes, taking in my surroundings. I feel like I've been asleep for about five minutes. Last night was insane. My body aches like it's been hit by a truck. My ankle is the worst, which has a low throb radiating up my leg. The painkillers must have worn off.

I look over to my side and see Fraser curled up asleep in the armchair next to me. His body is so big, it must have been one uncomfortable night's sleep for him, but he wouldn't leave me by myself even after what he witnessed at my apartment. We didn't talk about it at all, he was just focused on making sure I wasn't in pain and the baby was okay. They will send us for another ultrasound this morning, to make sure everything's all right, but the heartbeat was strong last night so it's a good sign.

The nurse came back at about 2am to take me for X-rays

on my ankle and it is fractured. They won't need to operate, thankfully, but I will need a moon boot to support it while it heals. Hopefully they will put that on today. Going to make styling houses interesting, but I'll deal with that when the time comes.

There's a knock at the door. We look over to see Indie's smiling face. She's holding a little brown tray with a paper bag over the top, the kind you get from the café.

"Hey, chickee."

"How did you get in so early?"

"I told them I was your lesbian lover, and they didn't want to ask any more questions. Works every time," she laughs.

"Hey, what am I then?" Fraser asks sleepily from the armchair beside me.

She shrugs. "Her fiancé. Isn't that what you said last night to get yourself in? I guess it's a whole modern polygamist thing." We both laugh at the thought, and Fraser rolls his eyes at us.

"I thought you might like this." She slides back the brown paper bag over the tray to reveal my favourite black forest cake. "Rachel sends her best."

My mouth salivates just looking at it and my tummy lets out a grumble, and I realise we totally missed dinner last night. No wonder I'm so hungry that I could eat cake for breakfast.

"Thank you, Indie, you're the best."

She smiles proudly. She searches the room for a chair and finds one in the other corner. She drags it over to sit next to the bed. "I wanted to tell you both as well, I've been doing some investigating, and I think I have cracked the case."

"What case would that be, Indie?" asks Fraser, as we both look at her, confused.

"The set-up of Elena Walker," she says, raising an eyebrow.

"Oh really, go on," says Fraser.

"I did some Facebook stalking because I'm Facebook friends with Luca. It was easy to find Tristan."

I can see Fraser's face harden and his fists clench at the mention of Tristan's name. He's still really mad about last night, but until now, hasn't brought it up.

She continues to tell us her story. "His account was private, so I thought it was a dead end, but I wasn't going to give up that easily. Then I set up a fake profile, finding a hot picture of some girl on Pinterest, and made friends with him, pretending to be someone new to the area, looking for a date. He fell for it hook, line, and sinker and we got to talking. Guess who his sister is."

We look at each other then back to her. "Who?" we both ask together.

"Shea! She's the one who set you up. Tristan told me the whole story. Shea was pissed at Fraser for not giving her a chance and dismissing her from working with them, and he was pissed with Elly for, in his words, 'being a cock tease.' So they joined forces to set you guys up. Shea called Fraser out to sign the fake documents, so he was out of the house while Tristan dropped by 'for a chat'," she says, using air quotes. "Tristan waited for Shea's text to tell him Fraser was on his way back, then he spilt the coffee on purpose, so he'd look the part, with no shirt on, and waited till he heard the key in the door to kiss you."

"That's why he apologised before he kissed me, saying he owed his sister a favour and I pissed her off."

"Yeah, it all makes sense now. Detective Indie solves the

case," she chants proudly, brushing her hands together like she's wiping away imaginary crumbs.

"Fuck. And that was what Shea was talking about at the pub last night. She said she had played matchmaker and now I would know what it felt like. That fucking bitch." Fraser's eyes are blazing with anger. I don't think I have ever seen him so angry.

"I can't believe they would go to all that trouble just to hurt us." It's a sickening feeling because I trusted Tristan and let him into my house. I thought he was a friend, and now look at me. I've wound up in the hospital with a fractured ankle. I could have lost the baby all because, in some weird twist of fate, they were hurting because they wanted what we had with each other. They could never have it, so they were out for revenge.

"Those two are going to pay for what happened to you," Fraser swears. "As soon as you're out of here I'm calling Theo so he can have them charged. I can't believe the two of them are so deluded that they think they can mess with other people's lives just because something doesn't go their way."

He's really mad about this. It is pretty fucked up. Who has the time to carefully create a plan like this just because the person you were into didn't want you back? It's so bizarre. I need to stop being so trusting of people, though, or this might not have happened in the first place. Tristan is one screwed up guy to go along with a plan his sister came up with for revenge."I know, Fray, but will having them charged really help the situation? What's done is done," I say, trying to defuse his anger.

"It might stop them from doing something to someone else. You can't let people walk all over you, Elly. They need to pay for what they have done."

"Yeah, you're right. We can drop over to Theo's on the way home, he wants to see me anyway."

"I'm sorry I didn't believe you last night, Elly, I should have straight away. You wouldn't be lying here in pain if I did," Fraser says, stroking my hand. I can see the sadness in his eyes, watching me in pain.

I look up to him and cup his face, "I can only imagine what it looked like, though, when you walked in. I understand why you didn't."

"Yeah, but I should have known you would never do anything like that. It's my fault you're here like this now."

"No, it's definitely not! It's Shea and Tristan's fault, no one else's. None of this is on you."

"She's right, Fraser, this is not on you. Those two are fucked up. Who goes to the trouble to set up someone else just to get back at them? It's the most immature thing I've ever heard. Fucking ridiculous!" says Indie, throwing her hands in the air.

"Thanks for working it all out. What would we do without you, Detective?" I laugh, offering my friend a smile. I'm so lucky to have a friend like her in my life.

"I don't know, I might just have to change my career!" Indie looks deep in thought, like she is actually considering the idea, then shakes her head. "Nah, I like painting too much. As long as I'm bridesmaid at your wedding, as payment for my detective services, that's all I ask. Or you could name the baby after me?"

"Is that right!" I look over to Fraser, and he shrugs. "How about auntie to our baby?" I suggest.

"Auntie Indie, yeah, I like the sound of that." She jumps up from her seat and lowers down to hug me. "Got to go, chick, glad you're okay."

"Thanks, Indie," Fraser says, "for everything, for being here when I wasn't."

She gives us a little wave as she walks out the door.

"I'm sorry about that," I say, a little embarrassed that Indie keeps bringing up us getting married. I don't know about Fraser, but I'm so not ready for marriage, even though I'm pregnant.

"For what?" He gives me a puzzled look.

"Indie. She keeps saying she will be a bridesmaid at our wedding. It's kind of early for wedding talk."

"Why? You're having my baby, and even if you weren't, I knew when we got back together this time, it was forever. I'm going to marry you, Elly. You're my girl, and I want the world to know it."

"Fraser Davis is going to settle down!" I fake a shocked look. "Let's not go rushing into anything. I'm not getting married while I'm pregnant."

"What, worried you won't fit into some amazing designer gown you just have to have?"

"No, it's not that, it's just, I don't know, it's just not how I pictured it, you know."

"Okay, gorgeous, no wedding while you're pregnant. But I promise you this, there will be a wedding in the very near future."

He smiles and pulls me into a kiss. "Careful of the ankle," I mumble into his lips. He adjusts himself on the bed, being as careful as he can not to bump my ankle. He threads his fingers through my hair, cupping my head, and bringing me in to kiss him. We pull back and that goofy grin is planted on my face. I can't help it, and he studies my face.

"You're my girl, Elly, I know the last few months have been crazy, and at times it probably felt like this was hopeless. But I have loved you for a very long time, and now we're going to be a family and I'm going to spend the rest of my life putting that smile on your gorgeous face."

They say that the universe works in mysterious ways. And I would have to agree. This year wasn't the perfect year I planned it out to be. But it did change my life forever in such a huge way. I know it won't always be some picture-perfect fairy tale, but it will be spent with the man I love by my side, and if we can survive this year, we will be able to get through anything together.

And I know one thing's for sure... I will love this man always.

EPILOGUE
FRASER: 12 MONTHS LATER

I watch Elly walk up the path, pushing the stroller, and it makes me smile. My little family. Today we're running through the final site inspection on our new house. Our dream house we designed together. I have been here all morning with Ash, making sure everything is going to be ready for the big move next week. So far so good.

Our son Cooper is six months old already, and he's just perfect, sitting in the pram smiling and babbling away. He's the spitting image of his mother with her blonde hair and fair skin, but he has my grey eyes.

He's full of energy, and even though he's only six months old, he's keeping us on our toes. He started crawling early, at five months, and is into absolutely everything. We have had to implement a few new design details for the house, with him in mind. Having a baby has definitely changed our lives for the better. Our life is full of laughter and happiness, and I can't wait till we move into this place next week.

Elly looks up and sees me watching her, and her face breaks into her signature show-stopping smile.

"Hey, gorgeous. How's your morning going?" I ask.

"Good, we're just on our way back from the park. I wanted to see how the site inspection is going."

"Can't help yourself, can you? Come on in. You just missed Ash, he's headed back to the office."

Elly parks the pram out the front and unbuckles Cooper, picking him up and putting him on her hip. He cuddles in, wrapping his chubby little hand around a bundle of her hair. I pat him on the head, messing up his soft blond spikes.

We walk through the front door, and I can see the tears welling in her eyes. Elly has been here many times throughout the building process, but it's always the same.

"You happy with everything, gorgeous? I hope they're happy tears."

"I'm lost for words, Fraser." She walks through the kitchen, running her hand along the eclectic tiled wall. "It's, it's just beautiful. Everything I could have hoped for and more. I can't believe we move in next week and this place is actually ours."

It is pretty amazing. The house is a mix of ultra-modern with a retro twist. Mostly white walls with recycled timber floor. There are pops of colour on the tiled splashback in the kitchen and the bathroom with beautiful retro-patterned tiles Elly found at an auction. My favourite part is the big hanging steel fireplace that features in the sunken lounge room. It's the centre of the house, and a place, I hope, we spend a lot of time as a family creating memories.

The kitchen has a large sliding door looking out over a courtyard that will be filled with native plants when the landscaping crew comes through in a few weeks. We couldn't wait for it to be done for us to move in. I'm too impatient.

Cooper wriggles out of Elly's arms, wanting to be put down. She places him on the timber floor, and he takes off crawling around, checking out the place for himself. I pull her into my arms, my hands going to her arse, cupping it as I pull her into a kiss. I could get used to this, holding her in my arms in our house with our little boy. Happiness overwhelms me.

I brush some stray hairs out of her eyes. She's distracted watching Cooper explore. "Are your parents still good for this afternoon?" I ask.

"Yes, but I'm not sure about it. What if Coop freaks out because I'm not with him?"

"He's not going to. You know that he loves your parents and it's only for a few hours. We'll be back before bedtime."

"Okay, I want to know what you have planned before we leave, though. You know how much I hate surprises."

"Yeah, I know, but there's no way I'm giving this one away. You're just going to have to wait and see."

She rolls her eyes at me and takes off after Coop, who's about to crawl onto the back deck.

Elena

We drop Cooper off to Mum and Dad and I make a run for the car. I don't want him to see me crying, but I can't help it. I know it's silly, but I haven't left him with anyone other than Fraser before, and I know it's only a couple of hours, but it makes me feel so anxious. I really should trust my parents because they were the ones that raised me and my brothers, but it's been a while. Maybe they've forgotten what to do.

One of the consequences of the accident is that I have

become very overprotective of him. Theo was just as furious as Fraser when he found out about what Shea and Tristan did to us and how it caused me to fall. He made sure they were charged and slapped with a restraining order. We haven't seen or heard from either of them again. Shea's reputation was completely destroyed and she's not working in this industry anymore, so I haven't even bumped into her. Thank god.

"Fraser, I'm not so sure about this," I say, playing with the hem on my skirt, as he drives out of town to our mystery location.

"Elly, it's only a couple of hours. They have our number if they need us, and we can be back within 20 minutes. It will be good for both of you. He didn't seem worried when we left, he was happily playing with your mum. I need you all to myself, just for a little bit, then we can come home to Coop."

"Okay." He's right, we do need to start claiming time back to ourselves. I've been working from home managing the business, while the staff Indie and I hired do most of the heavy lifting. Our little business is doing so well, we have made quite a name for ourselves here, and we're so busy we needed to expand almost immediately. We're now a team of five with two junior stylists and a coordinator, my old friend Janie from Project Reno.

Janie couldn't believe her luck when I rang her and offered her the job. The show had been cancelled due to bad ratings. When I left, they couldn't find a replacement and the Dragon was forced to do some actual work herself. She had no idea what she was doing and ran the show into the ground. Janie was working at a furniture shop while she looked for something better. She had nothing keeping her in Sydney, so she happily moved up here to join us. She has been a godsend since I had Coop. I get most of my work done while he sleeps, but now it's time to really go back to work. Probably just a few days a week to start with. Having a normal adult conversation sounds pretty awesome at this point.

This drive is starting to feel very familiar, and I look over to Fraser and smile. "Are you taking me to Ti Tree Lake?"

"It's a surprise, gorgeous. I can neither confirm nor deny that question," he says, with a little sideways smirk.

I let out a little excited squeal. I love it there, and it's where we had our first date. We've had picnics with Cooper a few times as well. It's kind of become our special family place.

As we pull up in the car park, Fraser is quiet, very quiet. He looks like he's got his own conversation going on in his head.

"Is everything okay?"

"Yeah, just realised I forgot to do something at work yesterday, all good, I'll fix it on Monday."

He grabs a basket out of the trunk, and we walk the winding track down to the lake. It's a stunning spring afternoon and the sound of birds chirping happy songs rings through the air.

I'm first to make it down the track, as normal, and as I get closer to the lake, I can see a picnic rug set up. My hands go to my mouth in shock. It looks like a romantic date scene out of a movie. There are cushions and candles and flowers in little jars. I look around to see if anyone else is here, but it's just us. I turn around to see Fraser's grinning at me like a Cheshire cat.

"So, I'm assuming you had something to do with this?"

"I may have had some of your fairy friends work their

magic for us." By 'fairy friends' I'm sure he's referring to my team of stylists. I recognise the set-up as some of our new bohemian accessories range.

"It's beautiful, Fraser."

"It's a special day, our first date back after becoming parents."

Hmm, seems like he's gone to a lot of effort for just a date. He sits on one of the cushions, placing the basket he brought down in front of him, and pats the cushion next to him. Holding his hand up to help me down to him. As I take his hand, I trip and fall a little, ending up on his lap. We both collapse in a fit of laughter.

"Why am I so clumsy?" I laugh.

"I have no idea, gorgeous. But I know where Coop gets it from. You sure you didn't fall on purpose just to get close to me? We can get straight to the happy ending now if you want."

I slap him away and pull out of his arms to sit next to him, still laughing.

"We're sitting here in a romantic set-up and that's all you can think about! Thought having a child that wakes all through the night would have you too tired to think constantly of sex."

"Not when I'm around you. It's all I can think about, you're just so fucking hot, Elly."

Now I'm blushing a little and remember what he just said. "Wait, what did you say about the 'happy ending'? Were you being dirty?"

"Well, I was going to wait till we had something to eat, maybe some wine, but..." He turns and searches through the basket he brought and pulls something out of it. Oh my, is he about to do what I think?

He opens the little navy-blue velvet box and inside sits

the most exquisite vintage sapphire ring, with a halo of floral-style diamond accents. Just like the one I've been eyeing off at the local antique store. But he didn't know that. Indie! She's totally in on this.

"Elena Walker, from the moment I met you I knew I needed you in my life. You are simply perfect and make me the happiest man alive. Will you marry me and spend the rest of your life with me so I can always be this happy?"

"Yes, Fraser, yes."

He slides the exquisite ring onto my finger, and with happy tears rolling down my face, I kiss his lips.

I may have been young the first time I ever laid eyes on him. But I knew the feeling he gave me was unlike any other I had ever felt. He was someone special and my life wouldn't be complete without him in it. I haven't always believed in fate or happily ever afters. But as long as I have known him, for me, it has always been Fraser.

The End

ABOUT THE AUTHOR

Thank you for reading my romances. I'm a mother of three who lives on the South Coast of New South Wales, Australia. I have always been a creative soul, with a background in fashion design, interior decoration, and floristry. I currently run a business as a wedding florist and stylist. With the pandemic in 2020 and all wedding work being put on hold due to lockdowns, I was given the opportunity to not only be a reader of my favourite genre, romance, but also to finally put pen to paper and bring a dream of writing my first series to life. I hope you enjoy reading them as much as I enjoyed writing them.

For all the news on upcoming books, visit A.K. Steel at:
    Facebook: A. K. Steel Author
    Instagram: aksteelauthor

ACKNOWLEDGMENTS

My partner, Kiel, you have changed my life in so many wonderful ways. Thank you for pushing me to start writing. Without your encouragement and love, I never would have put pen to paper and started this fantastic journey in the first place. I feel like I found myself this year, and I'm finally where I'm supposed to be. Without you, this never would have happened.

My amazing mum, Kay, thank you for your constant love and support. You read every word I write and have always been my number one fan. You put up with my meltdowns and endless questions, you are my best friend, and I'm grateful every day to have you in my life.

My dad, it's been six long years since you left us, but the outlook you had on life still inspires me every day. It's the reason I believe that if you work hard enough, you can achieve any dream, no matter how impossible it seems.

My kids—Hamish, Marley, and Quinn—thank you for looking at me like I'm amazing and can do anything, even when I don't feel like I can. Everything I do is for you. And I hope I have shown you that with a bit of determination and hard work, your dreams really can come true.

Karen, my friend and mentor, you made this dream feel possible. Every time I thought I couldn't do it, you encouraged me to keep on going. I couldn't have done any of this without your knowledge and friendship.

Lindsay, my editor, thank you for your patience with a new author. Your knowledge and expertise have made this book what it is.

Sarah, for my gorgeous cover design, and your patience with my indecisiveness. I love the cover you created for me.

My beta readers—Elise, Shelly, Kirstie, Bek, and Francesca—thank you for your time, honesty, and support. Without you lovely ladies I wouldn't have had the courage to publish and share my story.

My proof readers Shelly and Kay, thank you for double and triple checking every word.

To my friends and family who have been so supportive along this journey, you have all been so amazing—thank you.

And lastly to my readers, thank you for taking the time to give a new author a chance, and making my dreams become a reality.

Printed in Great Britain
by Amazon